Jay Russell was born in New York Cornell University and the University from which he received a Ph.D. in communications. He has worked for a Los Angeles detective agency, and as a researcher and editor. His short stories have appeared in such anthologies as *Splatterpunks*, *Still Dead: Book of the Dead 2* and *Dark Terrors 2*. His first novel, *Celestial Dogs*, is also available from Raven Books. Russell moved to England in 1993, and lives in London with his wife.

Jay Russell

RAVEN BOOKS
London

Robinson Publishing Ltd
7 Kensington Church Court
London W8 4SP

First published in the UK by Raven Books, an imprint of
Robinson Publishing Ltd, 1996

A copy of the British Library Cataloguing in Publication
data is available from the British Library.

ISBN 1-85487-466-7

Printed and bound in the UK

10 9 8 7 6 5 4 3 2 1

ACKNOWLEDGEMENTS

The author (that's me) would like to express his thanks and appreciation to:

Steve Jones, *mensch* par excellence, for his many kindnesses and generosity.

Louis Schechter for ongoing support, in spite of the dirty words.

And Jane Stokes for . . . everything else. Again!

For the bloody hell of it . . .

PART ONE

ONE

'Mu-thu-*fuck*-a!'

'Man! There be dead and there be dead, but that motherfucking shit is fucking *dead*.'

Dennis Reagan looked up from the bloated corpse. A couple of bums – *homeless people*, he reminded himself – had wandered right through the cordoned perimeter and flanked him as they evaluated the body.

'Ain't got no balls t'all,' the shorter one said.

'Maybe born like that,' the other suggested.

'Whachoo mean born like that? Motherfucker born wit'out no fucking balls? Suppose he born wit all them holes, too? Huh, motherfucker? Born wit the eyes torn out his head. That what you think?'

'Jes sayin' could be. Ain't sayin' t'is.'

'McKean! Morrison!' Reagan yelled. He glanced pleadingly at the sky, but saw only the thick morning overcast. The fine rain picked up again and Reagan took it as a snide response to his unspoken prayer.

The uniformed patrolmen tramped across the filthy sand. They came to a semblance of attention in front of Reagan, trying mightily and none too successfully to avoid eyeballing the corpse.

'Sir!' they said in unison.

'Would you get these bums out of here, please?' Reagan said. 'And let's see if we can't keep the fans in the bleachers? I mean, let's at least pretend we know how to follow procedure.'

'Homeless individuals, sir,' Morrison said.

'What?' Reagan whispered.

'Homeless individuals. Per current departmental directive, "homeless individuals" is the officially . . .'

'Jumping-Jesus-on-a-trampoline!' Reagan shrieked. 'Just get them the fuck out of here.'

'Yes sir,' the patrolmen again chorused, and prodded the two raggedy men back toward Ocean Avenue.

The voices faded into the distance as Witherspoon reappeared, keeping his back to the body. He looked deathly pale despite his tan, his thick hair dishevelled. *Why don't the assholes ever go thin on top?* Reagan wondered. Witherspoon had left his jacket and tie in the car, but several tell-tale vomit stains dotted the front of his shirt and bits of barf-encrusted sand stuck to a moist patch on his right shoe.

'Comedy team,' Reagan mused, shaking his head.

'The homeless individuals?'

Reagan looked to see if Witherspoon was making fun of him, but the young sergeant seemed dead serious. 'Yeah,' Reagan said, 'them, too.'

'Sir . . .' Witherspoon started.

'Forget it,' Reagan said.

'It's just that . . .'

'I said forget it. It happens. What about the meat truck?'

'It's on the way. There were some more drive-bys early this morning and the coroner's all backed up from the weekend.'

Reagan nodded. The gang shit was out of control. Again. Twenty or more homicides every weekend. Drive-bys, turf wars, random thrill-kills and endless Tunnel inspired lunacy. And not just in South-Central anymore. Shootings were up 30 percent over last year on Reagan's own Venice beat. And the media – the *fucking* media, Reagan corrected himself – were having a field day with it. The blow-dry pundits – who, Reagan noted, never suffered with receding hairline either – were set on chewing the department a juicy new asshole. Especially when it came to *Tunnel*. You couldn't turn on a television without some square-jawed pretty boy whining about how Tunnel was tearing apart the fabric of society. Christ! Had they already forgotten about crack? Whatever happened to the good old days?

And as long as the *fucking* media stayed obsessed, it was priority-one with the downtown suits who lived and died by the holy grace of the six o'clock news.

Reagan glanced back at the corpse through the thin drizzle.

He couldn't believe this one didn't connect with the gangs. Reagan hadn't made the tube for months and he needed a ticket. Hell, he'd only intercepted the call from Herbst because it sounded like a sure thing. But the victim looked lousy for it: too white, too old and no signature. When the gangbangers did a number like this, they signed their handiwork in letters big as the Hollywood sign.

No, this was shit and Reagan had stepped in deep. He'd called for it and now he'd have to live with it.

This one was a top-of-the-line sicko job and that meant silence. No press, restricted logs, everyone on a need-to-know basis. Strict departmental policy: no upsetting the citizens any more than necessary. Not with all the gang craziness and certainly not after the department's less than keen handling of the last couple of serial killers. And to top it off, he'd probably have to liaise with the goddamn Bureau. There was nothing worse than working with that stick-up-their-lily-white-ass bunch.

'Witherspoon.'

'Sir!'

Correction: one thing worse. Reagan had been saddled with a chuckle-headed partner. 'Special Duty,' they told him. Special *bullshit* was more like it. Nephew of Captain Alton 'Pencil-dick' Witherspoon of IAD. At first Reagan thought that the kid had been sicced on him as a wandering eye for Internal Affairs. But a week of partnering convinced him that ol' Pencil-dick had probably been desperate to get rid of the moron. Reagan was just unlucky enough to be the jackass the tail got pinned on.

'Keep an eye on our friend until the coroner gets here. I need smokes.'

Reagan started toward the row of tacky souvenir shops and fast food stands along the pier, but a patrolman flagged him down.

'Call for you, Lieutenant.'

Reagan sighed and popped a breath mint in his mouth. He slipped behind the wheel of his unmarked Chevy and dabbed at his face and thinning hair with a dirty towel he kept in back. It was raining *hard*. What a summer this was turning out to be. Reagan picked up the phone.

'Yeah. Reagan.'

'What d'you got there, Denny-boy?'

Donatelli.

'Raining like an open tap. Humid too. Christ, it's slick as the mayor's smile out here. I just know I'm going to catch a cold and there's nothing worse than a summer cold. Must be that global warming or something.'

'It's rough, I know. I can see the raindrops through the window. Can't hear it above the air conditioning, though.'

'Scumbag.'

There was a burst of something: laughter, static.

'So, what's the story?' Donatelli came back.

'We got us one ugly stiff. A floater. Everything you ever wanted in a hack-job and then some. The nephew blew chunks.'

'A Witherspoon from balls to ass. Talk to me about the stiff, Dennis. Paint me a picture with words.'

'The body's been in the water at least overnight. Maybe two. Multiple stab-wounds. Burns, gouges, skinning. No eyes, no dick. Somebody partied down on this guy.'

'Does it look like the work of our little friends?'

Reagan sighed. 'I don't think so, Carmine. This one is pretty nasty even by gangster standards. Nobody signed it, either.'

'Huh-boy.'

'Talk to me, baby.'

'All right. We're just coming up to speed on a break-in and hack-job at some lab over in Westwood. I knew you had something messy, but first word is that the Westwood job is a definite gang-related. I was hoping they'd be a set. You about wrapped up?'

'Just waiting on the coroner.'

'Okay. Why don't you leave the junior G-man to mind the store and get your dimpled rear over to Phaedra Pharmaceutical. Big complex off Ohio at Sepulveda. Take a hairy eyeball and let me know if there's any likely match on the stiffs.'

'Roger Rabbit. Hey! Who's fielding the scene at Sepulveda?'

'Ummmm . . .'

'Uh-oh,' Reagan said.

'Brolin's there.'

'Fuck me with a tampon, why don't you? Gargle me with a douche.'

'Make nice, Lieutenant.'

'Yeah, yeah.'

'And Dennis?'

'Yo!'

'This one's already leaked. The animals are swarming all over it, so behave yourself.'

'The media you say . . .'

'The *fucking* media,' Donatelli corrected. 'You're heartbroken, I know. Just get moving.'

Reagan did.

TWO

Reagan straightened his tie and chewed another mint. He affixed his gold shield to his breast pocket and elbowed his way through the mob of vultures swarming around the main entrance to Phaedra Pharmaceutical Laboratories, Inc. He noted two local TV vans already on the scene and a third just arriving. He slowed his pace, giving the cameramen a chance to swing around and record his entrance. He nodded paternally at the uniforms guarding the door and patted a blue shoulder. The managing editor at Channel 5 went apeshit for shots of cops looking confident and official. He paused before going in, turned and scanned the crowd with a detective's discerning gaze.

Another damn good shot, he thought.

A second set of uniforms stood guard just inside the entrance. One smoked a cigarette while the other stared blankly at a bank of small, closed-circuit video monitors set in the reception desk. The couch potato nodded semi-respectfully at Reagan. Reagan glanced at the monitors, saw Jenny Brolin talking to a short, bald man in a long hallway. He noticed Freddy Liebowitz lurking in the background with his forensics crew.

'Anyone else here from Homicide?' he said, tapping the screen.

The uniform looked up and yawned. 'Nah.'

'Which way to the action?'

The cop gestured vaguely to the left.

'Your name wouldn't be Witherspoon by any chance, would it?'

'Huh?'

'What I thought.'

Reagan shook his head and followed the trail of uniforms until he found the right hall. As he walked the sterile corridors he caught glimpses of nervous faces peering out of open doors. He saw oodles of expensive-looking equipment and curled his nose at the overpowering smell of chemicals and disinfectant. The entire wing seemed to be devoted to laboratory space. The gurgling racks of pyrex and whirling centrifuges put Reagan in mind of mad scientists, but he didn't see a single hunchback or arcing Jacob's ladder, nor was there a demented cackle to be heard.

He pushed through a set of double-doors posted with hazardous substance warnings and spotted Brolin at the end of the hall. He glanced over his shoulder at the closed-circuit camera above the lintel. He came up behind Brolin and listened in on the tail-end of her interview with the bald man.

'I gotta tell you,' Brolin said, 'you've got some pretty funny ideas about security. I mean if this stuff is so important and hush-hush as you claim.'

'I think, officer, that you do not entirely grasp my meaning. The work we do is highly proprietary, yes, but it can't be *stolen* in the way that *you*, perhaps, might understand. The samples in and of themselves have no particular value – they're potentially quite dangerous, in fact. And certainly they'd have no value to a bunch of . . . gang members. Even if they reached more, ah, sophisticated hands they would be useless without the accompanying documentation, no matter how carefully analysed. And most of the logs were not even in the lab – at least they shouldn't have been. We'll know more, of course, when Dr Bernouli arrives. And this is all assuming that theft is, indeed, what this was about.'

Brolin peered at Reagan with a sour expression. Reagan smiled falsely, but kept his eye on the bald man.

'You got any other ideas?' Brolin asked.

'As I've already told you – thrice now, I believe – I am at a complete loss to explain this incident. Nothing of this sort has ever happened here before. And as I understand it, speaking not only as a managing director of Phaedra Pharmaceutical but as a taxpayer, uncovering the whys and wherefores of crime is essentially your job. Hmmmmm?'

'And don't I just love it. That's speaking as a tax *spender*, of course. Okay, doctor, that's fine for now. We're still going to need to get something formal in writing, but that can wait until later.'

The little man turned briefly toward Reagan, scanning him up and down. He sniffed with what Reagan took to be disapproval and stormed off. Brolin jotted down some notes in a chicken-scrawl the CIA cryptography unit couldn't have done anything with.

'Nice, huh? And they say charm is a thing of the past. But then "these are matters that I might not understand," right?'

'Who is he?'

'Glanville. Head of the research group here. *Thrice.* Jesus Christ!'

'He's wrong,' Reagan said, watching Glanville disappear.

'So don't ask him for a date. What the fuck are you doing here anyway?'

Like most cops – like Reagan – Brolin was highly territorial. Maybe more than most, because Brolin thought that the old boys' network on the force had it in for her.

And in that regard maybe she wasn't too far wrong.

'What do I need, a password? How about "swordfish"? Donatelli sent me, what do you think? I found some head cheese floating under the pier in Santa Monica. Captain says you got some, too, and I'm supposed to see if they make a sandwich. S'alright?'

'Heeeey, since when does it matter what I think? I ain't the goddamn pope.'

Reagan just smiled.

'I need you like I need a pap smear, Reagan. I want you like I want cramps.'

'Just talk to me.'

Brolin took a deep breath. 'Sometime between midnight and four, perps, number as yet unknown – probably three or four – busted in through a skylight in the administrative wing. That's back the other way. These sons-a-bitches knew what they wanted, 'cause they made a bee-line for this lab. Diane Sommers, black – excuse me, *African-American* – 24, was working inside at the time. She probably surprised them, because she wasn't supposed to be there. They improvised. Had themselves a little party and sliced her up. Dollars to Winchell's they raped her, too. Trashed the lab, but good. Tagged gang shit all over the walls. Can't even tell what, if anything, is missing. We're waiting on the guy whose lab this is. Some hot-shot named Bernouli.'

Reagan nodded. 'I think I've heard of him.'

'Yeah, well, everybody here just about drops their drawers and genuflects when they say his name. He's been up in Frisco, but he's flying back down now.'

'Don't say "Frisco". It's very uncool.'
'Oh yeah? How about "eat me"? Is that cool?'
Reagan let it pass. 'Sure he was up there last night?'
Brolin grabbed a copy of the *L.A. Times* off a chair and handed it to him. Just above the fold on an inside page was a story about an international virology conference in San Francisco, accompanied by a photo of a dapper, handsome man speaking from an enormous dais. The caption identified the dandy as 'renowned' scientist Dr Samuel J. Bernouli.

'Hmmmph,' Reagan said. 'Could've flown back and forth.'
Brolin shrugged. 'We'll check.'
'How'd the perps get out?'
'They walked out the fucking front door.'
'Security?'
Brolin made a fish face and a one-handed, pumping motion in front of her crotch. Reagan nodded sympathetically.

'Donatelli was talking gangs, but this doesn't smell like their kind of shtick.'
'Yeah, well, we already got a list of the shit they keep here, and the place might as well be a catalogue showroom for do-it-yourself meth labs.'
'Oh boy.'
'Fucking-A. When word of this gets out look for hits on every pharmaceutical lab in the city. I give you five-to-one we find some deep-tanned scumbag on the inside who scoped this place as an easy mark.'
'I'd watch that kind of talk, if I was you.'
'Hey, if you were me I'd watch me eat my piece.'
Reagan shook his head. 'What about the girl?'
'Probably incidental. Wrong place at the wrong time.'
'Sounds right. I don't see any connection to my floater. Tell me about the stiff.'
For the first time since she saw Reagan, Brolin smiled. 'Uh-uh. This one's a blue-plate special. You look for yourself then we'll talk some more.'
Reagan followed Brolin down the hallway, nodding at Jack McLeod, Brolin's fireplug of a partner. They stopped outside a set of massive double-doors with frosted, opaque glass. A metal sign warned HAZARDOUS MATERIALS AREA in large red letters. In even bigger writing was a name: Dr Samuel J. Bernouli.
'I hope you didn't eat a colourful breakfast,' Brolin said and handed Reagan rubber evidence gloves.

He opened the door.

The smell hit him first. Thick, like a packed subway car in summer rush hour. But coppery and dizzying like only spilled blood can be. The odour overpowered Reagan's other senses. His brain was too shocked by the olfactory overload to register what his eyes were taking in. He pulled out a handkerchief and held it over his mouth and nose.

'The new Calvin Klein scent,' Brolin said. '*Exsanguination*.'

Reagan took two steps and froze as the picture developed in his head.

He saw a nightmare in red.

Pointillist, Rorschach patterns adorned the walls along with gangbanger tags painted in blood. The floor and lab benches were strewn with smashed equipment and splintered glass. Experimental flotsam and jetsam littered congealing multi-coloured pools.

Papers and mangled notebooks had been tossed about the room. The door to an industrial-sized refrigerator stood open, but the shelves were bent and askew. The punctured remnants of IV blood bags dangled from the shelves like fruit left too long on the tree. The steel door was tacky with gang slogans scrawled in drying blood. Splotches of red even tinged the fluorescent ceiling bulbs.

One wall had been tagged with an immense graffito: BLOOD 3–2.

Fred Liebowitz and his team wandered around the room scraping samples and taking pictures. They all wore thick rubber gloves, surgical face masks and plastic goggles. Liebowitz glanced up when Reagan entered, his goggles spattered with tiny red dots. Freddy's lips curled in a bleak smile, barely discernible beneath his mask.

It took another minute before Reagan's gaze lit on the crumpled sheet on a lab bench. He'd seen more than his share of mutilated bodies over the years – hell, the stiff under the pier was enough to put him off liver for the rest of his life – and had learned to deal with it. Like doctors, cops taught themselves to switch off a part of themselves on the job, or they didn't last. But Reagan felt more than the usual pang with this one. He just didn't want to see what lay beneath that cover.

He looked anyway.

The sheet clung to the body by several very wet, very red blotches. Reagan gripped a clean patch lightly between two gloved fingers, and snuck a furtive glance around the room to make sure none of Liebowitz's men were paying attention. He drew back the cover.

After a few moments he could tell that it had been a young

woman, but then he was a trained detective. At a quick glance it wasn't a sure bet. And who but a detective could bear to give it more than such a glance?

She had no face.

In its stead he saw a pulpy chasm of mashed bone and tissue. Swirling patterns of dark red and glistening pink intertwined in a cubist mockery of humanity. Twisted sinus cartilage lay enmeshed in a mound of chunky grey . . . *something*. Pearly chips of shattered teeth and silver fillings were sprinkled across the ruined face like raw gemstones in a vein. A jagged flap of desiccated blue tongue served as the only marker of what once might have been a full mouth.

The torso looked like the work of a retarded butcher's apprentice. Reagan followed the sloppy, serrated incision line from crotch to clavicle. Anatomy had never been his strong suit, but Reagan felt fairly sure that an organ or two was missing from the mass of diced tissue. He counted the ribs twice, but came up one short. He also noted that the thumb was missing from the left hand.

A few seconds later, he spotted the finger wedged into the bloody mess between her legs.

Liebowitz came up beside him and took off his mask. He pulled a gleaming forceps from his pocket and prodded at the girl's desecrated genitals. He gently twisted the instrument back and forth until he could remove the severed thumb. He deposited it in a marked, glassine evidence envelope. Liebowitz paused and furrowed his brow as he looked at the steel instrument, then held it up below his nose. He sniffed at it.

'What is it?' Reagan asked.

'Damn,' Liebowitz said. 'Now I'll never get the smell out.'

The lab team howled and Freddy shook with laughter.

Reagan forced an efficiently macho smirk, then turned and left before he threw up on a crime scene.

THREE

Rain.

When it rains in Los Angeles the streets bleed oil. The concrete and macadam bones of the city shudder and buckle under the barrage of strange liquid. L.A.'s vibrant facades clash bitterly with grey skies, even when touched by jagged, argent fingers of lightning.

The rain doesn't belong in L.A. It doesn't feel right or natural. It isn't understood.

It's not part of the *lifestyle*.

Expensive cars skid and slew like bumper cars at a boardwalk arcade. Steel and moulded fibreglass crunch and glass shatters as cocky, befuddled drivers go ten miles per hour too slow or too fast. Soft bodies carom across the slick freeways like fleshy pinballs, tilting in splatters of crimson.

Greymarch liked it.

He smiled grimly to himself as his Blazer hydroplaned up the Pasadena freeway en route to the cemetery. He allowed the funeral procession plenty of time to arrive ahead of him and get underway. He half-listened to the blather of a call-in radio programme – some crazy lady doctor spewing psychobabble – and unconsciously tapped his fingers on the steering wheel in counterpoint to the squeaky windshield wipers.

Funerals fascinated Greymarch. Everybody dressed in respectful blacks and sombre greys, all stiff and proper and long-faced. Sniffling and crying. Looking hard and stoic or wilted and pathetic. Soggy, tissue flower blossoms held in clenched fists, dabbing at runny, made-up eyes. Throat clearing and foot shuffling. Priests yapping and babies laughing. Long, black cars with bored drivers in stiff uniforms and silly caps.

The yin-yang stench of flowers and decay.

And for what?

Did they understand? Did they have even the slightest clue? Of course not.

Death was a mystery. The wall that couldn't be scaled, the chasm that couldn't be leaped. Death was the mind-crusher, the ultimate unknowable.

Greymarch knew better: death was highly overrated.

The traffic eased as he wound his way through downtown L.A., but the rain picked up in intensity. He had to brake hard as he came around a sharp turn in the old freeway when some asshole in a black and silver Porsche cut in front of him without signalling. Greymarch could see the driver yakking away on a cellular phone. The car's vanity plate read: IM BEST.

Greymarch turned down the radio and tapped the gas pedal, tailgating the Porsche. The other driver speeded up, but Greymarch matched his speed, maintaining a gap of mere inches between the two vehicles. The Porsche abruptly cut over a lane, but Greymarch followed as horns blared. The Porsche suddenly slipped back to the right, sliding recklessly into a car-length gap between two weaving vehicles, fishtailing slightly with the move.

Greymarch pulled up next to the Porsche and glared. The driver had a tiny head and red, shoulder-length hair. Pure rock and roll *manqué*. He looked back and forth between Greymarch and the slick road in front of him. His lips moved in a stream of bitter invective, the phone wedged in the crook of his neck. Beside him sat a Hollywood blonde, tan and plastic, all tits and hair. She leaned forward and peered at Greymarch. She looked nervous, her thick lips in a full pout. Greymarch nodded to himself.

Blow job city, he thought.

Greymarch smiled. He blew a kiss – with tongue – in the Porsche's direction.

The red-head freaked.

He started pounding the steering wheel and threw the cellular phone to the floor. He jerked out of his lane, angling straight for Greymarch, who cut into the fast lane as brakes screeched behind him. The Porsche missed him and hurriedly pulled back to the right. More horns bellowed in the background.

Greymarch slowed till the cars were once again side-by-side, but with an empty lane between them. He saw the blonde, looking scared, yell at the driver and pull at his arm. The red-head raised a fist and screamed at her. She flinched as he momentarily lost control and the car lurched onto the narrow shoulder.

The driver glared at Greymarch, his lips flapping like a grazing cow. He smacked the window with a tiny fist.

Greymarch reached into the glove compartment as a truck pulled up in the lane between them. It was full of Sunbeam bread, a cherubic baby's face painted on the side panel beneath the logo. Rain poured down its chipmunk cheeks like tears of joy.

Greymarch lowered the electric window on the passenger side.

The truck pulled on past, burning oil. Thick puffs of black smoke belched from the tailpipe, melting into the greater Angelino miasma.

Greymarch saw the Porsche through the smoke, still running even with him.

Seventy miles an hour.

Four thousand revolutions per minute.

Twenty-two calibre.

A Greymarch toy.

He nailed the Porsche's front tyre with his second shot. He felt bad.

He should only have needed one.

The Michelin exploded into strips of useless rubber and the driver lost control. The Porsche swerved left then right, crawling up the shoulder and bouncing off a cement rail in a fountain of sparks. The red-head jerked the car back into the slow lane, skidding badly on the slick pavement. The car started to fishtail and the driver jammed on the brakes.

Big mistake.

A vomit-green Ford ploughed into him from behind and sent the Porsche hurtling back onto the shoulder and down a slight grade. With an unfriendly cement barrier looming, the driver fought it and swerved left.

Mistake number two.

He hit the Ford mid-fender and caromed-off like a billiard ball. The Ford broke and skidded, immediately taking it up the ass from a black Saab, which in its turn wiped out a helmet-less biker to its left.

Metal screamed all around.

The Porsche jumped back onto the soft shoulder, weaving badly, but still moving much too fast. Greymarch decelerated and pulled into the slow lane to watch the denouement in his rear-view mirror. He saw the red-head looking dazed. Brakes screeched, rubber peeled, horns blared.

The red-head never saw the thick steel guard rail.

The Porsche came to a very abrupt halt and the plastic blonde exploded through the windshield.

Always wear your seat belt, Greymarch thought. *It's not just smart, it's the law.*

He stopped dead in the middle of the road. No cars could come up behind him through the tangle of steel and flesh that blocked all three lanes of the freeway. More crashes took place across the concrete divider as drivers heedlessly slowed down to catch a bloody eyeful.

Greymarch turned around and picked out the ruins of the rude Porsche. A spray of red marked the webbed windshield above the steering wheel.

Greymarch smiled. It was a deeper shade of red than the driver's hair.

And it dripped. Syrupy.

On the radio, the psycho-lady was discussing personal empowerment in co-dependent relationships. Greymarch turned up the volume. He was interested in this.

He tapped his fingers to the wipers' beat.

He drove on.

As Greymarch hopped the cemetery's chest-high stone wall, he wondered again if Bernouli would even come. And if he did, who might be there with him. Bernouli liked the public eye and was easy to keep track of, but some of his companions – his *masters*, not that Dr Sam would ever admit it – had been hard to locate of late. As much as anything, Greymarch had come to get a whiff of who might be minding Bernouli these days.

Would Titus show.

Greymarch landed in a crouch amid some brush. Thunder pealed in the distance like a great belch from the looming San Gabriel mountains. *Funny place for a South-Central family to have a cemetery plot*, he thought. The rain had dwindled to a fine mist that stung the skin like swarming gnats. Greymarch opened his mouth to the cool liquid, filling his gullet with its acrid taste.

He spotted the funeral party gathered around a plot fifty or sixty yards across the field of bones. He kept low, darting across the tangle of wet shrubs and brown grass, angling close enough for a better look-see.

He edged up behind an immense marble monument, topped with the carved statuette of a '68 Mustang. He glanced at the inscription, did a double-take and read it again:

GARY JONES, 1951–1986
He loved his mother.
He loved his car.
He loved to eat pussy.

Greymarch wondered, not for the first time, if there was any place else in the world quite like Southern California.

Thunder continued to roll through the valley as the graveside service droned on. Greymarch scanned the crowd of mostly black mourners. They looked disgusted, rain ruining the day for them. The nice suits and dresses would have to be dry-cleaned after this one.

Greymarch spotted him standing in the first row, between a tired-looking old black woman and a jittery teenage boy. It had been a while, but Bernouli hadn't changed a bit: tall and sturdy in an impeccable black suit. Square, strong jaw and aquiline nose. Stunning silver hair brushed back from a high, unlined forehead. Piercing blue eyes, remarkable even at that distance and through the gloom. He was holding the old woman's wrinkled claw in his own manicured hands.

He looked bored.

As Greymarch watched him, he felt an internal alarm go off.

At least one of the others must be near.

Greymarch dropped flat atop the muff-diver's grave. He checked his back then peered cautiously around the headstone. He craned his neck in a slow pan, through the crowded funeral party. He inched back off the grave, gliding snakelike across the sopping lawn and back to the cover of the bushes along the stone fence.

He crept along the edge of the wall, away from the mourning throng. His fingers curled around the grip of the Browning 9 mm in his pocket. He slipped an extra clip of hollow points from inside his coat to his left outer pocket. Wet brambles reached out for him, grabbing at his clothes as he crawled. The ground was sloppy mud that stained his black boots the colour of dried blood.

As he stepped out from behind a dense thicket, they spotted each other.

The blonde and the Asian stood amid a small copse of palms off to the mourners' left and out of their line of sight. The blonde, Heather, watched the service, but the Asian – Greymarch had never learned the man's name – stared right at Greymarch. Greymarch drew the gun from his pocket and held it at his side, out of sight amid the branches and leaves.

No sign of Titus.

The Asian nudged the woman, who picked out Greymarch and smiled when she spotted him. The Asian didn't seem amused. Heather's smile quickly faded as she bowed her head toward her collar and spoke into it. Greymarch saw a wire trailing out of her ear and into the neck of her jacket. The Asian was similarly outfitted.

Greymarch scanned the crowd looking for another earpiece or some sign of reaction, but the mourners were restless and several glanced casually about the graveyard.

Bernouli glanced around, too, but not in Greymarch's general vicinity. He looked even more bored than before.

Greymarch started slowly back toward his car, keeping an uneasy eye on his counterparts as he went. This wasn't the time or place for a scene, fun though it might be. And the sight of Heather and the Asian told him what he wanted to know. He stumbled over a bulging tree root and landed with a noisy exhalation and a slosh in a pool of brackish water.

He froze for several moments, face-down in the muddy culvert. Through the brush and vines he saw several people in the funeral party glance in his direction with puzzled expressions. Bernouli was looking, too, his gaze hard as a headstone. They started lowering the casket into the grave and all eyes returned to the business at hand.

Except for Bernouli's. He had located Greymarch amid the flora, his eyes wide with . . . what? Fear? Loathing? Regret?

Greymarch couldn't tell. He never could.

He crawled out of the ditch as quietly as he could. He glanced back at the grove. Heather and the Asian continued to watch him, but made no move his way. Heather was still smiling. She bent over and hiked up her dress to moon him.

No undies.

Greymarch saw the mourners file silently past the grave, tossing flowers as they went. Bernouli took his place in line, but kept glancing nervously around. The rain began to fall with greater intensity.

He started climbing back over the fence when a flash of lightning exploded across the sky. In a strobing instant, he was silhouetted against the looming grey and all heads seemed to turn his way.

Greymarch faded quickly into the shadows as the mourners departed and rolling thunder bellowed a final farewell to the dead black girl.

FOUR

Carmine Donatelli had more jowls than a pig farm. His nose was broad and round and fiery red with burst capillaries. Ugly tufts of salt and pepper hair sprouted from his nostrils and out of his enormous cauliflower ears. He was bald on top and paunchy in the middle and looked like he'd stepped straight out of a Tex Avery cartoon. And more than anything in the world, Donatelli hated having to get out of his comfy leather chair.

But he had bright eyes and a sharp mind and he didn't believe what he was hearing.

'No, I'm sorry but I can't accept that these are entirely separate incidents. You don't hardly get two like this in a year, much less on the same day. Even with the gang wars.'

Reagan and Brolin looked at each other. The final autopsy and forensic reports hadn't come in yet – the coroner's report was at least two days off with the back-log – but the preliminary investigation yielded no obvious connection between the cases and no indication of gang involvement had emerged from Reagan's investigation of the floater.

Brolin crossed her arms and looked the other way. She was convinced that the mutilations were just coincidence. Reagan tended to agree, but didn't want to admit it. He knew that Brolin had landed the spotlight case and he was reluctant to open any doors which might lead him off the stage and out of the media eye.

'We're not saying *definitely* no,' Reagan said, 'just that there's no immediate physical evidence to connect them. The damage was definitely inflicted with different implements. No indication of similarity in pattern or wounds and no gang tie-in for the John Doe under the pier. I mean, it is gang turf, but so far it's a no go. We're still looking for other possible links.'

'Do you have any kind of ID on the John Doe?' Donatelli asked.

Reagan shook his head.

'Prints?'

'No fingers.'

'Dental?'

'No teeth.'

'Jesus! Missing persons?'

'Shit, Captain. The guy probably matches a million general descriptions, but there's not a chance in hell of making this. I mean, the bastard was lashed to a piling, skinned, castrated and eviscerated. Then, to top it off, someone fired a flare gun down his throat. I'm telling you: this guy seriously pissed somebody off.'

'Stunning conclusion, Sherlock. You still canvassing?'

'Yeah, sure. But you know what it's like down there. It's mostly bums, whores and gangbangers. Hey, wasn't that a Cher song? Anyway, we're going to go back every day for a while and try to catch all the fishermen on the pier, but you know the play. They're three-quarters of 'em illegal and none too anxious to talk to the man even if they do habla Ingles.'

Donatelli slowly shook his head back and forth. He looked like an old basset hound.

'You check with the Feds?'

'Not yet. You want I should?' Reagan asked, already knowing the answer.

'I know they're pricks and I doubt they'll have anything, but maybe they can match an M.O. This kind of stuff is supposed to be their specialty, at least according to those neat Thomas Harris novels. I hate bringing them in, too, but for now I don't see where else to go with this. Do you?'

'You could lift the press gag. See if anyone comes in with anything.'

'No chance. We've got enough on the plate with the gangbangers.'

Reagan shook his head. 'Well, I'll fax the feds, but I wouldn't bet my daughter's cherry on anything.'

Brolin snorted but didn't look up. Still, Reagan scored it as one for him. Donatelli closed the thin file and opened another.

'What about you?' he asked Brolin.

Brolin looked up at him. 'The investigation is proceeding.'

'Where's McLeod?'

'Still taking written statements at the lab. Man, is he ever on the rag.'

'Wonder where he caught *that*,' Reagan sniped.

'Oooo, snappy comeback, Seinfeld.'

'Play nice, kids,' Donatelli warned. 'What do you have on the victim?'

Big sigh. 'She looks like a citizen so far. At least, she doesn't have a record on her. A couple of outstanding parking tickets is it. Lived alone in Los Feliz. Neighbours say she was quiet, but pleasant. They're shocked.' Brolin pantomimed gagging. 'She had a masters degree in organic chemistry from U.C. Davis. The people at Phaedra say she was a good employee, very dedicated to the job and to her boss. I'd say she just wasn't very lucky. Apparently she and her boss made the beast with two backs now and again.'

'That's Bernouli.'

Brolin nodded and glanced at her watch.

'What do you know about him?'

'Well, he's like the virus king or something. The world's leading authority and Phaedra's fair-haired boy. He used to be heavy into AIDS research, he invented that DPZ shit you're always hearing about. It made mondo bucks for the company. Now he's into some whole other thing, some kind of research into Gulf War Syndrome. Viruses is about all I could understand. He's got an iron alibi anyway.'

'How'd he take the news about the girl?'

Brolin laughed. 'He's a fucking iceman.'

Donatelli's eyes got a little brighter. 'How so?'

'He seemed more busted-up about the mess in the lab than about the girl. He said the perps trashed some big-time experiment. A bigger breakthrough than DPZ. At least, that's what *he* says.'

'How do you read him?'

'I think he's just an asshole. Obviously very taken with himself. Hell, maybe rightly so. What the hell do I know? I don't get any sense that he cared that much about the girl. She was maybe an okay assistant and a port in a storm. I think he banged her 'cause she was there which is maybe about as deep as his feelings go. I'm going to talk to him again when he can "fit me in". Those were his words.'

Donatelli nodded again, those Tex Avery jowls comically wobbling up and down. He stared mournfully at the tall stack of manilla folders on his desk. 'What next?'

'I'm going to interview the girl's family. Bet you wish you were me, huh?'

Donatelli pointed a fat little finger at Reagan. 'Take him.'

'Awwww . . . ,' Brolin started to protest. Donatelli cut her off.

'Until I'm satisfied that there's no connection here, you two will coordinate on all aspects of these cases. And you *will* make nice.'

Brolin looked pissed. Reagan smiled to himself then remembered.

'Hey, what about the nephew?' Reagan asked.

'What about him?'

'You can't do this to me, Captain.'

'Screw him,' Brolin said. 'Don't do it to me.'

Donatelli just smiled his jowly smile. 'Class dismissed.'

The two detectives glared at each other as they walked out of the office. Donatelli leaned back in his chair and watched them go. He knew Brolin was upset and Reagan pleased, Witherspoon notwithstanding. He was wary of Reagan's fondness for the limelight, but also knew that something smelled very bad here. And though he suspected that he was probably just being an old sexist, he didn't think Brolin, even with McLeod, had the experience to deal with it herself. The whole thing left him with a queasy feeling in his paunchy gut.

Donatelli leaned back, but not even the soft leather of his favourite chair could make that bad feeling go away.

FIVE

'Watchman!'

'Yo. I mean . . . number one.'

'What of the night?'

'It's down.'

'Watchman!'

'Number two.'

'What of the night?'

'Down!'

'Watchman!'

A faint crackle.

'Watchman!!'

Silence and static. Movement. Young black hands reach for guns and clips. Morgan clutching his Glock. Seventeen rounds in the magazine. Always ready.

A chirp on the intercom. An out of breath voice. 'Number three.'

'Where was you Curtiss?'

'Yo, Morgan, I had to hang Wallace.'

'I tol' you Curtiss, you tap the big black monkey when you off the watch. You down?'

'Ohhhh, man . . .'

'Don't let me be doubting you, Curtiss. If I have to cast my eye toward you – if even a question should enter my mind – that is something you would not like. I promise you that. Can you hear my words?'

A brief silence.

'I hear you Morgan.'

'And?'

'I'm down.'

Still a hint of defiance.

'You what?'

'I'm down.'

A note.

'You what?'

'I'm down.'

Defeat.

'Watchman!'

'Number three.'

'What of the night?'

'The night is clear, Morgan.'

'Tha's my boy, Curtiss. You stay frosty.'

The others had put away their weapons, but Morgan held onto the shiny Glock. He ran the smooth, dark barrel up and down his scarred cheek thinking about Curtiss. He didn't like that hesitation in the response. He'd never had a problem with Curtiss before, but Morgan liked to head off trouble before it arrived. A pound of prevention is worth an ounce of cure, his mother always said, and Morgan took her words to heart. Curtiss was expendable, a foot soldier. Countless others stood ready and very willing to take his place.

Morgan Carthay, on the other hand, was one of a kind. At least, that's the way he saw it. As leader of the Trey-Deuce Blood, Morgan was one of the most powerful people in Los Angeles. He smiled broadly at the thought. At the age of twenty he couldn't legally buy a six-pack of Bud at the Seven-Eleven, but with a word could order the death of anyone in the city.

No one even knew who he was. His picture never made it into the papers or on television. He didn't know if the cops were even sure of his name. But his power was absolute. He sometimes pictured himself in one of those old credit card commercials:

'Hi. You don't know me, but I had your mama raped and eaten by a pit bull. Sure, you don't recognize my black ass, but that was your baby whose head I blew off on his way home from school. That's why *I* carry this.'

Except there was no American Express card with the name M. Carthay embossed in sharp black letters. Only the Glock that was always at hand. Morgan once had his posse bring some drunken quack in because he wanted to know if the gun could be physically attached to his body. The doctor had been scared, but laughed at the suggestion. Laughed in front of the Blood.

So Morgan had no choice but to shoot him.

Fifty-one times.

After that he gave up on the idea, but the gun was rarely out of his hands and never out of reach. Guns were icons and Glock was Morgan's church.

But Tunnel was his salvation.

In little over two years, Morgan had elevated the Trey-Deuce from a minor Blood off-shoot to their present position as the most expansive and powerful gang in South-Central L.A. Their turf extended well beyond their small-time origins on 132nd Street. Morgan remembered how, when he first joined up at the age of nine, the Trey-Deuce were still fighting Crips for control of their own block.

He remembered very well the day he made his first kill – with a rusty, snub-nosed .38 lifted off a dead cop – when the Blood scattered the last of the C.C. Crips amid the now legendary slaughter in Athens Park. Morgan had been slit in the belly by a dude twice his age and size, but Morgan surprised the Crip with the .38 and blew the motherfucker's head off. Not a day went by that Morgan didn't finger the long scar that ran across his abdomen and exultantly play back the image of the Crip's brains spewing out on the dry grass.

Morgan and the Blood had come a long way since then. Straight out of Compton and across the city. With a gun in one hand and Tunnel in the other.

Just thinking about the golden drug made Morgan ache for another hit. He shot up as much as nine or ten times a day now and couldn't seem to stop.

Didn't want to stop.

Morgan glanced around the room. K'toma stood guard at the door, as always, but most of the others were sprawled out on the sofas or the floor, flying or watching the wide-screen TV. JuJu was working his way into the pants of some horse-faced Betty on the stairs. She kept her arms folded across her chest to stop him from grabbing at her floppy tits, but they were both laughing and there was no doubt but that she'd give it up to him before long. Why else would she be there? Lutece watched, looking a little jealous. Lutece's last girl had copped to soliciting a week earlier and he'd been moping around ever since.

Amid the empty Domino's pizza boxes and beer bottles, Tunnel hypos littered the room, their silvery needles glinting like cat's eyes in the roadway. Morgan gently laid the Glock on his lap and reached down and scooped up a hypo, casually pricking his finger on the dirty needle. Mindlessly, he touched the finger to his tongue dabbing at the tiny sphere of blood. Morgan's hands – like all the others' – were practically tattooed with abstract needle-prick designs. You didn't need to search for track marks to make a Tunneler, you just had to check their hands.

He twisted the hypo, separating the empty, rectangular syringe from the sharp, steel tip. He tossed the empty vial aside and pulled a full one out of his pocket.

He kept at least a half-dozen on him at all times.

He gripped the syringe between thumb and forefinger and held it up to the light. The Tunnel was pale gold and seemed to shimmer, almost magically, in Morgan's gaze. He twisted it slowly between his fingers, loving the feel of the flat, smooth container. Every perfect vial provided fifteen minutes of heavenly pleasure. The vials must have been made of plastic – they were almost impossible to break – but to Morgan the tiny beakers were worth more than the finest china or crystal. Morgan thought of them as little gold bars and himself as a pirate king awash in auric treasure.

Sometimes, in his rare, lucid moments between highs, Morgan had doubts about the drug and its hold on him. What was it doing to him? Would he ever be able to stop? And most of all, how come he and the Blood were lucky enough to be the only connection for it?

He never quite figured out how the man found him in the first place, or why he'd shed his grace on Morgan.

But Morgan's mother had another favourite saying: you don't give back a gifted horse 'cause he's got bad teeth.

Although this dude seemed to have some very bad bridgework indeed.

Morgan had taken the deal and taken the Tunnel and so far the trip had been a joyride. The cost to the Blood was negligible and the profits positively obscene. Morgan and his crew had everything and anything they wanted. They had respect and they had fear. If Morgan wanted a piece of ass, he snapped his fingers. If he wanted blood, he clapped his hands. You only dissed the Trey-Deuce at one hundred percent guaranteed risk to your life.

Morgan twisted the full syringe into the needle assembly until they joined with a satisfying click. Amazing design, Morgan thought. You could buy the works for a deuce, but replacements for the

Tunnel only went a nickel. The man insisted that the system work
that way and Morgan wasn't about to argue with him. The man
explained something about people using their own needles – some
AIDS jive – but it didn't seem to work out that way. There were
always needles around and when you could score four fresh pops
for the price of a new set of works, the clientele didn't worry too
much about where the needles came from.

But somewhere in the back of his mind, Morgan did worry.

Morgan tapped the needle, then slid it expertly into the skin between
the pinky and ring finger of his left hand. Within seconds the Tunnel
was burrowing into his brain and the entire world was cast in the
drug's ethereal golden glow. JuJu had finally managed to get the
horse-faced girl out of her shirt and was leading her upstairs to a
bedroom. Lutece, looking ready to cry, settled for a hit and joined
the other Tunnelers mesmerized by the TV.

Morgan tried to focus on the screen, but the pixels refused to
cohere into an image for him. The dancing dots of red, blue and
green twinkled like stars in his eyes. Morgan concentrated harder,
forcing the dots to melt into a pattern. The pattern formed a face.
He saw eyes as black as a raven's and a death's-head grin.

Lutece started laughing, the sound an ugly echo in Morgan's
ears. He tossed aside the spent hypo and fingered the Glock. The
feel of the gun in his hand soothed him. Morgan swam through
the ecstatic Tunnel haze, then fought his way toward the surface
and punched a button on the intercom.

'Watchman!'

SIX

Witherspoon hummed to himself in the back seat, slapping his thigh with an open palm as he admired the dull South-Central scenery. Reagan slowed for a red light and flipped his cigarette butt out the window. He eyed Witherspoon in the rear-view mirror then glanced over at Brolin who stared straight ahead with her arms folded. She was still sulking about having to ride shotgun and Reagan's refusal to not smoke in the car. Reagan had no problem with female detectives – well, none he would admit to – but that didn't mean he'd volunteer for the death seat while one drove. Or drive without smoking. Hell, you might as well not smoke after eating. Or sex. And it wasn't like he'd made her sit in the back or anything.

The light changed and Reagan again checked his partner in the mirror before tapping the gas: Witherspoon picked his nose, rolling the boogers between his fingers.

'I think Junior's being a very good boy today,' he said to Brolin. 'Don't you?'

'Just as long as he doesn't get carsick,' she said through clenched teeth.

'Heavens no. He hasn't done that in days. Right, Junior?'

'Hmmm?' Witherspoon said, trying to inconspicuously flick a juicy booger off his thumb.

'See, dear? Mother's special angel. I think we should get him some ice cream. Maybe even a Happy Meal.'

'Turn here,' Brolin said. 'And fuck off.'

Reagan followed half the instruction and hung a right off

Arlington onto Coliseum. He took another quick left onto Degnan and slowed down so they could scan the street numbers. A group of middle-aged black men sat along a concrete wall near the corner. Several of them clutched bottles in brown paper sacks. They warily monitored the car's slow progress up the street. On the opposite side, a group of black teenagers sat in the back of an old Chevrolet El Camino perched on blocks on a dead lawn. They, too, eyed the car with undisguised displeasure.

Three caucasians in a dark blue car in this part of town could only be cops. So as to leave no possible doubt, some jackass at the police garage had plastered anti-drug bumper stickers on every unmarked vehicle. The LAPD were the only ones in town who had them.

As Reagan pulled up in front of a small row house in the middle of the block, the group of old men all got up and ambled around the corner. One of them spat over his shoulder as he went. Reagan saw that the wall they'd been sitting on was heavily tagged with gang graffiti: Blood turf.

Brolin got out of the car before Reagan had the engine off. Witherspoon fumbled with the door handle, but Reagan turned around in the front seat to talk to him.

'I want you to stay with the car. If we leave it alone out here we won't be able to carry what's left home in an evidence envelope.'

It was a crock of shit, of course, but Witherspoon seemed to buy it. He nodded, then glanced nervously at the black youths idling across the street. Even at a distance and through the closed car windows, the bass echo from the speakers could be heard pounding out of the El Camino. Witherspoon dug down and found some courage in a pocket.

'I'll hold the fort,' he said.

'That's my boy,' Reagan said and got out of the car with a wink.

Brolin waited for him halfway up the walk to the little house. It was one of a series of identical cracker-box houses lining both sides of the street, cheaply constructed after the Second World War, but nicely maintained. A concrete bird-bath sat in the centre of the trimmed lawn and a narrow row of violet and pink flowers sprouted along either side of the cement path. Brolin watched a dirty sparrow frolic in the bath, but it flew away as Reagan came up beside her. Across the street, one of the kids turned up the volume on the music. Reagan glanced over and saw the El Camino rocking on its blocks. Though the sound had to be deafening, the youths who glowered back at him didn't so much as blink.

With Brolin leading, they proceeded up the steps. A black wreath hung from the front door and a murmur of voices could be heard inside. Brolin took a deep breath – jasmine was planted amid flowering bougainvillea along the side of the house – and rang the bell.

A tall, thin boy opened the door. He looked about fifteen with dark brown skin. He had large grey eyes and a wide, flat nose, but a small mouth with thin, sharp lips. His wiry hair was trimmed close to the scalp and a series of arcane symbols had been razor-cut into the left side. He wore baggy, over-sized trousers, slung low on his hips – Reagan couldn't figure out how the hell he kept them up; maybe his dick was permanently hard – and an electric red tank-top that billowed across his concave chest. A gold bracelet dangled from a wrist no thicker than a ginger root and his two-hundred dollar Nikes were unlaced. He eyed Reagan and Brolin with evident disgust.

'Yeah,' he droned.

'I'm Detective Brolin and this is Lieutenant Reagan.'

'So?'

'We're here to see Mrs Sommers,' Reagan said. He didn't like the kid's attitude.

'She busy.'

'Who is it, Arsenio?' A small, strong voice in the background. Arsenio turned his head slightly to reply, but kept an eye on Reagan.

'It's *po*-lice,' he said over his shoulder. Then, eyeing Brolin, spitefully added: 'Men.'

An elderly black woman came up behind the youth. The top of her head barely reached Arsenio's pecs, but he stepped away from the door at her slight touch on his arm. Her skin was black and worn as an old bomber jacket and her mottled scalp showed through her thinning, silver hair. Still, with her flat nose and small mouth, the resemblance to the boy was unmistakable. And in her stern posture and proud gaze, Reagan saw that the boy had inherited more than just his features from the old woman.

'How may I help you?'

Brolin held out her badge. 'My name is Detective Jenifer Brolin and this is Lieutenant Dennis Reagan. Are you Mrs Sommers?'

'I am Antoinette Sommers.'

'We're sorry to have to bother you at this time, Ma'am,' –

Arsenio growled – 'but we need to ask you a few questions about your granddaughter.'

The old woman hesitated for a moment – Reagan guessed that few if any white folk had ever crossed this particular threshold – then nodded slightly, but not at all deferentially. Arsenio continued to partially block the doorway, making no move to facilitate access. Brolin turned slightly to the side to squeeze past, but Reagan was of no such mind. For a moment the detective and the youth stood eye to eye.

'Arsenio, go and see to your Papa Jerome.'

Arsenio glared at Reagan for another moment. 'Yes, Nana,' he said and backed off.

Reagan and Brolin followed the old woman down a narrow hall with shiny hardwood floors, past a small living room and into the kitchen. A half-dozen or so black faces silently watched the small parade go past from the parlour, then picked-up their conversations in conspicuously hushed tones. Another slight, elderly woman hovered over the stove in the kitchen, while a little girl played with some pots and pans on the floor. Reagan breathed in the rich smell of barbecue sauce.

'Hi!' the little girl chirped.

'Well, hey there pretty one,' Brolin smiled.

'I'm Kelly. I'm four. Almost.'

'Really? My name's Jenny,' Brolin said.

'Heloise, would you please take Kelisha upstairs? It's time for her nap.'

'Naps are poo-poo,' Kelly said.

Heloise briefly eyed the officers with a mixture of fear and dislike, heavy on the latter. She turned down the flame under a large double-boiler and took the little girl's hand, silently leading her out.

'Bye-bye,' Kelly said. Brolin smiled again and waved to her as Heloise led her off.

'I must apologize for this setting,' Mrs Sommers said. 'I would have brought you to the sitting room, but as you see we have some company today in our time of grief.'

'That's all right, Mrs Sommers,' Brolin said. 'This is just fine. We're very sorry to have to bother you at all, but I'm afraid we need to ask you some things about Diane.'

At the mention of her granddaughter's name the old woman slumped a bit, but her voice never quavered.

'Go ahead then,' she said.

'When did you last see your granddaughter?'

'Diane came home for dinner every Tuesday evening. She never missed a Tuesday night.'

Brolin glanced at Reagan with eyebrows raised. The girl had been murdered late Tuesday night, early Wednesday morning.

'So you're saying that she was here this past Tuesday? The night of the murder?'

'Diane never missed a Tuesday dinner.'

'Did she say anything about going back to work afterward?' Brolin asked.

'She did mention it, I believe.'

'Did she say why?'

'She only said that she had a great deal of work to do and she appeared to be quite excited about it. I told her that she worked far too hard and that she was not sufficiently appreciated. Or remunerated. I told her that the man for whom she worked – that Dr Bernouli – was unworthy of her devotion.'

'Why did you think that, Mrs Sommers?' Reagan asked.

The old woman hesitated a moment before she spoke. 'Have you ever been to Africa, Officer Reagan?'

Reagan shook his head.

'I have been blessed with that privilege. It was my Diane who sent me there for my sixty-fifth birthday, for it had been my life's dream. And I was not disappointed by what I saw. It is a place of much rare beauty.'

'Mrs Sommers . . .'

'Please allow me to finish young man. Although I am no longer a spry thing, I was determined to avail myself of every opportunity to see all I could of my ancestral land. In Kenya, we were taken out into a wildlife preserve in a small . . . I believe it is called a Land Rover? There were only six of us and the vehicle broke down in the middle of the wild. While we were stranded, waiting on assistance, a pride of lions came upon our vehicle. One of those beasts pressed its face up to my window and stared right at me. It had tiny black eyes, like death's buttons, and I saw fresh blood matted in its fur and whiskers. Well, that lion gave me a good look over and, I could tell, dismissed me as unworthy of his attention. It was the look of a predator who could not be bothered with such feeble prey.

'Have you met Dr Bernouli, officer?'

'Not yet, Ma'am,' Reagan admitted.

'He shares that same predatory look. He is possessed of a

smugness and conceit – a dangerous and unattractive pride –
of one who thinks himself somehow superior to all he surveys.
I did not care for it. Such pride is an affront to the Almighty.'

'Do you know if Diane was involved with Bernouli in, umm,
other than a professional capacity?' Brolin asked.

'I did not speak with my granddaughter about such matters,
but I suspected so, yes.'

'Do you know if she was involved with anyone else?'

'I did not speak with my granddaughter about such matters,'
the old woman said again.

'Mrs Sommers,' Reagan began, 'we have reason to believe that
the individuals responsible for your granddaughter's death were
gang members. It's probably coincidental, but this *is* Blood territory
and Blood members may have been involved in her assault. Did
Diane ever have any gang associations?'

The old woman glanced down for a moment, seeming to gather
her thoughts. When she looked up her eyes were hard and her lips
tightly clenched.

'Mr Reagan. You do not have to tell me about the gangs. I lost
a child to that life. I see these young hoodlums on the street every
day and I curse them and their existence. They scrawl their profane
words on my walls and perform their foul deeds on my street. They
hurl insults and filthy language at me when I go to the store and
when I walk to my church. They leave me a prisoner in my own
home when the sun goes down.'

Reagan started to interrupt, but the woman wouldn't have it. 'I
raised my Diane for something better in this world. I raised her to
be a responsible person with good Christian values. I taught her the
meaning of dignity and raised her to respect herself and others and
God above all. I worked long days to see that girl through college,
to ensure that she made something of herself. To see her out of
this blighted place. And I succeeded.'

Her voice started rising in volume. 'And then you people come
and tell me that my little girl is dead. That some gang members
killed her in the night. You say that it was just bad luck. That she
was in the wrong place at the wrong time. Just a coincidence you
say to me now. Well, I say to you that there is no coincidence. My
little girl had nothing to do with those evil gangs. But she's dead
just the same. Dead as her brother who joined the gangs. So what
was it all for, Mr Reagan? Can you tell me what it was all for?'

The old woman turned away. She adjusted the flame on the
double boiler. Reagan wanted to ask her about Arsenio, but

he came up empty. Just then the boy appeared in the kitchen doorway.

'You all right, Nana?'

Mrs Sommers dabbed at her eyes with a tissue she pulled from her frilly sleeve. She nodded at the boy and waved him away, but he wouldn't go.

'I think you should leave now,' Arsenio said.

Reagan had been about to suggest the same, but didn't like it coming from the kid. He started to protest when Brolin grabbed his arm.

'We're sorry to have disturbed you, Mrs Sommers. And we're very sorry for your loss.'

The old woman had regained her earlier composure and nodded silently at the detectives. Arsenio followed them to the door and slammed it loudly behind them.

'Some fun, huh, Dennis?'

Reagan shook his head and reached for a cigarette, but froze in mid-gesture.

'Notice anything?' he asked.

Brolin looked up and down the street, then glanced at the car.

'Jesus Fucking Christ!' she said.

The hubcaps were missing.

Witherspoon was still sitting in back playing with the ceiling light. Reagan leaned over and tapped on the glass. Witherspoon fumbled with the handle but managed to get the window rolled down.

'So, uh, anything much happen while we were inside?' Reagan asked.

'All quiet on the western front,' Witherspoon smiled. He looked pathetically proud of himself.

'Didn't see or hear anything unusual?'

'Not a thing, boss.'

Reagan nodded and glanced across the street at the kids in the El Camino. The music had been turned down. They all stared at Reagan with broad grins. He fired up a Marlboro and got into the car. Brolin still stood there with her mouth open and her hands on her hips.

'That's my boy, Junior,' Reagan said.

SEVEN

'Mr Brain wi' see you now.'

A Chinese houseboy, Bernouli thought, *Jesus Christ!* Only Blaine would go for such an affectation. And only Blaine could get away with letting a man like Sam Bernouli cool his heels until he deigned to speak with him.

Bernouli followed the shuffling servant through the richly appointed halls of the Malibu mansion. The looking-glass floors were inlaid with a slightly disorienting mosaic with a vaguely Egyptian motif. The art work – all originals, of course – was more than a little impressive, even for this part of town: Warhol, Hamilton, a Rauschenberg combine. As he walked past the open door of the cathedral-like library, he marvelled at the immense Francis Bacon triptych that graced an entire wall.

The houseboy led Bernouli out through the back of the mansion and toward the pool. It was an Olympic-sized affair with low and high diving boards at the far end. The pool's tile work featured a colourful pattern of outrageously phallic sea serpents frolicking with lithesome mermaids.

The storm had blown itself out during the night, making way for another grade-A, standard issue southern California day. A naked blonde floated face-up in the middle of the pool, her long hair bobbing in a golden nimbus around her head. Bernouli didn't think he recognized her, but then with Blaine it was hard to be sure. Her breasts glistened in the noontime sun, the brown nipples large and erect. Her legs were languidly spread in a less than ladylike manner and her thick pubic hair waved in the water like a thatch of sea anemones.

Blaine was reclining on a deck chair by the shallow end. He wore a black Speedo swimsuit, turquoise flip-flops and black Wayfarers. He never looked up from his copy of *Daily Variety* as Bernouli approached.

'Sam the Sham,' Blaine growled. 'Where are your pharaohs? Take a load off.'

Bernouli continued to fume for a moment, then remembered where he was and pulled over a lawn chair. He picked that morning's *Hollywood Reporter* off the seat and tossed it onto the grass.

He studied Blaine for perhaps the hundredth time and marvelled. Blaine was really put together. His wild, thick shock of jet-black hair was wet and slicked straight back. His features were narrow and sharp, but not the least bit gaunt. He had wide, muscular shoulders and arms and a solid, expansive chest that tapered to a perfect V. Fat snakes of muscle rippled across his stomach as well as his legs and forearms. His fingers and toes were long and thin, though his feet were thick and square as cinder blocks. The Speedo barely contained the large bulge of his crotch. Bernouli glanced at the floating blonde and sighed.

Blaine finally put the newspaper aside and leaned forward. He inspected Bernouli through the sunglasses' smoky lenses. Though it was disturbing, Bernouli was glad Blaine didn't take the shades off. He knew those eyes all too well: they were black and cold as a winter night. They terrified him.

'Police,' Bernouli said to break the silence. 'A lot of them.'

'Problem?'

Bernouli shrugged as if to say: *What do you think?*

'You handled it.'

Bernouli nodded. Blaine leaned back in the chair.

'How was the funeral?' Blaine asked. His voice was smooth as chocolate mousse. 'Sorry I couldn't make it.'

'It rained.'

'I know. Had to use the sun bed. It's really not the same.'

'Greymarch was there,' Bernouli said, as casually as he could.

'So I hear.'

'And?'

'And my, but don't we live in interesting times?'

Bernouli had been furious, but the cold force of Blaine's personality struck him like a blast from a meat locker. Bernouli could barely move. Blaine seemed to sense it.

'What's the matter, Sammy? I can see you've got something on
your mind. Get it off your chest and we'll both feel better.'

Bernouli swallowed hard. 'I told you not to kill her.'

Blaine cocked his head to one side, grading the quality of the
sky's blue.

'You. Told. Me.' He exploded into laughter. 'Good one.'

The freezer got even colder. Bernouli crossed his arms over his
chest. 'You didn't have to do it. She was . . . I thought we had
an understanding.'

'Oh, please. Don't get maudlin on me, Sam, it's not your colour.
Neither are those earth tones you're wearing, by the way. The bitch
was nothing. Not a bad cut for dark meat, if that's your thing, but
there's always more tuna in the sea. I'm sure you'll find someone
else to play land-the-shuttle.'

'You don't get it, do you?'

'Get what, dude?'

Bernouli hesitated. He was scared. 'Nothing means anything to
you these days, does it? It's all just sick fun and games. I don't
even think you care about the money that much. Or *anything*.
Maybe you don't remember how all this started. What I did for
you. What I'm still *trying* to do.'

'I remember everything, Sam.'

'Damn straight!' Bernouli realized he was practically shouting
and restrained himself. 'I am not your puppet. I'm not like the
others.' Bernouli waved his hand in the blonde's direction. 'And
I won't stand for these arbitrary and dangerous moves of yours.
I wasn't through with Diane and I told you that. It's going to
cost you.'

'Cost how?'

Bernouli started to speak, but had to clear his throat. 'She
may have had something with her in the lab. Some of the
documentation.'

'Specifically what?'

'I'm not sure. Your *homeboys* . . .' – Bernouli snarled his lip –
'trashed the place a little too well. Maybe some of the delta phase
details. The new round of organelle modifications.'

Blaine leaned forward again and took off the shades. Bernouli
tried, but couldn't avoid looking into those eyes. They were crow's
eyes, the pupils like charred peas.

'I thought I told you to keep it in the family.'

'I thought that's what I was doing.'

'Anything there that could lead back to the Tunnel operation?'

Bernouli paused as if in thought, trying to play the power game with Blaine, who finally looked a little concerned.

'*Prob*ably not,' Bernouli said.

'Anything anyone else would *understand*?'

Bernouli snorted.

'Then it's negative perspiration, my man.' Blaine glowered a moment longer, then put the glasses back on. He lay back in his chaise longue. 'Totally negative perspiration. I'll have all the loose ends taken care of.'

'How? I told you, the cops are into it.'

'I have a way with men in uniform. It's covered, dude.' Bernouli didn't like the sound of that, but was too cowed to offer any further resistance. The two sat silently until a shadow crept over Blaine. The blonde, still nude, stood at the foot of the lounge. As she stretched her hands up over her head beads of water rolled slowly down her perfect body, understandably reluctant to let go of the golden skin.

'Titus,' she whined, 'I'm bored.'

Blaine pushed the Ray-Bans down his thin nose and peered at her over the lenses. 'Why don't you go inside for a while, Heather. It's almost time for your shows.'

The blonde glanced over at Bernouli. He felt like a lobster in a glass tank.

'Is this one for me?' she asked.

Titus smiled his devilish smile. He glanced at Bernouli. 'What do you say, Sammy? Want to play with Heather?'

Bernouli studied the blonde who casually scratched her labia. Her face and body were to die for.

He felt very certain of that.

'No. Thanks.'

Titus chuckled. 'Not today, babe,' he said. He winked at Bernouli and laughed. 'Another time, maybe.'

The blonde turned her back on the men and sauntered across the patio toward the house. Bernouli's eye naturally wandered to her exposed rear, but his gaze was frozen by the line of tumour-like pustules that formed a ridge along the small of her back.

'My god,' he whispered.

'What?' Titus said.

'The girl. You've . . . How many, Titus?'

'Whatever do you mean?'

'How many others are there now? With the organelles?'

Titus smiled and turned back to his newspaper. Bernouli knew

that no answer would be forthcoming. He also knew he was
dismissed, but dawdled a minute before getting up to go.

'Sammalah?' Titus said. He continued to read.

'Hmmm?'

'Repeat after me.'

'What?'

'I said repeat after me: I . . .'

'What are you talking about?' A note of fear crept into
Bernouli's voice.

'Do it!' Titus said. 'I . . .'

Bernouli still hesitated until Titus again whipped off the shades
and stared him down.

'I . . .' Bernouli echoed mechanically.

'Am . . .'

'Am . . .'

'yo-ur . . .' Titus sing-songed.

'Your . . .' Bernouli choked.

'Meat puppet!'

Bernouli glared down at his master.

'Say it, Sammy,' Titus teased. He smiled broadly, but there was
no humour in his flashing teeth.

'Meat puppet,' Bernouli spat.

'Always remember that. Like I remember everything. Or I may
just decide to let Heather have her *very* wicked way with you.'

Bernouli followed the houseboy back inside. *What have I done*,
he thought, not for the first time. He shuddered as Titus chuckled
behind his back.

EIGHT

'What would you do for me?' Morgan asked.

Arsenio kept his mouth shut. He understood that the question was rhetorical and wasn't about to interrupt. K'toma stood at the corner, stonelike as always. Only his eyes moved as he scanned the street. JuJu waited in the car, engine idling, doors open, pounding the wheel to the commanding beat of the stereo. The only other sound was the sizzle of fatty burgers on the grill.

'What would *you* . . .' Morgan touched a long, scarred finger to a spot between Arsenio's eyes, 'do for *me?*' He pounded his chest with a closed fist, let his hand drift down his body and squeezed his crotch à la Michael Jackson. Morgan leaned against the counter of the tiny burger stand and looked expectantly at Arsenio. He grabbed a handful of fries smothered in ketchup and stuffed them in his mouth.

'I do whatever you tell me,' Arsenio said. It sounded small and unconvincing even to himself.

Morgan threw his head back and sniffed at the air, like a dog. He glanced over at K'toma and beckoned the massive bodyguard over. K'toma stood at attention at Morgan's side, his eyes still moving, watching.

'Suck my dick,' Morgan said to him.

K'toma dropped to his knees. His expression never changed as he unbuttoned Morgan's pants and gently reached in and pulled out Morgan's flaccid penis. Arsenio shifted back and forth and looked around nervously. JuJu was still in the car, watching the street and listening to the music. The old grillman behind the counter kept flipping his burgers. He kept his back to the gangsters and Arsenio suspected that nothing short of tactical nukes could get him to turn around.

K'toma parted his lips and bobbed his head toward Morgan's groin.

'Stop,' Morgan said. 'Back to your post, Blood.'

K'toma gently let go of Morgan's cock and got up. He brushed the dirt off his knees and immediately began to survey the territory again. He returned to his position on the corner without once looking at Arsenio.

'That's called obedience. That's what your brother had and that's what it takes to survive in the Blood. That's the meaning of life. You do what I tell you?'

Arsenio swallowed hard and nodded. Morgan eyed him with a half-smile on his lips, his thick penis still hanging out of his open fly.

'Then suck my dick, homeboy.'

Arsenio glanced to his right, saw that JuJu was now watching events in rapt fascination. The grillman was all back-of-the-head.

Arsenio stood face to face with Morgan. The Blood leader stared icily into Arsenio's eyes. Morgan flicked his pink tongue across chocolate lips, snatching up a stray french fry crumb. Arsenio could practically taste the ketchup on Morgan's breath.

He looked down at Morgan's drooping cock, saw a large chancre on the circumcised head. He took a series of quick, shallow breaths and dropped slowly to his knees until Morgan's penis dangled right in front of his eyes. At close range, Arsenio saw that the sore wept a thin yellow-brown liquid. Closing his eyes, Arsenio slipped his hand beneath the warm organ and raised it to his lips.

As Arsenio opened his mouth, Morgan shot a stream of urine between Arsenio's lips. It was a short, sharp shock, but Arsenio gagged and twisted to the ground on his side. He tried to stop himself, but couldn't help retching onto the concrete. He heard JuJu's high-pitched laughter and started to look up, but had to turn away as another wave of nausea overtook him. Finally, he rolled onto his back and found himself staring at Morgan's upside-down visage.

Morgan handed Arsenio a stack of napkins and a Coke. He wiped his mouth and blew his nose and gargled with the soda. He drew up a wad of phlegm and spat it onto the pile of vomit. When he looked up again, Morgan held a hand down to him. Arsenio grabbed it and Morgan effortlessly pulled him to his feet.

'We'll see,' Morgan said. He walked back toward the car. Over his shoulder, Morgan yelled: 'Don't forget the burgers.'

It was well after midnight when Arsenio made it back to his grandmother's neat little house. He could hear the blare of a get-rich-quick real estate infomercial on the TV.

His grandmother was asleep on the couch in front of the television, her glasses pushed up on her forehead. She had taken her teeth out so that her wrinkled mouth sagged like an old balloon. A line of drool snaked down her chin. She clutched a picture frame to her stomach. It held Diane's college graduation photo, her crooked smile counterbalanced by the off-kilter mortar board on her head.

Arsenio used the remote to turn the television off and gently eased the silver frame from between his grandmother's fingers. He pulled the afghan up around the old woman's neck and looked long and hard at his dead sister's face. If what he'd heard on the street was true, Morgan and his crew were involved in Diane's death. He was determined to find out exactly which of them had killed her and why. The cost might be high, he knew, but he felt the cost of not finding out would be even greater.

He looked again at his dead sister's picture and then at his grandmother. He tasted Morgan's piss in the back of his throat and suppressed a gag.

'For you,' he vowed.

To the living and the dead.

NINE

Blood was everywhere.

Bodies filled all available space: sitting, kneeling, sprawled across benches, stretched out on gurneys, leaning against the industrial grey walls. The rhythmic blips and beeps of monitors and machines provided accompaniment to the near-constant whooshing of opening and closing automatic doors. Beneath the idle chatter and stern doctorly commands could be heard a pained undercurrent of moans and coughs, sobs and sniffles. The walking wounded, the sickly, the infirm, the wretched refuse, the poor, the *uninsured* waiting their turn.

Waiting and waiting and waiting.

The emergency room at County-U.S.C. Hospital had 18 beds and treated 500 patients a day. Greymarch curled his lip in a rotten-egg-stench sneer and pushed his way through the throng of rainbow coalition faces. An old Hispanic man with a compound fracture of the right wrist lay on the floor shivering and drenched in sweat, while a heavy-set nurse with a clipboard asked him questions about his mother's family. A slight Korean girl, who couldn't possibly have been more than thirteen, mechanically comforted a scrawny, jaundiced infant covered in its own crusty vomit. Two black youths in gang colours held up a teetering companion who bled profusely from a gash in his cheek. One of them screamed at a resident while the other kept a watchful eye on another cadre of teens garbed in rival rags sitting across the waiting room.

Greymarch unsuccessfully repressed a shudder. There was no place in the world he hated more than hospitals. Too many memories. He already had the shakes and had gone pale as egg white. He had to jam his hands in his pockets to stop himself from scratching and he swallowed rapidly and repeatedly in an attempt to keep his bile down. His mouth tasted of bad seafood.

At the main desk, Greymarch tried to insinuate himself in front of an enormous, middle-aged black woman, but admiringly stepped back when she refused to give ground and started swatting him with her pocketbook. After a brief shouting match with the receptionist, an orderly came along and escorted the woman off in a wheelchair. Greymarch stepped up to the counter. The receptionist was yelling at someone in the office behind her and typing into a computer terminal at the same time. She acknowledged Greymarch with a barely perceptible tilt of her head.

'Ewing,' he said.

'I what?' the receptionist asked.

'Ewing.'

'What you talking 'bout, mister?' The woman picked up a beeping telephone and attempted to carry on three conversations while continuing to type into the terminal.

'*Doctor* Judy Ewing. Where is she?'

'I tol' you, I don't *got* no urine,' she said into the phone. Then over her shoulder: 'You find that pee yet, Carmella?' Type, type, type. To Greymarch: 'Dr Ewing's in the on-call room. She asleep. You just take a seat and fill out the Medi-Cal papers and you get to see someone. Who's next?'

'Prole,' Greymarch muttered. He went looking for the on-call room, but the waiting room stood at the centre of a confusing octopus of corridors, each marked with faded coloured lines on the floor. The posted signs were about as helpful as the Scarecrow on the Yellow Brick Road. Greymarch's shakes were getting worse and the pain in his gut felt like a twisting knife. He tried hailing a couple of rushing nurses, but no one seemed to speak English. Finally, he grabbed the arm of a passing resident, a tiny Indian man who was trying to balance and read three patient charts and who looked as lost as Greymarch.

'Doctor's on-call,' Greymarch hissed.

The man did a double-take and dropped two of the charts.

'What is it you are wanting?'

'*On-call*. Where is the doctors' on-call?'

The resident glanced around and scratched his bald head. He looked at Greymarch, glanced around some more, looked back at Greymarch. 'Delhi?' he said, somewhat quizzically.

Now it was Greymarch's turn to be confused. 'What? Which deli? What are you talking about?'

'My uncle is in Delhi, thank you very much. What business is it of yours please?'

The resident scurried off without waiting for an answer, leaving Greymarch counting the ways he could kill the man using only his stethoscope.

'Yo, Mister.' Greymarch glanced down at a young black woman leaning against a pillar behind him. She had an enormous boil on her neck that forced her to hold her head at a canted angle. She'd overheard his exchange with the resident and was still laughing. 'The on-call room is down at the end of the blue hall. Follow the red line to the blue. It's across from X-ray. I used to work as a cleaner here, but I don't no more. Now I just come here to be sick.'

Greymarch nodded his thanks and followed the lines on the floor. The red faded out before he got to the blue, but he found a sign pointing the way toward X-ray. He spotted the on-call room at the very end of the hall. Ignoring the 'Authorized Personnel Only' sign, Greymarch went right on in.

The pale blue light of an old television dimly lit the room. An episode of 'I Love Lucy' was on with the volume turned down low. Lucy and Ethel were stuffing chocolates down their blouses. A red-eyed resident in hospital greens lounged in a tattered armchair beside the tube, playing with a hand-held video game that blipped and beeped and chirped a mind-numbingly happy little tune. The man didn't so much as look up at Greymarch.

A pair of bunk beds and metal lockers lined the far wall. A figure with flowing black hair was curled foetally in the lower berth of the second set of beds, face to the wall. Greymarch repressed another wave of reverse peristalsis and went over to the bottom bunk, kneeling beside the figure. He leaned over the sleeping form to verify her identity. At the touch of his breath on the back of her neck, her eyes shot open and she thrust an arm straight at Greymarch's throat, fingers rigidly poised to inflict maximum damage.

He caught her wrist with a trembling hand and smiled weakly. 'Snappy reflexes, Jude.'

She turned around to face him and her eyes were so full of rage that Greymarch instinctively tightened his grip on her wrist. Recognition set in after a moment and her features went slack, so Greymarch let her go and stepped out from under the bunk.

'Oh, Christ,' she moaned. 'It's getting so I can't tell the nightmares from my waking life.'

Greymarch tried another smile, but it wasn't a pretty sight. The contrast between his beaten-up face and Judy's delicate features couldn't have been more extreme. With her high cheekbones, thin lips, straight teeth and silver-blue eyes, she was a composite image of the perfect Seven Sisters alumna.

She stretched and yawned. 'What are you doing here, Calvin? Where have you been?'

Greymarch glanced over his shoulder at Dr Gameboy. Judy wore only a bra and panties and her cover had become snarled around her waist. The resident stared with unabashed lust at Judy's chest, the video game still chirping in his hand. Greymarch got up with a grunt and walked over to the man. He bent down and whispered in his ear. The doctor's face blanched and he started to get up, but Greymarch held him by the shoulder and continued to whisper. When he finished, the resident hurriedly left the room, leaving his game behind. Greymarch placed it gently on the floor then smashed it to bits under his heel. He squatted back beside Judy, who was now sitting on the edge of the bunk, pulling on some blues.

'What did you tell him?' she asked, trying not to smile.

'I said that if he so much as thought about your tits again, he'd be modelling for a revised edition of *Gray's Anatomy*.'

Judy chuckled in spite of herself, but her good humour quickly passed. 'You look like hell, Calvin. And you know you're not supposed to be here. I don't see you for . . . what is it? Six weeks? Eight? And then you show up here? What is your problem?'

'I came up a little short.'

'Christ!' Judy said. 'And you come *here*? What am I supposed to do for you? Take you up to a ward and turn out the lights?'

'C'mon, Jude.'

'Don't give me that!' she started to yell, then lowered her voice. 'I've got nothing here for you, Calvin. I can get you something later at the hospice, but I can't leave right now.'

Greymarch didn't say anything. He unzipped his green army jacket and fumbled open several buttons on his shirt. The sallow skin on his hairless chest was covered with sores and picked scabs. A halo of tiny black tumors surrounded each nipple, pulsing haphazardly like fairy lights on a Christmas tree.

'I'll hit the street if I have to,' he said. He looked beseechingly, pathetically at Judy. 'You know I will. If you make me.'

'How can you live like this, Calvin?'

Greymarch tried to rebutton the shirt, but his hands were shaking too badly. Judy reached up and buttoned it for him and rezipped his jacket.

'How can you?' he said.

They stared at each other for a moment. Judy looked away first. She went over to a tall locker and twirled the combination lock. Wrinkled jeans dangled from a hanger and several pairs of shoes and trainers and an old knapsack sat in a pile on the bottom. Judy pulled a small box off a shelf at the top of the locker and gestured to Greymarch who came up beside her.

Judy held a sewing kit in her hand. With an eye on the door she opened the box and flipped it upside down. As she gave it a shake, the moulded plastic bottom came loose, revealing two vials taped to the bottom of the box, one filled with red liquid, the other with light gold. She tore them from the box and, one eye still on the door, stuffed them in Greymarch's jacket pocket.

'For emergencies,' she said. 'It's not much, but it'll do you for a while.'

Greymarch grabbed her upper arm and squeezed it hard enough to leave a bruise. Judy smiled back at him, knowing it was his idea of affectionate thanks.

Greymarch pulled a needle assembly out of a pocket on his sleeve, but Judy stopped him. 'Uh-uh. Not in here,' she said.

Greymarch looked desperate, but put the needle away. He all but ran out of the room, then stuck his head back inside the door. 'You be there tomorrow?'

Judy sighed and nodded.

'You seen the news lately?' he asked.

'No,' Judy said and frowned. 'Why? What have you done?'

'We'll talk,' he said and was gone.

'Oh shit,' Judy whispered to herself.

Greymarch couldn't wait to get outside. He ran into the nearest men's room and dashed into the first free stall, slamming the door shut. He didn't even notice that the toilet seat was up and sat down on the dirty porcelain rim. He couldn't stop shaking long enough to fit the vials into the dual assembly and he dropped the needle several times. Finally, he took a series of long deep breaths and summoning a massive effort of will, snapped the vials into their slots.

Fumbling again with the buttons, he opened his shirt. He squeezed at one of the small growths around his nipple until it was bright red. He thrust the needle squarely into the growth and depressed the hypo. The mixture of Tunnel and tainted blood hit his system instantaneously. He slipped off the toilet and rested on the floor as the solution coursed through his system, bringing blessed relief.

He sat there briefly until he felt in control. He pulled the empty syringes from the needle works, broke them apart and tossed the pieces in the toilet. He flushed them away. The needle went back into the pocket on his sleeve.

He zipped the pocket with steady, sure hands and walked out of the hospital, whistling.

TEN

Reagan and Brolin sat side by side in the reception area of Glanville's office at Phaedra. Reagan was pissed about having to cool his heels, but secretly relieved that the meeting with Bernouli wouldn't take place in the lab. He couldn't seem to shake the picture of the butchered girl sprawled across the lab bench and didn't think he'd be at his best questioning the scientist with the memory of that scene so close at hand. And it had taken three days just to schedule an interview with Mr Bigshot. Nonetheless, Reagan had been about to get up and carp some more at the secretary, but Brolin held him back.

'Ixnay, Dennis,' she said. 'Kid gloves. Remember?'

Reagan knew she was right – Donatelli had actually risen out of his chair to deliver a speech about dealing gingerly with Bernouli – but he growled at her anyway. Brolin ignored him and continued browsing through a copy of *Psychoplasmics Today* that she'd picked up off the coffee table. Reagan fumed silently and turned his attention back to the secretary who wore a tight, revealing blouse. She was three-hole punching a stack of papers and jiggled entertainingly every time she pressed down on the punch.

'Pig,' Brolin mumbled and Reagan mentally awarded himself another point.

The secretary picked up her beeping phone. 'They're ready for you now,' she said, pointing at a closed door.

Reagan led the way into a small, neatly appointed conference room dominated by a round mahogany table. Bernouli, Glanville and a third man in a pinstriped suit sat in an arc around the table with Bernouli in the middle. The scientist didn't look up from his notebook computer as the detectives entered, and Reagan had the feeling that, whatever shape it might be, Bernouli's place automatically became the head of the table. Glanville gestured at the chairs. Reagan and Brolin sat down across from Bernouli. Everybody stared at each other for a while – except Bernouli, who still hadn't looked up – until Glanville, blinking and nervous-looking, broke the silence.

'Dr Bernouli is happy to give you thirty minutes today, then he has to leave for an important meeting. Shall we proceed?'

Bernouli finally glanced up at the cops, evaluating Brolin like a cut of steak before fixing his gaze on Reagan. Bernouli didn't *look* too happy to be there. He picked up a Mont Blanc pen with the thumb and forefinger of his right hand and tapped it gently against his manicured left thumbnail. He had devastating silver-blue eyes that reminded Reagan of the eerie children in *Village of the Damned*. Bernouli's good looks were powerful; he positively radiated authority and charisma. Reagan thought he heard Brolin say 'wow' under her breath and uncharacteristically felt he was beginning the interview at a disadvantage. He tried to stare Bernouli down, but felt himself start to drown in the silvery depths of his eyes. He looked away at the third man in the dark suit.

'Who are you?' Reagan snapped, finding a target for his annoyance.

'Brian Boyd,' the man said. 'I'm Dr Bernouli's attorney.'

'There's really no need for lawyers here,' Brolin started, but Boyd cut her off.

'Well, then it won't bother anyone if I stay. Will it?' The lawyer smiled beneath his bushy black moustache, but he somehow reminded Reagan of a small animal poked once too often with a sharp stick.

'No. No problem,' Brolin said, and Reagan felt them lose another piece of ground before the interview could even begin.

'Tick-tock,' Glanville said and Reagan got pissed. The hell with Donatelli, he thought, time to get off the defensive.

'Were you sleeping with Diane Sommers, Doctor?' he asked

Boyd immediately started to protest, but Bernouli quieted him with a slight raise of his pinky.

'It's okay, Brian. The officers have their methods and I'm eager to cooperate.' Bernouli spoke in hushed, even tones, like Mel Torme on downers. Reagan felt that his attempted step forward had landed him two steps back. 'Officer . . . Brolin was it?'

Reagan turned red. 'She's Brolin. I'm Reagan. Lieutenant.'

'Sorry. *Lieutenant*. To answer your question: Yes, Diane and I were intimate at one point in time. But that aspect of our relationship had been over for some while. We remained good friends, of course, and Diane was a treasured colleague.'

Reagan realized that he didn't have anywhere to go with that line and hesitated, but Brolin pulled him out.

'Dr Bernouli . . .' Bernouli turned his gaze on her and she stumbled for a moment then recovered. 'Can you tell us what Diane was doing in your lab on the night of the murder?'

'I'm afraid I don't know.'

'Surely you have some idea?'

'Officer, Diane was my primary research assistant and as such had full access to the offices and the laboratory. She was free to work her own hours and she was extremely devoted to her job. She didn't routinely work through the night, but she was as likely as not to be at the lab at any given time. Like myself, she placed the importance of the work that I do above everything else in her life. She was, again not unlike myself, something of a workaholic.'

'But what was she actually doing?' Reagan asked.

'I really can't say for sure. The vandalizing of the lab was so extreme that I can't tell precisely what she was working on that night, but in terms of the overall research timetable, we were concluding a series of histological analyses. So I would guess that she was dealing with those tissue samples on the night of the break-in. But she may well have been working on one of several papers or simply running some statistical analysis on the computer.'

'Analysis of what?' Brolin said.

Bernouli hesitated and glanced sideways at his attorney, who jerked his head in Glanville's direction. It looked a bit like a Three Stooges routine and Reagan half-expected Glanville to go, 'Nyuk-nyuk-nyuk.'

'I'm afraid that information is of a proprietary nature,' Glanville said instead.

'Proprietary,' Brolin repeated.

'Well,' Bernouli said, 'I think I can at least respond to the pretty officer in general terms. I am engaged in a large-scale research project which approaches the current epidemic of human immunosuppressive disorders in a somewhat radical manner. My own approach incorporates a consideration of HERVs . . .'

'Who?' Brolin asked.

Bernouli smiled the Webster's definition of condescending. 'Forgive me. Human Endogenous Retroviruses. We refer to them simply as HERVs.'

'Uh-huh,' Brolin said.

'HERV's are . . . how to make this simple . . . a common and vital co-factor in the manifestation of a range of dangerous syndromes and disorders which have come to light in recent decades: AIDS, CFS, so-called Gulf War Syndrome, many others. My research agenda is an effort to . . . re-prioritize the treatment of such disorders. It's vastly complex, of course, but we had progressed to an early, though promising stage in the project when the, ah, incident occurred.'

'How promising?' Reagan asked.

Bernouli took a deep breath and let it out. 'I can't really say without getting into technical details that would be far beyond you, but I would certainly call the work highly promising.'

'Promising enough to steal?' Brolin said.

Glanville twitched, but Brolin ignored him.

'No,' Bernouli said. 'No one other than myself would be able to make sense of any of the work. In point of fact, most of it was even beyond Diane's level of expertise.'

'Then how was she able to assist you?' Brolin asked.

'Officer. The man who repairs your VCR is quite able to do so without comprehending the theoretical basis of the integrated circuit. Diane performed largely mechanical lab work – sophisticated, to be sure – but essentially no different from that VCR repairman. *I* am the theoretician.'

'Is there anyone who would have it in for a theoretician like yourself?' Reagan asked.

Bernouli coughed and glanced at the lawyer who was again smiling that cold, wolverine smile. 'Many people, officer. I'm not the world's most popular fellow.'

'Give me a for instance.'

'In the past I've been picketed by several of the more militant gay organizations and activist groups largely because of my opinions about the role of HIV in AIDS-related syndromes. Incredibly, they seem to regard me as their enemy. More recently, some extremist veterans' groups have expressed their, ah, *discontent* with my position on the basis of Gulf War Syndrome and such. They've somewhat targeted me in their campaigns. "Against ignorance the gods themselves contend in vain." '

'You put yourself in nice company,' Reagan said.

'Targeted how?' Brolin asked.

'Oh, nothing violent. But they've staged a few protests and interrupted some public lectures. And there have been several . . . unpleasant telephone calls.'

'You report these to the police?' Brolin asked.

'He reported them to me,' Glanville said and started blinking again as all eyes turned his way. 'We decided that they were just attempts to garner publicity and that we'd be better off ignoring them.'

'Well,' Reagan said, shaking his head, 'I don't know who "we" is, but Diane Sommers sure isn't better off.'

The lawyer broke in. 'Detective, my understanding of the evidence at this point is that local gang involvement is suspected in this matter. Is there some reason to question that evidence?'

'Just exploring all the possibilities,' Reagan replied.

'Well, that's all very well, but I'm afraid Dr Bernouli's time is up for now.'

'We're not quite done yet,' Reagan started, but Brolin kicked him in the shin.

'Of course, Officer,' Bernouli smiled. 'I'll be only to happy to speak with you again. I want to do everything I humanly can to assist you in finding the animals who killed Diane. But I really do have other commitments just now. Why don't you arrange something with Dr Glanville.'

With that, Bernouli and his lawyer simply got up and left the room. Bernouli stole another appraising glance at Brolin as he passed, ignoring Reagan. Reagan and Brolin sat there and watched Glanville blink for a while, until he agreed to get back to them with another interview time.

The two detectives didn't speak as they left the building and walked to the car. Reagan lit a cigarette and lingered at the car door. Brolin crossed her arms on the roof and rested her chin on her wrists, staring at Reagan.

'What?' he finally said.

'How did he do that?'

'Do what?'

'Work us like that. We're supposed to be good at this.'

'He's pretty good himself,' Reagan said, nodding.

'Why would that be?'

Reagan took a final drag and tossed the butt away. 'Because Bernouli and his blinky friend have something to hide,' he said and got behind the wheel. Brolin took the passenger seat without argument.

'Maybe,' she said. She leaned over and inspected herself in the rear-view mirror. She seemed satisfied. 'But he is one good-looking cut of man. I tell you, I wouldn't kick *that* out of bed for eating pussy.'

Reagan blushed slightly and tried to cover. 'Isn't that expression supposed to be: "for eating crackers?"'

Brolin flashed a shit-eating grin. 'To each her own, sweetie.'

Reagan pursed his lips and grudgingly awarded a point to Brolin on the exchange.

Glanville caught up with Bernouli and Boyd in Bernouli's lab. The two stopped talking as the nervous little man approached. Bernouli nodded at the attorney who left without another word.

'What'd you think?' Glanville asked, blinking like a strobe light.

'Relax, Al. Everything's going to be fine. It's all taken care of.'

'But their questions. I don't think they buy it all.'

'They're just questions. It's all routine. *Don't* worry.'

'But . . .'

'Listen. Al. You saw what we have to deal with. They're just a couple of flunky cops. It's the LAPD, for Christ's sake. The geniuses who let O.J. get away. One breathes through his mouth and the other thinks with her tits. Not that they're bad little hooters. Did you notice? Probably a dyke, though.'

He patted Glanville on the back and sent him on his way. But alone in his lab, Bernouli's confidence wilted. He had more than a few doubts of his own.

ELEVEN

Morgan dabbed the sweat from his forehead with a paper napkin and ordered another Orange Bang from the geek behind the counter. The kid was deathly pale with purple and red hair and a stud in his nose. Morgan never could understand why white people did things like that to themselves.

The noon sun blistered the pavement and a steady stream of perspiration trickled down Morgan's back. He hated when the meets were set in Westwood, knew that the man knew that he hated it, and guessed that the man knew that he knew what the man knew. Morgan felt desperately out of place and off-balance in the predominantly white, UCLA enclave. Westwood wasn't what it used to be, largely because of the growing gang problems that touched the community; lots of the once trendy shops stood vacant and crowds were sparse when college was out of session. Still, it felt like alien territory to Morgan, especially without K'toma there to look out for him. No way could he bring K'toma along to meet the man.

He also felt constrained by the stiff fabric of his blue Oxford shirt and strangled by the conservative, striped tie he had to wear. His black wool pants were the best he owned, but too heavy by half for the weather. His plain black Florsheims pinched his toes and scraped his heel. He stuck a sweaty finger inside his collar to relieve the pressure on his Adam's apple and took another long swig of the cold drink. He was dying to at least roll-up his sleeves, but then his Blood tattoos would show, ruining the carefully manufactured image.

Morgan took another bite out of a Tomy's chili-burger, but he was too hot and uncomfortable to enjoy it. Every time he lifted the burger to his mouth another ball of cold sweat trickled down his armpit, making him squirm some more. He'd do a little dance which only reminded him how much his feet hurt.

There was no one else in the entire world for whom Morgan would submit to such indignity. And though it pained his pride to do so even now, he had learned the hard way the danger of not doing what Titus bid. Morgan had thought himself to be as hard as they come – as hard, as cold and as crazy – but the man had taught him different. And lest he forget, he could finger the scars that proved it.

A couple of UCLA girls eating at the other end of the counter kept looking Morgan's way and giggling. They both had long blonde hair and Malibu tans displayed to maximum effect by short shorts and halter tops. One of the girls glanced at Morgan out of the corner of her eye as she pressed a sweating can of Diet Coke to her chest, rolling it over the bronze skin. Morgan saw her nipples harden through the thin fabric of the halter top and thought about what he'd do to her if this were some other part of town.

'See a lot of white pussy, dude?'

Morgan wheeled around, upsetting his drink with a flailing elbow. It ignited another chorus of giggles behind him. Titus came up beside him, glowering down at the pool of orange spreading under Morgan's shoes. Morgan followed the gaze and performed another short dance out of the liquid.

'Damn,' he said. He never saw or heard the big man approach. Titus looked on without a hint of emotion, his dead charcoal eyes tracking Morgan's every move like a sniper's cross hairs. With his tailored pearl grey suit and paisley red silk tie, Titus might have stepped out of an Armani ad. And Morgan didn't detect so much as a drop of sweat on the man.

'My guess,' Titus continued, 'is that you don't.'

'Huh?' Morgan said.

'White pussy. Like that there. You know: the good stuff.' Titus eyed the UCLA girls with a lascivious smile. Morgan saw the girls trying very hard not to look at Titus.

'There's nothing like white meat, dude. Oh, I know how the brothers go on about the wonders of brown sugar, but that's all shuck and jive. I have been to the mountain and I know of what

I speak. Been to the jungle, too. The homeboys are just whistling past the graveyard of their own limitations.'

Morgan, as usual when in Titus's presence, found it hard to respond.

'On the other hand,' Titus went on, 'I suppose you can afford to buy as much pussy you want, these days, any colour. Business being what it is. But we both know that's not the same, don't we?'

'I do all right,' Morgan said.

'Yeah, poon-tang in the 'hood. But those scabby black bitches are a far cry from the fine white meat.'

'It's all pink on the inside.'

'You know who says that?' Titus laughed. 'Niggers and ugly white women. C'mon, dude, let's take a stroll.'

As they walked out of the fast food stand, Titus paused at the girls' table. He leaned over one of the blondes and whispered in her ear. Titus lightly placed his hand on the soft skin at the small of the girl's back and gently slid his hand down her rear. The girl's eyes went wide and her mouth gaped, and then Titus was at Morgan's side pulling him by the elbow. Two high-pitched shrieks went up behind them, but when Morgan looked back he saw that the girls were watching Titus's departure dreamily.

'What you say to them?' Morgan asked.

'I told them my cock was even bigger than yours and they call you foot-long.'

Still leading Morgan by the arm, Titus took them on a slow stroll past the half-empty storefronts. 'Keeping busy?' he asked.

'We doing what we doing,' Morgan said. 'Doing like you say.'

'Those are the words I like to hear. You keeping the word out about the drive-bys?'

'Yo, man. All god's children got Glocks. They all doing the deed. Shooting at every piece o' shit what ain't Blood.'

'Righteous,' Titus said. 'Now tell me about the lab.'

Morgan was nervous discussing the subject in a public place, but Titus showed no particular concern about being overheard.

'We was down,' Morgan said. 'Like you said, the security was a joke. We messed the lab up good and busted up everything we could find. We was in and out. Wham bam.'

'And the girl?'

'Yo! Like I say: it was wham bam and thank you little ma'am. We was, you know, improvising.'

Morgan couldn't figure out what Titus wanted to hear, so he went for the truth: 'You said we take care of business, do what got to be done. But you didn't say nothing about no girl.'

'Life is full of surprises.'

'You say. Anyway, we had us a little pussy party and then did her. Maybe she weren't no fine white meat, but she sure 'nuff gave up the pink. I tell you, cuz, it was on hit and the deed got done.'

Titus jerked Morgan around by the arm and shoved him up against the plate glass window of Tower Records. 'First of all, I ain't your "cuz" and you don't *ever* fucking address me like that. I'm not one of your little jigaboo, jungle homeboys, you understand? There's a million slick shines like you out there. All I have to do is nod and they'll be serving you up in a fish taco. The way it works is I ask you questions and you give me straight answers in the Queen's own English. You do what I say, when I say, how I say. You *down* on that, *homeboy*?'

'Yeah. Yes.'

'Better.'

Titus had been bouncing Morgan off the store window with every point. A teenaged sales clerk with inch-thick acne and a Green Day t-shirt stuck his head out of the front door and pointed a finger at them. 'Yaahhh, dudes. You break it, you totally bought it.'

Titus glowered at the kid who retreated inside the store. A moment later a beefy security guard came out, so Titus straightened Morgan's tie and pulled him on down the street. The plate glass was slick with Morgan's sweat.

They walked briskly, in silence. Morgan was rattled by Titus's always unpredictable behaviour and memories of lessons past. Finally, Titus came to a sudden halt in front of a frozen yogurt shop and pulled Morgan inside.

'What do you want?' he asked Morgan.

Morgan only wanted to get the hell out of there and sure as shit didn't need any yogurt, but he was afraid to say anything that might further piss Titus off. 'V-vanilla,' he stammered.

'Always a good choice,' Titus said.

Titus paid for the treats and handed a large cup to Morgan. They sat down in a quiet corner of the store and Titus went on as if nothing at all had happened. He got himself a sugar cone with chocolate sprinkles and started licking them off from the bottom.

'Did you happen to remove anything from the lab?'

'Nahh . . . No. We trashed everything in the place, like you said, but nothing came out.'

'You're certain? Maybe one of your boys?'

'Uh-uhh . . . No.'

'Good. I'm going to have some more work for you very soon. It's time to jack-up the heat in the 'hood another notch. Your boys are going to start to earn their pay. Are you ready?'

'We be . . . Yes. We're ready. What about the gold?'

'You running short?'

'Getting close.'

Titus nodded and finished the cone in one big bite. Morgan was stirring his melting yogurt with a plastic spoon.

'Don't you like it?' Titus asked

'Huh? Yeah. I mean, yes.'

Titus grabbed at Morgan's damp hand and inspected between the fingers. 'How much you using?'

Morgan shrugged. 'It's under control.'

Titus snorted, but didn't say anything. He let go of Morgan's hand and wiped his own on a napkin. He went up to the counter and bought another cone.

'You'll get a call tomorrow about the delivery,' Titus said and headed out the door. 'Just remember what I told you, dude, and everything will be fine. Maybe I even send a little white pussy your way. Give you a taste of how the better 80 percent lives.'

Morgan forced a smile and nodded at the departing figure. He wiped his sweaty palms on his itchy pant leg and pushed the yogurt away.

'One other thing.'

Morgan looked up. Titus was out on the sidewalk talking to him through the glass. He was lapping at the cone with his long red tongue.

'You sweat too much,' Titus said. 'Get some deodorant homeboy.'

TWELVE

Reagan found Brolin sitting in the precinct lounge with a couple of uniforms, watching a Dodgers game on the tube. She was munching peanut M&M's out of the big one pound bag and cleaning her piece, a department-issue S&W .38.

'Hey . . .' he started, but Brolin shushed him and gestured him into a chair. Reagan frowned, but complied. He watched with her as the Dodgers' latest rookie phenom struck-out looking, stranding runners on second and third.

'Motherfucker,' Brolin snarled and slapped her palm against her thigh. '*I* could get up there and strike out for the money he gets.'

'How can you watch this shit? Christ, it's the dullest damn sport in the world. And they're *all* overpaid.'

Brolin squinted and looked Reagan over, as if really seeing him for the first time. 'You got some kind of mental deficiency or something? You telling me you don't like baseball?'

Reagan snorted and laughed. 'College hoops is my game. Go Trojans. USC, my alma mater. God bless the crimson and gold. Also known as the blood and piss when they bust the point spread.' He pointed at the tube. 'You can't bet on this shit.'

'College basketball?' Brolin yelled. 'Haven't you got any fucking soul, Dennis? Don't you know that baseball *is* America? It's the perfect game. It's goddamn poetry in green. And you don't have to be eight fucking feet tall or weigh three hundred goddamn pounds to play it. Baseball's about skill and grace, hand–eye coordination.'

'You mean like the strikeout king there?'

'The exception that proves the rule. What's the matter, didn't you ever play catch with your dad? Haven't you ever seen *Field of Dreams?*'

'Uh-uh. My dad was a drunk. He used to toss empty bottles at me, but I never tried to catch them. And the last movie I saw was . . . uh, *Apocalypse Now*. I think.'

'Aaarrrgh,' Brolin said and turned her attention back to the play-by-play. Reagan watched with her as the Dodger starter yielded four consecutive hits before the manager yanked him for a reliever.

'Was that skill or grace?' he smirked.

'Eat me, scumbag,' Brolin responded automatically. She turned back toward him as a commercial came on. 'So where's the boy wonder today?'

'Witherspoon? I sent him over to Superior Court to hunt up some records.'

'Why?' she asked. 'LaRue or Washington could have done it on-line from here.'

'I know,' he smiled.

Brolin chuckled. 'Maybe you're not so fucking stupid after all.'

'Criminy, where'd you get that mouth?'

'What the fuck you talking about?'

'I'm just pointing out that it's not especially ladylike.'

'Well, excuse me your nibs. I didn't realize your virgin ears were so goddamn sensitive.'

'Hey, I'm cool,' he said. 'Just wondering what your husband thinks about it.'

'I guess you'd have to ask his girlfriend,' Brolin said, turning back to the television.

'Oh. Sorry.'

'Please. You can just eighty-six *that* tone of voice right now.'

They sat quietly for a while, watching one Dodger pitcher after another get pounded.

'That your only piece?' Reagan asked.

'I have a Glock 20 at home. Got it for Christmas last year. But I've always been kind of partial to the basic virtues of the Smith and Wesson.' She turned the revolver over in her hands. 'It's got a certain simplicity to it. Almost Zen-like.'

'Fuck that!' Reagan roared. 'Try that Zen shit on some gangbanger with an Uzi or a Tec-9. You'll have yourself a nice Zen funeral service with a twenty-one fortune cookie salute.'

'And what do you carry?' she asked. 'No! Let me guess: it's got to be a .45, but not an S&W. Too common. A guy who doesn't like baseball? Probably, hmmm, I bet you carry something goofy, like a Wyoming Arms or a Springfield.'

Reagan smiled and pulled his piece out of his shoulder holster. 'Ruger P89. A solid piece of work. Doesn't jam up like your Glocks, but packs the power you need. Especially with plated hollow-points.'

'Oh, Christ. I can't believe the department allows that. Hollow points should be banned outside of war zones.'

'What do you think we're in? Talk to me about it after you've been out there a little longer. I'd carry a bazooka if they'd let me and it had a 15-round magazine.'

'Ummm, Dennis,' Brolin said, 'don't you think the bone grip is a bit much.'

'It was a present from an admirer,' he said with a smile.

Brolin didn't rise to the bait, but turned back to the game. The Dodgers were up again.

'You married, Dennis?' she asked as the lead-off man walked. He vigorously shook his head. 'Shacked-up?'

'Nope.'

'Queer?'

'Something like that,' he smiled.

'More power to you. Unattached is the way to be. Especially in this miserable line of work.'

'That's what they say.'

More silence.

'How long you been separated?' Reagan asked.

'Couple of months. I'd give you the count in actual hours, minutes and seconds, but I wouldn't want you to think I'm dwelling on it or anything.'

'That bad?'

'Life's a bitch,' she said, 'and you know the rest. But that's not exactly a news flash, now is it.'

A couple of khaki officers wandered into the lounge and dawdled by the vending machines. One of them asked Brolin for the score, groaned loudly when she told him.

'Miserable sons-a-bitches,' he said as he walked out.

'Listen, Brolin,' Reagan said, 'what I actually came down here to tell you is that I'm going to ask Donatelli to turn the case back over to you. We've got nothing to tie Sommers to my stiff and it's clear that my floater ain't gonna make no way, no how. You're supposed to be working with McLeod, anyway, and I don't like stepping on toes. You don't need me hovering around.'

'Funny,' Brolin snorted, 'that's pretty much what my ex told me.'

'Yeah, well, I don't figure you'll be quite so upset to see me go. Though I know how much you're going to miss Witherspoon. Hey, maybe I can convince Donatelli to assign him to you. What do you think?'

A couple of Dodgers had reached base so Brolin's attention was riveted to the tube. She flipped Reagan the bird without looking away from the screen.

'Or not,' Reagan said and got up. 'Be good. Watch the mouth. Go Dodgers.'

Reagan was almost out of the lounge when she yelled at him over her shoulder. 'I see you around, huh, Dennis?'

He gave her a thumbs-up and headed back to the detectives' squad room. Reagan strolled by the captain's office, but Donatelli was in with a suit so Reagan went to his desk and started working his way through some old reports.

'The job's not finished till the paperwork's in,' he said out loud in a fair imitation of the roll-call sergeant. Somebody chuckled at a desk behind him.

'Detective Reagan?'

'Yo!' Reagan replied. A tired-looking little man with an armful of envelopes was staring down at him. 'What can I do you for?'

'I got coroner's reports for you on a Sommers, D. and a Doe, J., #117. You want 'em?'

'Actually, the Sommers report should go to Detective Brolin.'

'Where's he?' the man said, not at all happily.

'He's got tits. Ahh, it's okay. I'll take them both.'

'Whyn't you say so?' the messenger whined.

The little man handed Reagan a pair of thick envelopes, took another look at the labels and yanked them away at the last second. He leafed through the pile, sighing as he turned over each new packet.

'Anything interesting there?' Reagan said.

The little man looked up, blinked, looked around and then blinked again. 'Interesting?' he said. 'Interesting? Interesting is me at Santa Anita with my pony eight lengths in front on the home stretch. Interesting is me with a winning Lotto ticket and no wife and three kids hacking at my back. Interesting is *not* delivering reports for the goshdarn coroner. Here.'

The fellow threw the envelopes down on Reagan's desk and trudged off.

'Man!' Reagan said shaking his head. He heard Donatelli's voice from across the room and saw that he was out of his meeting. Reagan waved at him and Donatelli acknowledged by holding up two fingers, then waddled off toward the toilet. Reagan nodded back and opened the envelopes, starting with his floater. There were a couple of peculiar items in the blood work-up, but nothing that looked especially helpful for making an ID in the case.

A relieved Donatelli came out of the bathroom and headed back toward his office. Reagan had the sealed report on Sommers in his hand and started to get up to talk with Donatelli when he saw the Captain get waylaid by a phone call. Reagan sat back down and opened the second report.

It wasn't until he glanced at the fourth page that he shot off his chair. He ran for the steps, realized he'd forgotten the first report and dashed back to his desk. Donatelli approached from the other direction, an expectant look on his face.

'You want to talk to me?' Donatelli asked.

'Not any more,' Reagan smiled, and with both reports in hand made a bee-line for the lounge.

Reagan burst through the lounge door, practically bowling over a heavyset secretary carrying a couple of chocolate milks. Brolin was still watching the game and fiddling with her gun.

'Christ, Reagan. Miss me already?'

'I know something you don't know,' Reagan taunted. He fanned himself with the coroner's reports.

'How to pee standing up?'

'Uh-uh-uh-uh.'

'C'mon, give. The Dodgers are down by three and it's bottom of the ninth.'

'Well,' he began and stopped. He picked up the soda can that Brolin had been drinking from: a diet cola. 'You're eating M&M's and washing them down with diet soda? What do you, chase your bourbon with light beer?'

'Hey, it's another Zen thing, okay? It's all about balance. And what? You're a fucking dietician now?'

Reagan shook his head and put the cola back on the table. He also tossed the reports down in front of Brolin. They both glanced up at the game as a cheer came from the Dodger faithful.

'Never mind. I got coroner's reports here. Sommers and the

floater. It's mostly crap, but take a look at the blood work-ups
on each of them.'

Brolin thumbed through the report on the floater first. She
nodded as she read, 'mm-hmming' at the blood work-up.

She opened the Sommers' report and flipped right to the section
on the blood chemistries. She read it twice and looked up at
Reagan, who flashed a knowing smile.

'Motherfucker,' she said.

On the TV, a loud crack of the bat was followed by a raucous
ovation from the Dodger faithful. Brolin jerked her head toward
the screen and started to laugh.

She turned back to Reagan with a nearly orgasmic look on her
face. 'Blow me sideways. The phenom hit a 'tater,' she said.
'Dodgers win.'

THIRTEEN

Morgan licked a drop of blood from between his fingers and tossed the spent hypo under his chair. He closed his eyes, shuddering slightly as the Tunnel coursed through his bloodstream. As always, the drug seemed to race straight for his cock which stiffened as his balls grew taut. He took the energy back, drawing it into the muscles of his chest and arms, forcing the power up into his head where it exploded in golden fireworks on the silver screen of his closed eyelids. The Tunnel roared through his brain with the sound and fury of an uptown express. He screamed along with it.

K'toma merely glanced at Morgan, but Arsenio leapt up in panic. Lutece and the others laughed and JuJu playfully slapped at Arsenio as he sat back down on the couch.

'Easy, home,' JuJu told him, 'it's just the gold. Sometime the man do it on the *inside*.'

Arsenio nodded and tried to look cool, though his heart continued to race. This was his first visit inside Morgan's crib and he couldn't afford to look stupid. Morgan's crew acted good-natured enough, but he knew he was under serious scrutiny. K'toma, in particular, watched him constantly. Arsenio knew that there was no room for error and the slightest slip-up might mean a blade in the belly or a hollow point between the eyes. Morgan hadn't made any connection between him and Diane, and he figured – prayed – that he never would. Morgan knew him only as the ambitious little brother of the dead Nelson – Steel Door, to the Blood – not knowing that Diane was their half-sister. And that seemed

to be good enough. He turned back to the big-screen TV blaring
'Wheel of Fortune'.

'I do that Vanna White three ways from Tuesday,' Lutece said.
'Man, I do her so deep I come in her shoes.'

'Ahhhh, fuck you, sucker,' JuJu moaned. 'Every time you can't
solve the damn puzzle I got to hear about how you gonna do Vanna
deeper than a well. First all, she *way* too old. Bet she got that
cellulite. Second, Vanna wouldn't spread butter for your nigga
ass, much less her damn legs. I hear she hire bodyguards just to
shoot dumbass motherfuckers like you.'

'Fuck that shit. She ain't too old for me. And she take one look
at my pole, she be solving *my* puzzle and that ain't no trash.'

'You so full of shit you got to blow your nose with toilet
paper.'

'Yeah? Well you so dumb you'd *still* use it to wipe your ass.'

'Yeah? Well . . .'

'Enough!' Tamara screamed. 'You both so stupid you making
me sick. Can't neither you morons solve the puzzle.'

They both glowered at the screen and shut-up.

'The Fire Next Time,' Arsenio said, surprising himself.

'What's that?' JuJu asked.

'He's right,' Tamara said, pointing at the screen. 'That's the
answer.'

'What the fuck's "The Fire Next Time" supposed to mean?'
Lutece asked.

'That's a old TV show, ain't it?' JuJu said. 'With that dude from
Hawaii Five-O.'

'No,' Tamara said. 'Hawaii Five-O is the show with the dude
from Hawaii Five-O.'

They all looked at Arsenio, who swallowed hard and kept his
eyes glued to the television. 'It's the name of a, uhhh, book,' he
explained. 'It's by a famous black writer named Baldwin.'

'How you know that shit?' JuJu demanded.

'Uh, we were supposed to read it in school. I mean they gave
it out, you know? I didn't read it or anything.'

'Why not?'

Arsenio turned around. Morgan stared down at him from behind
the couch. He looked taller than before and more powerful. His
eyes were wide and alert and his face flush with blood. 'Why not?'
he said again.

'I don't . . . it's just bullshit, you know?'

'Don't reduce yourself to the level of these fools if that's not what

you be. And don't be ashamed of who you are, for that should stir
my wrath. Do you understand?'

'Yeah. Yes. I understand,' Arsenio said.

'Good. Then it's time to go. Time for you to earn the honour
of the Blood. Or die trying.'

Arsenio thought Morgan was being dramatic for the sake of a
little effect, but the sight of the Glock in the gang leader's hand left
fair room for doubt. Lutece and JuJu got up, but Morgan signalled
for Lutece to stay. The wiry gangbanger shrugged and plopped
back down on the couch, grabbing for the remote.

'Yo, baby,' Tamara said, 'you bring me back some of them
cakes. You hear?'

'We got business to attend to, bitch.'

'Then you take *care* your business and *then* get me some of them
cakes. And you watch that "bitch" talk.'

Morgan tried to stare her down, but Tamara wouldn't have it.
'Which cakes you want?' he finally asked.

'The Entenmann's. You know, the chocolate loaf.'

Morgan waved acknowledgement at her as they went out the
door, K'toma on point as always.

'Or the banana cream if they don't got,' Tamara yelled from
inside.

'Chocolate loaf, banana cream,' Morgan muttered, shaking his
head. 'She be sucking banana cream from my chocolate loaf
before the night's over.' JuJu laughed on cue and Arsenio made
a half-hearted attempt to join in. K'toma didn't crack a smile,
just scanned the street. When he was satisfied that it was safe, he
signalled the others to make their way to the car.

JuJu got behind the wheel of the black Ford, with K'toma riding
shotgun. Morgan gestured Arsenio into the rear and climbed in
after him. JuJu pulled away from the kerb and drove without
further instruction.

'The gospel,' Morgan said. K'toma pulled a CD out of a box on
the floor and slipped it into the player in the dash. The thunderous
roar of Public Enemy assaulted the interior of the car. Morgan had
to yell to make himself heard over the music. 'You strapped?'

'Like you told me,' Arsenio said and slapped at his right side.

'Let me see,' Morgan commanded and put out his hand.

Arsenio lifted up the tail of his washed-out Malcolm-X t-shirt
and pulled the .22 from his waistband, placing it in Morgan's
open palm. Morgan looked the gun over and started to laugh.
'Where you get this roscoe?'

'It was my grandfather's,' Arsenio said. He'd stolen it from his grandmother's dresser drawer where it had been gathering dust for years. Arsenio knew his Nana would never even notice it was gone.

'And here I was set to thinking you wasn't no Fred or Barney. What you gonna shoot with this here? Crip mosquitoes? You need to be holding some fire power, boy, you understand?'

Morgan tapped K'toma on the shoulder with the muzzle of the .22. K'toma glanced over his shoulder at the pistol, nodded and almost smiled. It was the most effusive display of emotion Arsenio had seen from the big man.

Morgan tossed the gun on the floor and pulled a small tab that poked out of the rear seat back. A whole section of the seat came loose and Morgan handed it to Arsenio to hold on his lap. Morgan stuck his arm through the gap leading to the trunk and pulled out a large leather attaché case. He flipped open the latches, revealing two handguns, a machine-pistol, three boxes of assorted ammo and some clips. Four vials of Tunnel also rolled loose in the case along with a few crumpled hundred-dollar bills. Morgan pulled out the smaller of the two handguns and gave it to Arsenio.

'Browning nine millimetre,' Morgan explained. 'Simple, efficient and powerful. It's well-made and it don't jam up. A Nine is a nice *first* gun. It ain't gonna do you against no Glock or Uzi, but then I don't see you as an automatic man just yet. And it's clean.'

Arsenio took the gun and hefted its weight. It was at least twice as heavy as the .22, but the dull metal felt solid in his hand. He tried to look like he knew what he was doing and managed to eject the clip on only his third try. He slapped it back in and chambered a round, targeting passers-by through the tinted glass. He feigned squeezing the trigger.

'Nice,' he said.

Morgan nodded and slid the attaché case back into the trunk. He started to replace the false seat, but eyed the .22 on the floor and tossed it into the trunk with the case. 'I take it out your first week's pay. Less a deuce for your granddaddy's hog leg,' he said and pounded the seat back until it slipped into place.

Arsenio hadn't been paying any particular attention to where they were going, but saw, as JuJu turned west on Martin Luther King Boulevard, that they were only a half-dozen or so blocks from his Nana's house. He even recognized one of his Nana's bingo partners walking out of a convenience store with a cart full of overpriced groceries.

'Eyes front, spud,' Morgan said.

They were coming up on a block of burned-out stores that had never been rebuilt after the Rodney King riots. The empty shells were a popular hang-out for local kids and aspiring gangbangers. A group of nine and ten-year-olds played in the charred ruins of an old liquor store. JuJu maintained a constant, lawful speed. The kids were too busy ragging on each other to pay the car any mind. As they passed by, Morgan narrowed his eyes and tightly gripped Arsenio's thigh. 'Red cap,' he snarled.

Arsenio studied the boy with a bright red Cincinnati baseball cap set sideways on his head. He was the tallest of the four, with dark black skin and closely cropped hair. As he slapped one of the other kids on the side of the head and laughed, Arsenio could see that he was missing two teeth in front. He wore a Nike t-shirt with baggy green pants and shiny white basketball shoes. Arsenio turned to watch through the rear window as JuJu continued on down the boulevard. JuJu went up as far as Crenshaw before he hung a left.

'We come around one more time from the south. That's when you do him.'

'The kid?' Arsenio's voice nearly cracked.

'That's the drill. You got the equipment?'

Arsenio wanted to pee very badly and his heart skipped off to the races again. He felt lightheaded, with another empty space forming in the pit of his stomach. He knew the price of initiation would be high, but he hadn't quite expected this.

'Just a kid,' he said, not really meaning to speak aloud.

'Do you question my orders?' Morgan said, staring right at him. K'toma turned around and gazed at Arsenio full-bore. JuJu continued to drive, but peered in the rear-view mirror.

'Uh-uh,' Arsenio said. 'No.'

'All right,' Morgan said, gazing back out the window

'It's just . . .'

Morgan's head snapped around and Arsenio saw fury in his eyes. K'toma looked almost stunned and JuJu swerved slightly out of his lane.

'Just what?' Morgan whispered.

Arsenio had trouble finding a voice. 'You know, it's just that people know me around here. I mean, I could be recognized pretty easy.'

'Really?' Morgan smiled. And Arsenio got the message.

JuJu had come back along Stocker and signalled left toward Martin Luther King.

Three blocks to the killing ground.

'You shoot fast and you empty your gun. You make up in quantity what you missing in quality,' Morgan told him. Arsenio's power window rolled down of its own accord. He glanced up front and saw JuJu's finger on the rocker switch. The opposing traffic thinned and JuJu completed the left turn. He cruised slowly up the street.

Arsenio switched the Browning to his left hand and wiped his sweaty right palm on Malcolm's angry face. He flexed his fingers and cracked his knuckles.

Two blocks.

He transferred the automatic back to his right hand and slid his index finger through the trigger guard. He started to chamber a round, remembered he'd already done it. He rested his right elbow on the open window ledge, his hand and wrist just inside the car, the gun dangling out of sight. He took a series of short, shallow breaths.

One block.

The rubble of the storefronts was visible from the corner. Arsenio saw the four boys standing in a ragged circle, poking at a small fire with shards of wood and metal crowbars. The tall boy with the red cap had his back to the Ford.

JuJu slowed down as the car was half a block away and turned down the volume on the CD player. The heavy bass echoes still pounded in Arsenio's ears; his thumping heart seemed nearly as loud. The circle of boys drew nearer and Arsenio raised the gun. He balanced his wrist on the window ledge and braced his right hand with his left.

The car's speed was down to a crawl when one of the boys spotted the gun. He pointed at the black car and started to run, but tripped on a twisted steel beam. The other two also started to flee, but Red Cap only turned around and stared at Arsenio.

Reality froze for an instant as Arsenio and the boy eyed each other like gunfighters on a dusty western street. Arsenio heard a voice beside him, but couldn't make sense of the words. He was suspended in the moment, unable to pull the trigger.

Unable to move.

A whirring noise broke the reverie. Arsenio recognized it as the sound of K'toma's window rolling down. He saw the tall boy start to bolt and closed his eyes. He heard a bang, felt his hands jerk up with the gun's recoil and smash into the top of the window frame. He opened his eyes and lowered his hands for another shot, but the boy collapsed slowly, like a teetering house of cards. The red cap had been blown off his head and a crimson fountain sprayed from his scalp. Arsenio saw the boy hit the ground hard and then JuJu gunned the engine, leaving behind a peel of rubber, a puff of white smoke and a dead child.

The window glass whirred under Arsenio's hands and he yanked them back into the car. Morgan took the gun out of his hand and placed it gently on the seat between them. JuJu drove slowly down the side streets in a cautious zig-zag route, but he was smiling and intermittently glanced at Arsenio in the rear-view.

Arsenio sat in stunned silence, still feeling the vibration of the recoil in his arm, still seeing the collapsing figure of the ten-year-old boy.

They drove out of the area without incident.

'Just so's you know,' Morgan said after a while, patting Arsenio's thigh, 'he was hassling my little sister. Tried to touch her titties in the schoolyard.'

Arsenio briskly nodded as if this somehow lent sense to what he had just done.

'Yo!' JuJu said, no longer able to contain himself. 'You see that? You see that, K'toma? Right in the eyeball. One shot, right through the fucking eyeball. My man here the Eyeball Kid.'

Arsenio looked up. Morgan was staring out the side window, but K'toma glanced back over his shoulder and half-nodded, almost smiled.

'Shit,' Morgan said, 'we still got to get them motherfucking cakes.'

'Eyeball Kid,' JuJu said again.

FOURTEEN

Bernouli smiled and nodded at the powdered crone and subtly tried to pry his hand free from her lacquered claws. She wore an embarrassingly revealing red evening gown that no sensible woman half her age would have *hoped* to get away with. Perversely, Bernouli found himself struggling to keep his eyes off the withered flesh of her sagging cleavage. The skin on her face had been nipped and tucked within an inch of its life and stretched taut as a drumhead. Her mien, he thought, was every bit as nauseatingly cadaverous as any final stage cancer patient. But her Hollywood mogul husband was poised to donate a cool six figures in start-up to Bernouli's proposed foundation, so he continued the smile and nod routine.

The woman went on and on about someone she knew who'd died in Vietnam. Bernouli didn't have a clue why and could only assume that the old hag didn't know the difference between Vietnam and the Gulf War. At last, Bernouli spotted an even bigger fish coming into the ballroom and finally managed to extract his hand. He made his apologies, knowing they'd be accepted without insult. The most fundamental of Hollywood protocols dictated that it was perfectly all right to snub a person so long as it was in order to suck up to someone even higher up the food chain.

Bernouli briefly greeted the newcomer, a middle-aged Valley real-estate developer toting his pneumatic blonde *du jour*. Fortunately, the tycoon was more immediately interested in the open bar than in absorbing Bernouli's greasy suck-up patter. Bernouli worked his way back through the throng, shaking hands, patting backs and kissing plastic cheeks. He laughed at awful jokes and feigned heartfelt agreement with every patently racist, sexist and homophobic remark and insipid opinion. His expression alternated between broad grin and deep concern as easy as flipping a switch. All just part of an evening's work for the host of a thousand-dollar-a-plate charity dinner.

Catching a brief respite between hand and wallet pumping, and with a little while to spare before he had to address the crowd, Bernouli snuck out of the ballroom and dashed down the hotel corridor to the nearest men's room. He was delighted to find that the toilet was deserted and the attendant away from his post. Bernouli had always had a slight hang-up about pissing in public and was most relieved when he could relieve himself alone.

He stepped down to the corner urinal and unzipped his fly. No sooner had he withdrawn himself from his pants than he heard the men's room door whoosh open behind him. He silently cursed, but ignored the newcomer, concentrating on the task at, or rather, *in* hand. As the first trickle spurted out, someone stepped up to the urinal beside him, resulting in a sputtering of the flow. Bernouli didn't look over, but continued to stare down at his business.

The continued silence was becoming obvious as Bernouli stood at the urinal with a bursting bladder and a bum tap. Still, no splashing sounds emanated from the adjacent urinal, either, and though Bernouli wouldn't turn his head he had a feeling he was being watched by the man beside him. Sure enough, as he tried to catch a sideways glance out of the corner of his eye he saw that his companion was not even facing the urinal, but leaned against it with his arms folded over his chest, staring at Bernouli.

Bernouli hurriedly tried to zip himself up as he angrily turned to face the man, but he was so shocked that he actually caught himself in his zipper and screeched in pain.

'Bashful bladder, Sam?' Greymarch said.

Brolin beamed from behind the wheel while Reagan sulked in the passenger seat. He tried to elicit maximum satisfaction from his cigarette, deliberately blowing the smoke Brolin's way, but she just cranked the air conditioner up another notch, adjusted the vent and silently gloated a little louder.

The final coroner's report had indicated that Reagan's floater had blood chemistry from another planet. The coroner noted that the man's blood and tissue samples showed a number of irregularities, most of which he couldn't make any sense of. The guy seemed to be some kind of walking chemical dump. The floater's blood also demonstrated an exceptionally high concentration of Tunnel. The best the coroner could come up with on preliminary analysis was that the floater's bizarre chemistry might have been a result of trying one of the many illegal back street cancer or AIDS therapies, though an HIV test had come up negative.

That a dead junkie scanned cock-eyed was no big deal, but what had sent Reagan running back to Brolin and the case was the report on the Sommers girl which showed that she, too, had some irregular and unknown trace elements in her blood; elements which seemed to match what they found in the floater.

And even more surprising, given what they knew about her, or thought they knew, the dead girl was a Tunneler.

There are eight million stories in the naked suburb, as Reagan liked to say of L.A., and perhaps it was just coincidence, but the twin result was disturbing enough that Reagan and Brolin decided to spring a surprise visit on Bernouli before splitting up the team.

Reagan actually thought that Brolin could handle things on her own, but he didn't want to let the case go. And Brolin herself suggested that, with McLeod unavailable, they confront Bernouli together at the fund-raiser and try to put *him* a little off-balance this time. As an approach, it wasn't exactly within policy, especially given Donatelli's kid-gloves warning, but Reagan agreed it was worth a shot. They'd worry about a lecture from the Captain after the fact.

'You ever been before?' Brolin asked.

Reagan tossed the butt out the window and turned down the air conditioner. 'Couple, three times. Rubber chicken lunches, Police Benevolent hoo-hahs, that sort of stuff. Nice hotel. Very high grade of hooker in the lounge.'

'I forgot. You're really into all that stuff, aren't you?'

'What? Hookers?'

'No. Well, I don't know about that. And *don't* tell me. I meant the political stuff.'

'You got to bring a ball if you want to play the game. Network, network, network. And being a white man with a wing-wang doesn't mean what it used to. Now that LAPD's got its female types and its black types and its brown and yellow and multicultural types all itching to move up the ladder without putting in the time.'

'Fuck you, Dennis. You saying I don't deserve my shield?'

'Did I say that? When did I say that? Have I ever questioned your abilities? Other than behind the wheel, I mean. All I'm saying is this: how many years you have in when you got your shield?'

'Three years and a couple months.'

'And how long at Junior Grade?'

'Eight months,' Brolin mumbled.

'Thank you. Even you're embarrassed by it. I was at J.G. three years before I got the big bump and I'm a brown-noser *and* damn talented. I'm not saying that you're not a good cop or that you didn't earn where you are or that there haven't been inequities in the past, blah-blah-blah. But it gets so that a dead white male like myself comes to question his place in the order of things. You see what I'm saying? And make a right here.'

Brolin cruised up the hotel drive and pulled into a no-parking area just off the main entrance. She sat at the wheel without turning off the engine.

'If you expect me to feel sorry for all the poor little white boys in the department, you're lifting your leg at the wrong hydrant, Dennis. This department was run by white men for years and years until it was run right into the ground. You forget that good old boy Daryl Gates already? I was practically still a rookie back when Rodney King went down, but when I saw the tape of that poor black bastard getting the living shit beat out of him by a circle of white cops, I wondered what the hell I'd got myself into. I remember – and I know you do – how it felt to be a cop in this city after that shit. Or after Mark Fuhrman and the O.J. mess. How suddenly it was like the badge and the uniform got turned inside out and suddenly stood for everything the opposite of what it was supposed to be. Yeah, women and blacks and Latinos and all the other colours are getting moved up in the ranks, and maybe it *is* at the expense of a few swinging white dicks. But seems to me that the department and the city are a hell of a lot better off as a result. And if you can't see that, then maybe you're not quite the detective you fancy yourself to be.'

Brolin got out of the car before Reagan could respond. He followed her out just as a young Latino valet in a red satin vest came running over, yelling 'No parking, no parking!' Brolin flashed her badge at him and smiled. The kid stopped in his tracks, but Brolin beckoned him over with a crooked finger.

'Official business,' she said. The kid clicked his tongue and started to walk away.

'Hey!' Brolin yelled. 'I come back and find a scratch on this car, I'll have I.N.S. on your ass before you can say "green card". Comprende?'

'Aw, man,' the kid said, 'I live in Sherman Oaks. I was born at Cedars.'

'Just mind the vehicle.'

'Yeah, yeah.'

The kid dashed off to another car and Reagan came up behind Brolin, lighting a cigarette.

'I do see your point,' he said. 'The veil has been lifted from mine eyes. I guess that's the kind of cultural sensitivity a dumb white man like me will never be able to grasp.'

With a sigh, she followed him into the hotel.

Bernouli tried to keep cool, but found it difficult with his shrivelled penis dangling from his half-open fly. Greymarch reached down and closed his hand around the organ, fingering the head none too gently. Bernouli grabbed at Greymarch's wrist just as the bathroom door swung open and an elderly man in a tuxedo walked in. Bernouli recognized him as one of the mayor's cronies and emitted a slight whimper. The small grey-haired man took in the scene before him and froze. Greymarch glanced over his shoulder. 'We'll just be a minute,' he said and winked. 'You understand.'

The man nodded as the muscles of his face contorted through an array of available expressions, culminating in a leer. He quickly retreated out of the men's room.

Greymarch started to laugh and loosened his grip on Bernouli's cock. Bernouli extracted himself from the situation and tucked himself back in his pants, his fear forgotten in a sudden wave of anger. 'What do you want here?'

Greymarch turned back to Bernouli, all trace of humour wiped from his face. He looked Bernouli over as if he was a used car. Greymarch didn't say a word. He just continued to stare until the doctor's anger faded and the fear once again returned.

'What do you want?' Bernouli whispered.

Greymarch held his thumb up in front of Bernouli's nose. Bernouli leaned slightly back and crossed his eyes, focusing on the ragged yellow hangnail.

'I got a problem, Doc,' Greymarch finally said.

He rolled up his left sleeve and pressed the yellowed thumbnail into the flesh of his forearm. He dragged the nail down his arm toward the wrist, tracing a thin dark line in the sallow skin. Crimson-black ichor slowly oozed from the rent flesh. Greymarch held his arm up and both men watched as stalactites of the viscous fluid formed on the skin, and heavy drops intermittently plopped to the floor.

'Doctor. It hurts when I do this,' he said.

*   *   *

Reagan and Brolin tried not to look too out of place as they milled around the black-tie ballroom, but they had to flash their badges repeatedly at dubious security guards and they received more than a few disdainful stares from the legitimate guests. Brolin didn't seem bothered and was happy enough grabbing handfuls of crab-puffs and caviar from passing waiters, but Reagan, ever mindful of his image, fidgeted with his tie and pulled at his tweed sports coat with every baleful glare.

'Pretty fucking ha-cha-cha,' Brolin said between bites.

'Damn. This is like one of these dreams where you're naked in public and can't do anything about it. I told you we should have stopped to change first.'

'Nah,' Brolin said, grabbing a couple of flutes of champagne from a passing waiter. 'It's an edge on Bernouli. Says that even though we're on his turf, we play by our own rules.'

'I still don't see him. But I do see big money here. Industry types, politicos, wheeler-dealers from all parts of town. Goddamn, but rich people are ugly! You ever notice how they always look like caricatures of themselves? Check out the nose on that guy with the pinky ring.'

'What?' Brolin said. 'And poor people are pretty? You walked a beat around MacArthur Park lately? Get a clue, Dennis.'

'Well, your handsome doctor definitely plays with the big boys. Man, Donatelli'd pitch an embolism if he knew we were here.'

'So? You've been fouling them off for years. What's the problem?'

Reagan pulled some more at his tie and scanned the room. 'I don't know. I've been feeling hinky all day. Like someone's been following us or watching us or something.'

'I didn't get that feeling.'

'Call it white man's intuition.'

'Eat me, Dennis. And you just dribbled crab-goo on your tie.'

'Shit!' he said. 'You know how much this thing cost? I've got to find a men's room.'

'Mention my name,' Brolin said and grabbed another drink.

'Listen, Calvin, I . . . you know this isn't the place for this. There are people out there.'

Greymarch ran his arm under the tap, washing the dark blood down the drain. The slow flow had already ceased and the skin was starting to heal. Greymarch dabbed at the wound with some paper towels and inspected the arm.

'You do nice work, Sam,' he said. He held the arm up palm forward, like a cigar store Indian. 'But the job's only half-done. Jude's been waiting to hear from you, but it's been a while. Me, too. You suddenly forget your old friends?'

'Christ, Calvin! You think an hour goes by I don't remember that you're out there? That I don't have nightmares about you? I'm doing the best I can, but it's not that simple. And there have been some complications. Some problems at the lab.'

'Yeah, I heard about that. Quite the little tragedy you had there. Bummer about the girl, too. Who you fucking now? I mean, besides me and Jude and the others.'

'Calvin . . . a great deal of work was ruined. I'll have to start all over again. The project to correct . . . well, you know.'

Greymarch grabbed Bernouli's arm and squeezed tight. 'You're full of shit, Sam. I've been on your ass, watching and listening. You're sucking Titus's dick. Again. And now you're pissing me off. You're riding the Tunnel express and living the good life while the rest of us are still in the shit.'

'I . . . you're hurting me Calvin.'

Greymarch tightened his grip and pulled Bernouli close to him. Bernouli struggled, but Greymarch forced him to the ground with a flick of his wrist. The doctor was kneeling in a slick of Greymarch's blood. He was shaking and moaning.

'You don't know from hurt, Sam. You don't even know the smell. But we've learned a lot about hurting and I think maybe it's time to teach you some of what I know. Just like Quince learned. Do you ever think about him? Or Aliosha? Do you ever really think about any of us or what we have to go through?'

Greymarch yanked Bernouli back to his feet and drew his sweaty face within inches of his own. 'You don't know what it's like when the shakes come and the pain starts in your belly and just grows and grows. You don't understand the *need*. And I think you don't care, any more. If you ever did. So maybe it's time you got a whole new kind of motivation.'

'Calvin . . .'

The bathroom door whooshed opened again and Greymarch shoved Bernouli aside. The doctor fell back to the floor with a thud.

'Yah, dudes,' Titus said. He smiled and glanced back and forth from Greymarch to Bernouli. 'Is this a small fucking world or what?'

FIFTEEN

Greymarch threw himself at Titus, catching him in the solar plexus with a squared shoulder. Titus stood five inches taller than Greymarch, but he emitted a stunned 'ooomph' as the smaller man lifted him off the ground and drove him into a mirror on the far wall. The impact of Titus's head shattering the polished glass reverberated across the tiled room. Titus slumped to the ground in a pile of jagged silver and covered up, but Calvin immediately began to pummel his face, launching a non-stop flurry of fists at his temples.

Titus curled up tighter and managed to roll onto his stomach. A thin sliver of glass jutted out of a gash in his side. Greymarch kicked at it, driving the shard deeper into the leathery flesh. Greymarch stepped back and aimed a series of vicious kicks at the back of Titus's head. The staccato clicks of his steel-toed boots connecting with bone sounded like an exploding mat of firecrackers. Greymarch felt Titus's nose crunch like a walnut shell as a well-aimed kick penetrated the bigger man's defences. Thick blood oozed from a dozen cuts on Titus's head and face and his tuxedo was smeared with blotches of black mucus.

Titus tried to crawl away and reached for the edge of a sink to pull himself up, but Greymarch grabbed him by the ankle and jerked him back. Titus screamed as he landed broken-nose first on the ground and Greymarch quickly let loose with a full-force kick between Titus's legs. Titus vomited something green on the floor.

Greymarch drew his leg back to deliver another kick to the groin, but somehow Titus swept his leg around, tripping Greymarch up as he was off-balance. Greymarch went down hard and Titus was on top of him, lightning-fast, clawing at his eyes. Greymarch managed to bring his knee up and catch Titus in the groin again. He grabbed the lapels of Titus's tux and flipped him over his head. As Greymarch scrambled to his knees he saw Titus roll over and pull a small cylinder out of his jacket pocket. Greymarch rolled to his right as Titus hurled the object at the spot on the floor where Greymarch had been. A small burst of flame went up as the micro-charge detonated, ripping a hole in the tiles.

Titus grabbed another device from his pocket when Greymarch pivoted on his knees and mule-kicked him in the kidney. The charge flew out of Titus's hand and exploded against the wall of a toilet stall, igniting the wood and cheap paint. As the flames crawled up the wall, Bernouli was shocked into motion and ran for the exit, but slipped on a splotch of Titus's blood and skidded head-first into a urinal.

Acrid smoke from the fire set off the automatic sprinkler system. Greymarch got to his feet and saw Titus rise as well. His sharp nose was flat and off-centre and his face dripped with dark blood washed down by the cold shower from the sprinkler. He bared his teeth at Greymarch and made a noise low in his throat. Although he held another charge in his hand, he made no move to throw it. Bernouli seemed to be out cold in the urinal, but a shrill alarm was ringing in the background and Greymarch knew it would be a matter of moments before others came rushing in.

'Let's do this again real soon,' Greymarch said.

'Have your people call my people,' Titus smiled. He dropped the charge back in his pocket and straightened his tuxedo.

Greymarch whirled as the door opened behind him. Reagan sauntered in glancing behind him for the source of the ruckus. He pushed the door open with one hand and held his tie in the other. As he turned and took in the messy scene in the bathroom, he started to reach for his gun, but had barely let go of the tie when Greymarch barrelled into him, sending him ass-over-teakettle back into the hall. A group of hotel employees came running toward the bathroom from the lobby, so Greymarch took off down a different corridor. Reagan tried to get to his feet, but a scurrying bellboy stepped on his hand and they both went down in a pile.

By the time Reagan thought to yell, 'Stop, police,' Greymarch was long gone.

*   *   *

Bernouli was just coming round when Brolin walked into the bathroom, drink still in hand. The fire had been quickly extinguished and the maintenance man finally found the cut-off valve for the sprinklers. Reagan, drenched to the bone, helped Bernouli out of the urinal while Titus cleaned the blood off his face, grunting as he tried to realign his nose.

'Christ, Dennis,' Brolin said, 'what the hell did you do in here?'

Reagan just glared at her. Bernouli was sitting on the floor with his back against the wall, groaning and holding his head where it had met up with the hard porcelain fixture. His hand came away slightly bloody.

'Damn,' Bernouli said.

A crowd had gathered around the rest room entrance as rubberneckers craned for a peek inside. Brolin put her drink down and pinned on her badge, ushering the crowd away and closing the bathroom door. She pulled a pen and notepad out of her bag and started jotting down information, starting with the time. Bernouli was still holding his head, but he squinted at Reagan as recognition set in.

'You're . . .'

'Lieutenant Reagan. Brolin,' he said, pointing toward his partner. 'Can you tell us what happened?'

Bernouli pulled a wet handkerchief out of his breast pocket and pressed it to a soft spot on his head, where it quickly turned red. He inspected it, turned it inside out and pressed it back against the wound. He winced again. 'What are you doing here?' he asked.

'Bathroom patrol. To serve and protect,' Brolin said. 'You want to tell us what happened, Doctor Bernouli?'

'Ca . . . Calvin,' Bernouli said. He glanced around, slightly disoriented. He did a double-take as he saw Titus watching him in the mirror. Titus's eyes went wide and he all but imperceptibly shook his head from side to side.

'Calvin. Calvin who? What Calvin?'

'I think Dr Bernouli is referring to his assailant,' Titus said, turning around.

'And who are you?' Brolin asked.

'Titus Blaine. I came for the benefit, but unfortunately – or perhaps fortunately for the doctor – walked in and interrupted the assault.'

'Assault?' Reagan asked.

Titus walked over and looked down at Bernouli and Reagan,

who was squatting on the floor beside the doctor. Reagan didn't much like the perspective and stood up, but Titus still towered over him.

'When I walked in,' Titus explained, 'the fellow who bowled you over was roughing up the doctor. I tried to intervene, but he was a little more than I could handle. We had at it a bit, but,' Titus touched his swollen nose and smiled, 'I think he got the better of me.'

'Looks busted,' Reagan said.

'Won't be the first time,' Titus said and smiled. 'Don't worry.'

'I didn't plan to,' Reagan said.

'You know who attacked you?' Brolin asked.

'Greymarch. Calvin Greymarch. He followed me in and started ranting at me. I . . .' – Bernouli vamped – 'I'm not even sure what he was talking about now. He started pushing me, then he hit me. Then Mr Blaine came in and they started fighting. The next thing I knew I was out cold in the . . . porcelain.'

'Who is this Greymarch?' Brolin asked.

'He's a . . . nut. An . . . oh, I suppose he calls himself an activist.'

'For what?' Reagan asked.

'Some radical veterans' group. I forget which one he represents. For all I know he's the only member. He's harassed me at lectures a few times, but nothing like this has ever happened before. I believe I mentioned this problem during our last conversation.'

'As one of his most ardent supporters, I can attest that Dr Bernouli has been a frequent target of these lunatics,' Titus offered.

'So he said,' Brolin frowned. 'But he also said that the threats weren't taken seriously. Well, now you've got a dead assistant, a vandalized lab and a direct attack on your person. Do you think maybe it's time to take things seriously, Doctor?'

'I think,' Bernouli said, still holding his head, 'that perhaps I need to get to a hospital.' Bernouli looked up at Brolin, who was stunned by the anger in his eyes. She glanced at Reagan, saw that he caught it as well.

'Ambulance is on its way,' Reagan said. 'Why don't you just relax till it gets here and we'll talk more about this Greymarch character later.'

Reagan turned to question Titus when the rest room door crashed open and a couple of paramedics rushed in with a gurney. Bernouli managed to get to his feet on his own power, then started to wobble.

He didn't object when the paramedics strapped him down and wheeled him out. Titus started to follow, but Reagan grabbed him by the arm. He felt Titus tense at his touch and almost started to reach for his gun again.

'We still have some questions for you,' Reagan said.

'Like how did the fire start?' Brolin asked. Reagan raised his eyebrows and nodded. He had forgotten all about that.

Titus loosened up and smiled at the detectives. 'I assume that it was the work of this Greymarch person. I noticed he was holding what looked like a large firecracker. M–80s, we called them when I was a kid. Better than cherry bombs. Anyway, the fire was already burning when I walked in. I suppose he was using them to threaten Dr Bernouli.'

'How do you . . .'

'Forgive me, officer, but despite my earlier courage, I'm feeling some serious pain in my nose and I think that maybe it would be best if I went to the hospital with the doctor. I'll be happy to answer any questions you have later, but I'm hurt and I'm wet and I think this can wait until I've seen a doctor.'

'Of course, Mr Blaine. We'll talk later. Do you need a hand?' Reagan asked.

'No, thank you. I can make it to the ambulance on my own.'

Reagan nodded at Titus, who headed for the door. As he turned his back on Brolin she inhaled sharply. 'Fuck!' she said.

Titus turned back around. Brolin was pointing at his left side.

'You've got a piece of glass stuck in you,' she said.

'Jesus,' Reagan said and stepped toward him. Titus smiled and held up his hand. He reached down and grabbed the jagged edge of the sliver between two fingers and eased it out. Reagan winced and Brolin gasped. He inspected it, dropped it into his pocket and strolled on out the door.

'Motherfucker,' Brolin said.

SIXTEEN

Arsenio lay in bed, listening to the music of the South-Central night. A police helicopter circled overhead, then drifted off to the south. Within minutes another chopper moved in from the east, hovering directly over Arsenio's street. The sharp edge of its searchlight beam briefly cut straight across the window of his bedroom. The Sharrats next door were having another knock-down drag-out. Mrs Sharrat's shrill voice pierced even the thunk-thunk echoes of the whirring chopper blades. From down the hall the theme music of the network news blared from Nana's TV. Arsenio knew that his grandmother would be settling into her spot on the couch for the evening, a tall glass of lemonade in her hand.

The searchlight briefly flashed by again as the helicopter moved off in another direction. Arsenio glanced toward the window at the fading sound. No sooner had a brief silence set in than it was shattered by the pop-pop of gunfire. Arsenio judged it to be small calibre, Saturday Night Special, and there were only two shots so he didn't bother to go to the window and check it out.

Arsenio stared at the shadowy patterns formed on the ceiling by the headlights of passing cars. As a kid, he used to lie in bed at night, after his Nana tucked him in, and look for pictures in the grainy whorls of stucco above him. He'd squint his eyes and try to force the patterns into the faces of his favourite heroes: Magic Johnson, Mike Tyson, Michael Jackson. Hard to believe now that he'd once thought that trio was special. Sometimes, he'd lie there and listen to the voices from Nana's TV programmes and make up his own pictures to go along with overheard snippets of music and dialogue and canned laughter. Sometimes Diane would come in – she always seemed to know when he was sleeping and when he was just faking it – and he'd point the pictures out to her and she'd laugh and stroke his head and sing to him until he really did fall asleep.

Tonight he saw only the face of the boy he'd killed.

Arsenio tried to recall the boy's face before he pulled the trigger, but in his mind's eye he could only see the child as he tumbled to the ground, his toothless mouth a circle of surprise, a fountain of blood pouring out of the wicked hole where his eye had been. Arsenio closed his eyes, but the image of the falling boy lingered. The baseball cap that had been blown off his head hovered in mid-air like one of LAPD's ubiquitous choppers. Arsenio opened his eyes and slapped his hand to his forehead in an almost comical gesture of disbelief. He found himself repeating the gesture every time he thought about the shooting, as if he could somehow slap the picture out of his head, or perhaps slap some sense into himself.

He tried to keep things straight in his own mind, tried to remember the plan, but it was getting more and more difficult. It was Diane's picture that he needed to hold onto, to remind him of what he had to do and why. Arsenio knew that Morgan's crew were involved in the hit on the lab, but he still didn't know exactly who or why. Lutece, who had a tendency to get loose at the mouth – especially when he was high – had let slip mention of the lab score a couple of times, but K'toma was always there to shut him up with a glance. Arsenio was sure that if he could get Lutece alone he could pry him for information, but no opportunity had arisen. The crew did almost everything together: eat, sleep, get high – hell, everything, but shit. Arsenio had been shocked when Tamara got down on her knees and blew Morgan in front of everybody when he brought her the goddamn cakes, but the others just went about their business as if she'd given him a peck on the cheek. Arsenio had established some credentials with his lucky and literal bull's eye shot, but he had a way to go to become part of Morgan's inner circle. He knew it wasn't a place he really wanted to be, but he also knew that there was no other way to even the books for his Nana.

Another chopper wandered into range. Arsenio again reran the images of the falling boy when something chirped. Arsenio rolled off the bed and grabbed a fold-up cellular phone from the pocket of a jacket hanging on the back of his bedroom door. Morgan had given it to him the way you might toss a nickel to a homeless person. He'd been given a pager, as well, but Morgan didn't like to use them. 'Every grade school bottle dealer got a pager,' Morgan said.

He flipped the phone open with a flick of his wrist. It made him feel way cool, the kind of buzz you can only get from a really smooth piece of technology. He put it to his ear upside-down. He turned it around and closed the bedroom door.

'Hello?'

'Yo! Eyeball?' It was JuJu. He'd started calling Arsenio 'Eyeball' after the drive-by and Morgan seemed to approve, so it stuck.

'Yeah,' Arsenio sighed, 'it's me.'

'What down? We got business little brother.'

'What's going on?'

'We got . . . What? Yeah. Eyeball.' JuJu was talking to somebody off the phone. 'Yeah. Okay. Okay. Okay!'

Two helicopters circled overhead now, so Arsenio had to shut the window, propping the phone between his shoulder and his ear. The window stuck in the frame and when Arsenio tried to force it, the phone slipped out and bounced on the floor.

'Shit!' he said. He picked up the phone, which seemed to be all right.

'Eyeball! You still there, man? What the fuck you doing?'

'I dropped the damn phone.'

'Shit. That motherfucker worth ten of you. Morgan say you come strapped, hear?'

Arsenio sighed and slapped his hand to his forehead again without even realizing. 'Yeah. At the crib? What time?'

'No. We gonna come by for you. You be ready at . . .' JuJu again conferred with someone in the room. 'Ten.'

'Got it,' Arsenio said and JuJu hung up without another word. Arsenio sat down on the edge of the bed. He folded up the phone and held it in his palm, pressing the cool plastic against his cheek. 'Come strapped' JuJu had said. Arsenio felt the start of a headache coming on. He tucked the phone back in his jacket pocket and rubbed his temples with his fingertips. He opened the door and glanced down the hall, catching a glimpse of his grandmother already asleep on the couch.

He closed the door softly and slid open the door to his bedroom closet. He pulled out some cardboard boxes filled with X-Men comics. He ripped the tape off a VCR box and carefully withdrew a stack of well-thumbed Batmans. At the bottom of the box was a smaller, homemade wooden box secured with a padlock. The lock was a joke – the box was shabbily built and could easily have been pried apart with a screwdriver – but it made Arsenio feel better.

He spun the numbers on the combination, mis-dialling it the first couple of times, and popped open the lid. On top lay a small stack of porno magazines with titles like *Sister Slit* and *Black Bazookas*, and a pirated videotape with the handwritten label *African Desires* that his friend Joey Ramos had given him for his twelfth birthday. Those were the days, Arsenio thought, as he gently put the tape aside. Joey had been killed by an off-duty cop six months earlier during an ill-fated rip-off of an El Pollo Loco drive-thru.

At the bottom of the box lay the Browning that Morgan had given him, along with some ammo. Arsenio hesitated, then picked the gun up and held it in his right palm. He stared down at the gun, feeling the cold steel against his dark skin. He turned it around, holding the grip in both hands, pointing the barrel directly at his left eye, closing his right.

'Pow,' he said.

He turned the gun around and gripped it in his right hand, hefting its weight and staring off into space. He pressed the muzzle up against the underside of his chin and squeezed the trigger.

He hadn't chambered a round.

A car passed by and he looked up at the ceiling, seeing his victim's face quickly form and dissolve again in the stucco.

He pressed thirteen bullets into the clip and slapped it into the gun. He tucked the Browning into his back pocket and pulled his dark blue sweatshirt down over it, checking in the mirror that the bulge didn't show. He stared for a while at his own image.

'Eyeball,' he said, over and over. 'Eyeball.'

The maroon LTD pulled up at exactly ten. Arsenio knew because he could hear the anchor man from the channel 5 news reading the headlines. With one hand on the gun, Arsenio jogged down the walkway to the waiting vehicle. The back door swung open and JuJu patted the seat beside him. The car pulled away before Arsenio could even close the door.

Arsenio expected to see Morgan and K'toma up front, but he didn't recognize either of the Blood. He nodded at them and JuJu made the quick introductions – the driver was Kiki, the big man was Endzone – but no other words were exchanged. Kiki drove slowly and carefully, signalling as he turned left on King Boulevard, frequently checking the side and rear-view mirrors as he went. Endzone rapped his knuckles against the window glass and nodded his head along to some secret song.

'Where we going?' Arsenio asked.

'Business,' JuJu said. 'Got us some major league business.'

'Where's Morgan at?'

'He be along.'

JuJu offered no other details and Arsenio knew better than to ask. JuJu rested his feet on a crate covered with a swatch of cheesecloth. Something inside tinkled as the car took a sharp turn and Arsenio caught a strong whiff of gasoline.

They continued east on King Boulevard, right on past the dark Coliseum and Exposition Park. JuJu didn't speak again until they had passed under the Harbor Freeway and into the fringes of East L.A.

'You got a lighter?' he asked Arsenio.

'Huh? No. I don't smoke.' That brought a chuckle from Endzone, but JuJu let it pass.

'Here.' JuJu handed him a disposable butane lighter. Arsenio turned it over in his hand, saw that it didn't even have an adjustable flame.

'What's this for?'

'Business,' JuJu said again.

Kiki slowed down and cut the headlights as they approached a ratty looking building in a deserted commercial district off San Pedro. He pulled over to the kerb and Arsenio saw figures waiting in several other parked cars. Even in the dark, he spotted K'toma sitting in the passenger seat of an old Chevy across the street. As always, K'toma seemed to be magically watching him. Arsenio leaned back, putting JuJu's silhouette between himself and the big bodyguard.

'The middle building,' JuJu said. 'With the busted gate. Sagrados think they can cook them some magic dust under the Blood's nose. Piece of shit Salvadorans. They 'bout to learn they wrong.'

JuJu pulled a syringe out of his pocket and snapped a vial of Tunnel into the hypo. He glanced back and forth out the window as he rolled up his sleeve, and satisfied that nothing was in the offing, jabbed the needle into his arm. He exhaled a deep moan as the golden fluid entered his veins. Kiki shot up as well, rolling up his shirt and sticking the needle into his skinny belly, but Endzone abstained. JuJu offered Arsenio the syringe, but he shook his head. JuJu shrugged and tossed the works aside.

A radio crackle broke the nervous silence. Endzone finally

stopped rapping on the window and grabbed a small walkie-talkie off the seat.

'Number 5,' Endzone said.

'*En*-gage,' the voice over the radio replied. Morgan.

JuJu bent down and pulled the cheesecloth off the crate. He slid the lid off, revealing a dozen Cobra malt liquor bottles with rags stuffed in the necks, sealed with wax.

'Time to serve up the drinks,' JuJu said and handed three of the bottles to Arsenio. JuJu gave another three bottles to Endzone and took three more himself. Kiki watched, but stayed behind the wheel. JuJu and Endzone each stuffed two of the bottles into their jeans and held the third, so Arsenio followed suit. He pulled the lighter out of his pocket and gripped it tightly in his hand.

As they alighted from the car, a dozen other shadowy figures did the same. JuJu nodded his head and Arsenio followed him through an alley and around the back of the warehouse, with Endzone bringing up the rear. There was no other traffic and not a sound to be heard except the omnipresent background rush of the city. Another group of Blood emerged from an alley on the other side and the two groups fanned out around the building. Arsenio spotted more Blood on the roofs of adjacent buildings and caught glints of the dim street lights reflected in the bottles in their hands.

Within moments everything went still and Arsenio guessed that everyone was where they were supposed to be. Another echo of static crackled from the radio and a gallery of tiny flames was struck. JuJu nodded at Arsenio who thumbed his own lighter and readied to set it to the greasy rag. Like a row of veteran archers, the Blood on the roof launched a round of Molotov cocktails in unison, followed by a less organized volley from the Blood on the street. Arsenio's thumb was slick with sweat and slipped off the lighter, dousing the flame. He quickly flicked the lighter back into use and touched it to the rag, tossing the lit bottle at the warehouse even as JuJu and the others launched their second round.

The rear of the building exploded into flame as the bottles detonated against the decayed wooden structure. The Blood on the roof had spent their ammunition and were already climbing down and heading back to their cars. Arsenio quickly lit and tossed his second cocktail, hurling it at a boarded-up window. The wood ignited in a burst of Halloween orange and Arsenio got so caught up in the visceral thrill of the act that he dropped the third bottle, splashing gasoline on his shoes and pants. JuJu glared at him and shook his head, but indicated for Arsenio to follow him around to the front. Arsenio hated to walk away from the beauty of the crackling flames, but a shove from Endzone got him moving.

Thick smoke clogged the air, though the front of the building had not yet caught fire. Most of the Blood got back in their cars and took off, but JuJu headed for the front entrance where a smaller group of Blood stood guard. JuJu went inside the building and pulled Arsenio along, while Endzone waited outside with the others.

Morgan and K'toma stood over several convulsing bodies sprawled on the floor just inside the gate. Blood poured out of bullet holes. Morgan held the Glock in his hand, while K'toma clutched an Uzi to his chest. Morgan's eyes were wide and his teeth bared. Arsenio could tell he was deep in the Tunnel. One of the bullet-ridden figures tried to crawl away from Morgan in the direction of the now visible flames. Morgan stepped on the small of the man's back, grinding his heel. He bent down and fired two shots into the back of the Latino's head, sending a shard of bone pinging off a stone pillar.

The roof collapsed in the rear and muffled explosions could be heard at the far end of the building. Morgan seemed not to notice. Arsenio heard the creak of straining wood and eyed the ceiling above them, but no one else made a move.

Lutece held a small Hispanic man from behind. The man wore glasses with shattered lenses and trembled visibly. He looked distinctly South American. Morgan strode over to them and leaned over the captive.

'The cooker,' JuJu whispered into Arsenio's ear.

Morgan flashed a crazed smile at the man and then nodded at K'toma. The big man strode over and pulled a butterfly blade out of his jacket, handing it to Morgan.

The fire roared no more than a dozen feet behind them. A spark of flame had jumped to one of the corpses and the stomach-churning odour of burning flesh wafted in the hot breeze.

Morgan took the blade and delicately sliced the chemist's pants and shirt until they fluttered off his thin body. The chemist's shrivelled genitals were visible in the firelight.

'Hermano, no,' the chemist said, 'por favor.'

'Por favor?' Morgan asked and shook his head. 'Poor hermano.'

Morgan smiled again as the little man peed down his leg. Morgan shook his head and plunged the knife deep into the cooker's belly.

'Oh, snap!' JuJu gasped, but his eyes were alight with wonder.

The cooker screamed and bucked, his blood splattering Morgan and Lutece, but Lutece continued to hold him up. Morgan twisted his wrist right, left, right, left, drawing a fresh, but weakening scream with each twist of the blade.

No sounds, only blood poured out the cooker's open mouth as Morgan forced the edge of the knife up toward the cooker's chest. Arsenio had never seen so much blood, couldn't believe the cooker was still alive.

Agonizingly, he was.

The other corpses smouldered now and bits of the roof started to give way just over their heads. The fire sucked the air out of the room and though all the Blood dripped with sweat, no one made a move to leave. Arsenio didn't want to see any more, didn't want to be there, but found that he couldn't look away.

Morgan, covered in the chemist's blood, withdrew the blade and held it up for all to see.

He plunged the point into the little man's eye.

Morgan nodded at Lutece who finally let the cooker go. He collapsed to the floor, dead. Or so Arsenio hoped.

No one moved until a great piece of flaming wood came crashing down almost on top of K'toma. The big man ducked it with ease, but the sudden clatter served to break the mood and the Blood quickly ran out of the collapsing building. Morgan was the last one to move, walking at a leisurely pace as flames lapped toward the front gate. Arsenio followed JuJu to the car, but stopped as he looked over his shoulder and saw Morgan standing there, his back to the flames, his arms raised high.

Hell, Arsenio thought. *I'm in hell, and the devil is a black man.*

SEVENTEEN

'Never heard of him,' Donatelli said and took another bite out of his crueller.

'Yeah,' Brolin said. She tried not to stare at the crumbs on his chins. 'That's the whole problem: seems like *no* one's ever heard of this asshole. He's got no driver's licence, no local or federal raps – the schmucks at the bureau were their usual delightful selves, by the way – no court records and no state property listings. At least not under 'Blaine'. He lives in one of those enormous glass and stilt mud traps up in the Palisades, but the ownership is registered under a management company. No credit history, either.'

'IRS?' Donatelli said. 'He's gotta have beaucoup bucks if he's living up that way.'

'Not to mention getting an invite to Bernouli's shindig. It was strictly high rollers. We're working on Internal Revenue, but it's, you know, pulling teeth.'

'Let me see what I can do,' Donatelli said and scribbled a note to himself on his doodle-covered desk blotter. 'So go on with the story.'

Brolin glanced at Reagan who picked up the thread.

'There's not that much more to tell, really. We hung around the men's room for a while – fortunately Brolin knows the terrain . . .'

'Eat me,' Brolin mumbled. Reagan smiled, Donatelli cleared his throat.

'Anyway, we canvassed the crowd for a while, but nobody saw a thing. There's supposed to be a men's room attendant on duty, but he was on an unofficial break, too bad for him. None of the hotel staff came along until the fire alarms went off.'

'Explain that part to me again.'

'Can't,' Brolin said. 'Blaine said he thought that this Greymarch character had some M–80s with him, but we didn't find any traces of them if he did. The guy had some mean little explosive and whatever it was triggered the sprinkler system.'

'And what have we come up with on Greymarch?'

'Calvin Greymarch,' Reagan said, flipping through his notes. 'DMV kicks out a Bay Area address. Walnut Creek, to be exact. Born November 23, 1960. Five foot eleven, hundred seventy pounds. Brown hair, brown eyes. A ton of speeding tickets. A DUI in 1988. Registered with an '81 Datsun. His licence and registration expired in '92.'

'Does he have a sheet?' Donatelli asked.

'Nope. He looks like a citizen. Or he used to be. He comes up as co-owner on a condo that got foreclosed on just over a year ago by B of A. He's got plastic up the wazoo, all of which was cancelled a while ago for payment in arrears. We're working on getting his bank records and I've got a friend up in the Alameda Sheriff's office who's sniffing around for information.'

'McLeod's out checking with some of the local veteran's groups to see if anybody knows him or will acknowledge him,' Brolin added. 'I checked with the department's Liaison for Gay and Activist Affairs – man, is that a title, or what? – but he's never heard of Greymarch. I've got a call in to the Sheriff's office, too, but their guy doesn't have a nifty title.'

'Did you mention Blaine's name to our guy?' Donatelli asked.

'No,' Brolin said, 'it didn't really occur to me. Why?'

Donatelli leaned back and started stroking the well-worn leather on the arms of his chair. 'I don't know. Just something that doesn't sit right. So finish the story.'

'We mopped up at the hotel,' Reagan said, 'and then went over to the hospital to follow up with Bernouli and Blaine. Bernouli's doctor wouldn't let us anywhere near him. Said he was waiting on a CT and that Bernouli'd be spending the night at least for observation. So then we went looking for Blaine, but he never showed at the hospital.'

'Didn't you say he got cut by some glass?'

'Pretty nasty looking, too,' Brolin nodded, 'but the paramedics said that Blaine never got on the ambulance at the hotel. He told them he was okay and would go see his own doctor. The paramedics also mentioned that Blaine did stop to have a chat with Bernouli. The driver said that Blaine did most of the talking while Bernouli nodded. Didn't overhear any of it, though.'

'Interesting,' Donatelli said, stroking the leather a little harder.

'Maybe,' Reagan shrugged. 'Anyway, from there we split up. I had to come back and do the paperwork. Say, did you know that the job isn't finished till the paperwork's in?'

Donatelli sneered.

'And Brolin went looking for Blaine.'

'I took a run up to Blaine's place in Malibu,' Brolin continued, 'but it was no go. Fucker's got a houseboy who no speak English.'

'So? Don't you speak Spanish?'

'*Asian* houseboy.'

'No shit?' Donatelli said.

'Yeah. It was like walking onto the set of *Chinatown*. Hell, in that neighbourhood I wouldn't be surprised if Jack Nicholson lived next door.'

'Follow-up?' Donatelli asked.

'I've got Witherspoon staked out at the hospital,' Reagan said, 'probably in the gift shop. He's supposed to let me know if Bernouli gets released this morning. My friend up in Alameda won't have anything before the end of the day, at the earliest.'

'McLeod's out in the field now,' Brolin said. 'Me and Dennis are gonna take another shot at Blaine. And we thought we'd maybe interview some of the dead girl's KAs again, now that we know about her Tunnel habit. It may be just that the gangbangers shot her up when they did her, but the coroner seemed to think she was a more regular user.'

'And the floater?'

Reagan offered a wet Bronx cheer and turned his thumb down. 'Dead issue,' he said.

They sat in silence for a while. Reagan swirled the coffee dregs in his styrofoam cup and Brolin vacantly watched him while Donatelli finished jerking off his chair arms. Finally, Donatelli cleared his throat.

'You're out of it,' he said, pointing at Reagan.

'What?' Reagan snapped. Even Brolin leaned forward in surprise.

'I'm sorry Dennis. There's lots of dangly, loose ends here, but nothing that Brolin and McLeod can't tug on their own. There's still no direct tie-in to the floater, right?'

'Except for the coroner's reports,' Reagan said, but Donatelli shook his head.

'Not enough,' Donatelli said. 'At least, not for now. I've been up to my eyeballs with Command all morning. They've got fresh intelligence that a major gang confrontation is coming down the pike. Word is out that all treaties are off and Sagrados are on the warpath after that massacre at their lab. I swear, Tunnel is going to send me into early retirement. As it is, gang-relateds are already up better than 20 percent over last month and downtown is pretty sure that something big is imminent.'

'Like what?' Reagan said.

'They're not sure.' Reagan started to protest, But Donatelli waved him off. 'I know, Dennis, but the big boys are running scared. They can't have the city burning in an election year. You're my main gang guy, so I can't very well expose myself by letting you linger on this Sommers thing. Not if there really is a shit storm coming down at us.'

'By all means, don't expose yourself Carmine,' Reagan said.

'Look, Dennis, I'm sorry. I know you're invested here and I expect you and Brolin to reach out. Especially regarding your friend up north. But Brolin and McLeod can handle Bernouli and Greymarch and whatever follow-up there may be on this Blaine character. Frankly, I don't even know what you have there. It could just be Blaine's an eccentric rich guy and he picked the wrong time to take a piss. It's not like there's any shortage of them in this town. In any case, a floater and a dead junkie – ah, ah! Don't start on me, Brolin: Sommers was a Tunneler – a floater and a junkie don't stack up against an incipient gang war. Tell me if I'm wrong.'

Reagan took a deep breath, let it out as a heavy sigh. 'No. No, of course not. I just . . . there's something about Bernouli that rings my bell, you know? And this guy Blaine. Maybe you're right. Maybe he just chose the wrong moment to tap the vein. But you had to see this motherfucker pull that piece of glass out of his gut. It was like he smiled as he did it. It's . . .' – he looked at Brolin, who shrugged, then back at Donatelli – 'I don't know. I've just got one of your queasy feelings about the whole shebang.'

'Listen,' Donatelli said, 'I believe in a cop's instinct as much as anyone, and any other week I keep you on with Brolin, no question. But this ain't any other week. Like I say, I expect you two to keep in touch, but other than that . . .' Donatelli shrugged.

Brolin walked Reagan back to his cubby hole to collect his

files and notes. He plopped into his squeaky chair while Brolin straddled the corner of the desk.

'I thought you'd be happy, Dennis. A little gangbanging maybe puts you back in the headlines.'

'Fucking media,' he said. 'Yeah, I suppose . . .'

'But . . .'

'But I've got a feeling about Blaine. How do you get to live in a mansion like that with a goddamn Chinese houseboy and not leave any paper trail? And what the fuck did he tell Bernouli in the ambulance?'

'Well, gee! Sounds like a job for a detective. Duuuuhhh . . .' Brolin said.

'Right. Sorry. Listen, when I hear from my goombah in Alameda about Greymarch I'll let you know. And I'll give him your number for anything else he comes up with.'

'Thanks Dennis. And don't look so glum; the cameras beckon.' Reagan half-smiled and nodded.

'And besides,' Brolin added, 'you're forgetting the best part.'

'What's that?'

'Now Witherspoon is all yours again.'

Reagan's smile faded. Brolin's wicked cackle echoed loudly as she disappeared down the hall.

PART TWO

EIGHTEEN

Reagan lit a cigarette, took three long drags on it, snuffed it out.

Ten seconds later he lit up another.

He stood up as best he could in the small van, cricking his neck back and forth until the vertebrae popped and he 'ahhhed' with relief. He rolled his fists along the small of his back and did a series of jerky deep knee bends, his joints creaking with every squat. He stood up too quickly and smacked his head on the low roof, then ducked back down, banging his elbow into a bank of electronic gear affixed to the wall of the van. Voicing a series of short curses, Reagan sat down on the hard swivel stool, slipped the lightweight headset over his ears and started to light another cigarette.

He sniffed at the air and turned up his lip.

'Witherspoon!'

'Sir?' The younger man had trouble meeting Reagan's gaze.

'I thought we were straight on the ground rules of this operation: No unauthorized radio contact. No watching Dodgers' games on the surveillance monitor. And most importantly, *no farting in the goddamn command vehicle*!'

'Yes, sir. Sorry.'

'Criminy! How many times have I told you not to eat at Taco Hell?'

'I know, sir. But they have this new bargain menu with . . .'

Mercifully, a call came through and Reagan was able to wave Witherspoon off as he spoke into the mouthpiece.

'Deathstar,' Reagan said.

'Unit Three in place,' came a scratchy voice over the radio.

'Copy Three. Unit Four?'

'Unit Four. Still establishing, Deathstar.'

'Copy Four. How much longer?'

'Five more minutes.'

'Make it three, Powell,' Reagan said.

'Copy, Deathstar.'

Reagan checked in again with the other units and satisfied himself that everyone was ready to go. He glanced at his watch and decided to give Powell two minutes. He swivelled the microphone away from his mouth and lit a cigarette just as Witherspoon let loose another silent but deadly burst of wind.

'Make a ru-uu-un for the border,' Reagan sang to himself and punched up the video signals. Powell's group was still off-line. One man in each unit was outfitted with a tiny fibre-optic camera mounted in his helmet. The image quality was dark and grainy, but good enough for Reagan to track and direct the operation from inside the van.

They had lucked out on a tip: a couple of uniforms busted a wimpy gangbanger named Li'l Bone on an early morning Tunnel buy at Dockweiler Beach. Li'l Bone had an outstanding manslaughter warrant in Nevada and more importantly, a monster Tunnel jones. He was talking deal before the uniforms could finish reading him Miranda. He gave up the location of the Blood storage facility in exchange for expedited extradition – according to Bone, it was easier to score Tunnel in the Nevada pen than on a Los Angeles street corner – and a convenient failure to conduct a full body cavity search when he went into lock-up. It was a long way out of policy, but Reagan would trade a possible jailhouse OD for a media-scale Tunnel bust any day of the week and twice on Superbowl Sunday.

Reagan glanced at his watch and started to call Powell when Unit Four's camera blinked on-line. The cameraman was glancing down, adjusting his Cermet body armour, then looked over at Powell who flashed a nervous thumbs-up at Reagan. The camera whip-panned over to the rear of the building and the thick steel door that was one of only two ways out of the place.

'All units get ready,' Reagan said. He glanced again at the row of monitors. Units One and Two were perched outside the front entrance of the building, a U-DO-IT self-storage operation. The structure was made up of a series of rectangular metal boxes joined together at the ends like a tableau of dominoes, sprawled over a half-acre of land on the fringe of Mar Vista. Unit Three, composed of five sharpshooters, was positioned on the roof of the closest neighbouring building. Although the warehouse had only a single front and rear entrance, several of the prefabricated boxes had small emergency exits built into their roofs. Reagan sighted down the barrel of a rifle at one of those roof exits with the cameraman/sniper.

Reagan took a last drag on his butt, snuffed it out and smiled at Witherspoon who looked back dumbly.

'Go,' Reagan said.

Unit One burst through the front door like a hurricane. The camera tracked a fat black man at the front desk who instantly did the wrong thing, reaching under the counter. The image shuddered with the recoil of the cameraman's gun as the clerk went down in a spray of bullets.

Reagan glanced at the Unit Two monitor. They came in right behind the first unit. Unit Two went down a corridor to the right, while Unit One took the corridor to the left. Reagan looked back and forth between the monitors, like watching a tennis match, as the officers proceeded down identical halls, cautiously checking every locked door along the way, yelling instructions to each other as they went.

A hail of Uzi-fire riveted Reagan's attention to the Unit Two monitor. The officers were exchanging fire with a pair of Blood barricaded behind a steel mesh door at the end of the hall. The Blood sprayed Uzi-fire in the direction of the camera. One officer was down on the floor in front of the cameraman, but it was impossible to tell if he was still alive. The cameraman and the rest of the Unit returned fire as best they could without exposing themselves to the seemingly endless stream of bullets.

Just as one of the Blood went down with an explosive shot to the chest, Reagan saw that Unit One had engaged with a cadre of Blood armed with Glocks and SKS–46s on the other side of the building. Reagan watched as three of the Blood went down in succession before the fourth zoned-in on the officer with the camera.

Reagan saw what was coming before it happened and realized the officer must have known it as well. He tried to yell into the microphone but his lips couldn't form the words fast enough, nor his throat generate the sounds before the Blood eased his finger back on the Glock and the bullets exploded out of the barrel directly into the face of the officer with the camera.

The gangbanger with the Glock immediately took a series of

quick hits, but his image receded in double time as the cameraman took the impact of the bullets. Reagan was suddenly looking up at the ceiling as the officer's head snapped back with whiplash fury and he flew backward through the air. Something dark and billowy spurted up from just below the camera and with a sick feeling, Reagan realized that it was blood spewing from the officer's neck or face. The picture shook as the cameraman thudded to the ground on his back. For a moment, the billowy liquid seemed suspended in space above the camera until gravity drew it down, washing over and mercifully blacking out the tiny lens.

'Officer down! Officer down!' someone screeched over and over on the radio.

'Shit,' Reagan screamed, but before he could bark a command to the Unit One leader, his eye was caught by the picture from Unit Three's rooftop vantage.

Although the cameraman sighted down the barrel of his rifle, the distance to the warehouse was great enough that Reagan could see three of the emergency exits in the frame. A body, pistol in hand, was already slumped across one of the exits and two more were opening up. The Unit leader bellowed a tinny, bullhorned order to freeze, but the Blood members rising out through the roof raised their weapons. The unit leader whispered the order to open fire.

The image barely shook as the sniper/cameraman squeezed off three rapid shots, impacting in a precise crescent pattern across the would-be escapee's chest. The Blood's corpse dropped down into the hole and though the cameraman kept his rifle at the ready, no one else emerged. The other gangbanger managed to squeeze through his exit and bound out onto the roof before a different sharpshooter took him out with a single, very messy head shot. Reagan quickly glanced at the picture from Unit Four in the rear, but the steel door was still tightly closed and nothing was going down.

Back inside the warehouse, Units One and Two had converged on a large, central storage area without further confrontation. A half-dozen of the Blood lay face-down on the floor at gun point while squad members roughly searched and cuffed them.

'All secure, Deathstar,' came the voice from Unit One leader.

'Copy, Unit One. Hold till I get there. Units Three and Four, maintain position.'

From the rooftop camera Reagan saw the first ambulances arrive on the scene. He directed the paramedics to the location of the downed men and crossed his fingers. With nothing left to see on the monitors, Reagan slipped off the headset and handed it to Witherspoon who had gone white as cotton balls.

'Take charge, Junior,' he said and dashed out the back of the van.

Reagan went directly to the area where the cameraman had gone down. The Unit One leader, a tall sergeant named Conway, was already on the scene looking over the shoulders of the paramedics who applied CPR to the injured officer. Conway glanced up as Reagan approached the scene and shook his head. Reagan saw that Conway had tears in his eyes. He watched as the paramedics hustled the injured man onto a gurney and hurriedly wheeled him out toward the ambulance, still pumping at his chest. Conway turned back toward Reagan with a look that said *this better be fucking worth it* and stalked off after the paramedics.

Reagan followed another pair of paramedics into the main storage area where Ross, the Unit Two leader, stood over the Bloods who were still kissing floor. The paramedics went straight over to the one gangbanger who was sitting up, braced against the wall and moaning. His leg was twisted at an awkward angle and gunshot wounds in his chest spurted red. Reagan saw the open emergency exit and realized that this was the Blood he'd seen on the monitor. Ross looked expectantly at Reagan.

'Man down in Unit One. Looks bad,' Reagan said.

'Who is it?'

'I don't know,' Reagan mumbled.

'Didn't you fucking ask?' Ross snarled.

Reagan just sighed. 'Report.'

Ross snorted and shook his head. 'This group didn't have much fight in them. Unit Three scored the hit on the scumbag with the leg and the others surrendered without a shot.'

Reagan nodded. 'Let's see what we've got then.'

The storage area was stacked to the rafters with small, unmarked wooden crates. Reagan found a crowbar lying on the floor and pried the top off of the nearest box.

'Yee-haw,' he said and smiled. 'Alert the press.'

The crate was filled with glinting golden vials of Tunnel, neatly arranged in layers of ten, four layers to a box. Reagan randomly selected a different crate from the other corner of the room and popped the lid open. The contents were identical to the first.

'This is the mother lode,' Reagan said, 'and all ready to ship, too. I make it, what, about 200 crates in here? We got us some serious weight. All right, let's start to inventory the rest of the premises. Get Powell's people in here to help out.'

Ross walked up behind Reagan and peered down at the amber vials. 'Congratulations,' he said, without enthusiasm and went off to coordinate the clean-up operation.

The paramedics continued to work on the injured gangbanger, but the others were being prodded off the floor and herded out of the room. Reagan glanced at them, saw that they looked mad as hell. They were all going to be in deep shit for fucking up once they hit lock-up. One of the Blood conspicuously looked away from Reagan, but the little light bulb didn't flash until the group had been moved out of the room.

'Hey,' Reagan yelled as he made the connection. 'Hey! Hey! Hey!'

He ran out after the prisoners, still yelling, until the guards drew the group to a halt and looked at the detective with annoyance.

Reagan ignored the officers and strode directly up to the one gangbanger who was trying to bury his face in his armpit. Reagan grabbed the Blood by the chin and yanked his head around till he could look him straight in the eye.

'Arsenio, my man!' Reagan beamed. 'What it is, asshole?'

NINETEEN

The Semper Fi Hospice occupied a mock-Victorian mansion on a tree-lined street at the base of the hills above West Hollywood. Despite the gung-ho name, the hospice provided service to more than just jar-headed marines. It had been established in the eighties as a refuge for destitute Vietnam vets, especially those suffering from effects of Agent Orange, but had more recently played host to those suffering various Gulf War effects. Since Judy Ewing took charge, Semper Fi was open to anyone with a HERV-related complex.

The way Judy heard it, the house had been designed and built in the twenties by silent-screen star Gilbert Roland before the world discovered that he had a voice like Mickey Mouse and his career hit the skids. Another story, probably apocryphal but a particular favourite among the staff, had it that Lupe Velez's legendarily ignominious suicide had been acted-out in an upstairs bathroom. The Big Flush, they called it.

The basement had been converted into an examination room with a small working laboratory, but the upper floors had been kept as homey as possible. Judy thought that with its cathedral ceilings, thick leaded windows and baroque carvings and banisters, the house eerily evoked *Sunset Boulevard* and she sometimes wondered about the therapeutic value of the decor. Once, as a joke, one of the patients – a middle-aged ex-Green Beret with CJD, who also happened to be a drag queen – did himself up as Gloria Swanson, parading up and down the staircase calling for his close-up. Judy laughed along with others at the time, but the image of the frail, wasted man in a cheap wig and flowing gown haunted her. The place was full of ghosts –

some still breathing – and no matter how hard she worked, how many hours she devoted to her charges, Judy couldn't quite make her guilt go away.

As she worked in the lab, the thought that she needed to be tougher, like Greymarch, danced fleetingly through her mind and she shuddered. She already had as much in common with him as she cared to and secretly feared that it would take only the slightest shove of circumstance to push her out over the ugly edge where he lived. They all of them walked that line, she knew, between control and madness. The horrible need was a constant factor not to be denied. Greymarch dealt with his pain by turning it outward, unleashing it on his enemies. Or at least those he perceived as such; Judy wasn't always so sure. She dealt with it in her own way. Through the work. And the guilt.

Judy noticed that a panel light was flashing for Peter Cullen's room. Peter was in the last stages of AIDS and in near-constant pain. A heroin addict, he had developed such a high tolerance to opiates that nothing short of near-lethal doses of morphine had much effect on him. Peter's only known friend had been a fellow junkie who'd OD'd a few weeks before and Peter was scared and lonely and cried out for constant attention. Judy did what she could, but every bed was occupied and each patient could tell an equally tragic story.

She wearily punched the intercom button: 'This is Judy. What is it Peter?'

'Judy?' the thin voice came. 'It hurts.'

'I know Peter, but it's not time for your medication.'

A brief silence. Then: 'I'm thirsty, Judy.'

'There's a pitcher of water on the table beside your bed.'

Another silence.

'I can't reach it, Judy.'

Judy closed her eyes and rubbed her temples with her latex-gloved fingertips. She sighed. 'All right Peter. I'm in the lab, but I'll come up just as soon as I can. Okay?'

'Okay.'

Judy turned back to her work, but was interrupted by another crackle from the intercom.

'Thank you, Judy.'

'Uggghhh,' she said, throwing her head back and letting the guilt wash over her.

'How do you stand it?' Greymarch said.

Judy spun around, dropping a small vial of blood which shattered on the floor. 'Goddammit, Calvin! Do you have to be such a fucking creep?'

Greymarch flashed an evil half-grin and bent to help her pick up the broken glass. He dropped the tiny slivers in a hazardous substances disposal bin and then licked the blood off his fingers. 'Actually, I think "ghoul" is probably closer to the truth.'

'What do you want, Calvin? Christ, how many times have I said those words?'

'No one's ever happy to see me.' Greymarch attempted to pout at her, but the look didn't work.

'Oh? And who else do you ever visit?' she asked with a half-laugh.

'Just the other night I paid a visit on old Dr Sam.'

Judy was washing the blood off her hands, but froze in mid-motion. 'Oh Jesus, Calvin. Please tell me it wasn't you who attacked him. Please tell me you're not that stupid.'

'Who'd you think it was?'

'I didn't, I suppose. Think. What, exactly, did you hope to accomplish?'

'Just a little sand in the machinery of the world, as the poet said. And I didn't attack him, by the way. Well, I did, but not on purpose. Sort of.'

Judy turned her back on him and pulled another test-tube out of the rack. 'Just an accident, huh?'

'Titus was there.'

CRAAAASH.

'Goddammit!'

An entire rack of test-tubes shattered on the floor. A thousand points of jagged glass glinted in a thick spill of red. Judy stared down at the mess, but seemed to be a million miles away.

'You dropped something,' Greymarch said.

By the time Judy returned from Peter's room, Greymarch had more or less cleaned up the lab. There was a suspicious, tell-tale, crimson smear on the tip of his nose, but she decided it was best not to question his disposal methods. One of the hospice volunteers reported in and agreed to keep an eye on things, so Judy led Greymarch into her tiny office and locked the door behind them. They glared at each other for a while, but Judy was no match for Greymarch who could out-stare a cigar-store Indian. He grinned when she looked away.

'Tell me about Titus,' Judy said.

'Not much to tell, really. Sam and I were having a nice chat in the men's room when he walked in. I beat the shit out of him. Busted his nose.'

'What was he doing there? Since when has he become a public figure again?'

'How the hell should I know? Holding the leash on his boy, I suppose. I didn't take the time to ask him. But shit *is* going down.'

'Like what?'

'Sam the man is onto something. I don't know what, but he would have coughed it up if Titus hadn't showed. I think maybe he's refined the new organelles.'

Judy's eyes went wide. 'Do you know that for a fact?'

'No, but what else could it be? You know that's what Titus has him working on, what they've been playing with. Titus wants it as bad as we do. Sam tried to feed me a line about his lab getting busted up, but fuck me if that wasn't a Titus operation, too.'

'Do you know *that* for a fact? Jesus, they did the girl . . . what's-her-name.'

Greymarch slammed his hand down on the desk top hard enough to rattle the shelves. 'Get a clue, Jude. Diane was never more than Sammy's little love doll. Disposable as a used condom. And half as useful.'

'I always thought he liked her.'

'Fucking hell. You must be getting soft working in this place. We're talking about Victor Von Bernouli here, remember? The man who sidestepped all known medical ethics to make us what we are.'

'I suppose,' Judy offered.

'You suppose. He's dancing at the end of Titus's string. Again. But he better watch his fucking ass or Titus is going to pull it tight around his miserable neck.'

'He can't,' Judy said. 'Sam may be a turd, but he's a brilliant turd. And Titus still needs what Sam's got.'

'Well, maybe he already has it. 'Cause Titus is seriously on the move.'

'How so?'

'He's got himself a major operation. I mean, impressive even for him. He's linked up with some badass street mothers. Has them moving Tunnel like it's soda pop. You watch the news? Read the papers? All the gang shit that's been going down? It's Titus that's pushing the buttons.'

'How can you know this, Calvin? How do you find these things out?'

'It's the information society. You need information, you bust open a head or take a hammer to a kneecap. There's a whole city full of information out there. Who needs the Internet?'

'Charming.'

'Fuck you,' Greymarch said, standing up. 'Who are you to judge me, anyway? Maybe you and the others can cope with this . . . lifestyle . . . by martyring yourself to the local lepers, but that doesn't cut it for me. Maybe who I used to be wasn't so terrific, but at least it was me. Now . . . I don't know what the fuck I am, but I don't like it. And if I have to cripple some Tunnel-dealing street-scum to get *me* back, well then bury me and fuck 'em all but nine. And fuck Titus most of all. God help him if he stands in my way.'

'Nice speech. A little heavy on the self-pity maybe, but not bad.'

Greymarch stared nails at her for a moment more, then broke into his evil grin. 'Think so? I spend a lot of time making stuff like that up in my head.'

'You need a hobby.'

His grin faded. 'I've got one. I mean what I said.'

'I know you do. And I . . . appreciate it. In my way. But I can't sanction your methods.'

'I want absolution I'll find a priest.'

'So what do you want from me?'

'What do you think? Blood.'

TWENTY

Reagan eased a cigarette between his lips then offered the pack to Arsenio who shook his head without looking up.

'Kids today,' Reagan chided. 'You shoot-up T between your toes, but you won't smoke a cigarette. I don't know, I think it's television. What do you think?'

Arsenio sat on a hard wooden chair in the interrogation room. His hands were cuffed behind him. He stared down at his fuzzy reflection in the dented, stainless steel table top, shifting slightly when Reagan leaned forward to exhale smoke in his face. He refused to meet Reagan's gaze.

'Yeah, I blame the fucking media,' Reagan continued. He affected the voice of a crotchety old man. 'You darn kids with your crazy rock and roll music!'

Arsenio kept his head down, but Reagan saw him raise an eyebrow and steal a glance at the detective.

'Yeah, I know. Rock and roll is white boy music right homes? You a *gangsta*. You listen to rap. Rap, rap, rap. Let's rap.'

Arsenio did glance up now and saw that Reagan didn't even seem to be paying any attention to him; was, in fact, dragging on his cigarette and staring off into space as he spoke.

'Let's rap. Man, I remember when people used to say that all the time and it had nothing to do with that noise you call music. Yeah, *rap sessions* we used to have. Once a week in the academy we had to meet with this shrink – man, was he ever goofed-up, with his granny glasses and pony-tail and sandals. With socks, yet. Unbelievable. Every week we had to meet with this shrink for a rap session. Or was it an encounter session? I can't remember the difference now. Huh!

'Anyway, he'd try to convince us we were the reincarnation of the SS and we'd nod and *rap* about our inner feelings about the city and violence and disadvantaged minorities. The fucking sixties, son, those were the days. When people actually used to worry about marijuana. Can you believe that shit?'

Reagan dropped the butt on the floor and ground it out beneath his heel. 'Gone with the wind, huh, Eyeball?'

Arsenio's eyebrows arched.

'Yeah, scumbag, I know your street name. I heard a story about how you got it, too. People been keeping their eyes on you. You been making yourself some interesting friends. Moving on up the Blood line mighty fast. See, we like to keep up with your Mr Morgan Carthay and his little sewing circle.'

Reagan got up and walked around behind Arsenio. The boy strained to keep the detective in his sight, but he couldn't turn around handcuffed to the chair.

'Now I'm not a stupid guy,' Reagan said, 'and while I'm not a bleeding heart, I'm not exactly Pat Buchanan, either. I've got no illusions about what it's like out there. I hate you fucking gangbangers, but I can kind of understand you, too. You do what you got to do to live in this city. A man can only eat so much shit before he has to spew it up.'

Reagan completed his circuit around the table and sat back down. He leaned forward again, getting right in the boy's face.

'The thing I can't figure out is this: how do you look your sweet old granny in the eye when you're running with the gang that killed your sister? What's proud old Nana gonna think about you after I tell her that?'

'Motherfucker!' Arsenio screamed and jerked in his chair, fighting the restraints. Reagan sat back and let the boy struggle.

'You motherfucking . . . I fucking kill you, motherfucker!'

'Tsk-tsk,' Reagan chided. 'Such language. I'm afraid I'll have to make a note of that, too.'

Arsenio continued to curse and struggle. Reagan simply lit another cigarette and waited until the boy tired himself out. A uniform opened the door and stuck his head in to see what the ruckus was, but nodded and withdrew when Reagan winked at him. Arsenio finally gave up the fight and again stared down at his reflection, having succeeded only in working up a good sweat.

'Ain't what you think,' Arsenio whispered after several minutes of silence.

'How's that?' Reagan said. The boy looked Reagan squarely in the eye for the first time and the detective was taken aback by his intensity.

'I said it ain't what you think.'

'Well, then enlighten me, Mr Eyeball.'

Arsenio took a deep breath and looked up at the ceiling. He tried to figure out what to do. There was no way in hell the cop would believe he joined the Blood just to find out who killed Diane. Not after the shoot-out at the storage place. And especially not if the cop really knew the Eyeball story. It was all such a crazy idea that sometimes Arsenio lost sight of things himself.

On the other hand, even as a juvie he was looking at stiff time just for being on the scene at the Tunnel bust. The cop who got shot had died and they were making noises about accessory charges for everyone who'd been taken in. Under the circumstances, the idea that a jury would ever buy his story about being an undercover Blood was completely insane.

Hell, it *was* completely insane.

Arsenio thought of his Nana and what it would do to her when she found out about him. She was no dummy and he'd had to assuage her suspicions about his recent nighttime activities by telling her he'd got a job at a fast food joint. He even managed to swipe a McDonald's uniform which he sometimes wore out of the house to make it look good. If she learned he'd been running with the Blood, it would shatter her. She'd close her mind and her heart to him and never even give him a chance to explain things. He knew, in the end, that it wasn't the detective or any twelve of his supposed peers that mattered to him.

It was a jury of one.

'Listen up,' he finally said, looking Reagan eye-to-eye.

Reagan told a uniform to keep an eye on Arsenio while he went to look for Brolin. She wasn't at her desk, but he found McLeod who told him that Brolin was out in the field. McLeod offered to page her, but Reagan declined. As much as he would have liked her input, Reagan knew he had no right to bring her into this if he decided to do what he was thinking about doing. Right or wrong, it would have to be his play and his alone.

He walked past Donatelli's office, but the Captain was away as well. He certainly couldn't tell Donatelli if he went ahead with it, though he would have greatly welcomed the advice. Even if the Captain privately thought it was a good idea, he could never give it official sanction. The kid's idea wasn't just out of policy, it was out of this world.

Reagan continued to stroll around the precinct, mulling over the possible outcomes. As he went by the lounge he saw himself on television. The local news was playing a clip from one of the interviews he'd given following the warehouse bust. He'd already received word that he would be up for a commendation for the operation and that, even with the loss of one officer, the downtown suits had all but creamed their pants over the size of the Tunnel seizure. He stared briefly at his picture on the tube, admired how good he looked and moved on.

He walked back to his desk and plopped down heavily in his chair. He crossed his arms over his chest, leaned back and closed his eyes. Much as he hated to believe it, because he didn't like the kid, Reagan had a gut feeling that Arsenio was telling him the truth. It wasn't just that the kid had a tear in his eye when he talked about his sister – Reagan had met more than one perp who could act; this was L.A., after all – it was the palpable rage that emanated from him when he talked about his supposed Blood brothers. The kid had spilled some valuable details about Carthay's operation, enough in fact, to get him seriously killed, but he talked about it all as if it meant nothing. Arsenio seemed consumed by a desire to avenge his sister's murder and Reagan just didn't believe that anybody could act so convincingly in that situation. Especially since the kid didn't even have a sheet. And the kid had spoken about a mysterious connection who channelled the Tunnel to the Blood. The kid didn't know who it was, but as soon as Arsenio mentioned it, Reagan felt his alarm wires trip.

'Yo! TV star.'

Reagan opened his eyes. A fat detective named Brooks waved a pocket TV at him from across the room. Reagan saw that yet another of his interviews was on the news.

'Looking good, Gorgeous George,' Brooks yelled, 'but next time remember to zip your fly. Nice bust, champ.'

Reagan forced a smile and covertly glanced down at his closed fly. He took a long look around the room and made his decision. He grabbed a micro-cassette recorder from his locked desk drawer and headed back to interrogation.

'Here it is,' he said to Arsenio after dismissing the khaki officer.

'I'm putting my goddamn career on the line with this, but I'm letting you back out.'

Arsenio's whole body seemed to relax in the chair. Reagan unlocked the cuffs and sat down across from the boy who rubbed furiously at his wrists. Reagan removed the tape recorder from his pocket and set it on the table between them.

'But first, I got to hear the Eyeball story.'

Arsenio froze, his left hand tightly squeezing his right wrist. 'I . . . can't,' Arsenio said. He was shaking his head slowly back and forth. 'I can't give you that.'

'You got no choice. That's the deal. You come through on your end and I burn the tape. You burn me and you take a murder rap. Direct line to the lethal injection table. One needle, no waiting. It's my only insurance.'

Arsenio shook his head, but it was clear that he was thinking.

'How do I know I can trust you?' he asked.

Reagan offered a faint smile. 'I could ask you the same question. This is a pure trust deal, both ways. Either of us fucks up, it's the other one's ass.'

Arsenio's head shake gradually transformed itself into a nod. He pointed at the tape recorder and Reagan switched it on.

'My name is Arsenio Sommers,' he said hesitantly. Reagan nodded at him. 'My street name is Eyeball. I got the name after I shot a little kid right through his eye with one shot. I done it for my initiation into the Trey-Deuce Blood. I don't know who the kid was, but he dissed Morgan Carthay.'

Arsenio pressed his hand to his forehead as if he couldn't believe what he was doing. Reagan marvelled, too, knowing that the tape was a certain death sentence for the kid if it was ever made public.

'I didn't want to shoot him, but I had no choice. I . . . I just shot. I hit him in the eye, but it was just . . . lucky.'

Arsenio's voice actually broke on the last word. Reagan's surprise level went up another notch as Arsenio finished the confession in tears and broken words.

'I didn't want to do it. I didn't . . . he just fell over . . . in the eye. Just fell over. I got . . . a lucky shot. In the eye.'

Arsenio fell silent, wiped his runny nose with his sleeve. Reagan fished a monogrammed handkerchief out of his pocket and tossed it to the kid who studied it like it was some alien artefact. Reagan turned off the machine.

'That'll do me,' Reagan said.

Arsenio blew his nose in the hanky and then offered it back to Reagan who made a face and shook his head.

'I get it cleaned for you,' Arsenio said sweetly and in that moment Reagan thought he saw the boy that his grandmother probably knew. 'Can I go now?'

'Back to lock-up,' Reagan said.

A look of anger flashed across the boy's face, but Reagan stemmed the outburst with a gesture.

'Think, Arsenio. I can't just let you walk out of here. Even if I could convince my superiors, what would Carthay think? He'd assume you gave him up and he'd cut you into little chunks. No, I've got another idea. Are you quick? No bullshit now.'

Arsenio thought a moment and then nodded. 'I ain't that strong, but I can move. I did a little track in school. Hurdles.'

'All right. You're going to have to escape from an officer. Ah, ah! It won't be hard and he won't be armed.'

Arsenio looked doubtful, but Reagan reassured him.

'Just don't hurt him,' Reagan said. Thinking about Witherspoon he added: 'Well, don't hurt him *too* bad.'

TWENTY-ONE

'What are *you* looking at?' Reagan asked.

Brolin continued to inspect him. He nervously glanced around
the squad room as she looked him up and down and then walked
a circle around his chair. She reached over and grabbed his chin,
turning his face to the right and then to the left. She grunted to
herself.

'What?' he demanded.

'No,' she said, sitting down on his desk, 'it's just . . . I've never
seen an asshole that big before.'

'Ahhh, give me a break, Jenny.'

'*Give* you a *break*? Have you gone out of your fucking mind?
How could you let that kid go? Do you really think you're ever
going to see him again?'

'I've got his confession on tape. He names Carthay.'

'So what?' Brolin asked. 'Man, I bet he's out of the state by
now. Out of the damn country!'

'Jenny, he's fifteen years old and lives with his grandmother.
Where the hell's he going to go?'

Brolin continued to shake her head. 'Jesus! I don't know. He
may be fifteen, but he's a gangster and a killer. With you on one
side and the Blood on the other, he sure as hell ain't gonna hang
around and wait on the big squeeze.'

'I think you're wrong. I think he was giving it up straight about
his sister and that he's really onto something with Carthay and the
Trey-Deuce. And I think he meant it when he said that he didn't
want to shoot that kid.'

'Didn't want . . . ?' Brolin seemed at a loss for words. 'He capped a ten-year-old kid on a street corner just for fun! That's called a stone killer, buddy-boy. What the hell, Dennis? You couldn't fucking stand this kid before. Where'd this incredible bond of trust suddenly come from? Did he read to you from Kahlil Gibran or something?'

'I don't know,' Reagan admitted. 'It really comes down to a feeling, I guess. I keep getting them about this mess. Maybe it's desperation, but there's a bell ringing here and I can't figure out what for. I know I can't exactly put that in a report, but it's all I have to go on. Besides, what do we gain if we hold him? Six months in juvie?'

Brolin flashed him a sceptical look.

'Look: we know it was a Blood crew that did the job on the kid's sister at the lab. The kid thinks it was the Trey-Deuce and he says that's why he went in with them.'

'Yeah?' Brolin said, 'so why would Carthay bring him in so fast?'

''Cause the kid had an older brother who was an OG. He ran with Carthay back when the Trey-Deuce were still part of the Athens Panthers. The brother went down in a drive-by about three years ago. It's like a college fraternity, the kid gets an automatic pledge.'

'That's pretty thin, Dennis. That's fucking Kate Moss is how thin that is. Honour is not what these scumbags are about.'

'Ohhhh, don't underestimate them, Jenny. You haven't been around the scene that long. The "dumb nigger" impression that gets laid on the gangs suits a lot of people, including the gangbangers themselves sometimes. But it couldn't be further from the truth. Honour runs a lot deeper than you think. Especially with the Blood.'

'Maybe so, Dennis, but I still think you're kidding yourself about the kid. And, frankly, I don't see how you're going to cover your ass on this.'

'Not to worry, me and my ass go way back. You know, S.I.S has been trying to slip someone inside the Trey-Deuce for a year and they got nowhere. The kid's already inside and the way I see it, he's the only way we'll ever get a line on Carthay. Correct me if I'm wrong, but we still don't have squat. Right? I mean the follow-ups have gone nowhere.'

'I like to think we'll always have squat, Dennis.'

'Cute,' he said. 'But check the replay. One: the dead girl is doped to the gills with Tunnel, even though everyone who knows her swears up and down that she's right as spring rain. Two: we've got a flood of the shit washing through the city courtesy of the Trey-Deuce. Now my little buddy Arsenio comes along and not only confirms that the Blood hit the lab at Phaedra, but tells me that the Trey-Deuce are working the Tunnel trade through some mystery man.'

'Jesus,' Brolin said, 'that sounds like a *total* crock of shit. It's out of a Dolph Lundgren movie. Exactly who is this mystery man?'

'The kid says he doesn't know, but he's going to try and find out. All he knows is what he's overheard and that is that there's some heavy-hitter white dude who's setting up the Blood's Tunnel trade and that even a crazy motherfucker like Carthay dances to his tune.'

'Well, that sure cuts it down to size. Maybe we should go question David Geffen or Michael Eisner. Hey, maybe Pee-wee Herman's back in action.'

'Try this on for size: how about your lover-boy Bernouli?' Reagan said.

'Say *what*? You connected those dots a little too fast for me, Dennis.'

'He's in the middle of this somehow and he's got all the credentials. Tunnel came out of nowhere, what, a year ago? I mean, it's all over the place now, but the Feds trace its origins right here to L.A. The good doctor obviously knows his way around a chemistry set, maybe he cooked the shit up. You can't tell me that Bernouli doesn't stink.'

'Christ on a crutch, Dennis. I maybe agree the man's got some BO, but that's a hell of a long way from making him mastermind of the Tunnel trade. You're making this up as you go!'

'I admit that, but stay with me. Why the hell did the Blood hit Bernouli's lab in particular? They could have had their run of that place after they broke in, but they head right for a lab with all kinds of nasty warnings about contamination and lethal substances. If you're a gangster looking for a quick score or a good time is that where *you* go? No way, not even for some do-it-yourself meth. They had another reason to be there. Maybe payback on Bernouli for something we can't know about, but something to do with Tunnel. Hell, maybe Bernouli sent them himself to lose some evidence. Bernouli has the means and the money to be behind this.'

'And the dead girl?'

'An accident,' Reagan shrugged. 'Even Bernouli didn't know she'd be there after hours. She was a throw-in for the Blood.'

Brolin was still shaking her head. 'Even if I grant you all that – which I don't – what's Bernouli's goddamn motive, Dennis? People sell drugs for money, not for fun. You yourself admit that he's already got money and you saw who turned up for that benefit. I bet he raised a million bucks at that dinner. Maybe more.'

'Motive is an overrated concept. It's strictly nineteenth century and it doesn't cut it in a postmodern world of freeway snipers and militia bombers. "Shit happens" isn't just a bumper sticker in Los Angeles; it's a way of life.'

Brolin cocked an eyebrow and made a fish-face.

'Okay,' Reagan laughed, 'so I don't know what his motive is. Maybe he needs *more* money. Maybe . . . he needs it to do good, to find a cure for AIDS. Maybe it's for his sainted old mother who's got female trouble and needs full-body electrolysis. Or maybe he's just a greedy, power-hungry bastard who wants to be richer than God. It's not like there aren't plenty like that walking around, doing nasties. And they don't all produce movies. I'm just offering a plausible . . .' – Brolin snorted – '. . . theory that fits the limited facts at hand. And I'm saying it's worth the shot of losing the kid to send him out and maybe came back with something we can use.'

Brolin absently rifled through some papers on Reagan's desk. She started shaking her head again and opened her mouth to speak when Reagan's phone rang.

'Yeah, Reagan . . . Hey! How you doing? . . . uh-huh . . . uh-huh . . . no, I don't . . . yeah . . . yeah . . . yeah . . . *What*?'

Brolin hadn't been listening, but Reagan suddenly dug a claw into her thigh to get her attention. He looked up at her, eyes wide, as he continued to talk on the phone.

'You're sure about the name? No chance of mistake? . . . No, I know, I just . . . I know, Jerry . . . I know . . . yeah, you've got my fax number, right? . . . As soon as you hang up . . . Who?' Reagan shot a glance at Brolin, then broke into a smile and quickly looked away from her. 'Yeah, I'd say so. Smarter . . . Smarter . . . not that smart . . . ummmm . . .' Reagan peeked at Brolin, who saw him steal a quick glance at her chest. 'Smaller. Bigger . . . not *that* big. You got it.'

Brolin felt herself blushing, but managed not to turn away.

'Okay. Thanks, Jerry . . . yeah, I will . . . when pigs fly, scumbag. Thanks again.'

Reagan wiped the smirk off his face before turning back to Brolin whose face was still bright red.

'Anyone I know?' she asked with clenched teeth.

'That was my buddy with the Sheriff in Alameda. He finally did some checking into Greymarch.'

'It would seem he checks everything out very thoroughly.'

'Yeah,' Reagan said, suppressing another smile, 'Jerry's pretty much a perfectionist.'

'Hmmm,' Brolin nodded, 'and how big are *his* tits?'

It was Reagan's turn to blush. 'Right. Anyway. He found one interesting tidbit.'

'Let me guess: Greymarch has a sister and she's stacked.'

'Greymarch has a military record. He was a corporal in a tank division that saw action in the Gulf.'

'Figures. Bernouli basically said he was a vet with a gripe.'

'Well, Jerry was able to get a hold of his V.A. medical records. Supposed to be confidential, but like I say, Jerry has a way with these things. Greymarch was checked into a San Francisco veterans' facility as recently as November of 1994.'

'Gulf War Syndrome?'

'Seems that way. The V.A. doesn't officially recognize it so they don't call it that, but the records say he had a whole host of "unspecified" virus-based conditions. They also did a major psych work-up on him. Something about violent tendencies.'

'That's not so surprising. Hell, if I'd been exposed to what they gave those bastards without telling them, I'd probably be a little violent myself.'

'I agree,' Reagan said. 'But it doesn't explain his being dead.'

'Say what?' Brolin said.

'Yeah. The V.A. has a death certificate on file. Jerry followed up with state records and it's on file there, too. Calvin Greymarch died of complications arising from pneumonia on December 10, 1994.'

'God*damn*!'

'And here's the really interesting part: the death certificate bears the signature of a Dr James Beniger.'

'So?'

'Well, Jerry did a little more checking and found that Beniger was part of a group practice.'

'Uh-oh,' Brolin said.

'Yeah, it's one of those medical corporations with about a dozen offices around the state. The individual practices all have different names, but they're tied together under a parent company.'

'Don't tell me . . .'

Reagan nodded. 'Samuel Bernouli and Associates, Incorporated.'

'Ooooh,' Brolin said with a wicked grin. 'Now the fun begins.'

TWENTY-TWO

Arsenio tried to bear up under Morgan's scrutiny. The gang leader lay on his king-sized bed, scratching his nose with the shiny barrel of the Glock. His eyes were lit up with the rush of a Tunnel high. Arsenio saw a drop of blood ooze out from between the knuckles of Morgan's gun hand and trace a lazy red line down his hard skin. Morgan wore only a pair of brightly patterned boxer shorts. Arsenio noted that Morgan looked thin and drawn, even sickly, and suspected the gang leader's ever growing appetite for Tunnel had something to do with it. Scaly red patches mottled his legs and his formerly pitch-black skin was taking on an ugly grey cast. K'toma, as always, stood at Morgan's side, Uzi in hand, surveying the terrain. Lutece and Endzone shifted nervously behind Arsenio, waiting on Morgan's judgement. Lutece mentioned that JuJu had been picked up by the cops in an overnight sweep.

At first, Arsenio didn't know if he could face up to the encounter with Morgan. Or even if he should. He hadn't believed that the detective would actually allow him to escape, had figured it for a set-up where he'd end up shot in the back. He was old enough to know not to trust LAPD. He'd seen and heard enough stories of black suspects who'd been shot and killed 'resisting arrest' or 'attempting to flee,' but he couldn't see where he had any real choice. If he'd kept his mouth shut and done the time, he might never have been able to work out the truth about his sister and take his revenge. And if the cop leaked word that he gave up the Blood, he'd end up in a can of dog food.

For an instant, after he'd escaped from the cop – and he couldn't

believe how easy *that* turned out to be; apparently *any* old white
dude could make the force in Los Angeles – he thought about
just taking off, grabbing the first bus out of town. But even if he
hocked the cellular phone and the gun he'd only have a couple
hundred bucks to his name and nowhere to go. His only other
family was in Chicago, but, no matter how bad the situation, he
couldn't imagine just running away from his grandparents without
a word. He could never bring himself to break his Nana's heart like
that. Not after she'd lost her other grandchildren to the streets. So
Arsenio tried to go home. But he found out that isn't something
you can always do.

Reagan had warned Arsenio that his escape would have to
be on the record and that he'd be making himself a fugitive.
The detective told him that given the circumstances, Arsenio's
re-capture wouldn't be a priority item, but that it was out of
Reagan's immediate control. Reagan warned Arsenio that he would
have to keep a low profile, but basically he'd just be another felony
warrant walking the streets, okay so long as he didn't get picked up
for anything else. The detective also told him that his grandmother
would certainly be informed about both the arrest and the escape.
Arsenio had demanded that Reagan find some way to keep his
Nana out of it, but the cop just shrugged and said that was the
deal, take it or leave it.

Arsenio was careful to approach the house from the back. He
cut across another lawn, his Nana's backyard neighbours, thankful
that their noisy terrier was locked up in the house. He crept up to
the honeysuckle-draped cyclone fence that separated the properties
and peered through the foliage toward a familiar scene on the rear
patio of his house.

His Nana sat on a wicker chair feeding his Papa Jerome. Jerome
had suffered a paralysing stroke two years earlier and was confined
to a wheelchair. Jerome couldn't even speak and was barely able to
move his mouth and tongue enough to take solid food. Sometimes
Arsenio would feed Papa Jerome. After a while he had come not
to mind the chore, but his Nana seemed to relish the task and
would wheel the old man out into the yard at mealtimes. She
spoke softly to him as she slowly spooned oatmeal or thin soup or
finely blended whatever-it-was into her husband's mouth. Jerome
never responded to Arsenio, but occasionally when his Nana fed
the old man, Arsenio thought he saw a dim spark of life in his
grandfather's eyes.

Arsenio just sat for a minute and took in the scene. His gaze roamed over the small vegetable garden full of blood red tomatoes and oversized peppers and cucumbers that sprouted beside the patio. A patch of vibrant flowers, bold colours clashing, stretched across the rear half of the yard. His Nana was forever trying to get him interested in the garden, but he'd never have any part of it, agreeing to help out only when he felt guilty.

But now Arsenio wished that he'd spent a little more time working on the flowers and tomatoes with his grandmother, for he feared he'd never have the opportunity again. With a time-to-face-the-music sigh, Arsenio hauled himself over the shoulder-high fence, careful not to tread on his Nana's vivid, blooming flower bed.

His grandmother looked up. She glanced fearfully at him for a moment until he entered her nearsighted field of focus. She sagged with relief, then drew herself up again to a stiff posture, still holding the tray with Papa Jerome's lunch. A thin line of dribble trailed down the old man's chin and his lips continued to flap up and down, though there was nothing in his mouth.

'Hi, Nana,' he said meekly, but she didn't respond. She put the tray down on the floor, slopping some soup over the side, and released the brake on her husband's wheel chair. With the practice of years she opened the back door with one hand and spun the chair around with the other, manoeuvring the steel frame up and over the slight bump at the base of the doorway. Arsenio reached over to hold open the door, but she slapped at his hand and got her husband in the house on her own. She whispered a few words to Papa Jerome, but Arsenio couldn't quite make out what she said.

She returned to the patio door, but didn't step outside. She reached for the open screen door and pulled it closed in front of her, staring out at her grandson through the torn wire mesh. Her features were harder than diamond, but her eyes were moist and her hands shook.

'Nana . . .'

'I don't know you,' she said.

Arsenio felt a pressure in his chest, like the weight of a big old fat man. 'Nana, please, I know what they told you, but . . .'

'You don't know nothing. I thought I taught you, boy, but you don't know nothing. And I don't know you.'

The fat guy started jumping up and down. Arsenio swallowed hard, struggling to keep his voice steady. 'It's not like you think, Nana. Please. I . . . I can't tell you now, but it's not bad like you think.'

'I had a boy,' she said, staring more through him than at him. 'His name was Arsenio. But he's gone. Gone like the others.'

Arsenio was sobbing now, pressing his hand against the old screen, reaching for his Nana's touch. But her arms stayed at her side and her hard look never faltered.

'It's *for* Diane, Nana. You don't know . . . it's for Diane. It's not how you think.'

The old woman looked truly *at* him, now, her eyes brimming with tears. 'She's gone, boy. Nothing to do for her now, but weep. Nothing but grief.'

'Please, Nana,' he said. He pushed his little finger through a tear in the middle of the screen and waggled it toward his grandmother's hand. She looked down at it as tears fell across her cheeks. She gently touched his finger with her own, then quickly drew her hand away and resumed her Beefeater stare.

'All gone,' she said again, then walked away.

Arsenio stood there sobbing for several minutes. Finally he turned around and dashed back through the yard, leaving a trail of trampled flowers in his wake.

Arsenio had wandered aimlessly for a time, cursing Reagan, Morgan and himself, unable to shake his grandmother's rejection. He paid no attention to where he was going until he looked up and saw that he was standing across the street from the lot where he'd earned his street name. Almost laughing at the irony, he wandered across the road and onto the junk-strewn patch of ground. He tried to find the spot where the boy in the red cap had gone down, but the only traces were a few tattered pieces of yellow plastic crime scene tape strewn across the debris.

'Eyeball,' he said to the dirt. 'Arsenio.'

'*Eyeball*,' Morgan said, casually pointing the Glock at Arsenio.

With no place else to go and no other choice to make, Arsenio had hopped an RTD bus and made his way across town to the Blood crib. Lutece was surprised to see him and Arsenio felt the Blood eye him suspiciously. They'd had him wait in the living room with Tamara while Endzone went looking for Morgan, and even she was uncharacteristically quiet. He watched a rerun of The Cosby Show with her, but every time she started to laugh at something, she'd quickly glance at Arsenio and stifle herself. Finally, Endzone and Lutece came back in to escort Arsenio up to Morgan's bedroom.

'How'd you get on the street?' Morgan asked, still waving the Glock.

'Escaped,' Arsenio said. He remembered that Reagan told him to stick as close to the truth as possible. 'Damn cop's so stupid, he didn't snap the cuff. I caught him from behind and ran away.' He didn't mention the fact that Reagan slipped him the key ahead of time and made sure Witherspoon went out without his gun.

'Why wasn't you with the others?'

Arsenio was ready for that as well, again with a rough version of the truth. 'The cop knew me. The detective. He come by my Nana's house one time making trouble and I got in his face. He kept me at the station after the others got sent on. Slapped me around a little, but he didn't do no damage.'

Morgan nodded, but the barrel of the gun tracked precious bits of Arsenio's anatomy. 'What he want?'

'Nothing, really,' Arsenio lied, thinking it sounded all right. 'Just getting in *my* face. He asked a couple questions about who I ran with, but mostly just pushed me. I didn't give him nothing so he gave it up after a while. Sent me out with the other dude and he's the one I messed up.'

'Come here,' Morgan said and patted the mattress beside him. Arsenio glanced up at K'toma and back at Lutece and Endzone, but there was no sympathy to be found. He practically tiptoed to the side of the bed and gingerly sat down on the edge.

'No,' Morgan said. 'You climb on up here.'

Tentatively, Arsenio pulled himself up on the bed and lay down at Morgan's left. Morgan draped a sweaty, muscular arm around his shoulders. Up close Arsenio could see a thousand tiny Tunnel pinpricks. Morgan's body smelled foul and feverish, though the skin felt cool to the touch. Arsenio wasn't sure if Morgan was sick or if it was the permanent redolence of Tunnel abuse.

'You gonna fuck me up the ass?' Morgan asked.

Arsenio sort of cleared his throat but didn't know what to say. He finally managed a partial head shake.

'I didn't catch that,' Morgan prompted.

'No,' Arsenio said. 'No way.'

'Okay,' Morgan nodded. They lay there quietly for a moment, Morgan still squeezing Arsenio's shoulder. 'You sure now?'

'Huh? Yeah. I mean yes.'

'Yes, you gonna fuck me up the ass?'

'No!' Arsenio exhorted. 'I wouldn't mess with you. You got to know that.'

'Okay.' More silence. Then: 'Cause if you want to fuck me up the ass, you do it here and now. I roll over and you go on and shove it in. 'Cause later I find you fucked me with the po-lice, well . . .'

Morgan reached over with his Glock hand and rested the barrel of the gun on Arsenio's shoulder. 'You see that?'

Arsenio craned his neck to look at a dirty, brown splotch on the wall at the end of the barrel. He nodded.

'See, that's the last dude what thought he could fuck me up the ass. You know what I'm saying?'

Arsenio nodded again.

'I'm sorry,' Morgan said. 'I missed that.'

'I hear you,' Arsenio said, very deliberately.

'Good. Good.' Morgan twitched his wrist and the Glock's cold muzzle scraped Arsenio below the ear. 'So you ain't gonna fuck me up the ass, now.'

'No. I will not.'

'And you did not fuck me up the ass with the po-lice.'

'Uh-uh. No way.'

'That's nice. All right. You done good with the one-times. You go back on down and tell . . .'

Morgan looked over at K'toma. 'Lanise,' the big man said.

'Yeah. You go tell Lanise I said to give you some sex. But you best hold tight to her big titties or you gonna fall right on in. Go.'

Arsenio tried to summon a smile and hurried out of the room, followed by Lutece and Endzone who were once again laughing with him, slapping him on the back.

'What you think?' K'toma asked after they departed.

'Ahhhh, man. He gave us up. That nigger's sucking serious pig dick. That's all right, though. We use it to our advantage.'

K'toma nodded and headed for the door.

'And another thing,' Morgan said, pointing at the wall behind the bed, 'do something about this here. This don't look nothing like no dude's brains.'

TWENTY-THREE

Reagan desperately wanted to follow-up on Bernouli with Brolin, but he had to spend the morning dealing with the morass of paperwork from the big bust, along with all the separate reports about Arsenio's escape from Witherspoon. Much as he couldn't stand the little geek, Reagan felt a twinge of guilt over his role in engineering the situation and he did what he could in the report to make Witherspoon come off as at least marginally competent. He'd convinced Witherspoon that, for his own good, it was best not to mention the fact that he was unarmed at the time of the kid's escape and to 'exaggerate' some of the details of the mishap. Typically, Witherspoon seemed more confused than embarrassed by the whole thing and was so concerned about how his uncle would react that he gratefully accepted Reagan's ostensibly brotherly advice, vowing eternal friendship in return. It was almost enough to make Reagan feel really guilty, but the pair of shiners that Arsenio had dealt Witherspoon in the course of the escape reminded Reagan that the moron really did deserve whatever he got.

There was also the matter of the escalating gang war. West L.A. normally had the lowest level of gang activity in the city, but what was left of the old Blood–Crip truce had fallen apart during recent weeks and there had been nearly a dozen gang-related homicides – mostly drive-bys – in Venice alone over a ten-day period. Two known Blood Tunnel-houses in the Oakcrest area had been burned over night, probably by Crips, but maybe by the johnny-come-lately Sagrados, and the division was braced for what would likely be an indiscriminate Blood response come sundown.

Reagan spent the afternoon in strategy meetings with S.I.S. and Division and in-between had to rush back to West L.A. to update Donatelli and attempt to keep pace with Brolin. Reagan tried to keep his mind focused on his assigned duties, but he couldn't stop thinking about and polishing his Bernouli scenario. He also had more than a few worries about Arsenio and how that decision might boomerang on him, but he figured either it would work out or not and, thus compartmentalized, he was able to shove it to the back of his mind. He was so distracted by the Bernouli affair, though, that he couldn't even enjoy a late afternoon press conference on the precinct steps in which the happy-talk reporters tossed up grapefruit-sized questions for him to swat over the cameras and out of the park.

As he finished up the last of a series of 'exclusive' interviews with the local TV stations, Reagan spied Brolin and McLeod pulling into the precinct lot. He noted that McLeod got out on the driver's side and chuckled slightly to himself. He had to stand and pretend to talk for a few more minutes while the camera crew shot fill-ins over his shoulder of a lady reporter nodding engagedly. As soon as they were done, he dashed into the precinct and found Brolin staked out in her favourite spot, watching a Dodger game in the lounge and sipping from a can of Diet Yoo-Hoo.

'Hey,' he said from the doorway.

'Hey, yourself. Come to see how us working stiffs live or is there an autograph session scheduled in here?'

'We all have our bears to cross.'

'You're a real fucking stoic, Dennis. I only hope that someday I might be lucky enough to give my life, so that you can go on giving interviews.'

'Amen,' he said. 'What's the score?'

'Zip-zip. They'll lose.'

'Ah, how quickly they forget,' Reagan said, shaking his head in mock-exasperation. He pulled a chair around, straddling it backwards. 'What's happening on the Bernouli front?'

'And here I thought you just missed me. I'm crushed.'

'Yeah, yeah,' he said, 'spill.'

Brolin yawned and leaned her elbow out over the table, resting her head on her palm and arching her back. Reagan's gaze wandered on its own down to her chest before he caught it and yanked it back to her eyes. He hoped she hadn't noticed, but the barely perceptible upturn of her lips told him that she had and he reluctantly scored a mental point in her column.

'Bernouli blew us off again this morning,' she said. 'Well, his rat bastard attorney did, actually, so I haven't had a chance to ask him if he's masterminding the Tunnel trade.' Reagan offered a sarcastic smile. 'No, seriously. Bernouli did blow off a meeting, but agreed to reschedule for tonight. I'm supposed to interview him at his place at eight o'clock with McLeod. The attorney's supposed to be there, too, so it's going to have to be good cop, good cop.'

'Damn! I wish I could be there.'

'You can tag along if you like. I don't mind and McLeod's a pussycat.'

'No way,' he said. 'Not with the Blood on the warpath tonight. We've got a situation room put together downstairs for response. Coordinating with Division, South Central and Valley. Donatelli'd tear my head off if anything went down and I wasn't there.'

'The life of a star,' Brolin shrugged. 'Anyway, if I should suddenly, like, get my period or something, I think McLeod can back me up okay. And I'll try to ask Bernouli a pertinent question or two.'

'That's not what I . . . you know . . . I'm not saying that.'

Brolin laughed out loud. 'Christ, Dennis, take it easy. I'm just jagging your wires. Man, what happened to your sense of humour?'

'Sorry. There's just something about this mess that's dug its way deep under the skin. I keep thinking about it like an itch that you can't find so you have to scratch all over. This case stinks like a dump from top to bottom. That scene at Bernouli's benefit dinner didn't play right by half. Did you come up with anything more on Greymarch, by the way?'

'McLeod tried to follow-up on the doctor that signed the death certificate. Beniger? Turns out he's deceased as well. Car accident last year in Berkeley.'

'Suspicious?'

'Berkeley P.D. have it as a hit and run. No witnesses, no suspects. It's still open, but they told me it's a dead file.'

Reagan nodded in response.

'Then McLeod tried to track down Greymarch's records from the medical practice. It seems Beniger was a lousy administrator and Greymarch's records have somehow been misplaced.'

'Motherfucker!'

'Tell me about it. McLeod thought maybe they were just giving him a hard time so he pressed it. He says he's convinced that there's no trail to follow there.'

'Anything to tie Bernouli in with Beniger?' Reagan asked.

'Nothing directly. McLeod tried to wheedle some info out of the practice, but whoever he talked to claimed not to know Bernouli except by name. It was just, like, the office manager he talked to, though, so it doesn't mean much.'

'It would be nice to get up there for some face-to-face,' Reagan mused.

'Dream on, TV-boy,' Brolin said. 'They ran out of toilet paper in the ladies' room two weeks ago. You think the department's going to spring for a ticket to Frisco for something like this?'

'No, I suppose not. And I told you never to call it Frisco.'

'Well thank you Herb friggin' Caen. This from a man who refers to women as gash.'

Reagan felt himself blush and cleared his throat.

'Thought I didn't hear that the other day, huh?' she said. 'Just mind your own P's and Q's, Nosy Parker.'

'Yeesh! I'm sorry. Okay?'

Reagan didn't say anything for a while as Brolin turned her attention back to the ball game. The Dodgers were suddenly down three to nothing. Reagan waited for the end of the half-inning before picking up the conversation.

'What about Blaine?' he asked, as a beer commercial came on.

'Another fucking mystery man,' Brolin said. 'He obviously has major bucks, but he keeps his name out of the system. Donatelli connected with someone at I.R.S., but it didn't add much. He files some very complicated corporate returns that let him get away without paying any taxes – ain't that always the way? – but none of it shed much light on him. Donatelli's guy forwarded a list of some of the dummy corporations he uses, but I haven't had a chance to go through it yet.'

'Any medical or pharmaceutical companies?'

'I don't know, Dennis. I just told you I haven't had a chance to look through it. It's pretty low priority at this point.'

'Get me a copy of the list?'

'Whatever,' she said.

'Thanks.'

He watched the game with her for a few more minutes before getting up. 'Call me after you talk with Bernouli?'

'If I get a chance,' she said, still staring at the screen. He sighed loudly and started out of the lounge, but Brolin called his name before he was out of earshot. 'You'll be here all night?' she asked.

'Till early morning, anyway.'

'I'll call,' she said and winked at him. He smiled in return and went back up to his desk.

Reagan fussed with the paperwork for a while before heading down to the situation room to prepare for the evening's gang festivities. By seven o'clock, with the sun still hovering over the lip of the Pacific, there had already been two gang shootings near the Pavilion in Venice and a small explosion at a Crip crack-house in Mar Vista. Reagan was on a conference call with S.I.S. when a khaki officer Reagan didn't know came into the situation room.

'Lieutenant Reagan?' the officer said.

'Yo!' Reagan said, listening to the S.I.S. commander with half an ear.

'This came in from Liebowitz at S.I.D.' The officer handed Reagan a manilla envelope. The arrival time was stamped on one corner: 1.15 p.m.

'Hey,' Reagan said, 'why am I just getting this now?'

The officer shrugged as if to say *why does the sun rise in the east?* and left the room.

Reagan mumbled a few 'um-hmmms' in the teleconference as he tore open the envelope. Before he could read what was inside a sergeant passed him a note indicating that another shooting had just occurred near Santa Monica Community College. Reagan shook his head as he read the note and used the excuse to bow out of the phone conversation. He buzzed upstairs to Donatelli and got approval to redeploy some officers. By the time the new orders were communicated and implemented it was 7.30 and Reagan had forgotten about the message from Liebowitz. He was paged to come back into the teleconference and spent the next thirty minutes arguing with Division about the redeployment.

Reagan hung up on Division at eight o'clock, feeling exhausted and irritable. He was about to head over to the lounge for a Coke and smoke when Liebowitz's envelope again caught his eye and he picked it up. His eyes grew wide as he read the cover letter from the S.I.D. man:

Yo Denver,
    Nice face-time on the Tunnel bust. You're really much too pretty to be a cop (but next time zip your fly). Maybe someday you'll send me an autographed glossy.

I don't know what the hell is going on out there these days, but the shit you landed in the raid is *fucked*. We ran the standard analyses on samples of the Tunnel (prelim report attached) and got some impossible results. Nobody here could make it (lost me a sawbuck to Manusov), so on a lark I sent a batch to our med-lab. To make a long story short, *they* couldn't figure it either so they sent it external.

The stuff is fucked. The samples are contaminated with some kind of live virus. The lab thought it was HIV at first, but they can't make a true match, something about the protein structures being off (I know you don't know what that means, but trust me: it's weird). It's going off to CDC in Atlanta marked PDQ, but I don't count on hearing back from them anytime this month. The outside lab guy said whatever it is to handle with extreme care.

So, handle with extreme care, Dennis.

What I don't get is why the fuck would anybody want to sell contaminated shit? Chances are the fucking junkies are going to die of AIDS anyway, but who'd push stuff like this? I tell you Denver, this is one goofy town. Anyway, give a call if you need anything else. I'll try and press CDC for help. Let me know if you figure out what the hell this is all about, will ya?

X's & O's
Freddy

Reagan quickly scanned the computer print-out in the report and then re-read Liebowitz's note. He glanced at the clock – ten after eight – and heard somebody calling his name, but he was a million miles away.

What did it mean that the Tunnel was contaminated? Why in the world would the Blood want to push shit like that on the streets? What could they possibly hope to gain from it?

Unless even the Blood didn't know that the Tunnel was bad. Unless someone was using them to get the shit out.

But the question still remained: Why?

Five more minutes had passed while Reagan sat in silent reverie, the S.I.D. report still clutched tightly in his hand. The sergeant was tapping him on the shoulder and looking at him oddly. Finally, Reagan turned to him, but didn't hear what he said.

Why? Reagan wondered.

He could think of only one person who might be able to provide the answer. It was almost twenty after eight. Brolin had said that her appointment with Bernouli was for eight o'clock. Bernouli's place was over in Cheviot Hills, maybe a fifteen-minute drive.

'I got to go,' Reagan said.

'What?' the sergeant responded. 'Lieutenant, you can't leave. Who's gonna supervise?'

'Call Donatelli. Get him down here. Tell him . . . I'll fill him in later. But I got to go.'

Reagan didn't wait for the sergeant's reply. With the report still in his hand he ran out of the situation room and up to his car. As he turned the key in the ignition he glanced at the blinking digital clock.

It was 8.27.

TWENTY-FOUR

The fifteen minute drive to Bernouli's place took Reagan nearly half an hour. He had a hard time negotiating the unfamiliar winding streets of Cheviot Hills. Although not as upscale as Bel-Air or the Palisades, Cheviot Hills was comprised of impressive if not quite palatial homes, set on what was more like a series of gentle rises than real hills. The neighbourhood always came as something of a surprise to the uninitiated, for while its relatively meagre elevation was too slight to notice from afar, the houses were perched just high enough to afford sweeping vistas of the Los Angeles basin.

It was just after nine o'clock when Reagan finally found Bernouli's place, a two-storey mock-Tudor affair surrounded by a six-foot-high redwood fence. The house sat at the apex of one of the highest rises in the area, with a brilliant western exposure. Behind the house, the last purple streaks of dusk dipped into the ocean in the distance. He had worried that he might already have missed Brolin and McLeod, was relieved to see both their cars parked out in front. There were few other vehicles on the street and, typically, Reagan had yet to spot a single pedestrian. Of course, the fact that there weren't any sidewalks served to discourage those unworthy enough to lack internally-combusted locomotion.

Reagan hesitated as he got out of his car, musing on how dislocated the area was from the rest of the city. He fantasized about how nice it would be to live up here. The quiet, tree-lined streets with their stately houses, pretty gardens and immaculate lawns wouldn't have been at all out of place in some small town. They were, as Reagan knew all too well, no more than five miles away from one of the highest crime areas in the entire country, but from up here it was hard to believe that these houses, these people, were really a part of the same city that saw forty-plus homicides a week, enough drugs to narcotize the third world and a gang war that made Bosnia look like a church social.

Perhaps that was exactly the problem, he thought: perhaps if the people who lived on these perfect little streets were even occasionally touched by the daily horror that raged just outside the rarefied confines of their enclave – with its neighbourhood watch patrols and rolled-up sidewalks – maybe then some of them would finally care enough to *really* remake Los Angeles and not just trot out such sentiments for the sake of catchy slogans.

Reagan glanced back at the Bernouli stead and exhaled a sour half-laugh. Then again, he thought, maybe these fine little neighbourhoods are touched more than people know – or care to admit – by events outside. Just maybe it's those very events that make the existence of such enclaves possible.

Reagan found that he felt better about his cramped Venice apartment.

He strode up to the heavy wooden gate at the entrance to Bernouli's house and was about to ring the bell when he felt a tingle race down the back of his neck to the small of his back. His internal klaxon started to shriek and Reagan spun round, certain that someone or something was coming up behind him.

There was nothing there.

He carefully scanned the bushes and hedges that trimmed the surrounding houses, even glancing up into the dense tree line that formed a green canopy over the middle of the street.

Nothing.

Reagan had had a sense that he and Brolin were being followed on-and-off for several days, but the feeling had never been as strong as this. He turned back toward Bernouli's gate and reached for the bell, then quickly turned round again, hoping to catch a hint of motion out of the corner of his eye.

The quiet street scene might have been a painting.

Reagan pulled out a handkerchief and mopped his brow, annoyed by his jumpiness. A small video camera was mounted high above the gate and Reagan prayed that Brolin hadn't been watching his antics on a surveillance monitor or he'd never hear the end of it.

Reagan pressed the doorbell and straightened his tie, then looked up at the camera. He waited for the crackle of the intercom, but a full minute passed without response. The tingle ran down his spine again and he was reaching inside his sports jacket, toward his shoulder holster when he heard a door open and the soft shuffle of footsteps approach the other side of the gate. He withdrew his hand from his coat, but left it unbuttoned as a latch was thrown and the heavy door swung inward.

Reagan looked down at a small Asian man. The Asian had pin-prick black eyes and tightly cropped hair in a bad bowl cut. Reagan glanced over the man's shoulder down a cobblestone path through a garden that led to the front door.

'What is?' the man asked.

As Reagan reached into his pocket for his shield, the little man tensed and took a half-step away from him. Reagan flipped open his ID and held it out for the man to read.

'Lieutenant Reagan. I'm with Sergeants Brolin and McLeod.' The little man returned a blank look. 'I'm here to see Dr Bernouli.'

The Asian continued to stare vacantly at him. Reagan again glanced up the pathway looking for some help, but the front door was closed. He looked back at the little man and remembered Brolin mentioning that Blaine had an Asian houseboy. He reckoned it must be the happening thing among the L.A. trendoids.

'This way,' the Asian finally said and gestured for Reagan to precede him up the path. Reagan dropped his shield back into his pocket. As he headed toward the door he felt the houseboy right on his heels and another tingle ran down his back. He stopped midway up the path, ostensibly to admire Bernouli's garden, though it was a bit difficult to see in the dark. He preferred to keep the smaller man in front of him. But the houseboy stopped too, staying a half-stride behind Reagan.

'Pretty garden,' Reagan said, taking a step back.

'Pretty,' the houseboy agreed, moving backward with Reagan.

'Say, how come you didn't use the intercom out there?' Reagan turned to face the smaller man, who slid half a step further to Reagan's left.

'No work,' the houseboy said.

'I see,' Reagan said, moving again to his left so that he was facing back toward the gate. The dance continued as the Asian maintained his relative position and Reagan was torn between concern and amusement. Reagan feigned a half-turn right then left, but the little man moved with him. Reagan had to suppress a slight smile and decided that the man was probably being duly subservient and that Reagan was making it unnecessarily difficult for him to do his job. He did another brief two-step with the houseboy and smiled broadly, then continued up the walk.

As he neared the heavy oak door, Reagan noted that it was slightly ajar. He felt another slight tingle as the houseboy rushed past him, relaxed again when he saw that the Asian was merely hurrying to push the door open for him. With one hand on the knob, he gestured for Reagan to enter. Reagan nodded at the man and flashed a brief smile, then glanced down as he stepped across the threshold and into the house.

Only the softest squeak of an un-oiled hinge served to warn Reagan of what was coming. He looked up just in time to see the heavy door looming large in his field of vision. Then it struck him full in the nose, breaking bone.

Reagan fell backward, landing hard as his wrist cracked against the jagged cobblestone path. He felt a wet warmth pour over his lips and an electric fire radiate out from the middle of his face. He saw a bright red blotch drip slowly down the middle of the door, but it didn't immediately register that it was his own blood. He opened his mouth to take a gasping breath and nearly choked on a viscous gob of mucus and blood. He hacked it out of his throat. He started to reach for his gun, but the Asian was quickly on top of him.

Reagan could only observe as the little man's lips curled back from his teeth and his almond eyes narrowed to furious slits. Reagan even marvelled at the grace of the Asian's movements as he drew his right arm back in a short, powerful arc before thrusting it forward, two fingers extended like a bayonet from a hard yellow fist. A spray of spittle geysered out from the little man's mouth along with a high-pitched shriek as the slits of his eyes opened wide with killing fury.

Reagan saw the fingers dart toward his neck like a striking cobra. The spittle spray became a fountain of explosive light.

Then darkness.

TWENTY-FIVE

None of the Blood questioned the fact that Arsenio had more or less moved into Morgan's crib. The house, an immense, run-down Victorian building, dating to the late nineteenth century when South-Central was the good part of town, had half-a-dozen bedrooms along with various sitting rooms and parlours, most of which were occupied. Different Blood members and their girlfriends were always crashed out or strung out on available beds, couches and floors. Only Morgan's room was off-limits, enforced by K'toma. Arsenio's sudden semi-permanent presence around the house seemed perfectly natural.

Arsenio was inwardly discomforted by the new digs, but kept it to himself. More than anything, he wished he could return to his real home, to his Nana's house. He still felt her rejection as a dull, near-constant ache. He wondered if he would ever be able to make it right with her; if he could find some way to explain the necessity – the compulsion – of what he was doing.

Somehow he doubted it.

He wasn't sure he could even explain it to himself anymore. He had managed to convince the cop, but he knew that Reagan regarded him as a tool to use toward his own ends and that ultimately the detective would walk over him or toss him aside once Arsenio had fulfilled his purpose. And even as he had tried to explain his mission to the detective, Arsenio felt a kind of emptiness inside. It still *sounded* right – avenging Diane's murder – but the fire that had driven him down this path had abated. It happened, he realized, after he shot the kid for Morgan and became Eyeball.

Arsenio still hated the name, didn't think of himself as Eyeball, but at the same time couldn't deny that he wasn't the person he had been before he pulled that trigger. In the end, it didn't matter that he didn't *want* to shoot the kid, hadn't *meant* to kill him. The deed was done and couldn't be undone. Like cutting your hair too short, there was nothing to do but wait for it to grow back.

But Arsenio felt sure that his new do – the new *him* – would never look the same.

In the meantime, he staked out a cot in a third-floor bedroom and did what he could to make his own space out of it. He had managed to sneak back into his Nana's house and grab some of his clothes and things and tried to recreate his old room. Frequently, though, he would retreat upstairs only to find strange people shooting up Tunnel or screwing madly on his clothes.

There was so much activity at the house that it was hard to do much snooping. Reagan had told Arsenio to search for any hard evidence he could find concerning the identity of Morgan's mystery man or for details of the Tunnel operation. Arsenio warned the cop that the Blood weren't real big on writing stuff down and the detective nodded, but told him to look anyway. Arsenio tried to casually check out every room, but hadn't found much besides used condoms, fast food wrappers and spent Tunnel hypos. He figured if any kind of paper evidence did exist it would probably be somewhere in Morgan's room, but remembering that stain on the wall above Morgan's bed, he hadn't yet mustered the courage to try to sneak into the gang lord's sanctum sanctorum.

At the same time that he kept an eye out for information to feed to Reagan, Arsenio continued to do what he could to find out which of the Blood might have been involved in Diane's murder. The crew were always going on about their supposed exploits. He'd heard plenty of bragging about drive-by kills and patently outrageous exaggerations of sexual prowess, criminal scores and superhuman substance abuse. But not a word about what went down at Phaedra. He'd tried to casually bring the subject up with Lutece and JuJu, but quickly gave up upon seeing their sullen reactions. He *had* once overheard Endzone angrily refer to 'a Betty they done bad,' but again Arsenio's effort to follow up was met with suspicious silence and he backed off.

At least, Arsenio thought, he had managed to avoid a Tunnel habit so far. Most of the Blood were addicted and some, like Morgan, shot up almost constantly. Only K'toma seemed never to use the stuff, but then K'toma showed few signs of being human at all. Although the man was six and a half feet tall and must have weighed close to 250 pounds, Arsenio had never even seen him eat. He was always on-guard and alert. Within a matter of days of joining the Blood, Arsenio had managed to observe all of Morgan's regular crew having sex with one or more of the many girls who wandered in and out of the house – Tunnel seemed to be a fierce aphrodisiac – with the exception of K'toma.

Arsenio himself had tried Tunnel only once, and unwittingly at that. It happened right after Morgan's cross-examination. Arsenio had no intention of obeying Morgan's instruction to find the girl, Lanise, and make her give it up to him, but Lutece and Endzone got in his face about it.

'Ooooh,' Lutece had teased, 'Eyeball still a cherry nigga.'

'Lanise gonna *swallow* that cherry and spit it out,' Endzone said.

'Shit, Lanise don't never spit *nothing* out,' Lutece said, slapping Endzone's hand,

Arsenio tried to scoff it off, but in fact he *was* more or less a virgin; once, one of Diane's girlfriends, stoned out of her gourd, had wandered into his room and casually blown him, but he didn't think that really counted against his cherry status. He didn't much care for the idea of losing it to Lanise – despite what the others said about her skills – especially with Lutece and Endzone in audience. He was pleased and surprised when the others relayed Morgan's orders to Lanise and then left the two of them alone. Arsenio fumbled for an excuse to get away, but Lanise turned out to be really nice.

'Relax, sugar,' she said, pulling him down with her on a mattress. 'We don't got to do nothing if you ain't in the mood.'

Arsenio felt his pulse start to ease, but it quickened again when Lanise reached out and casually placed his hand on her breast. He squeezed it so hard that she winced, but she didn't say anything. He continued to maul her breasts, his penis straining against his pants, until she again took his hands and lifted them off her, kissing the palms as she let him go.

Lanise gracefully pulled the green top over her head revealing long, cone-shaped breasts. Arsenio couldn't take his eyes off the dark aureoles, big as ginger snaps, and felt sure he'd come in his pants. As she laid back on the mattress to slip off her jeans – she wasn't the underwear type – Arsenio climbed around beside her and tickled the palm of his hand with her pointy nipples. They both giggled. As he leaned in to taste them he saw that the aureoles were pockmarked with a circle of tiny track marks, and he felt his erection wilt as he realized that Lanise shot-up right into her tits.

Arsenio regained some enthusiasm when Lanise pulled down his pants and urged him to climb on top of her. He quickly and clumsily started thrusting wildly in the direction of her pussy, but she pushed him gently away.

'Easy, baby, easy. First things first.'

Arsenio leaned back and ran his hand up and down the inside of her dark brown thighs, tentatively allowing his pinky to brush the furry wetness of her cunt. She giggled every time he brushed her and slapped playfully at his hand. Then she reached into a box beside the mattress and pulled out a hypo and a vial of Tunnel. She offered it to Arsenio, but he shook his head; he'd seen enough to know he didn't want to touch the stuff.

'You sure, baby?' she said with a pout.

Arsenio just nodded and turned his attention back to her thighs.

'Makes it so much nicer,' she said.

Lanise twisted the vial into the needle assembly. Arsenio was afraid she was going to shoot up in her nipple, but she slid the dirty needle between the pinky and ring finger of her left hand and depressed the plunger. She immediately fell back against the mattress and exhaled a long, orgasmic sigh. She opened her thighs wide and thrust out her hips, pressing Arsenio's face to the rent between her legs. Obligingly, Arsenio went into action face-first, licking at everything he could find, hoping he was doing the right thing.

He'd closed his eyes and buried his face in her sticky warmth when he felt the prick in his neck. He bolted backward, nearly yanking the hypo out of Lanise's hand. He slapped at his neck and rubbed the tender spot, saw that Lanise had managed to shoot almost an entire vial of Tunnel into his system.

He got to his knees and started to get mad, but the Tunnel lit him up before his anger could become articulate. He swayed slightly in his kneeling position as the drug coursed though him. His mouth and throat went dry and he found he couldn't swallow. He felt electric charges shoot up and down his legs and arms and out to the tip of his erect penis. Every colour in the room grew more vivid and the sounds so acute he felt like a deaf man hearing the world for the first time. Lanise's dark skin took on the character of melted milk chocolate and her big green eyes looked like limes picked fresh from the tree. His own body felt bigger and stronger and more alive than he'd ever known. Merely rubbing his fingertips together was a sensual act and he could hear the ridged whorls of his fingerprints grating against each other like sandpaper on ground glass.

He looked back at Lanise who smiled and ran her fingers over her breasts. 'See, baby,' she said and the words ping-ponged inside his skull.

His breath came in gasps and he felt an energy bolt build up inside of him. His cock was harder and bigger than he'd ever felt it, the tip already smeared with oozing ejaculate. Lanise parted her legs and spread her labia with two fingers. In an instant, Arsenio was on her and inside her, squealing with every thrust.

He exploded in her almost immediately, but his cock stayed hard. He continued to push inside her, encouraged by her pleasured moans. He felt her tighten around him as she came, but even then he couldn't stop thrusting. He heard her yip of displeasure, but ignored it. He felt like an overwound toy that frantically jumped about until all its energy was spent. Lanise was trying to push him off her now. His vision was dark inside the pressure of the Tunnel and all he could feel was his own violent need to continue. He could hear her crying and shrieking, knew somewhere deep inside that he was hurting her, but it still wasn't enough to make him stop. He felt her scratching at his face and chest with her nails and bucking to toss him off, but in the blindness of his fury he struck back at her, slapping her hard across the face.

He exploded inside her again.

And then it was over.

Just as quickly and madly as it came the fury, like his passion, was spent. He opened his eyes and the appearance of the room, of Lanise, of himself had returned to normal.

He lay on top of her as she sobbed. He pulled out of her and fell onto his back on the mattress. He glanced down at his penis and gasped because it was covered with blood. Lanise was crying and doubled over. Blood spilled down her thighs.

Arsenio's breath came in short, frightened rasps. He didn't know what to do and couldn't believe what he had done. He tried to reach over to her. She shrieked at his touch. His penis had shrivelled. He glanced over at the spent vial of Tunnel, at Lanise still curled in a ball, naked and weeping and bloody. The dirty sheet was stained with a hand-sized badge of wet red. Arsenio looked again at the empty needle and whispered to himself, 'Never again.'

Morgan hadn't needed him for anything since then so Arsenio mostly stayed in his room, afraid that he'd run into Lanise or that she'd said something to the others. He had been terrified by what the drug did to him, the kind of animal it turned him into. Still, as he lay on his bed thinking about the incident, about Lanise's big brown nipples and warm cunt, the feeling engendered by the hit, he found himself getting hard. It made him ashamed, but that didn't make him soft.

He pulled his cock out of his pants and started tugging at it, thinking about the Tunnel rush and the animal ecstasy of what he had done. He was about to explode when a throaty chuckle startled him. Morgan stood in the doorway, grinning broadly, the Glock, as always, in his hand.

'Business, Eyeball,' Morgan said. '*Serious* business.'

He went out, then stuck his head back in the doorway. 'Bring your dick.'

TWENTY-SIX

Reagan opened his eyes and beheld a blurry angel, halo and all.

Her fine blonde hair tickled his cheek as she bent down to examine him. Her pale skin was smooth as a polished pearl, her eyes a deep, navy blue. With a delicate gesture she reached up a tiny hand and brushed her trailing hair back behind a perfect, studded ear revealing a neck as alluring as a milk bath. She flicked her pointy pink tongue out between collagened lips and he felt her breath skip across his cheek. A tell-tale red blotch stained her otherwise flawless round chin.

She stepped back and crossed her arms over her chest, framing her decidedly ample breasts in the crooks of her elbows. Reagan traced the trail of red down her chin, through the channel of her cleavage beneath a tight tube top and back out to her pea-sized navel (an 'outie'). She wore revealing short-shorts and stood with her long muscular legs spread apart in a pose of conquest.

Reagan squeezed his eyes shut, opened them and blinked again.

The halo disappeared on second glance and he was pretty sure that the drying red trail running down her neck and chest was blood.

Reagan tried to move and found that he was hog-tied, his hands and ankles expertly bound behind his back. He was perched precariously on the edge of a black leather love seat, facing out into a large study. The wall behind the blonde was lined to the ceiling with neat shelves of hardcover books. An enormous video screen took up another wall. Reagan tried to shift his weight backward, but he couldn't get any purchase against the smooth leather. His squirming only brought on greater discomfort as his right arm, pinned underneath him, bore the brunt of his body weight.

He blinked again, but his vision still didn't seem right. It took a moment before he realized that the problem was that his nose had swelled to massive proportions and loomed in his vision like a big-haired woman in a movie theatre. Remembering the blow from the door that laid him out, he was surprised it didn't hurt more. He'd been breathing through his mouth and tried to take a normal breath. Something shifted in his sinus cavity as he inhaled, triggering a minor explosion of pain. He panted for air then took a series of deep breaths as the blonde laughed at him.

Reagan pulled at his bonds, confirming that he had been secured by a pro. The thin plastic cord wrapped around his wrists and ankles had a sharp edge that tore his skin, leaving his hands cold and numb. His calf and thigh muscles had cramped from the unnatural contortion of his position. He tried twisting his wrists back and forth, to work out some of the numbness, but there was no give at all and he succeeded only in deepening the cuts drawn in his flesh by the plastic twine.

'He up?' a voice said from the doorway. Reagan couldn't see the speaker, but the male voice sounded young. The inflection was definitely black and a little bit nervous. The blonde nodded.

'Then you supposed to bring him,' the voice said. The speaker hesitated for a minute – taking in the blonde, Reagan imagined – before the sound of footsteps disappeared down the hall. When the blonde woman turned toward the doorway, Reagan gaped at the tumour-like pustules that formed a ridge beginning somewhere on her otherwise flawless rear and running up the small of her back.

The blonde stepped forward and reached for Reagan's groin. He gasped as she grabbed his belt. She used it to lift him off the small couch as if he was a piece of luggage. He croaked in pain as his spine bent and the back of his head smacked against the floor. Even so, staring straight up at the ceiling, he marvelled at the prodigious strength it took to carry him in such a manner. The woman looked lean and fit enough, but her strength was astonishing. She carried his bulky 200 pounds with one arm.

She shrugged her shoulder and hefted him up so that his head and knees didn't scrape the floor. Reagan thought for sure his spine would snap and he strained to straighten his lower back as best he could. It was difficult under the circumstances, especially when his head and knees smacked against the frame as she squeezed through the door. She momentarily lost her balance as she stepped out into the hall and tipped him head first into a wall with a tooth-crunching jolt. She was able to right herself and again tried to heft his weight, but his belt broke as she jerked him up and Reagan fell heavily to the hallway floor. His ankles and wrists took the brunt of the fall and he heard an ugly snap followed by a knifelike pain in his right forearm.

Reagan gasped. The blonde stood over him, lips pursed and hands on hips, like it was *his* fault that he fell. She reached down and lifted him by the waistline of his pants, but the material ripped and he squealed as she again dropped him on his broken wrist. Reagan moaned, but it had no effect on the blonde. She stared down at him with evident displeasure and after thinking for several seconds, rolled him onto his stomach and used the plastic cord that bound his hands and ankles to pick him up.

Reagan actually screamed as something else snapped in his arm, but the blonde ignored it. He flexed his thigh and upper arm muscles, trying to take the weight off his fractured wrist, but the pain just kept on coming. The polished floor slats glided by below his eyes as the blonde carried him down the hall. As she turned a corner into another room, the wood floor was replaced in his vision by a thick shag carpet that cruelly tickled his swollen nose. The point of his right shoulder smacked into the back of a table as the blonde brought him into the middle of the room. She dropped him face-first onto the floor, detonating another pain charge in his face. The white carpet filled his mouth and he couldn't breath. Then a steel-toed boot dug into his gut and flipped him over as he gasped for air.

Reagan was too immersed in pain to take in the situation immediately. And when he did realize what he had been brought into, he longed for those halcyon moments on the leather love seat.

He lay on the floor of a sumptuous living room that was bigger than Reagan's entire apartment. Bernouli's decor was out of a magazine spread, with lots of shiny glass and chrome furniture and a high contrast black and white colour scheme. The divans and easy chairs were black leather, as was an immense couch that must have taken an entire herd of cows to stitch together. One wall was dominated by sliding glass doors leading to a semi-circular redwood deck with a panoramic view of the city and the Hollywood hills. An enormous duochrome Rothko canvas, highlighted by secreted spots, dominated another wall.

Several smaller, but equally impressive and pedigreed, abstract expressionist paintings dotted the room. The wall with the Rothko gently sloped up toward a pair of skylights in the beamed cathedral ceiling, thirty feet overhead.

Dr Samuel Bernouli dangled from one of those beams by his ankles.

Bernouli had been stripped naked. He slowly twisted and turned in the slight breeze that wafted in through the open skylight. As he twirled in a macabre pirouette, Reagan saw that the doctor had been crudely gutted and castrated. A red gash across his neck glistened wetly and Bernouli's face bore a look of startled befuddlement. No wonder. Blood had congealed in the matted strands of his no longer distinguished looking silver hair. The white carpet below him was spongy with blood.

'Oh, shit,' Reagan said. He briefly forgot his own discomfort. A sharp kick to the gut reminded him.

Reagan's assailant was a well-built young black man wearing baggy black trousers and an oversized Georgetown sweatshirt. The youth's round, scarred face and razor sharp flat-top were maddeningly familiar, but it wasn't until Reagan locked onto the cold brown eyes that the tumblers clicked and he was able to make the ID.

'Morgan,' Reagan croaked with a half-nod.

Morgan drew his leg back and launched another kick at Reagan's mid-section. There was no way to avoid it.

'They call me *Mr* Carthay,' Morgan said. He smiled up at someone behind Reagan who the cop couldn't see. 'Yo! You ever see that movie? With what's his name? The old dude what look like Danny Glover. "They call me *Mr* Tibbs." That scene be dope.'

Reagan did what he could not to vomit. Only the fact that he was hog-tied kept him from doubling over. He tried to rock backward and brace himself against a leather chair, but he tipped all the way over, exacerbating the agony in his broken arm. Morgan drove a toe into Reagan's rectum for his efforts, then rolled him back over.

Reagan caught a quick look at the scene behind him as Morgan spun him around. There was no sign of Brolin or McLeod. He caught a glimpse of several of the Blood positioned around the room behind him. Their attention was largely riveted on the blonde, who sat on the couch. She had popped a tit out of her top and was shooting a vial of Tunnel into the nipple. She tossed the spent hypo aside then lay back and peeled off her shorts. Incredibly, she began to masturbate. Reagan, dumbfounded, stared at her, too, and for a surreal moment everything – Bernouli's spinning corpse, his own pain and injuries, the grave danger of the situation – was forgotten as everyone watched the blonde bring herself to a quick and furious climax. She curled up into a ball and seemed to doze off on the spot. Even Morgan stared at her, slack-jawed, until a new voice broke the reverie.

'For Christ's sake!' Titus said. His lips were drawn back in a snarl, his sharp, white teeth stained blood red. He wore only black low-rise briefs which inadequately contained him. A matte of wiry black hair stretched from his navel to his crotch like steel wool. One nipple was pierced with a dime-sized gold ring.

The Asian houseboy entered the living room behind him, prodding Brolin along at Glock-point. Her hands were tied behind her back and she looked pale and scared. Correction: terrified. Dark half-moons of sweat showed under her arms and across her blouse, but she didn't appear to be injured. There was no sign of McLeod. Brolin glanced over at Reagan and looked even more frightened. Reagan took that as a bad sign.

Titus strode over to the definitely sleeping blonde and ran his hand roughly through her hair. She stirred and purred slightly, but didn't open her eyes. 'Fucking junkie bitch! I told her she could have the *cop* in a minute!'

Reagan shot a nervous glance at Titus who grinned back at him.

'Not you, pork chop,' Titus groaned. 'You belong to me.'

TWENTY-SEVEN

Arsenio didn't know what to do.

His heart was beating so fast that he peered down at his chest to see if the thumping could be seen through his t-shirt. He hopped from foot to foot, stopped out of fear of drawing attention to himself, then started again to avoid peeing in his pants. He had to crap, too, and kept farting – as silently as humanly possible – but Endzone, who stood three feet to his right, kept curling his nose, glancing unhappily in Arsenio's direction.

The cop, Reagan, lay in the middle of the room with his back to Arsenio. It took everything Arsenio had not to bolt when he saw the blonde carry him into the room. He didn't think the detective noticed him, but he couldn't tell. He wasn't sure what difference it made anyway. He knew that the lady cop had recognized him and thanked god she didn't say anything. He'd never seen the other Five-O before and hearing the man's screams after Titus led him away, guessed that he wouldn't be seeing him again. Arsenio reckoned that Reagan and the lady cop were headed for a similar end.

Arsenio held a Mac–10, the stubby barrel pointed down at the floor. His fingers and palms were slick, but nothing could have pried that gun out of his hands. He had reached for his Browning when Morgan came to get him for the run, but Morgan told him to leave it, that the job called for more firepower. K'toma handed him the square automatic pistol with brief instructions on its use and a stern warning about the lack of a safety and keeping the barrel pointed down.

'Just don't shoot your motherfucking feet off,' the big man had told him, proffering Arsenio a very uncharacteristic smile. Arsenio tried to smile back at him, but K'toma's grin was joyless and even more unnerving than his normal stony look.

Arsenio, Morgan and four other Bloods piled into two cars and headed west on the Santa Monica Freeway. The west side of town was truly alien territory for Arsenio, who, like almost everyone he knew, rarely crossed La Cienega Boulevard, the city's unofficial class border. He'd gone to see a movie in Santa Monica once, but the many harsh looks he'd earned from the cops and the mass of white shoppers at the mall kept him from ever going back. Though he'd been born and lived all his life in Los Angeles, he'd only been to the beach a handful of times, mostly when he was a little kid and his mother was still alive. He remembered that she loved the sun and the water and that, along with Diane, the three of them once built an elaborate sand-castle only to watch the ocean wash it away.

Arsenio got to ride with Morgan and K'toma and supposed it was an Honour, though he'd rather have been in the other car with Lutece. He gawked at the expensive houses as they exited the freeway at National and cruised through the labyrinthine streets of Cheviot Hills. Arsenio had never been there before and was astonished that this tranquil bastion was part of the city he lived in. He tried to imagine growing up in one of these enormous houses, but realized, with sudden and heartfelt anger, that he couldn't even begin to grasp what it might mean, how different life here must be. As he seethed about it, he started to relax. Morgan hadn't said what the night's plan was, but Arsenio hoped that it would offer him a chance to get a measure of satisfaction for the life that he had missed.

It wasn't working out that way at all.

Arsenio emitted a particularly noxious fart and heard Endzone mutter something under his breath. He looked over at Morgan, but the gang lord stood across the wide room talking – listening, actually, with his head bowed – to the white dude in the underwear who was very clearly in charge of whatever sick shit was going down. Arsenio assumed that the white guy was Morgan's big connection, because he'd never seen Morgan listen to, much less take orders from anyone before. At one point, Morgan froze Arsenio with an ice-pick glance. Arsenio felt his heart start to pound a little harder and he squeezed out another small fart, desperate to prevent anything more substantial from slipping out. Arsenio couldn't hear what Mr BVD was saying, but he took in the nervous conversation between Reagan and the lady cop.

Brolin had been shoved to a black leather chair behind Reagan and manhandled to a sitting position with her hands still tied. She glared at the small Asian and took a hard slap across the face for it. Though the sharp crack echoed across the room, neither Morgan nor Titus paid it any heed. The Asian stepped around behind the chair and lazily rested his gun on Brolin's shoulder.

'You all right?' Reagan grunted over his shoulder.

'Yeah,' Brolin replied. 'You?'

'Been better. Where's McLeod?'

Brolin didn't answer right away. Reagan tried to twist to the right to catch a glimpse of her, but she was only a blur in his peripheral vision. Arsenio took a couple of steps to his left so he could see her profile and caught a scowl from K'toma.

'Dead,' Brolin finally said. 'Christ, Dennis, you wouldn't believe . . . we're in deep fucking apple sauce here.'

'No shit,' he groaned and leaned forward slightly. He heard her gasp and froze.

'What?' he said.

'Fuck! Your arm . . .'

'It hurts like a motherfucker. Oh shit! Is it compound? Please say it isn't.'

Brolin nodded as she stared at the jagged edge of ivory protruding out of his arm. She saw that his fingers had turned morning-sky blue. Just a few hours earlier the sight might have made her gag, but compared to McLeod's ordeal Reagan's injury looked like a schoolyard scratch.

'Well?' he said.

'Huh? Sorry, Dennis. Uh, yeah. It's . . . that's . . . you got yourself a problem there.'

Arsenio hadn't noticed the cop's wrist and leaned over to catch a look. His view was obstructed by the Asian, who seemed to sense Arsenio's gaze and glowered fiercely back at him. Endzone watched, too, and pointed down toward something with his chin. Arsenio realized that the barrel of the Mac was aimed almost straight at Morgan and Titus. He quickly lowered it.

'What happened with . . . OOOOFF!'

Reagan's question was interrupted by a kick to the chin from Morgan. Reagan's head snapped back, the force bowling him over backward. The bone jutting out of his wrist struck a chrome chair-leg with a hollow chime, followed by an agonized cry. To add insult to injury, Reagan's torn pants had slid down his waist, exposing his ratty, grey briefs in what might have been, under different circumstances, a slapstick antic. Brolin instinctively started to go to him, but she was forced back down by the houseboy who pressed the barrel of the gun behind her right ear. Arsenio whined, but the other Blood were too intent on the action to notice.

Morgan grabbed Reagan by the hair and yanked him back to his knees. His torn pants slipped the rest of the way down his legs and Reagan took some slight comfort from the fact that his baggy shorts concealed the extent to which his genitals had shrivelled with fear. He opened and closed his jaw, thankful that it wasn't broken. Of course, it was early yet.

Titus came up beside Morgan and rubbed his hands together in an expression of pure, greedy delight.

'All right,' he said. He looked back and forth from Reagan to Brolin. 'Time to play fuck the pig. Who wants to go first?'

No one said anything, but Reagan shifted slightly to take some weight off his ankle and groaned as he moved.

'Excellent!' Titus chirped. 'We have a contestant. Come. On. Down.'

Titus smiled broadly, but his black eyes were lifeless as old cherry stones. He told Morgan to cut Reagan's bonds. The gang lord pulled a switchblade out of his pocket and slid the blade through the taut plastic cord, taking a slice of skin off the back of Reagan's hand in the process. Reagan's nerves were so numb that he didn't even feel it.

Titus winked at Brolin who squirmed in her chair. 'Not to worry, darling, you'll get a chance, too.'

Reagan uncoiled on the floor. He felt a hundred sharp points of pain as blood rushed back into his deadened hands and feet. He clutched his fractured right wrist and almost fainted at the sight of the jagged bone that poked out through the torn blue-pink flesh. Blood spurted liberally from the open gash. The hand dangled uselessly at an ugly angle, though he could also feel a little blood coursing through his dead fingers. Some feeling had returned to his left hand and he tried to use it to knead sensation back into his other digits, but they were cold as garden slugs.

'You don't call them pigs any more, do you?' Titus asked.

'Huh?' Morgan said. 'Yeah, sometime.'

'What's the phrase now?'

Morgan seemed slightly confused. 'Uh, different. "One-times." "Five-O" mostly.'

'That's the one I was thinking of. Yeah! Very postmodern.'

'Uh-huh,' Morgan said. 'For these here you could just say
"187".'

Reagan forced himself to a sitting position as feeling returned
to his legs and feet. The ankle hurt like a son-of-a-bitch, but he
tested it gingerly and decided it was sprained and not broken.
His right wrist continued spurting blood, but not so quickly. He
pressed the arm to his chest and held it as tightly as he could bear.
He almost swooned from the pain and had to catch his balance
against the floor with his left hand as he fell to one side.

It was at that point that he locked eyes with Arsenio, standing
wide-eyed behind him.

Arsenio felt his heart stop as the cop finally noticed him. He
expected the detective to lift the broken arm and point him out
with the jagged bone shard, like the pod-people in *Invasion of the
Body Snatchers*, betraying him as a traitor to the Blood. He saw the
policeman's startled look, then the cop turned away and Arsenio's
heart slowed to a mere salsa beat.

Though Reagan was stunned to see Arsenio, he had the presence
of mind not to stare. It had never occurred to him that Arsenio
might be there, though it made sense once he thought about it.
What he didn't know was how he could use it to his advantage.
The kid held a machine pistol, probably retro-fit to full automatic.
It was enough to take out everyone in the room if only he could
get his hands on it. Or Brolin. From what he knew, he doubted
the kid had much experience with that kind of weapon. Would
the kid take action on his own? Or know what to do? Would he
even *want* to help Reagan out?

'Over here,' Titus said.

Reagan's thoughts were interrupted when Morgan grabbed him
by the hair and hauled him to his feet. His knees buckled and his arm
sang with pain. With his pants around his ankles he had to shuffle
forward as if on a chain-gang. Morgan half-dragged, half-pushed
him to the large couch.

Titus casually walked over to the far end of the living room and
sorted through a small bag on the floor. He pulled out Reagan's
service revolver, briefly inspected it and then brought it over to
Reagan. He pressed the Ruger into Reagan's dangling right hand,
evoking another wheeze and groan from the detective. Reagan
could feel the bone grip against his palm and desperately tried
to exert control over the weapon, but his fingers simply didn't
work. The gun would have dropped to the floor if Titus hadn't

been supporting Reagan's grip in his own hands. Titus forced Reagan's index finger between the trigger and the trigger guard and slid back the receiver.

'Just so you fully understand the situation,' Titus said.

In a smooth, sudden gesture he raised up Reagan's hand, pointed the gun at Brolin's face and with his finger on top of Reagan's, squeezed three times.

The move was so quick and Reagan's arm so dead that he never had a chance to resist. He saw Brolin's eyes go wide and her lips formed a brief 'O' of surprise before the first hollow point blew her face away. The second bullet took the top of her skull off and the third all but decapitated her in an wet explosion of pink and red. Her headless body held its seated pose for a moment before sliding slowly down the black leather, leaving a chunky trail behind. The Asian, still standing behind her, was drenched with her blood and brains. Titus let go of Reagan's hand and the Ruger slipped from his fingers and fell to the floor with a thud.

Reagan continued to stare at Brolin's corpse. He began to shake with fury. He swivelled his hips to launch a kick at Titus's midsection with his left leg, but he telegraphed the move. Titus easily swept Reagan's weak right leg out from under him and he went down in a pile. Reagan reached for the gun with his good hand, but Titus kicked it under the couch and out of reach.

Arsenio observed the action in stunned paralysis. He thought about opening up on Titus with the Mac, but it was over so quickly that he was afraid to react. He also feared that if he did shoot, he'd hit the cop. Mostly, though, he was too scared to do anything to help Reagan. He was too damn scared to do more than breathe.

Multi-coloured fluids continued to gurgle out of what was left of Brolin's head and seep into the thick white carpet.

'Tiiii-tuuuus,' the naked blonde whined. She was up again and on her knees on the couch, her breasts resting atop the couch back. Her lips pursed in a little-girl pout as she stared at Brolin's corpse.

Titus smiled and nodded at her. The blonde jumped off the couch and grabbed another hypo full of Tunnel from the coffee table. She squatted down beside Brolin and slipped the needle into her leg above the thigh. She then thrust her face into the ruined mass of tissue atop Brolin's neck and sucked at the dark fluids.

Reagan had made it back to his feet. He felt himself start to gag and turned away. Arsenio continued to look, but felt detached, like none of this could be real. He watched the way he would view a horror movie, telling himself it was just so much latex and chocolate syrup and damn! couldn't they do some mean special effects these days.

Endzone threw up on his shoes. K'toma was a blank.

Morgan laughed.

The blonde lapped at Brolin's neck until the blood stopped flowing. Reluctantly, she pulled herself away from the corpse and lay down beside it on her back. She emitted a loud belch and a contented sigh. She closed her eyes, stretching out on the soft carpet. Her face and chest were smeared with blood.

Titus snorted to himself then turned back to Morgan.

'Bring him over,' Titus said.

Morgan dragged Reagan across the floor by his good arm and deposited him in a pile at Titus's feet. Reagan tried to resist, but the gang leader grabbed Reagan's injured right arm and twisted it behind his back. Reagan briefly lost consciousness as another half-inch of bone slid out through the torn skin. Morgan let go of the arm, but Reagan couldn't make it work at all. It dangled behind him like a strip of toilet paper stuck to his shoe.

Reagan looked up and saw Titus looming over him. For the first time, he noticed the maw-shaped circle of tiny pustules that dotted Titus's thighs and disappeared under his shorts. They were red and blistered and matched the ridge he had seen on the blonde's back. Titus had a straight razor in his hand.

'It's like this, pigshit: I want to know everything you know about Dr Sam, there, and what he's been up to. What you know, what you think, what you imagine. And especially what's written down. It's time to squeal, little piggy.'

Reagan summoned his remaining energy to straighten up and direct a blow at Titus's balls with his good arm, but Titus danced easily away and grabbed Reagan's dangling right hand. He twisted it. Hard.

And harder.

And harder still.

Reagan heard the bones break and his flesh rip like silk. He screamed himself raw as Titus continued to twist and tear at the hand while the blonde watched and giggled. The pain was beyond anything he had ever imagined or could comprehend, yet a part of his brain commented on the fact that he hadn't passed out. He could even distinguish the sound of someone, Endzone as it turned out, vomiting voluminously behind him.

Titus continued to wrench at Reagan's wrist, huffing a little with exertion. With a final CRUNCH and an exultant yell, Titus ripped the hand off the end of Reagan's arm and pressed it to the cop's face. Reagan could taste his own fresh blood and the stale sweat from his palm. Titus, laughing, picked at Reagan's broken nose with the dirty, overlong nail of his finger. Woozy, Reagan peered up through his stiffening digits to the sight of Bernouli dangling above him, seeming to grin over the fact that Reagan would soon share his fate.

Clinging to consciousness, Reagan saw Titus flick open the straight razor.

'Pig fuck!' Morgan squealed in the background. 'Hrrralll! Hrrralll! Hrrralll!'

That's when Arsenio opened fire.

TWENTY-EIGHT

Arsenio held the trigger down, strafing the room. He gritted his teeth and swivelled in a half-circle, fighting the recoil, just like Arnold Schwarzenegger. He tried to hold the line of fire steady as he cut a swathe directly across Titus's and Morgan's mid-sections. He saw the blonde look up from Brolin's body in surprise, then throw herself to the floor. He didn't drop the barrel for fear of hitting Reagan. The cop was still doubled over, clutching the gushing stump of his right wrist. The grue-splattered houseboy gaped at Arsenio as the smoking muzzle of the Mac cut him in two.

The clip was empty before Arsenio could complete his sweep of the room, but the Mac felt warm and solid in his hands. He started to laugh, until he realized that something was very wrong with the picture before him.

No one was down.

No one was bleeding.

No one had been shot.

'I told you the nigger was sucking pig dick,' Morgan said to K'toma in the stunned silence.

K'toma and the other Blood were just getting up off the floor. Neither Morgan nor Titus had so much as ducked while Arsenio strafed the room with blanks. Titus still held the razor out in front of him, though his grin had drooped. Reagan had slumped to the floor behind the couch, looking somehow white and green at the same time, trying to staunch the flow of blood from his wrist with his chin. He appeared to be crying.

Morgan narrowed his eyes at Arsenio and drew his lips away from his teeth in a lupine approximation of a smile. 'Hmm-mmm-mmmmm, we gonna have a time with you, boy. You gonna die like a Crip. You done tied the wrongest rags there is.'

Like Wile E. Coyote sheepishly realizing that he has run off the edge of a mesa, a gaping chasm of terror opened up under Arsenio's feet. K'toma quickly came up beside him, ignoring the rigged machine pistol, and grabbed him painfully by the back of the neck with one massive hand. The other Blood nervously trained their weapons on him. They all looked very pissed. K'toma actually hoisted Arsenio several inches off the ground while Morgan continued to appraise him from across the room. Arsenio peed in his pants, but was too horror-struck to be bothered by the warm liquid that raced down his leg.

Titus hadn't said a word, just scratched the tumours on his thigh with the fingers of Reagan's severed hand and scowled at Morgan. 'I don't really like surprises,' he said.

Before Morgan could explain, the sliding glass door to the patio exploded in a hail of very real bullets. The first volley practically sliced Endzone in half as explosions of red formed a line across his chest. The impact hurled him backward into the wall, adding a fresh, expressionistic drip to a Jackson Pollock painting.

In a series of staccato, slow-moments Arsenio watched the line of blood get traced across Endzone's torso from right to left, as it moved in his direction. He dropped a load in his pants as the first bullet struck him in the right elbow. He heard the bone shatter. It sounded like a foul tip off a broken bat. The arc of bullets that followed ricocheted off the useless Mac still clutched to his chest, driving the frame of the gun into his sternum hard enough to crack three ribs. He turned his head to follow the line of fire off to his left as another volley of bullets caught K'toma across the throat. The big man dropped both Arsenio and his gun, and clutched at his neck, but the very force of his grip opened his veins even more and he fell over as a tide of blood gushed down his torso.

Lutece started moving and was almost quick enough to evade the stream of bullets that poured into the living room.

Almost.

Arsenio was drenched with K'toma's blood. He looked down at himself and marvelled that the only direct hit was to his arm. He tried to draw a deep breath and found that he couldn't seem to swallow any air. He heard a mushy, sucking noise and saw a ragged, nickel-sized hole in his chest where a second bullet had caught him. He managed to stand there and stare at it, fascinated by how the loose strips of black skin billowed in the wound like reeds in a red tide. He pressed the tip of his left thumb to the hole and slid it in as far as the knuckle before he fell backward. He slid slowly down the wall until he was sitting on the floor in his own loose excrement.

Reagan, though lightheaded from loss of blood, kissed the carpet as soon as he heard the glass break. He saw Arsenio and the other Blood go down in a torrent of bullets. He silently cheered to himself as he saw the houseboy drop into a classic shooter's stance only to take a dozen or more rounds directly in the mouth and somersault over backwards amid a confetti-like shower of his shattered teeth.

Reagan spied his gun lying on the floor beneath the couch and started to slither toward it. Morgan dropped down beside him and pulled the Glock out of his waistband. He emptied a clip in the direction of the patio and then saw where Reagan was headed. As bullets whizzed over their heads, Morgan tossed the spent Glock aside and the two men struggled to get to Reagan's piece. Morgan was closer and kicked at Reagan's head, missing, but connected with his left shoulder. Reagan grabbed Morgan's ankle with his good hand and pulled himself closer to the gang lord. Morgan shot a fist out and landed a blow to Reagan's broken nose, but the detective was too numb to react to the pain. He responded by shoving his oozing stump directly in Morgan's face, briefly blinding him with blood.

Morgan replied with a bony knee to Reagan's crotch that doubled the detective over. Morgan delivered another short, hard kick to the back of Reagan's head, then looked up as the sound of gunfire abated. He still couldn't see who was shooting and started to reach for the gun, but pulled his arm back when a new round of firing commenced. Morgan quickly decided it wasn't worth hanging around and crawled on his belly in the direction of the hall when the line of fire shifted.

Titus had watched as the gunman on the terrace took out the Blood foot soldiers before he sprang into motion. He wanted to get to the guns stashed in his bag, but the move would leave him too exposed. He tucked and curled and rolled toward the hallway that led to the study, out of the direct line of fire. He threw over a mahogany coffee table and dropped behind it, peering out around the side. His fists were clenched so tight, that they broke through the cooling skin of Reagan's hand, still clutched in Titus's fingers.

There was a brief lull in the fire, during which the blonde started to get up.

'Heather, no!' Titus yelled from behind the table, but it was too late. The still-invisible gunman had found enough time to drop a new clip in his weapon. The blonde was facing the patio, her arms at her sides, her tongue poking through her lips, when the next volley came.

The line of fire traced red lines up and down her torso. The gunman was unrelenting, using the spray of bullets like a carving knife to gut her from crotch to chin. Incredibly, she stood her ground against the monumental impact of the assault, her body dancing in place as bullets shredded her perfect skin and her organs exploded outward. Thick, brown blood sprayed in every direction, like water from a spinning lawn sprinkler, splattering the room all the way up to the cathedral ceiling. Even Bernouli caught a comical spurt in a dead eye.

Another brief lull in the assault ensued and weaving, still alive, the blonde reached for her dangling entrails. She ran her hand along a length of dripping intestine and, swaying precariously, held her filthy palm up before her face. Through broken teeth she poked out the stubby remains of her tongue and lapped at her palm.

The gunfire started again and she collapsed to the carpet.

'Heather!!' Titus screamed and jumped out from behind the table. 'I see you, fucker! You're meat in my mouth.'

A new stream of fire came at Titus who took two hits in his right shoulder before retreating down the hall as the walls exploded behind him.

The gunman finally stepped through the broken doors and into the living room. He wore black Reeboks, black denim pants and a black, long-sleeved sweatshirt. Shoeblack was smeared over his face, camouflage-style and he wore tight leather gloves.

The sudden silence was broken only by the muffled sound of Arsenio's sucking chest wound, followed by the distant scream of sirens. Reagan managed to pick his head up without vomiting and gasped at the carnage around him. He heard the front door slam, but couldn't tell if it was someone coming in or going out.

The gunman looked around, keeping one eye peeled for other foes. He slowly walked over to the hall, kneeled down and simultaneously poked his head and gun out for a quick look. He grunted to himself and walked back to Reagan. The barrel of his smoking AK–47 was pointed at a spot in the middle of the

detective's sweaty forehead. He glanced at Arsenio, who held his
chest and blankly took the scene in, then his gaze shifted back to
the sight of Reagan's ruined right stump.

'Need a hand?' Greymarch asked.

TWENTY-NINE

A car engine roared to life, followed by a squeal of rubber as the vehicle tore out of the driveway. And the sirens were getting louder.

Reagan propped himself up against the couch. He squeezed the stump of his wrist closed with his good hand and fought to hold onto consciousness. Greymarch glanced around the room, the barrel of the assault rifle still pointing at Reagan's face, before dashing to the broken venetian blinds by the shattered patio doors. He reached back behind the slats, yanked out a clear plastic rod and then threw it aside.

'Goddamn Levolars,' he said.

He panned around the room again and ran over to a telephone sitting on a coffee table. He picked it up and then threw it hard against the wall.

'Cordless piece of shit,' he mumbled and took another look around.

'Screw it,' he said. He yanked an electric cord out of the wall, tearing the other end out of the base of a standing halogen lamp. He pulled a six-inch knife out of a sheath strapped to his ankle and cut an eighteen inch length out of the cord. He tossed it to Reagan.

'Wrap it tight as you can. Just below the elbow.'

Reagan picked the cord up and tried to bind it around his ruined arm, but he didn't have the strength to pull it tight. His breathing came in ragged gasps. It was a tough battle just to hold his head up.

'For Christ's sake,' Greymarch complained. He squatted beside the detective, drew the cord tightly around his slick upper forearm and tied it off in a quick, sloppy knot. The flow of blood from the severed wrist dwindled to a slow trickle.

The sirens sounded like they were coming up the block now. Greymarch glanced nervously toward the front door and secured the assault rifle over his shoulder by its strap. He slipped a 9 mm revolver out of his waistband. 'We got to get moving, chief.'

Reagan tried to shake his head, but the effort was too much for him. 'Police,' he whispered. 'I'm . . . a cop.'

'Hey! No shit, Sherlock.'

'Under . . . arrest,' Reagan squeaked.

'Gee, chief, I don't think so. And I can't afford having you file any reports just now. So you can come along with me or I can put a bullet behind your ear. It's pretty much the same to me either way.'

Reagan forced his chin up and looked Greymarch in the eye. He thought he spied a hint of amusement, but there was less than a trace of anything like pity. He glanced down at the revolver, loosely held in Greymarch's grip, aimed in Reagan's direction.

The sirens were wailing right outside now and the red and white shadows cast by the spinning dome lights of arriving squad cars flashed on the walls of the hallway. Officers would be bursting in within seconds, but Reagan had a feeling that he wouldn't be alive to greet them if he tried to wait Greymarch out.

'I'll . . . unnhhh . . . come,' Reagan said.

Greymarch nodded and hauled Reagan up to a standing position. The detective swayed, feeling like he'd left his stomach back on the floor. He attempted to take a step on his own, but his ankle started throbbing again and his legs simply wouldn't stand for it. Greymarch caught him before he fell, grabbing the cop around the waist. He pulled the detective along toward the patio doors. Reagan's pants still hung around his ankles so Greymarch sliced them off with a flick of his wrist. At least Reagan still had his socks and shoes on. He almost laughed out loud thinking that he looked like he'd just walked off the set of a Benny Hill show, but the shoes saved him from further injury as Greymarch danced them across a carpet of broken glass.

It was an awkward way to walk, like contestants in a three-legged race, but Greymarch supported Reagan's bulk with no apparent effort. Greymarch maintained a tight, if uncomfortable grip on

Reagan's body and even in his foggy state of quasi-awareness, Reagan registered that the man was uncommonly strong.

As they stepped across the threshold onto the patio, Reagan jerked back around toward the living room.

'No games, asshole!' Greymarch said. The pistol still waved in his other hand.

'The . . . kid,' Reagan managed, gesturing back toward Arsenio.

Greymarch hesitated a moment. He hadn't given any of the Blood a second thought, though as he watched events unfold from the patio it had become clear that one of the Blood had betrayed his brothers. It hadn't occurred to Greymarch that the cop might know the kid, but it certainly made sense. He couldn't see Arsenio from their present vantage point, though he could still make out the sound of the kid's sucking chest wound. He knew the cops would work their way around to the back of the house in minutes.

'Nothing I can do there, chief,' Greymarch said. 'I think he's dead already.'

A tiny groan escaped from Reagan. Greymarch wasn't sure if it was a reaction to his pronouncement about the gangbanger or just an expression of pain. Maybe both. In any case, there wasn't any more time to waste.

Greymarch dragged Reagan across a small patch of grass at the end of the patio. The grass trailed off into a dirt track which marked the edge of the steep slope that afforded the house its magnificent view. The seventy-foot hill leading to the street below wasn't sheer, but it was pretty damn imposing. It had been no problem for Greymarch to scale it on his own, but carrying Reagan back down wasn't going to be so easy. The cop would have to hold on for dear life and Greymarch wasn't sure that Reagan had the strength left to do it.

He thought again about putting a bullet in the cop's eye and having done with it, but it just didn't sit right with him. And he was anxious to know exactly what the detective knew and what he had told his superiors. It didn't matter all that much to Greymarch in particular, but he knew that Judy and the others would be pissed if he wasted him. If nothing else, it might prove useful ammunition against Titus.

The front door of Bernouli's house slammed open at that moment and Greymarch's decision was made for him. He hefted Reagan onto his back, wrapping the detective's arms as tight as he could around his own neck. Reagan groaned again, but at least he was still conscious.

'Better hold tight, otherwise you're road pizza.'

Reagan grunted and squeezed Greymarch's neck for what little he was worth, biting his lip to keep himself awake.

As the first cop walked into the carnage of Sam Bernouli's living room and immediately threw up, Greymarch, with Reagan riding piggy-back, dropped down over the edge of the slope. He grabbed onto a network of tree roots poking out through the dry dirt and lowered himself as quickly as he could, shifting Reagan's weight a bit, blindly feeling for toeholds.

The top half of the hill wasn't too bad, between the roots and weeds, but they were still a good thirty feet off the ground when Reagan's grip started to loosen. Greymarch knew right away that the cop had finally surrendered to unconsciousness. He snapped his chin down on Reagan's arm before it could slip away entirely. Fortunately, he was in a position with a decent foothold or he would have lost Reagan completely and likely gone down with him.

'Hey!' Greymarch croaked, trying to speak and hold onto Reagan's arm at the same time. 'Hey! Hey!'

It was no use. The cop was out of it.

Greymarch froze for a minute, his neck muscles shuddering from the strain of supporting Reagan's entire weight. He couldn't look up, but he knew it couldn't be too much longer before one of L.A.'s finest got the bright idea to glance down the hill.

He looked down at the ten-yard drop along the rough slope to hard concrete below, mentally measuring it against his durability.

He thought again about just ditching the detective.

He peered out of the corners of his eyes and satisfied himself that no cars were approaching either way on the street below. With a smooth movement he raised his chin, let go of the hillside and grabbed hold of the cop's arms.

They fell.

THIRTY

Donatelli waddled out of his car – a '76 Chrysler New Yorker: 155,000 miles, polished like a new apple and still going strong – and through the crowd of upscale rubber-neckers massed along the police lines in front of Bernouli's house. A dozen squad cars, roof lights swirling like strobes in a disco (did they still have discos? Donatelli wondered), were parked willy-nilly up and down the street. A few of the cherry-tops had been driven right up onto the neighbouring lawns and Donatelli knew, homicide or no, in this neighbourhood there'd be messages of complaint on his desk come morning. Probably even the threat of a lawsuit or two.

A half-dozen patrolmen stood on the lines, kibitzing back and forth with the onlookers and each other. A couple of the cops looked bored and annoyed, but the crowd was wild-eyed and excited, pacing like expectant fathers. Blood always brought them out and they could smell it by the bucketful tonight. Donatelli made a mental note of the officers who looked disinterested. There were dead cops here, and everyone should be looking frosty or angry, no matter how dull their particular role in the investigation.

Donatelli wasn't one to take anything for granted.

He recognized one of Liebowitz's S.I.D. team fussing over the front door and nodded to her. The woman nodded back and continued scraping a sample of something wet onto a glass slide. Donatelli left her to her work.

Two more patrolmen waited just inside the door. They were shifting on their feet with arms crossed over their chests, nervously glancing back and forth around the room and back outside.

More like it, Donatelli thought.

Another S.I.D. man was going about his business in the foyer and Donatelli sighed as he spied Witherspoon standing at the end of the hall, chewing his nails. As he got closer, the Captain saw that Witherspoon was white as new-fallen snow and quite obviously scared out of his wits. Donatelli was prepared to chide the pathetic sap until he turned the corner and took in the sight of Bernouli's living room.

Donatelli went a little pale himself.

The assistant coroner, a heavy-set Chinese man named Chang, stood below Bernouli's still twisting corpse, scratching his chin and shaking his head. Another group from S.I.D. collected samples and dusted for prints, while Liebowitz yelled instructions from the patio. He was smoking a cigarette, tapping the ashes into his cupped palm so as not to contaminate the crime scene. Every few seconds he stuffed the collected ash into the jacket of his old suede sports coat.

Gaffney and Kerr, both gold-shields, supervised the operation. Kerr studied Chang staring up at Bernouli, while Gaffney longingly watched Liebowitz smoke his cigarette. Donatelli gently patted the antsy Witherspoon on the shoulder and stepped into the middle of the disaster area.

The pile of machine-gunned flesh that had been Heather caught his attention first. Having served two early tours in 'Nam, Donatelli was quick to recognize the signature of an assault rifle. He registered the fact that the dead woman was half-nude and he sniffed at a curious odour that wafted from the corpse. He'd been around a lot of dead bodies in all conceivable stages of decomposition, but he'd never smelled anything quite like it before. He stored away the information and moved on.

Next up was the body of a small man with his face blown away. From the yellow skin of the exposed hands Donatelli made the man as Asian. One of Chang's assistants knelt over the body. He gingerly lifted the head up so that Donatelli could see the back. The exit wound was the size of a Florida grapefruit. And the same curious odour drifted up from the open wound.

'What the hell is that?' he asked, wrinkling his nose.

'Nasty, isn't it?' the coroner's man said and shrugged. Donatelli moved along.

The bodies of three black youths lay sprawled along one wall. Each was riddled with bullets and the biggest one's head had pretty well been shot off. His dead eyes were still open, though, and seemed to follow you across the room, like a black-velvet Elvis.

Liebowitz came back inside and Donatelli grimaced as he stubbed his cigarette out in his palm. It went into his pocket with the ashes.

'Where are they?' Donatelli asked.

Liebowitz coughed and covered his mouth. He sighed as a tiny shower of ash blew off his palm and fluttered to the floor. 'McLeod's in one of the bedrooms. It's the most awful goddamn thing I've ever seen. They . . . well, you're going to have to see it for yourself. I don't know the words.'

The S.I.D. chief shuddered. Donatelli had never seen that before.

'What about Brolin?' he asked.

Liebowitz cocked his head, squinting at the fat little Captain. 'She's right there,' he said softly, nodding toward the middle of the room.

Donatelli turned around and let out an audible gasp. Everyone in the room stopped and looked at him, but no one said a word. Their reactions had been about the same.

Brolin's mostly headless body lay at the foot of the leather lounger where the bullets from Reagan's gun had taken her life. Donatelli recognized the conservative, powder blue suit – a typically unflattering Brolin choice – and the white-gold wedding band that she hadn't had the heart to stop wearing. He didn't know how he could *not* have noticed her there as he came in, then considered that perhaps he had, but had been unable or unwilling to acknowledge the sight.

He squatted down on his hefty haunches in front of her, staring at the unrecognizable cavity that had once held her brain.

'Oh, Jesus,' he whispered. 'Jesus, Mary and Joseph.'

Arsenio guessed he was on his way to heaven. He enjoyed the smooth sensation of floating and no longer felt any pain. Not in his arm or his chest or even his heart which, since Diane's murder, had really been the source of his deepest hurt. And though his eyes were closed – at least he thought they were closed, it was a little hard to tell and perhaps that was part of heaven, too – he saw what could only be a divine light. Then the light faded and the gentle movement abruptly stopped.

The slamming door at the back of the ambulance and the rising wail of the siren sent him hurtling back to reality like Lucifer in free fall.

A paramedic knelt beside him, adjusting the drip on an IV. Arsenio followed the plastic line up to a sac of clear fluid dangling from a tiny steel hook in the curved roof of the vehicle. The paramedic was a short Latino man with a pony-tail. His face was severely pock-marked and he wore a thin moustache that looked like it had been pencil-drawn on his upper lip. A tiny silver crucifix dangled from his left ear lobe.

'Haaa . . . thhhffff . . .' Arsenio tried to form words, but he couldn't make his lips work. His mouth was so dry he could barely pry his tongue off his palate.

This is *not* heaven, he thought.

'Don't try to talk,' the paramedic said. 'We on the way to the hospital now. Just enjoy the ride, eh?'

Arsenio tried to swallow, but couldn't even manage that. The paramedic – *Francisco* was stencilled in blue across his breast pocket – shook his head and reached for something out of Arsenio's sight. He squatted beside Arsenio and pressed a wet Q-tip to the boy's lips. Arsenio poked his tongue at the cool wet stick and though he came away with a piece of the fuzzy cotton end, it was worth it for the precious drops of water that rolled past down his tongue. Francisco wetted the Q-tip twice more before announcing, 'Enough.' Arsenio tried to smile at him, but Francisco was stone-faced in response.

'Little fucker's up?'

Arsenio searched for the source of the voice, but had trouble focusing. Francisco took a step back revealing a uniformed officer sitting on a tiny fold-down seat. The cop held his service revolver in his hands and looked mean as a hungry Rottweiler. His cap was tilted back on his head, revealing a shock of curly red hair. He had a bushy red moustache and beady eyes. Arsenio couldn't quite read the ID plate on his uniform, but was pretty sure the cop's name was 'O something.

'Little nigger cop-killer,' O'Something said, gesturing at Arsenio with the barrel of his .38. 'Little cocksucking, cop-killing, dead nigger bastard.'

'Hey!' Francisco said.

'What?' O'Something demanded. 'You got a use for this piece of shit? You know there are two dead cops back there? You know that one 'em had her damn head blown off and the other was cut into a pile of bits no bigger than your damn fist?'

'S'not my problem,' Francisco said. He showed the cop the same blank face he offered Arsenio.

'Not your fucking problem, Pedro? Maybe next time I get a back-up call for one of you candy-ass motherfuckers, I don't have my radio on. Maybe then it's *your* problem.'

Francisco shrugged. 'I just do my job. Maybe you should too.'

'Fucking beaner,' O'Something mumbled and turned his attention back to Arsenio. 'Don't you worry nigger, you're still dead.'

Arsenio thought that he probably should be scared, but he didn't feel much of anything at all. He suspected it had something to do with whatever it was that dripped down the plastic tube and into his arm. He knew he was in serious shit, but he couldn't keep his eyes open a second longer.

Definitely not heaven, was his last thought before consciousness fled.

The bodies had all been carted away and Liebowitz and his troupe were finishing up around the house. Cutting Bernouli down had been the hard part, Donatelli thought, but then he wasn't the guy who had to scoop the little bits of Jim McLeod into little plastic bags. Even so, the M.E. hadn't spotted the incision that had been drawn under Bernouli's crotch and around to the anus. A stinking glop of innards came sliding out once they'd cut him down and set him right-side up.

Donatelli stared out at the hypnotic field of twinkling lights that extended to the ocean in one direction and the dark hills in the other. On a clear night – yeah, right – you could probably even see the tip of the downtown skyline from Bernouli's deck. Donatelli strolled out to the edge of the property and stole a downward glance. He swayed slightly as he was overtaken by vertigo and took a step back from the edge of the slope.

Liebowitz had collected over 150 shells from the patio area, which at least accounted for the abattoir in the living room. Still, whoever had been shooting it out here, it was clear that it had been a battle royal. It was going to be hard to piece together, but it looked like the Blood had been having themselves a party with Bernouli when Brolin and McLeod walked in on things. *What the hell were Blood doing in Cheviot Hills?*, Donatelli asked himself again. Then someone else joined the party with a major assault from the patio. It obviously connected to the mess at Bernouli's lab, but Donatelli didn't have a clue as to how. With Brolin and McLeod both dead, that left only Reagan to fill in the blanks.

So where the hell was he?

Donatelli went back inside and for the fourth time since S.I.D. found it under the couch, picked up the clear plastic evidence bag containing Reagan's gun. He wished he could pretend it belonged to someone else, but Reagan was one of the few cops the Captain knew in the department who walked around with a Ruger. And certainly the only one to carry a Ruger with a custom bone grip. It made Reagan look like something out of a John Ford picture, but then it had been good for some media attention, which Donatelli always assumed to be the point.

'Looked good on camera,' Liebowitz said, apparently reading the Captain's mind.

'Yeah,' Donatelli sighed. He didn't comment on Liebowitz's use of the past tense. 'Slick son of a bitch.'

'Listen, he may be all right. I mean, better than if we found *his* body, too.'

Donatelli nodded, but his queasy gut was dripping acid double-time. Witherspoon had contacted gang command and they confirmed that Reagan tore out of the command centre like a bat out of hell after reading Liebowitz's report. Liebowitz filled Donatelli in about the contaminated Tunnel. The two agreed it was a strange finding, but couldn't explain why it might have set Reagan off. They'd found Reagan's car parked across the street, but other than the gun there was no sign of him.

'FUCK!!!'

The scream came from another room. Liebowitz went running and Donatelli followed as quickly as his short legs and fat belly would allow.

An S.I.D. woman, a squat, sexless red-head named Sipson, stood by an open window in a small bedroom, one hand pressed to her forehead and the other clutching her chest.

'What?' Liebowitz demanded.

She turned around and blushed slightly, stood up straight and cleared her throat. 'Sorry,' she said, 'it just, it caught me by surprise. I thought we'd found everything we were going to find. Sorry.'

She pointed at a spot on the floor behind a toddler-sized potted plant.

'What? What is it?' Donatelli puffed, standing on his toes to peer over Liebowitz's shoulder.

Liebowitz went over to his team member and squatted down.

'Fuck,' he said. 'Are all the M.E. guys gone?'

Sipson nodded. 'I'll get one back. Look, I'm really sorry . . .'

Liebowitz cut her off. 'No, it's okay. It would have made me yell, too. Go and call.'

She left the room as Donatelli bent down beside Liebowitz. He felt a new pool of acid bubble and churn in his stomach.

'Recognize it?' Liebowitz rasped. He poked at the fingers with his pen.

Donatelli nodded. The M.E. would take prints, of course, but it was a foregone conclusion.

Donatelli would have recognized Reagan's U.S.C. school ring anywhere.

THIRTY-ONE

Reagan opened his eyes and beheld a blurry angel.

Again.

But this one wore a white coat, tortoiseshell glasses and a look of moderate concern.

'Hey,' she said softly.

'You're not blonde,' Reagan whispered.

'Uhh, no, I'm not.'

'Thank you,' Reagan said and fell back to sleep.

'What was that all about?' Judy asked.

'Titus's punching board, I think,' Greymarch answered. 'The new one, what's her name?'

'What? Did you . . . Is she dead, too?'

'Didn't I mention it? Cut the bitch right down the middle.' Greymarch smiled. 'Only took 70, 80 rounds.'

Judy let out an admiring whistle and shook her head. 'Man, oh man, Calvin. Titus must have a major hard-on for your ass. If he got away.'

'He got away,' Greymarch said. A truly evil smile crossed his lips. 'Took a couple of hits, though. Mosquito bites, really. But I'll bet his boner was fading fast as he ran.'

Judy continued to shake her head, impressed but scared. It was the way Greymarch usually made her feel. As always, he acted nonchalant and unfazed, flexing and unflexing his muscles and admiring Judy's stitchwork.

Both Greymarch and Reagan had gotten torn up some during the long tumble down Bernouli's hill. Fortunately the damage was mostly skin-deep. The cop's other injuries were far more severe, though Judy was pretty confident that he was stable for the time being. He'd lost an awful lot of blood and was in shock, but was otherwise in reasonably good shape. And while he belonged in a real hospital, that just wasn't a possibility.

Fortunately, Semper Fi was equipped for minor surgery and well-stocked with blood. Judy's fix-up job on the cop's severed hand was crude, but it would keep him alive and save the arm. And though she didn't like to think about it, the detective's long-term prognosis was in Greymarch's hands more than hers.

Greymarch had been banged up some himself, but nothing his constitution couldn't handle on its own. Incredibly, he hadn't broken anything, although something seemed to be rattling around in his left knee. Though it was uncomfortable, he could walk all right so he didn't bother mentioning it. He didn't like for anyone, even Judy, to have any more information about him than was absolutely necessary. Besides, he was already on the rebound. The skin on his arms and legs that had been ripped during the tumble down the hill had already gone pinkish and was visibly starting to mend.

The Bernouli touch.

'You're going to stay here, right?' Judy asked.

'For now,' Greymarch said. He glanced over at Reagan, sleeping on the bed. 'Until he can talk, at least.'

'I mean you're going to stay *right* here. In the guest house.'

'Uh-huh,' Greymarch sort of agreed.

The small bungalow was located behind Semper Fi, at the rear of the property. Ostensibly, it was Judy's unofficial living quarters and thus considered sacrosanct by the in-patients. In actuality, the house served as a storage facility for the needed supplies of blood and Tunnel which Judy used herself and distributed to Greymarch and the others in the circle. People came and went at odd hours, which did not escape the notice of the hospice patients, and which was explained by them via a blossoming and rather elaborate mythology concerning their favourite doctor's sexual appetites. Judy was initially embarrassed when she caught wind of the rumours, then decided it served as good cover for what was really going on. For, in practice, the little house was nothing more than a shooting gallery for a very unusual group of junkies.

Judy would have liked to know what Greymarch had planned – for the cop, for Titus – but she knew better than to ask. He had said he would stay in the guest house and, if nothing else, Greymarch was a man of his word. The presence of the injured policeman made her very nervous, but there didn't seem to be anything else she could do for now.

'I have to go,' Judy said. It was getting on 8.00 a.m.

'Have a nice day, dear. Kiss-kiss.'

She glanced at her watch and saw that she was never going to make it to the hospital in time for rounds. And there was still one not-so-small matter to take care of.

She didn't think she'd ever get used to it. Most of the others seemed okay with it, a few came to love it, but perhaps because she *was* a doctor it just didn't sit right with her. Every time she took out the hypo assembly she thought of all the godawful treatments and therapies that she had prescribed over the years to frightened patients. 'You'll adjust,' she would tell them. 'You'll get used to it.'

Insulin injections, colostomy bags, glass eyes, plastic hips, chemotherapy. It had all been so simple from the other side of the examining table.

It wasn't so easy taking the treatment herself.

Greymarch watched her every move, making her feel even more uncomfortable. He knew she didn't like him to watch, but it made *him* feel better to see her do it. Misery loves company and all that. She had learned the hard way that he was impossible and that the best course of action was to ignore him. She unlocked the large refrigerator and removed a fresh ampoule of blood from a rack on the shelf. She opened another locked steel case on the wall and withdrew a golden vial of Tunnel, snapping it into the hypo next to the blood. Ignoring Greymarch, who couldn't resist a tiny smile, she sat down and unlaced her right cross-trainer, slipping off the white anklet. She gently slid the needle between the third and fourth toes and depressed the plunger. The two vials emptied at an even rate, the gold and crimson liquids swirling together as they entered her vein.

She threw her head back and slumped in the chair, dropping the hypo to the floor as the elixir sped through her system. Warmth radiated from the point of injection, up her leg and around her body. She groaned deeply as her clitoris engorged with blood and her nipples hardened into tiny bullets. The warmth rushed up into her face and her cheeks flushed as the fine hairs on her nape stood on end. She moaned loudly, closing her eyes and fastening a death-grip on the chair arms as a long, deep orgasm racked through her. It lingered and deepened and grew so intense that she couldn't breathe.

And it was over.

She looked toward the floor as she opened her eyes and though he didn't say a word, she knew that Greymarch was still watching. She took several deep breaths as the peak of the high faded, leaving a residual warmth and sense of intense well-being. She put her sock and sneaker back on, picked up the spent hypo and got to her feet. She could see Greymarch's fuzzy reflection in the dull finish of the metal refrigerator door. He was still watching her.

She put the hypo away and grabbed her bag.

She left without saying a word, locking Greymarch and Reagan in from the outside.

Reagan drifted in and out of sleep all morning. He never quite made it around to consciousness, but was restive, knowing somewhere in the back of his injured, drugged mind that he wasn't in Kansas anymore.

Greymarch kept a silent watch over him as he twisted and turned. Flashes of fever-like dreams filled with images of blood and gore disturbed his rest. One scene kept recurring: Reagan dog-paddled in an immense pool of warm water, thick as honey. Bernouli and Brolin floated at the other end, the doctor licking furiously at Brolin's crotch. Brolin looked at Reagan the whole while, a broad smile on her face, her tongue lolling out of her mouth.

'Can't throw him out of the pool for eating pussy,' she slurred. And then she started to gag and convulse. Bernouli thrust his head all the way inside Brolin's cunt and blood oozed down her thighs. Reagan frantically tried to paddle toward her, but he couldn't make any headway through the thick water. He had to struggle just to stay in place. Brolin screamed with pain/pleasure as Bernouli burrowed into her. The doctor was only visible from the waist down as he ate his way up inside her.

Reagan suddenly found himself standing on top of the water, tiny waves tickling the soles of his feet. Somehow his Ruger had physically melded with the stump of his right wrist. He pointed the gun at Bernouli whose naked ass loomed above the supine Brolin as he tried to wriggle his midsection up into her. Reagan's gun went off on its own. Bernouli's feet slipped inside Brolin's contracting cunt with a slurp and she floated alone atop the gentle rolling waves.

But her head was gone, replaced by a veiny stump that was twin to Reagan's own.

Reagan heard laughter and looked up to see Titus bouncing up and down on a diving board at the end of the pool. He pointed at Brolin's headless corpse and flashed his sharp teeth. Reagan raised his wrist to aim the Ruger at him, but the gun had vanished and only the shredded flesh of the wrist remained.

Titus continued to laugh and bounce, growing bigger with every leap. Reagan continued to point his fractured wrist at him and croaked: 'Bang, bang. Bang, bang.'

Titus soared higher and higher. The laughter stopped and Titus's smile dissolved into a snarl as he leaped off the board, directly at Reagan. Titus's shadow blocked out the sun as his face grew impossibly large in Reagan's vision.

'Whnnnnhh!!' Reagan yelled, waking himself up.

'Good morning, sleeping beauty,' Greymarch said.

Reagan dozed throughout the day. Thankfully, the dream didn't recur, but twice he awoke with a burning need to urinate. Greymarch responded by bringing him a bedpan, taking it away and cleaning it without complaint or visible disgust. He seemed to be practised in it. Greymarch brought the detective a cup of ice water with a flex-straw (Reagan was also hooked up to an IV-saline drip) and a moist towel with which he mopped Reagan's face, though he made no effort at conversation.

By late afternoon Reagan started to feel a little like himself. He was still tired and hurting, but some of the fogginess had lifted from his mind. At one point, Greymarch appeared to be napping in a chair, his gun tucked loosely in a shoulder holster. Reagan tried to get up, but the effort was far too much and too soon. He fell back heavily against the pillow and when he could again open his eyes, he saw Greymarch carefully monitoring him.

Reagan avoided any and all reference to, or thought of, his right hand. He knew it was there – or rather that it *wasn't* there – but mentally compartmentalized the thought and sealed it off. He felt the anxiety pressing at its mental vault, but he kept it at bay. The arm itself he kept under the cover and out of sight.

At five o'clock, Greymarch turned on an old black and white television that he'd dragged out of a closet. He set the TV on an overturned carton a few feet from Reagan's bed and plugged it in. As the set warmed up – it was *that* old – he sat down on the edge of Reagan's bed and they watched the local news together.

The anchor-woman, a visibly ageing blonde whose plasticized face bore a terrifying resemblance to the hockey-masked Jason of horror movie fame, feigned as much sober concern as her unnaturally taut skin would allow as she read the lead. Hovering over her right shoulder was a lurid graphic exclaiming 'Massacre in Cheviot Hills' in bold red letters.

'Wasn't a goddamn massacre,' Greymarch muttered. 'Perfectly fair fight. All things considered.'

They cut away to a location reporter standing in front of the Bernouli house. A couple of tired-looking uniforms idled in the background. Reagan leaned forward a little when they played back footage from the previous night of the cops and onlookers crowding the crime scene. His heart sank as he saw the tape of bodies being carted out and into the meat wagons and, though the reporter didn't indicate which corpse was which, Reagan could tell from the faces of the cops which gurneys bore the remains of Brolin and McLeod. They briefly flashed an out-of-date Academy snapshot of McLeod and a photo of Brolin with her husband that Reagan remembered seeing on the corner of her desk. She'd kept it there even after the divorce.

There was a another cutaway to the reporter, then some file footage of Bernouli speaking at some AIDS forum. The reporter casually mentioned the earlier trouble at Bernouli's lab and cautiously speculated on a connection between the two incidents. Reagan's spirits briefly rose as they cut back to footage of Arsenio, still breathing, being loaded into an ambulance and he shot a look at Greymarch, who just barely shrugged to communicate: *So I lied, so sue me*. The live voice-over reported that Arsenio was the only survivor of the massacre and that the latest reports indicated that he was in 'guarded' condition in the prison ward at County-U.S.C. Hospital.

Reagan's heart fell back into his stomach when his own picture came up on the screen. Bizarrely, the reporter mispronounced his name – Ree-gun, he said, perhaps so as not to confuse Dennis with the former president – and noted that Reagan was believed to have been at the scene of the crime, but was now reported missing. To add insult to injury, the photograph they used was particularly unflattering. Reagan knew and disliked the reporter and suspected the choice was deliberate.

'Awww,' Greymarch confirmed, 'now that's not right. You're much better looking than that.' Reagan cocked his head and studied his companion, but Greymarch was still attending to the news and seemed perfectly serious.

The news report finished up with the usual blather about violence on L.A.'s streets and how no neighbourhood was immune to trouble, followed by some idiotic banter between the anchor and the reporter in which the anchor got to shake her head knowingly and cluck her tongue. They moved on to a story about brush fires in the Valley, so Greymarch flicked off the set.

Reagan, tired from the mere act of sitting up and watching the story, laid back down and let out a heavy sigh. They knew he had been at Bernouli's, which meant they'd be looking for him. He didn't see a phone in the room, but he had to find a way to contact Donatelli and let him know what was going on.

Whatever the hell *was* going on.

It was interesting, Reagan thought, that there was no mention of gang involvement in the news story. There couldn't have been any mistaking the dead Blood for what they were and then there was Arsenio. It figured that no one but the cops and the coroner got to see the bodies, but the cameras had caught Arsenio getting wheeled away. What the hell would a black kid be doing in a neighbourhood like that if it *wasn't* gang-related?

But what *were* the Blood doing at Bernouli's place? And why had they killed – killed? – hell, *butchered* Bernouli. And Blaine had been there as ringmaster. Again.

What the fuck was going on?

Reagan turned to Greymarch, but he had disappeared into the other room. He emerged a few minutes later carrying a small plate with some stale-looking crackers. They were dry as sawdust, but Reagan discovered that he was a little hungry. He started to pull his right arm out from under the cover to reach for a cracker and then caught himself. He locked eyes with Greymarch who studied him without expression and continued to hold out the plate. Careful not to dislodge the IV-tube, Reagan snatched a cracker with his left hand and slowly nibbled at it. Greymarch put the plate down on the floor next to the bed and pulled a chair over from across the room. He sat down.

'Want to hear a story?' he asked.

THIRTY-TWO

Titus reconnoitred the area before approaching his Manhattan
Beach duplex. He didn't know whether Greymarch had taken out
the cop, but he couldn't risk going back to the Malibu house now.
Other than a small stash of blood and Tunnel, a few guns and the
ocean view, there was nothing there worth salvaging anyway. And
if the detective was still alive – despite his anger, Titus grinned
thinking about the scumbag's hand – cops would be swarming all
over the estate.

He went right for the locked fridge and shot up with a double-
dose from the twin hypo. As the Tunnel and tainted blood sped
through his system, he lay back on a sofa and thought over the
events that had brought him to his present state.

Titus fumed some more about the ignoble manner by which he
had been forced to exit Bernouli's house. He'd gone out a window
and streaked to his Mercedes, which he managed to hot-wire and
shift into gear even as the first squad cars roared around the corner.
The bullets in his right shoulder hurt like a son-of-a-bitch, but he
took it slow and easy driving out of the area, carefully pulling over
to the kerb each time a racing emergency vehicle came roaring up
the street at him. Between the darkness and the typically blasé
attitude of L.A. drivers, no one even noticed he was wearing only
his underpants.

But he had an Uzi under the seat, just in case anyone did.

By the time he pulled onto the westbound Santa Monica Freeway, his anger had risen beyond his ability to contain it. He floored
it coming off the entrance ramp and gunned the engine to 110

mph, weaving through the traffic in kamikaze style. As he zoomed under the towering ramp that led onto the San Diego Freeway, he stabbed at the buttons on the CD controller and punched up an Iggy Pop disc. He cranked the volume and screamed along, pushing the German engine to the limit until he was forced to slow down where the freeway turned into Pacific Coast Highway. Frustrated by the line of slow-moving traffic, he sped across the road, screeching to a halt in one of the deserted beach parking lots south of the Santa Monica Pier.

Leaving the engine on and the stereo blaring, Titus threw open the door and ran toward the sea. With every heavy stride across the dirty sand he saw himself killing Greymarch in a new way. Oh, how he regretted his failure to tear the man apart during the mêlée in the men's room. Not to mention their encounters in times past. As his anger continued to build, he thought of all the occasions they'd been together, from their very first meeting in the Gulf, and all the chances he'd had to throttle, smother, garrotte or just plain eviscerate Greymarch, but hadn't done the deed.

So great was his fury that he half-expected steam to rise off his body as he plunged into the cold water of the Pacific. The icy waves brought his internal temperature down to tolerable levels.

Until he thought of Heather and heated right back up again.

With the picture of her face in his mind, he waded out to waist level and crouched down. The salt and bacteria stung the holes in his shoulder. He reached around with his left hand and fingered the entrance wounds, about an inch apart just above the shoulder blade. He crouched down again and dug into the first wound with his index finger, wriggling it around until he felt the tiny shard of flattened lead a quarter-inch below the skin-line. He worked it loose, like pulling the last olive out of a narrow jar, and eased the bullet out of the wound. He dropped it into the sea where it vanished with a soft plop!

He stood up and took a deep breath, then wedged his finger into the second hole. This bullet was lodged much deeper and his finger slid in up to the second knuckle before he found the lead. He swayed a bit as he pulled the finger out.

Titus took a deep breath and fell to his knees. The water-line rose to his neck and the polluted waves washed up over his nose and mouth. He jammed two fingers back into the wound and forced them in until he could grab the bullet between his fingertips. He lost his grip several times when the pain grew too fierce, but finally managed to snag the prize.

Twisting his hand and squirming his shoulders he got a solid grip on the bullet and, with a glass-shattering yell, popped it out, collapsing backward into the water.

He floated there for some while, letting the salt treat the wound, feeling his supercharged system already starting to heal. Good old Sam the Sham, he thought, and howled into the night sky at the delightful memory of Heather gutting Bernouli with her bare hands.

Hanging by his heels from his own living room ceiling, dripping blood like a slaughtered sow, that was the way Titus wanted to remember Bernouli.

And blood on her lips, his cock in her mouth was the way Titus would always think of Heather.

Beaten to a grey pulp, skinned alive and skull-fucked was the way Titus *planned* to remember Greymarch.

Titus had just floated there for hours. Long enough for the traffic to thin and his injuries to heal. Only when the hunger came upon him did he get back in his car and make for the safe house in Manhattan Beach.

As the Tunnel rush subsided, Titus put aside the memories. He got up from the sofa and went into the bathroom to examine his wounds and clean himself up.

And to make new plans.

Arsenio stared at the dirty ceiling. There really wasn't too much else to do other than sleep, but he'd dozed through most of the morning and afternoon and didn't care to revisit the ugly pictures that haunted him when he closed his eyes.

The prison ward at County-U.S.C. was spartan, utilitarian and dull. A row of eight beds was lined up along each wall of the long room, with a pair of shotgun-bearing Corrections Officers at one end and a nurse's station in the middle. Only half the beds were occupied, but two of the inmate/patients were junkies forced into cold turkey, and when one wasn't moaning or screaming the other filled in the silence. All the prisoners, including Arsenio, were manacled to the heavy steel bed frames by ankle cuffs and chains. If a patient had to be turned or moved, a guard would accompany the nurse and unlock the cuffs, trading his shotgun for a semi-automatic pistol.

Upon arrival, Arsenio had been taken directly to surgery. He had drifted in and out of consciousness during the journey, and vaguely remembered the cop and the paramedic betting on whether he'd last till they made it across town to County. He didn't remember much else until he woke up in the ward with a large dressing draped across his chest and his right arm in a light cast. The dressing smelled rank, but the doctor who eventually came by told him that the surgery had gone well and that the damage looked worse than it was. As the anaesthetic slowly wore off, the chest wound itched like mad and hurt like a bastard at the same time. His arm felt sore, too, but it was a mere annoyance in comparison. He'd asked for some painkiller, but the nurse told him he'd have to grit it out for a few more hours.

'Shouldn't be no problem for a tough cop-killer like you,' the middle-aged black woman had snarled. One of the guards had grunted agreement and after the nurse walked off, hawked up a grey lugie and spat it on Arsenio's pillow.

Arsenio sighed. He was in very big trouble, here. He wasn't entirely sure of what had gone down at the doctor's house, but he knew who was going to take the fall for it. He remembered the hellish screams that came from the other room after Titus had taken the first cop away, and he all too clearly recalled the way the lady cop's brains had exploded out her head when Titus made Reagan shoot her. The terror he felt when his own act of would-be heroism fizzled was also keenly etched in his mind, but everything after that, from when the gunfire exploded through the big glass doors, was fuzzy. He definitely remembered K'toma clutching onto his head as if to keep it from falling off, but he didn't recall the moment that the spray of bullets had torn through him. He could recapture fleeting snapshots of the events that followed, especially when the dude who shot him stopped to look his way before leaving, but why the man didn't kill him, how it was Aresenio had managed to survive at all was a mystery.

Less mysterious was what lay in store for him. All of the doctors and nurses referred to him as 'cop-killer' and the guards obviously agreed. He'd only had one exchange with another prisoner. The Crip – an older guy with a bandaged head in the cater-corner bed – smiled at him in a very unpretty way and mentioned how he was looking forward to meeting Arsenio in the shower.

Although hardly a seasoned criminal, Arsenio had been around enough to hear some stories. He knew that the cops had ways of beating prisoners without leaving any marks. He knew that special lock-ups were commonly arranged in which unpopular perps were assigned to cell-mates with unpleasant habits.

And he knew that if you'd been marked for a shank-job, sooner or later you took a shiv in the belly.

It was Morgan who worried Arsenio more than anything else.

Arsenio tried to coyly pry some information about Morgan's fate out of one of the friendlier nurses, but she either didn't know or wouldn't say. The guard's ears pricked up at the attempt and he offered a savage grin when Arsenio looked his way. It wasn't an answer exactly, but Arsenio got the message.

Clearly, Morgan had figured Arsenio for a plant, though Arsenio didn't know how he knew. He wondered why Morgan hadn't wasted him on the spot, not that it mattered. Arsenio reckoned that his life expectancy had grown very short. Arsenio was a dead man as soon as he went into the general prison population. That is, *if* Morgan was still alive.

A nurse came by to change his dressing and take his temperature. She pulled the old dressing off slowly and painfully, causing Arsenio to exhale sharply and issue a high mewling noise.

'So sorry,' she said, but couldn't hold back a laugh.

The guards laughed, too.

As she roughly poked and prodded at his chest, Arsenio's thoughts turned back to Morgan.

Is he alive?, he wondered.

Morgan lay on his king-sized bed amid a litter of spent vials of Tunnel. The highs seemed to be of progressively shorter duration and he found it harder and harder to function without them. His left hand looked like a pin cushion from all the injections he'd given himself since returning from the disaster with Titus. More disturbing to him, though, was that he wasn't reaching the highs he used to feel. The sense of power and the clarity of vision that he'd always gotten with Tunnel were harder to achieve.

Morgan had always regarded Titus with a deep fear rooted in his belief that the man was something like omnipotent; that belief had been shattered by the events of the previous night. The slaughtering of Bernouli and the cop had been a righteous enough gaffle – Morgan got *stoked* when Titus tore the cop's hand right off his arm – but things went sour after that. Morgan had expected that that bastard Eyeball would nark him and he'd been ready for it. He had planned to offer the little chickenshit up to Titus as a sacrifice to cap off the evening. He knew that Titus's squeeze had a thing for dark meat and felt sure Arsenio would score him some extra points in the big man's eyes.

He couldn't believe it when the hail of bullets tore the Blood apart. Not that the loss of Lutece and Endzone was all that tragic.

But K'toma hurt.

Morgan didn't believe in friends, didn't think he needed them or was in a position to afford them. Tamara was an okay Betty and talented with the tongue, but he wouldn't go crying a flood of tears if she fell under a Blue Line train.

K'toma was different, though.

They'd been together since kindergarten, always watching each other's back. They'd seen and caused a lot of trouble over the years and they'd both taken their share of hits. Yet, they'd made it through together. K'toma wasn't just *a* Blood, he *was* blood. And now some motherfucker had stolen Morgan's only real blood from him.

Morgan felt his focus fading and the pain start to well up again in his belly so he reached for another hit. He rolled the vial between his fingers and pictured K'toma's watchful eyes in the golden fluid. He snapped the Tunnel into the hypo and jabbed the needle into the palm of his left hand hard enough to draw tears from his eyes.

The Tunnel exploded into his body, filling Morgan with another brief moment of orgasmic strength in which he could forget his lost brother.

JuJu knocked on the half-open door and stuck his head in the room. The charges against him had been dropped for lack of evidence and he'd been released by the cops just that morning. JuJu wasn't all that bright, but Morgan was glad to have one lieutenant he could more less trust.

'Yo,' JuJu said, 'it's coming together like you say.'

Morgan nodded and dismissed him with a gesture. JuJu went back out pretending not see the tears in the gang lord's blood-shot eyes.

THIRTY-THREE

Greymarch thoroughly grilled Reagan on what he knew about Bernouli and Tunnel and the whole situation. It rubbed hard against Reagan's trained detective grain, but as he thought about what exactly he should tell his captor, he realized that he knew so little – and nothing solidly, at that – that there seemed no harm in reporting most of what he did know. It was more likely, he figured, that he would gain from the exchange than reveal anything significant. He tried to be cagey in his phrasing, especially when talking about something he knew absolutely *nothing* about, guessing that Greymarch would assume that Reagan wasn't being entirely forthcoming.

Because that's what Reagan would have assumed if their positions were reversed.

It didn't take Reagan very long, even with padding and augmenting his meagre story and when he was done Greymarch looked at him a little sadly. Reagan abashedly recognized the look: he'd seen it plenty of times in locked precinct rooms, when the interrogation team realized that their perp was just another dumb street kid with a third-grade reading level, who couldn't manage an escape if they unlocked the door for him and knocked themselves unconscious.

'And Titus?' Greymarch asked softly, after a while. 'What, exactly, do you know about him?'

Reagan tried to rally some dignity, but it wasn't easy when you were flat on your back in a hospital johnny with an IV-tube stuck in your only good arm. Even harder since he really didn't know a thing.

'We were just starting to look into him,' he said. 'He seems to be an . . . umm . . . a somewhat secretive fellow.' Reagan vamped: 'We were working with Internal Revenue to . . .'

Greymarch interrupted him with a cutting burst of laughter. 'I.R.S.? Jesus Christ! You don't know jack-shit about him, do you?'

Reagan pursed his lips in a schoolmarmish way and sighed. He shook his head. 'No. Not a clue.'

'Well, that's Titus.' Greymarch leaned back in the chair and crossed his arms over his chest. Reagan fidgeted in the bed, making himself comfortable as Greymarch began to tell his tale.

'You remember, what was his name . . . Robert Vesco?' he began. 'The old Nixon scumbag. Embezzled millions, hundreds of millions, and skipped off to some non-extraditable desert isle. Had a hand in every dirty deed from JFK to Watergate. Pure Oliver Stone stuff. Been living on a beach smoking Havana cigars and sipping paper umbrella drinks for decades.

'Well, Titus makes Vesco look like a jaywalker. And Titus never had to skip. Because Titus is *connected*.'

Reagan furrowed his brow. Greymarch smiled and went on before the detective could ask a question.

'I don't know where his money came from originally – probably smack, maybe weapons – but he's had his finger in a lot of muddy pies. He's a fixer, connected everywhere there's trouble: selling Stingers in El Salvador and Afghanistan, stolen grain in Somalia and Sudan, heroin in Ukraine and everyplace else you can imagine. He's one of those invisible men who make the world of Black Ops turn. The agencies, the powers-that-be know him – they couldn't exist without his type – but there's never a paper trail. You can always follow the dead bodies, though.'

Reagan didn't have a clue what Greymarch was talking about, but he hung on every word.

'Titus's main talent is always staying that little bit ahead of the curve. He was long out of Nicaragua before Ollie North and his boys ever moved in. He's got a nose for these things, Titus does. Hell, I'll give him his due: it's a a fucking talent. That's how he sniffed out Bernouli, hooked up with him. Way I heard it, they linked up back in the eighties when Titus was playing footsie with Savimbi in Angola and Sam was breeding Ebola bugs in Zaire. Supposedly they met on an endangered species safari in Kenya. They both liked killing things.'

'*What?*' Reagan said.

'Don't know much about Sam, either, do you?' Greymarch shook his head. 'Pathetic.'

'We checked up on Bernouli . . .' Reagan whined. But as he said it he felt like the captain of the Titanic trying to defend the decision to take a closer look at that iceberg.

'Yeah?' Greymarch said.

'He's been with Phaedra for years. University of California before that. He's never even had a parking ticket.'

Greymarch laughed uproariously. 'Neither have I,' he said. 'Hey, I hear Jeffrey Dahmer was a terrific driver.'

'And Hitler loved his mother,' Reagan sighed.

'But maybe a little too much,' Greymarch suggested.

'And Sam Bernouli?'

'I don't think Sam loved Hitler's mother. Then again . . .' Reagan made a face.

'Sam is Company man. And Phaedra is a Company company.'

'Company? Now you're going to tell me that this is all some CIA plot?'

'No,' Greymarch said, 'it's not as simple as that. The CIA is bullshit, a cover. If the CIA counted for shit you think Ames or those other losers could have got away with what they did? No way. The CIA is strictly for public consumption, a little Tom Clancy, Harrison Ford rah-rah.'

Greymarch pulled his chair a little closer to Reagan's bed and leaned forward.

'I read this thing once, by some French dude. Jean something-or-other. Batshit crazy but right on the mark like only batshit crazy people can be. Anyway, he said that Disneyland is really America because it disguises the fact that all of America is really Disneyland.'

'Oooh, deep,' Reagan sniped.

'You bet your ass it's deep. Think about it for a while. Because that's the way things really are. The CIA exists to make you think that the rest of the government isn't the CIA. But that's exactly what it is. Everything is corruptible. Anyone can be bought. And everything's for sale.'

Reagan was finding it hard to focus. Between the drugs Judy had given him, the pain in his arm they couldn't quite control and Greymarch's paranoid conspiracy theories, his head was swimming like a salmon moving upstream. But he felt sure that amid the lunacy there was something to Greymarch's story.

'What does this have to with Bernouli?' Reagan asked again.

'Phaedra lives on Department of Defense money. They do all kinds of other shit – it's all Disneyland, remember? – but DOD research is their bread and butter. And Sam is . . . heh . . . *was* their blue-eyed boy. Sam started out researching biological weapons when he was still a prof. He was the virus king of UC Davis. Except the university wasn't too thrilled with his project even with all that DOD money he brought in. So they canned his ass and the Company . . .'

'The company that isn't the CIA,' Reagan interrupted.

'The *government* – does that make it sound better? – the government set him up with Phaedra. Which was just another one of their operations anyway. 'Cause the *government* isn't supposed to be working on biological weapons agents anymore, 'cause we signed a fucking treaty and it ain't politically correct. Except *they* are still making their nasty little viruses, so someone's got to do it here, too. It's called keeping up with the Husseins. Enter Dr Bernouli, stage right.'

Greymarch suddenly sat up straight and looked toward the door, though Reagan couldn't hear anything. The gun was in Greymarch's hand before Reagan even saw him move. A key turned in the dead bolt. Greymarch put the gun away when he saw Judy's face and Reagan felt a sense of relief with the woman's return. Greymarch was clearly nuts and Reagan didn't rate his survival under Greymarch's care.

Judy was carrying a couple of bags of fast food. She handed the sacks to Greymarch and came over to examine Reagan. She checked his dressings and the IV and nodded at Greymarch, as if impressed.

'How do you feel?' she asked.

'Hostage-like,' Reagan answered.

'Hungry?' was her only response.

'A bit,' Reagan admitted.

'Good sign.'

She took Greymarch by the arm and walked him into the other room. Reagan strained to hear, but couldn't make out anything they said. He heard Greymarch loudly curse at one point.

Greymarch came back a few minutes later carrying a plate with a drumstick, a smattering of Spanish rice and a corn tortilla. He helped Reagan up to a sitting position and handed him the plate and a sweating cupful of iced lemonade. Reagan naturally grabbed the plate with his left hand and reached for the plastic fork with his right, stopping in mid-gesture.

There was an awkward silence as Reagan stared at his bandaged wrist and then down at the plate. Greymarch reached for the fork, to feed him, but Reagan growled, 'No!'

He balanced the plate on his legs and picked the drumstick up with his left hand. Greymarch watched for a minute then put on his jacket.

'I have to go out for a while. Jude here will look after you while I'm gone.'

Greymarch headed for the door and almost as an afterthought added: 'Oh yeah. Jude's almost as good a shot as I am. So don't be fucking stupid.'

Reagan glanced over at the doctor, who was gnawing on a wing. A Smith & Wesson .38 dangled in her hand.

Reagan turned back to his dinner. In spite of everything, the pain, the exhaustion, the insanity, he couldn't help but marvel at how wonderful the greasy chicken tasted.

THIRTY-FOUR

In spite of his anxiety about his captivity and a growing urgency to *do* something, Reagan's physical woes and exhaustion got the better of him and he dozed for several hours after devouring his dinner.

The television was on again when he woke up. There was neither a window nor a clock in the room, but Letterman was on so Reagan knew it must be around midnight. The woman Greymarch referred to as Jude was out of sight, and though Reagan held his breath and listened for signs of life, he didn't think she was in the house with him.

Reagan pulled himself up to a sitting position and swung his legs out over the edge of the bed. He went a bit lightheaded and had to brace himself to avoid falling over. He reached up to touch his fingers to his forehead, only to rediscover, yet again, that the hand that he was certain he could still feel wasn't there anymore. He whimpered slightly at the recognition, but was determined not to let it stop him from taking advantage of his opportunity.

He slowly eased himself off the bed, testing his wobbly legs. His right ankle was tightly taped and a sharp line of pain shot up to his hip as he daintily put some weight on it. Using the IV-stand as a crutch, he hauled himself fully upright. He took a tentative step and found that he could walk, though not very well.

Unfortunately, he didn't notice that his IV-tube had snagged on the edge of the bed frame. As he experimented with a second step, the plastic tubing jerked him back toward the bed, upsetting the IV-stand in the process. He frantically reached out for the stand before it fell, pulling himself backward yet again and losing his balance.

The floor rose fast in his vision before everything went dark.

'I guess what they say about cops is true,' Judy said.

It took Reagan a minute to reconstruct what had happened and figure out that he was back in bed. The IV had been removed from his arm, but a new bandage had been affixed over his right eye and he had a dull headache. He groaned slightly, more over the memory of his bungled escape than any immediate physical discomfort.

He smacked his lips and Judy handed him a plastic cup of cold water. He took a small sip, then glugged the rest of the water.

'Easy,' she warned.

'Ahhhh,' he exhaled. He furrowed his bandaged brow. 'So what *do* they say about dumb cops?'

'How many L.A. cops does it take to screw in a light bulb?' she asked. Reagan shrugged.

'Seven.' She paused. Reagan held his breath. 'One to screw in the bulb, four to beat the light socket into submission and two to get doughnuts.'

'That's not funny,' Reagan said. 'You know, some cops don't even like doughnuts.'

'Eight,' Judy muttered.

'Huh?' Reagan said.

'Nothing. That was a pretty stupid stunt in your condition. You could have really hurt yourself.' Reagan guffawed. 'Well. I didn't think you'd be able to get up at all. How do you feel?'

'My head hurts.' He started to finger the new bandage with his phantom hand and sighed as he caught himself again. He stared at the dressing on his wrist. 'And my hand is gone. My fucking hand is gone. Christ, this is going to take some getting used to.'

Judy started to answer him, then stopped. He could see her biting off the words.

'Or is it?' he asked. 'You don't know what that maniac has planned for me, do you?'

'I . . .' Judy thought about it for a minute, then just shook her head. She couldn't meet his gaze as she did it.

'Sort of rubs against the grain of that old Hippocratic Oath, wouldn't you say?'

'It's not as simple as that,' she said. 'Calvin isn't so crazy as you think. He's . . . out there. But he's definitely not crazy.

There's a lot more at stake here than ... well, than you could know.'

'So tell me,' he said. 'You think I don't realize I'm chin-deep in the shit? For Christ's sake, some goddamn lunatic slaughtered two of my partners and ripped the hand off my arm last night. *He ripped my fucking hand off!* Your little joke notwithstanding, I'm not an idiot. Just give me some idea what the hell it is I'm into. Please. Greymarch started to tell me before he took off. But he doesn't make a lot of sense.'

'How much did he tell you?' she asked.

Reagan briefly recapped Greymarch's somewhat rambling conspiracy theory. Judy listened, sitting in a chair beside the bed, propping her chin on the knuckles of her interlaced hands. The .38 didn't appear to be on her person and Reagan thought about making a move, but decided he couldn't possibly take her in his condition. She looked to be in terrific shape. And Reagan still needed to know the rest of the story.

'Bernouli wasn't entirely a villain,' Judy said, after gathering her thoughts. 'But what Calvin says about him is true. Sam was a brilliant, brilliant man, but he wasn't big on conscience. He worked for the Department of Defense on viral weapons research. He could have worked anywhere for anyone – I've heard Calvin's Disneyland theory, by the way, and I don't buy it – because no one in the world knew more about virology than Sam Bernouli. There isn't a hospital or university that wouldn't have opened their doors to him and written a blank cheque. His work on DPZ alone guaranteed that. Genuinely amazing stuff. I believe that if anyone could have cracked the AIDS problem it was Sam. He was really onto something.'

'So why didn't he stick with it?'

'Because something more interesting came along.'

'*More* interesting than a cure for AIDS?' Reagan asked.

'You have to try to understand the way Sam looked at things. He was a big picture kind of guy. DPZ was quite a breakthrough in AIDS treatment, but Bernouli knew that it wasn't really the answer. Most of the AIDS research community are either working on vaccines for prevention or on stronger palliatives, but because of the strong mutagenic properties of HIV, Sam didn't believe that a specific vaccine would ever be possible. And truth is he didn't think it really mattered all that much. He was much more interested in the broader importance of HERVs, Human Endogenous Retroviruses, and the nature of their relationship to new exogenous retroviruses.

HIV was just a little stream to him while he wanted to cross an ocean. So he broke off the AIDS work and embarked on a whole new course of research rooted in the genetic engineering of HERV proteins.'

'Engineering? You mean DNA stuff?' Reagan asked.

'Yeah,' Judy laughed, 'DNA stuff. This'll be so much easier since you know the technical jargon.' Reagan blushed and Judy laughed a little harder. 'You see, vaccines are based on introducing either live or inert forms of a culture into the body to foster an immunity to a virus. But because of rapid mutation, Sam concluded that it was a waste of time for the new diseases which he believed were arising as a result of HERV mutation. So instead of pursuing a vaccine, which is what most everyone else is after, he started looking for a way to target the viruses *after* they'd breached the cellular defences and to eliminate them before they could completely break down the host's immune system.'

'Eliminate? You mean like piss away?'

'Actually, that's sort of what he had in mind. Let me try to explain this simply: once it's in a system, a virus works by binding, or attaching itself, to certain proteins that are located on the membrane of individual cells. Once it binds with the protein, the virus can enter and infect the cell and then use that cell to begin to reproduce itself. It multiplies geometrically. You follow?'

'So far, so good.'

'Okay. Viruses and retroviruses, even the nasty new kinds of HERV, aren't real bright, but they're incredibly persistent. Like cops.' Reagan frowned, but didn't say anything. 'They know exactly what they're looking for, and once they think they've found it they don't look any further. In the case of HIV, for instance, the virus looks to bind to a specific cell protein called CD4. In fact, CD4 turns out to be a key receptor site for a series of related exogenous retroviruses. Some other similar proteins can figure as well, but Bernouli's idea was to introduce, well, call it a more attractive version of the CD4 family into infected hosts so that the viruses would mistakenly bind with *it* and not to vital cells in the immune system. Then, the engineered CD4 cells, with the virus attached, could be eliminated from the body. Possibly in as simple a manner as just urinating them away.'

'This is all interesting, I'm sure, but what the hell does it have to do with the price of Tunnel in Los Angeles?'

Judy held up a finger. 'I'm explaining this to you as if it's all fact, but the reality is that Bernouli's brand of research is highly controversial. And no one else does it. Did it. Sam made his name with DPZ, but really it was an accident.'

'I don't follow,' Reagan said.

'Bernouli wasn't *looking* for an AIDS treatment at that point, it just dropped out of the research. A little bonus from out of the blue. He was actually working on a research project for the Defense Department when he stumbled onto DPZ. See, he'd been fiddling around with HERVs for years, mostly trying to figure out how to utilize their action in developing biological weapons for the Pentagon, but also how to protect our forces from anyone who might be messing with them someplace else. There's always a balance of terror element that figures into this stuff. We may not want it, but we *have* to have it, 'cause if we don't *they* might.'

'They being . . .'

'They being the evil empire of the day. You know: whoever provides a good enough reason to allocate big bundles of money.'

'Disneyland,' Reagan muttered.

'Whatever,' Judy shrugged. 'Bernouli always was a lucky bastard. Well, until recently, anyway. He was hot off his DPZ find and heavily into a new round of research into HERVs when Saddam Hussein handed him the keys to the kingdom.'

'How's that?'

'The Gulf War. If Sam had been god himself – and believe me, he sometimes thought he was – he couldn't have designed a more perfect scenario on such a massive scale. Half a million troops heading into what looked like a certain chemical/bio-warfare situation. The Defense honchos were frantic about the kinds of stuff the troops might encounter, how the folks back home would react to seeing their boys and girls coming back looking like lepers and plague victims. They gave Sam carte fucking blanche.'

'To do *what*?' Reagan asked. 'I still don't get it.'

'Like I said, Sam's research agenda after DPZ was already . . . unconventional. If he hadn't been working for Phaedra, with their own dubious connections, it would never have flown. See, his solution to the big HERV problem was to foster the growth of, oh, think of them as *designer* organs – organelles he called them – into people with HERV-associated conditions. These organelles were genetically engineered by Bernouli to produce CD4 and its variants in very precisely controlled amounts. The point was that the organelles would attract the invading virus, without doing other damage to the host. He devised a way to affix the organelles to the appendix, making a useless organ a useful one.

'It was an incredibly radical idea, but it was brilliant. The thing is, for any other researcher it would have taken years to get permission to proceed even on animal tests, much less humans. But Sam wasn't any other researcher. He was connected up the wazoo with the Defense boys and so was Phaedra. And when the Kuwait thing went down, so did *any* obstacles to Sam trying out whatever he wanted. I still can't believe that there wasn't someone, somewhere in that murky Black Ops hierarchy who didn't think: uh-oh, maybe this isn't such a hot idea. Maybe there was. But Sam Bernouli wasn't the kind of guy to take no for an answer.'

Judy got up and went into the kitchen. She came back in with two cups of lemonade and handed one to Reagan, who nodded his thanks.

'Maybe this is a naïve question, but how is it exactly that you come to know about all this?' Reagan asked.

'I thought for sure you'd have figured that out by now.' Judy smiled grimly. 'I was Sam's henchman.'

THIRTY-FIVE

'Sounds like one of those fifties movies, doesn't it? *I Was a Teenaged Werewolf*. I suppose hench-*person* would be more politically correct, these days,' Judy said.

'So, what are you saying?' Reagan asked. 'You dug the bodies out of the graveyard at midnight?'

'Nothing quite so honourable,' she said. 'I was Sam's assistant.'

'Fuck me,' Reagan whispered.

'Tell me about it. It was just one of those crazy old things, like the song says. I was serving in the Gulf . . .'

'Whoa! You were in the service?'

Judy nodded. 'The army paid my way through med school. I was still paying my way back out when Uncle Saddam decided to embark on his less than excellent adventure. Saddam Hussein and Sam Bernouli. Who'd have thought even that desert was big enough for two such egomaniacs.'

'What was Bernouli doing there?'

'Experimenting, of course. He had a hell of a theatre of operation for his laboratory. Seven hundred thousand white rats is how he must have seen it. You must have heard about how the army shot up every soldier who went over there with a whole cocktail of chemicals. They didn't know what they were doing. It was criminal, really. Even if they really thought it was for the troops' own protection, they should have been more careful.'

'And Bernouli was involved in that?'

'No. Sam showed up later. The first cases of what they're calling

Gulf War Syndrome manifested themselves almost immediately.
Complete autoimmune failure in the worst cases, and there were
a lot of them. That's not what the death certificates said – there
were a whole lot of "jeep accidents"; man, the army was scared –
but that's what the poor bastards were dropping from. The army
panicked, for good reason I suppose. They quickly changed the
cocktail they were delivering, but it had already been administered
to a couple of divisions of troops. They had visions of hundreds,
hell, thousands of body bags shipping back before the fighting had
even started. No way the folks at home would stand for that. So
they brought Bernouli in to do his thing. But because they don't
trust anybody, they also insisted he have a minder. Sam wouldn't
have it at first, but they finally found a mutually acceptable choice
for the job.'

'Don't tell me . . .'

'Mr Titus Blaine.'

'Goddamn!' Reagan said.

'Titus is neck-deep in every bit of nasty shit you think of. He
already knew Sam; he knew the shadow boys in Washington. Both
agreed they could work with him, 'cause both thought they could
control him. Joke, huh?' Judy stared down and shook her head.

'It was just chance that I got involved,' Judy continued. 'Bad
chance. The whole damn thing was bad luck from start to stop.
Except for Bernouli. He'd already been developing his organelle
therapy, had performed some experiments, and was aching to
take things to the next level. You remember that hantavirus scare
in '93?'

Reagan shook his head.

'In the southwest. It was all over the papers for a couple of weeks; Four-Corners Virus they called it. A bunch of
Navajo Indians and some other folk died from some mystery
ailment.'

'Oh, yeah,' Reagan nodded.

'It was a hantavirus, spread by rodent vectors. It was another
Sam Bernouli special. On the road to organelles.'

'Jesus,' Reagan whispered.

'I didn't find out about that one until recently. Sam kept things
compartmentalized. I don't even know if anyone in the army other
than Titus really knew what was going on with the organelle project,
but they sold the programme on the basis that it could possibly cure
those soldiers already affected *and* provide immunity for everyone
else still at risk.'

'But why would the army go for it? They're not idiots.'

'Maybe not, but I think that all they could see was the picture of those body bags coming off the planes. You have to think back to how quickly the whole Gulf thing developed. Decisions were being made on the hoof, elections weren't too far off. And the first phase of the programme was extremely limited.'

'But what about you?' Reagan asked. 'You're a doctor! Why did you go along with it?'

Judy looked Reagan square in the eye. He could see the pain of the memory.

'At first, because it was my job. I got shipped out because of my basic doctoring skills, but Sam took an interest in me because of my background in oncological research and I got assigned to him. I thought it was weird at the time, but I'd certainly heard of Sam Bernouli and was thrilled at the chance to work with him. A once-in-a-lifetime opportunity.' Judy shook her head. 'I knew it was rotten almost from the start, but I was cowed by Sam. And Titus. You follow orders in the army. Ours not to question why and all that shit. But I should have . . . no, I *did* know better. But by then it was too late.'

'Why too late?'

'Because I was dying,' Judy said.

'What?'

Judy glanced away now, staring at the wall, but seeing something else. 'Life's a funny old business. I was one of the first ones sent over to the Gulf and I received the same drug cocktail as the others, but somehow it didn't affect me. It worked like that; the reactions to it were very mixed. As it turned out it wasn't *just* the cocktail that triggered the condition, but a tainted batch of pyridostigmine bromide that caused most of the early fatalities. Chances are I was immunized from an okay batch. That's the irony of it: the Syndrome's been fairly widespread, to be sure, because the army screwed up big time, but the worst panic turned out to be over nothing more than a bad lot of drugs. The kind of thing that could have happened anywhere. Sam's programme need never have been initiated.'

Reagan felt exhaustion once again seeping through his bones. He tried to raise himself up against the headboard, but couldn't seem to shift himself one-handed. Judy helped him to sit up.

'Thanks,' he said, taking a deep breath. She offered him a thin smile. 'So if you didn't contract the Syndrome . . .'

'Life is a *very* funny business,' Judy sighed. 'I didn't contract it off the initial immunization, but I pricked myself with a contaminated needle.' Judy shook her head back and forth. 'Just as dumb as that. I was thoughtless for one second and then I was as good as dead.'

Judy didn't say any more, just stared at the floor. Reagan cleared his throat until she looked back up. 'Not to be indelicate,' he said, 'but . . .'

'Yes?'

'Well, how come you're still alive?'

'This is where it gets complicated,' Judy sighed as she sat back down. 'You see, the organelle therapy worked.'

The statement hung in the air for a minute. 'Huh!' was the only response that Reagan could manage.

'But the cure's worse than the disease,' she added.

Judy leaned forward in her chair, dropping her head almost between her knees, arms crossed over her chest. It never even occurred to Reagan to take advantage of her potential vulnerability in that moment. He was too caught up in her story.

'Sam had already had some success with animal trials. He had tested on rats – thus the hantavirus – and found that the engineered organelles produced CD4 in massive quantities. Too much, in fact. The organelles were hard to control and went cancerous very quickly. Nothing seemed to solve the problem of exponential protein production. Sam concluded that the problem wasn't with the organelles, but with the rats. You see, rats are pretty good proxies for human chemistry, but not perfect. Especially since Sam decided that the problem with the organelles had to do with protein structure, specifically with agents known as prions. Sam believed that if he could manipulate the shape of the prion protein, he could resolve the other problems. He developed a chemical treatment to force the prion changes that were needed to correct the dysfunction of the organelles.'

Reagan squinted off into the distance. He reached to scratch his cheek with his right hand, caught himself, and tucked it back under the cover. 'Prion sounds familiar to me, but I don't know why. I mean, I don't know the first thing about biology.'

'CJD,' Judy said. Reagan shook his head. 'Creutzfeld-Jakob Disease? You know, Mad Cows? British beef? Prions were all over the news because of that.'

'Oh, yeah!' Reagan said. Yet another sick feeling came over him. 'Bernouli didn't . . . he wasn't . . .'

Judy shrugged. 'I'm not sure. But it's a small world and nothing surprises me anymore.'

'Fuck me,' Reagan said, yet again.

'Sam had been working on the prion problem before the Gulf. He had even managed to scrounge up a few human subjects. AIDS patients, mostly. People who were so desperate they'd volunteer for any experimental study on a one-in-a-million prayer. Sam owned an interest in a chain of medical clinics, so he had no problem tracking down candidates.'

'We know about the clinics,' Reagan nodded.

'They provided him a ready source of subjects and Phaedra covered him for everything else.'

'But cover for what?' Reagan asked. 'This is all . . . fascinating, I suppose, but I'm still in the dark here. What does this have to do with what's going down here and now? Why was the girl butchered at Phaedra? And how the hell do the Blood fit into this?'

'Don't you understand?' Judy snapped. 'Bernouli used his resources at Phaedra and his initial experiments on AIDS patients to develop the first batches of Tunnel. Tunnel is the drug that Bernouli concocted to affect prion shape and control organelle growth. Obviously, it wasn't *called* Tunnel back then. It was intended to have an analgesic component within its general use context, yes, but it was *never* intended as a recreational psychoactive.'

'Oh. Wow,' Reagan said. 'Goddamn.'

'The Gulf situation came along at the perfect moment for him. He had just refined a new variation of the organelle/Tunnel therapy and needed test subjects. I don't know that much about the gang angle, how the Tunnel thing got so out of hand. I think Greymarch knows more. Actually, I know he does, he gets around. I don't really want to know. But naturally it all ties in through Titus.

'See, I got involved because . . . what else could I do? I was looking at a short, very ugly death from autoimmune failure. Everyone who took the organelle therapy agreed to it, but we were all facing death sentences. I'd only worked with Sam for a few weeks, but I knew his reputation, what he could potentially achieve. As a doctor I had a better idea of what was going on than the others, but I was in bad shape. And because I had the knowledge, I also understood better than anyone just how hopeless the situation was. The stark choice was to try Sam's magic elixir or die. Even though I wasn't entirely sure of what the treatment entailed – Sam always played his cards close to his chest – I clutched at the one straw he was offering.'

'But you must have understood the dangers,' Reagan said.

'Up to a point,' she said, 'but what would you have done? With days, maybe weeks to live and no other hope. I was a good doctor, an ethical woman. But I was about to die and Sam Bernouli held out the only hope in the world of staying alive. Of course, I realized it was extreme, but . . . no, I won't cop out and say my judgement was impaired by my condition. I just wanted to stay alive. Simple as that. Would you have done differently?'

Reagan tried to hold Judy's gaze, but it was too intense. He looked away. 'No, probably not,' Reagan said. Then: 'So what went wrong?'

'*Every*thing,' Judy said. 'I was actually treated with the third wave of subjects. None of the first wave, all of whom had been treated at Phaedra before the Gulf, had survived implantation of the organelles. Apparently they went horribly cancerous very quickly.

'The second wave, who were the first to be treated when I was assigned to the project in the Gulf, showed a lot of improvement, though. Bernouli had worked out the gist of the Tunnel therapy for managing organelle growth, but still hadn't managed to generate sufficient CD4 production to fully block the action of the retroviruses. Even so, four out of the second group of subjects were still alive when I came in. But there were . . . complications.'

'What exactly does that mean?'

'You see,' Judy explained, 'the organelles provoked some unexpected effects. They were binding the retroviruses, yes, but they were interfering with other essential chemical functions as well, especially with regard to the thymus gland. Do you know what that is?

Reagan started to nod, then shook his head.

'It's located up here,' she said, tapping a spot above her breastbone. 'It's important in the development of the body's immune system up through puberty. Then it gets smaller and becomes essentially insignificant in adults. Atrophied.

'Well, something about the action of the organelles reactivated the thymus in test subjects. It seemed like a good thing, provoking a dormant aspect of damaged immune systems. After all, these retroviruses kill primarily by breaking down the body's immune reactions and leaving the host susceptible to any opportunistic infection. Pneumonia, tuberculosis or what have you.'

'I understand that,' Reagan said.

'Good. Well, the thymus is normally inactive in adults. But the reactivation by the organelles initiated immune responses that were out of all proportion to the task at hand. The subjects didn't only fight off the retroviruses as intended, but attacked their own bodies. Some subjects grew allergic to their own skin or battled the functions of their own kidneys or livers. The physical manifestations were often quite grotesque. Greymarch was in that second group of subjects.'

'Ahhh,' Reagan said.

'Calvin was Bernouli's first true success. It didn't make any sense, at first, that he should be doing so well when the others faded, but Bernouli's ego explained Calvin as well.'

'I don't follow you,' Reagan said.

'Bernouli kept toying with variations on Tunnel as soon he saw that he needed a way to check the organelle growth in the second wave subjects. The precursor he had used on the first wave of subjects was a complete wash-out. The second variation was better, but most of the subjects were still dying. Late into the second round of tests, he hit on a new variation. Any good scientist would have refined it and held it back for the next set of trials, but obviously Sam wasn't one to be bound by the rigours of experimental protocol. Of the second round subjects who were still alive, Calvin was by far the healthiest. So Bernouli started feeding Calvin, and Calvin alone, the new Tunnel variant. Without, of course, telling Calvin or anyone else what he was doing.'

'And it worked,' she said and then glanced down at her feet. 'Sort of.'

Reagan was beyond exhausted. He felt thirsty and asked Judy for some more lemonade and she got up to oblige.

By the time she returned to his bedside, Reagan was asleep.

THIRTY-SIX

Titus knew that he had lost face. He could see it in Morgan's eyes, in the change in the gang lord's demeanour. Where before Morgan had always seemed slightly off-balance and ill at ease around Titus, always seeking to maximize the distance between them, now he had no fear of coming right up in Titus's face. Titus didn't like it, knew he'd have to deal with it severely at some point, but couldn't let himself worry about it just now. Besides, though he hadn't fully settled on the decision, he didn't think that Morgan was looking at a long tenure in the organization.

The Glock never left Morgan's hands these days. In the past, he would not have considered even flashing it in Titus's presence, but with K'toma dead Morgan trusted no one to watch his back other than himself. He had thought Titus to be invulnerable, and though Titus had wasted the cops impressively enough, he let one get away, his plans shattered, it seemed, by a single man. Morgan wouldn't have believed that anyone could be Titus's equal, but the assault that wasted K'toma and the other Blood proved otherwise. He never quite figured out exactly who or what Titus was or where the hell he'd come from, and had never stopped to consider that there could be anyone else like him. But the dude who'd smoked the Blood was more than righteous enough to set Morgan to thinking.

Titus insisted that Morgan vacate his South-Central crib after the fireworks in Cheviot Hills. Once the dead Blood were identified there was too big a chance that the cops would trace their way back to Morgan. Morgan insisted that no way did the cops know where the Blood holed-up, but Titus only laughed.

Morgan and his crew were now living in the Tunnel lab they ran out of an old factory building on Jefferson Boulevard, just below Baldwin Hills. The area consisted of warehouses, factories and small auto repair garages that shut down promptly at six every day. There were no residential properties nearby, only light traffic at night and few passers-by or prying eyes. The building's high windows had all been painted over and the space inside divided into separate processing and packaging areas, with an immense loading dock at the rear. An upstairs loft had been converted from office cubicles to surprisingly luxurious living quarters, affording a view of the entire interior of the facility. The living area was Titus's private domain, however, and Morgan had to grudgingly make do with sleeping on a sofa-bed in a small storage space on the main floor. He wasn't happy about it, but Titus promised that it was a temporary arrangement. His fear of Titus remained healthy enough that he wasn't willing to argue. Yet. At least he had room for his TV and PlayStation, while the other Blood slept on air mattresses on the cold cement floor. For food, they alternated between Jack in the Box, Kentucky Fried Chicken and take-out from an Ethiopian joint.

Titus watched as several Blood loaded a delivery van with cartons of Tunnel bound for San Bernardino. Morgan supervised, pointing and scratching his balls with the barrel of the Glock. When the van pulled away and the loading bay door was lowered and locked, Titus thumbed the button on the intercom and whispered into it: 'I want you.'

Morgan glanced up at Titus's window and ran the gun barrel under his chin. One of the other gangbangers said something and laughed and slapped hands with another grinning youth, but Morgan's dour expression didn't change and the Bloods quickly lost their smiles. From above, Titus saw them exchange grins again and one grabbed his crotch after Morgan turned his back.

Morgan trudged up the metal staircase and, Titus noted, entered the room without knocking. He didn't sit down until Titus gestured at a chair, but Morgan's impudence seemed to go up a notch every day.

'We have some shit to take care of,' Titus said.

'That last load . . .' Morgan forgot what he was saying as he happened to glance through an open doorway into the adjacent room.

A large bed dominated the tiny space. Morgan regularly
fantasized about sneaking-up and getting some decent sleep on
it when Titus was away, but had never conjured the nerve to take
the chance. Sprawled across the bed, on her back, was a lithe and
very young looking girl with the palest white skin Morgan had ever
seen. He couldn't see her face, which was turned in three-quarters
profile the other way. He would have guessed she was no more
than 13 years old, except that she had absolutely enormous tits.
They hung off her torso like a thrift store suit. Several thick pillows
had been propped under the small of her back such that her body
arched like a frown. One massive tit flopped backward; it looked
as if the meaty tissue grew out of her shoulder. Her eyes were
open, but she didn't blink or move and Morgan wasn't sure if
she was awake or asleep, alive or dead.

'You were saying?' Titus prompted.

'Huh?'

'About the shipment.'

There was something sort of creepy about the girl, something freakish about her proportions, but she riveted Morgan's
attention.

'Dude?' Titus laughed.

Morgan finally turned back to his boss, his mouth agape.
'Whah?'

'Earth to Morgan. Shipment. Drugs. Money.'

'Yeah,' Morgan said, shaking his head, sneaking another glance
at the supine girl out of the corner of his eye. 'The cooker say that
last batch wasn't so good. He say it had impurities.'

'Awww,' Titus said. 'Poor little crack-heads.'

'Just telling you,' Morgan shrugged.

'Fuck 'em. Let 'em die. That may be the last batch for a while,
anyway.'

'Say what?' Morgan said.

'We're slowing down production for now,' Titus nodded.
'Gonna make all them crystal critters crawl.'

'What the hell you talking about?' Morgan was so stunned that
he forgot about the girl, didn't even realize the tone he'd taken
with Titus. Titus noticed it, but let it slide.

'You ever hear of supply and demand? Econ 101, homeboy.'

Morgan just shook his head. He didn't know what to say.

'Look,' Titus said, 'we've been flooding the market with Tunnel
for six months to drum up business, keep the price down. We
got competition out there selling everything from crystal meth to

Drano and calling it Tunnel, but it ain't the real thing. And like they say: ain't nothing like the real thing, baby. The supply dries up, the price goes through the roof and we come back in for twice the score.'

'Yo, you don't got it straight. The network will fall apart. These are some hinky motherfuckers we dealing with.'

'They ain't going to go no place,' Titus said.

'How you know that?'

'Because you and your Blood are going to keep them all in line. If you have to make an example or two out of some uncooperative-type dudes, then that's what you do. I mean, that is what you do, isn't it?'

'This gonna rile up some serious shit,' Morgan said, shaking his head.

Titus shrugged, his lip curled in a knowing smile.

'And that's what you want?' Morgan asked.

'That's what *we* want,' Titus corrected. 'After all, we're a team. Aren't we?'

Morgan had a feeling that Titus was dissing him, but he ate it. He stole another glance at the little girl on the bed. *Was she alive?*

'Item number two on the agenda,' Titus said. 'Your little ratfuck buddy.'

'Huh?'

'The dime-dropping scumwad you brought to Bernouli's.'

'Oh,' Morgan said softly. 'Eyeball.'

'I don't give a whale's cunt what you call him. All I know is he's still alive.'

'Naw,' Morgan said, 'no way. He went down.'

'He's in the prison ward at County.'

'How you know that?' A scowl rose on Titus's features, and Morgan continued: 'Yeah. So what you want me to do?'

'What do you think?'

'I take care of it.'

'You sure you can handle it?'

Titus saw Morgan's grip tighten on the Glock, expected an explosion, but Morgan held it together. 'I say I take care of it,' Morgan said, holding his breath and staring some more at the naked girl.

'Better do it soon,' Titus said. He turned back toward the window that looked out over the factory and Morgan knew he'd been dismissed.

But he didn't go.

'Something else?' Titus asked. He didn't turn around.

'What about the cop?' Morgan said. 'And the Mac what wasted my crew.'

'That's not your problem,' Titus said coldly.

'Yo, they was my boys, you know what I'm saying? K'toma was my tight. There's justice involved here.'

Titus turned around slowly and crossed his arms over his chest. 'I said it's not. Your. Concern.'

He said it softly, but Morgan saw that the subject lit a fire inside of Titus. The urge to get up and leave was intense. He held his ground.

'They was my *boys*,' he said again.

Titus's eyes went wide and for a moment, Morgan was sure Titus would attack him. He almost brought the Glock to bear, but the moment passed. A trace of a smile played at the corner of Titus's lips and Morgan had the feeling that the white man was impressed by his bravado.

'There'll be justice,' he said. 'Count on it.'

Morgan didn't press his luck. He bolted to his feet, taking a step toward the bedroom on his way out. He craned his neck to catch a better look at the girl.

'Do you want a taste?' Titus asked. He poked the tip of his tongue out between his lips. It looked a little redder than normal.

Morgan looked over his shoulder at Titus, not sure if he was serious. He ran his gaze once more over the girl's bountiful tits, tried to detect the slightest movement of her chest, some sign that she was breathing. Her eyes were open and a bit glassy, but she could just be riding through the Tunnel.

'She alive?' he finally asked.

'What do you think?' Titus said, teasing.

Morgan honest-to-god didn't know.

THIRTY-SEVEN

'Let's go! Get up!'

Reagan opened his eyes, but the fog took a while to lift. Gradually he saw Greymarch standing over him, a revolver tucked into his waistband. It all came roaring back. Horribly. Reagan dragged himself to a sitting position and made several ugly, early-morning snorting noises.

'Oh, you'd be a charmer to wake up next to,' Greymarch said.

'You're not my type,' Reagan yawned and started to stretch, pulling back as a jolt of pain ran up his injured arm. Judy was nowhere to be seen. He cradled the arm against his chest, gently rubbing it with his good hand. He eyed the gun again, but Greymarch made no move to cover it.

'I knew a guy on the force used to carry his piece like that,' Reagan said. 'He saw Jimmy Smits do it on some TV show. Shot his balls off one day when he tripped walking down a flight of stairs. Ended up eating his gun. Closed casket. Nice flowers.'

'Your concern is noted,' Greymarch said. 'Now get up. We're moving.'

Reagan examined the dressing on his arm, poking at a spot that looked a little yellow. 'What? Where we going?'

'Out of here. Jude says you're okay to move and this place isn't secure.'

'I ain't going no place,' Reagan said and lay back down, smoothing the covers over himself.

Greymarch seemed taken aback. Reagan noted his expression with some glee until Greymarch pulled the gun out.

'You don't get a vote,' Greymarch said.

'So fucking shoot me,' Reagan said. 'I don't think you'll do it. If you were going to kill me, I'd be long since dead. You're looking for something here, but I don't know what it is. Frankly, I can't make you out. I mean, you iced those bastards the other night without blinking and then you went and saved my ass. At the very least you're accessory after the fact in the deaths of two other cops. Not to mention the half-dozen or so of those cocksuckers you wasted first-hand. Not that I'm going to miss them. Between you and your girlfriend I get some half-assed, cock-and-bull story that's got more holes than a discount whorehouse. So if you're going to shoot me, just do it. Otherwise, if you want any kind of cooperation from me, you tell me what the fuck I'm caught up in here and where the hell we're going.'

Reagan surprised himself with the force of his little spiel. Greymarch didn't move or blink and, for an instant, Reagan didn't know if he was going to shoot or not. Then he spun the gun around on one finger by the trigger guard – *I'll never be able to do that again*, Reagan thought – and returned it to his waistband. He handed Reagan a shopping bag from the Broadway. Inside was a pair of black jeans, a dark blue work shirt and some Calvin Klein underwear.

'Wow. This is better than what I usually wear,' Reagan said, examining the briefs.

'You dress,' Greymarch said. 'I'll talk.'

Greymarch helped Reagan to the bathroom. He wouldn't let him close the door, though he half-turned his back while Reagan did his business. Between grunts, Reagan briefly recounted the part of the story that Judy had told him during Greymarch's absence.

'Yeah, Bernouli's treatment worked,' Greymarch began, after the flush, 'but not the way it was supposed to. Jude could give you the medical explanation – at least as much as they've been able to figure out – but what it comes down to is that Bernouli's organelles took on a kind of life of their own.

'It became clear right away that the Tunnel was addictive, but they were so buffed when the virus got wiped that Bernouli figured they'd worry about detox afterward. When Bernouli shot me up with his new version of the shit, the others had already died and I was so weak with pneumonia I could hardly lift my ass off the bed to slide a bedpan underneath. Within a week I was practically dancing around the room.'

'Magic bullet, huh?' Reagan wheezed. He was having a hard time getting his feet into the underwear with just one hand. Greymarch allowed him the dignity of not offering to help.

'That's the way it looked. And Bernouli was so fired up about it that he went ahead and began the treatment on another group of subjects. They were all pretty far gone and he said they couldn't wait or it might not work at all.'

Reagan managed to get the shorts on and decided he needed a little breather before starting with the trousers.

'Problem was,' Greymarch continued, 'the remission from the virus didn't last. A week or so later I was on my back again. The organelle was doing some funny shit to my body. Bernouli claimed it was still looking for more virus to munch and went after other stuff when it couldn't find any. He designed the shit himself, but I don't think he really knew what he'd created.'

'Are you saying the organelle thing cured you in a week?'

'It looked that way, but they couldn't be sure. He was going to remove the organelle again as an experiment.'

'Yeah?'

'Except it turned out the organelle itself had grown inside me. It had wrapped itself around some other organs. Like a fungus on a tree, Bernouli said. And it raised these funny external growths too.' Greymarch unbuttoned his shirt and showed Reagan the now-familiar pustules on his chest. 'No way to remove it without killing me. He came up with another solution though.'

Reagan had been struggling with the jeans, which were a size too small. He looked up when Greymarch paused in his story. Greymarch was staring blankly into space, rubbing a finger over the pustules.

'What'd he do?' Reagan prompted. He sucked his gut in about as far it would go and fastened the button at his waist.

'He re-infected me with the virus.'

That gave Reagan pause. 'He what?'

'Yeah,' Greymarch nodded. 'He didn't tell me that's what he was doing until after, but he did it. He decided that the organelle needed a steady supply of the virus to work. So he pumped me full of infected blood.'

'Jesus!' Reagan whispered.

'Had nothing to do with it. But by now you must have guessed the punch line.'

Reagan took a deep breath, but couldn't let it out without undoing the pants. Greymarch was studying him quite intently now, his head cocked like a parakeet. It took Reagan a minute to get it.

'It worked,' he said.

Greymarch smiled. 'Give that a man an epiphany.'

'Jesus, Mary and Joseph,' Reagan marvelled.

'Moe, Larry and Curly is more like it,' Greymarch said. 'See, the organelle kept the virus in check, but only as long as there were viruses in the system to sustain it. As long as I was infected, I was cured. Catch-22 therapy. By the time, Bernouli figured things out, the others had already had the treatment. The organelles grew like dandelions in an open field. No way to get rid of them. But as long as the organelles are nurtured with a steady diet of virus and Tunnel, they keep us all healthy. *Very* healthy.'

'What do you mean?'

'The organelles had some unexpected side-effects. The way Jude tells it, Bernouli designed them to bolster weakened systems. They do that double-time. Greater strength and endurance. Quickness. And amazing recuperative abilities. Like a turbo-charged immune system. As long as we keep our habits fed, we're like a step up the evolutionary ladder. That's when Titus got interested.'

'How do you mean?'

'It's like I told you: Titus has a sixth sense for these things. I figure that's what interested him from the start. He monitored the programme, but he had all kinds of other scams going on. Allah knows how much money he made on drugs and pornography in Saudi. But when he saw the side-effects of Bernouli's treatment – the strength, the new immunities – he decided he wanted in. So he made Bernouli give him a dose.'

'He deliberately infected himself?' Reagan asked.

'He's a sick motherfucker. Is that news to you, lefty?'

'How many others are there?' Reagan asked.

'There were twenty-five to start with, counting me and Jude. Four died of complications right off the bat. Two more went Kevorkian. I wasted the Asian at Bernouli's place and I did another one of Titus's cronies last week.'

'The floater!' Reagan gasped.

'Huh?'

'The one you killed. Was it out by the pier in Santa Monica?'

Greymarch nodded. 'Weaselly little bastard. Used to stake out the carousel for little boys. I couldn't have it anymore.'

'Hot damn! File closed,' Reagan said.

'Trouble is, Titus has been experimenting on his own. Doling out the therapy like candy to a party of favourites. That luscious blonde lady I gutted at Bernouli's place wasn't one of the original subjects. I don't know how many others there are now. Obviously, Titus decided he didn't need Bernouli any more. Though we were still waiting for him to come up with some solution to our addictions.'

'What about the Sommers girl? At the drug lab. She had Tunnel in her system. And all kinds of other weird shit. Was she . . . one of you?'

'No. She wasn't part of the original group and if she'd gotten the treatment from Titus, he wouldn't have taken her down like that. She was just a junkie, I think. A punching board for Bernouli definitely. He's got . . . had ravenous tastes.'

'So why was she killed?'

'I don't know. You'd have to ask Titus. Just for the fun of it, most likely.'

'By Titus?'

'Yeah. Indirectly, though. I'm sure it was Blood who did her, but that's a Titus scam, too. Titus always finds the angle in things.'

'Tunnel,' Reagan said. Greymarch nodded and hauled the detective to his feet by his good arm.

'It was a gold mine waiting to be tapped. It's cheap to produce, incredibly addictive and a better high than crack. Titus took the gift horse by the mouth and yanked out all the teeth.'

'Pardon?'

'I told you: Titus has been giving the treatment to a select group of friends. Suddenly, he's the leader of this group of . . . supermen with a franchise on the next great human vice. He was already dealing crack and smack through the Blood for pocket money so he had a distribution system just waiting for product. Bernouli was so far out on the limb that he was completely under Titus's thumb. He had no choice but to cough up the formula for Tunnel. What was he? Gonna go to his masters and 'fess up about Titus? They'd have iced him on the spot.'

'But the Tunnel we found was all infected,' Reagan said. 'With . . . we never figured out what. Strange shit.'

'It wasn't at first. Titus only just came up with the idea.'

Reagan shook his head in confusion

'Don't you see that Titus is literally killing two birds with one stone? The demand for Tunnel has gone through the roof. It's serious shit, after all. And he's the only one who knows how to make the pure stuff. Especially with Bernouli out of the way. By infecting the Tunnel with some of the viruses, Titus guarantees a permanent, massive source for his . . . for *our* addiction. Jude's been working on something better here and she's great, but she's not Bernouli. But at least it's a way for us to source viruses from contaminated blood along with pure Tunnel. Titus improvised his own solution. Need a hit? Hey, grab some piece of street trash and drain him. The virus and Tunnel in one neat package, plus a hefty, tax-free profit from selling the shit to begin with. It's two, two, two treats in one.'

'God in heaven,' Reagan said. He teetered a little on his feet. Greymarch reached out to steady him, but Reagan drew away from his touch.

'Vampires,' Reagan croaked. 'You're a bunch of fucking . . . you're vampires!'

Greymarch continued to hold his hand out toward Reagan. A sadness swept across his face as he drew back his arm. He didn't look away, just offered a tiny, pained nod of his head.

'Time to go, Renfield,' he said.

THIRTY-EIGHT

'Fuck me! We're in Hollywood,' Reagan observed. He stood outside the cottage and glanced around at the twilit hills behind the mansion. The short walk from his bed to the door left Reagan winded.

'So how is it you and Titus come out on opposite ends of this thing?' Reagan asked. He paused to take a heavy draught of the cool night air.

Greymarch started to walk away, then stopped and stared into the night. 'Despite what you've seen, what you might think, I'm not an animal. Not a savage. I used to be a decent guy. I was a professional soldier and I thought I was a pretty good one. I was taught how to kill and I have killed, but it's not an act I ever took for granted. Until I met Titus.'

Reagan didn't answer.

'Titus *is* an animal,' Greymarch said. 'He revels in this new . . . condition. It's somehow enabled him to become what he always was inside. It's what he'd been waiting for, somehow. Titus has a heart like a pit, nothing but cold and black. I won't . . . can't let him draw any more down in there with him.'

Greymarch grabbed Reagan by the arm and guided him across the lawn. Reagan estimated his chances of making a break for it, discarded the notion when he found himself feeling lightheaded after only a few steps. Greymarch half-dragged him down the long gravel driveway and around to the front of the mansion. Reagan had to lean against his captor just to stay on his feet. He stopped to catch his breath, examining the small dedication plaque in front of the mansion.

'Fucking hell!' he said as he read it. 'Talk about the fox guarding the henhouse.'

'Not like you think,' Greymarch said, surveying the street in both directions.

'Uh-huh,' Reagan said. Before he could say another word, Greymarch was again pulling him toward a steel grey BMW. He leaned Reagan up against the fender and fished for his keys.

'Not stolen?' Reagan asked. 'I'm impressed.'

'I lifted the keys, too,' Greymarch smiled.

'Listen,' Reagan tried, 'before we go any further why not . . .'

A burst of automatic gunfire cut-off his words. Greymarch dropped to the ground, gun in hand, before Reagan even realized what was happening. An instant later, Greymarch roughly yanked him down as well. Reagan instinctively reached for his piece, smacking his bandaged stump against the open car door in the process. He screamed bloody murder as lightning bolts of pain raced up his arm.

Glass shards exploded above their heads and bullets ricocheted around them. Lead penetrated German steel, pinging like coins spilling from a one-armed bandit. Reagan saw a pebble-sized piece of glass tear a divot out of Greymarch's left cheek. Greymarch didn't even blink, just raised the gun up over the edge of the hood and fired blindly across the street. When the clip was spent, he expertly popped it out and slapped in a new one.

Reagan wasn't sure where the gunfire was coming from or what the hell Greymarch was shooting at. Back in the mansion he saw several pale faces staring down from second-floor windows in stunned amazement. Tears involuntarily poured from his eyes as he clutched his arm and rocked back and forth on the ground.

Greymarch took advantage of a momentary lull in the attack and crawled over Reagan and into the open passenger door. He had the key in the ignition and the car in gear before Reagan could turn around. Greymarch reached out and grabbed at Reagan's collar, roughly hauling him into the vehicle. Bits of glass littered the interior, the jagged slivers tearing Reagan's too-tight jeans. Reagan's right leg still dangled outside the car when Greymarch floored the accelerator, tearing away from the kerb with a squeal. Reagan lost some ankle skin to the asphalt and would have tumbled right back out had Greymarch not pulled him in with cobra-like reflexes.

Reagan sat on a pile of shattered glass. He clutched the console for balance and managed to drag his leg up into the car. He started to reach for the open door when a new spray of gunfire exploded around them. He ducked his head below dashboard level as bullets mulched his headrest. The car door swung shut on its own as Greymarch shifted through second and into third and took a sudden, hard right through a stop sign.

'How many?' Greymarch said, scanning back and forth between the spider-webbed windshield and the rear-view mirror. He gunned the motor harder as he headed south toward Hollywood Boulevard.

Reagan raised his head up from between his knees and warily peered back through the empty frame of the rear window. A black Lexus sedan with dark-tinted glass was gaining fast, weaving treacherously in and around the other traffic. A black hand clutching an Uzi dangled out of the passenger window. Twenty yards behind it, a big American sedan was zooming up the wrong side of the street amid screaming horns.

'Two cars, both black and moving fast. I can't see how many inside.'

Greymarch had to brake as they came up on a red light at the corner of Franklin. A steady stream of traffic came at them across the yellow line. He glanced into the rear-view.

'They ain't stopping,' Reagan prompted.

Greymarch didn't need it. He gunned the engine and cut the wheel to the right, clipping the fender of a parked car as he climbed up the kerb and onto the sidewalk with a nasty scrape of the undercarriage. L.A. being L.A., there were no pedestrians around, but it was a tight squeeze between the glass storefronts on the right and the kerbside row of parking meters and signs.

At the corner, Greymarch cut right onto Franklin then left, bouncing the car back off the kerb and into traffic. He sideswiped an old pick-up truck full of Mexican labourers, sending a kid in a Lakers sweatshirt flying off the flatbed and under the wheels of an oncoming semi. Reagan winced at the retreating sounds of peeling rubber, crumpled steel and screams.

'Goddammit,' he yelled.

'Ought to slow 'em down,' Greymarch said, one eye on the mirror.

'Nope,' Reagan said, 'here they come.'

Traffic had massed back around the accident, so the two black cars followed Greymarch's lead and rode up the sidewalks on either side to get around the snarl. Reagan saw the Lexus clip a bystander who'd wandered out a doorway, but they were too far away for Reagan to learn the poor bastard's fate.

The chase cars pulled up nose-to-nose fifty yards behind the BMW. Reagan heard the distant staccato pulse of Uzi-fire, but none of the bullets came anywhere close. As they approached another busy traffic intersection at the corner of Franklin and Highland, Greymarch cut the wheel and zipped across the road, making for a gas station on the corner. He bowled right through a series of standing signs advertising Big Gulps and hot dogs. He swerved around the narrow pump islands, hardly slowing at all. Reagan followed the progress of the black cars behind them when Greymarch yelled: '*FUCK!*'

Reagan spun around as Greymarch twitched the wheel to the left, but it was too late. Looming fast was a fat black woman in a white nurse's uniform pushing an old man in a wheelchair. Reagan saw her eyes widen at the sight of the approaching car and then the right front fender caught her across the back of the thighs, launching her into the air. Greymarch briefly lost control of the wheel and jammed on the brakes as the car spun out in a full 360 degrees. Reagan lost sight of the nurse and scanned around for her, like an outfielder looking for a pop-up in a high sky. He didn't spot her until she landed with a boom, smack in the middle of the hood, spraying the remains of the windshield with a fine red mist before rolling off to the right and into the street.

'Fuuuuck!!' Reagan gasped, but Greymarch didn't miss a beat. He up-shifted and punched the wiper-washer button in one smooth motion. There was no washer fluid, though, so the wipers only smeared the woman's blood across the webbed glass.

Greymarch cursed to himself. Behind them, the two black cars zoomed through the gas station in hot pursuit. They bounced over the sidewalk, one after the other, passing within inches on either side of the man in the wheelchair. The man's head darted right then left at the passing cars, then straight up toward heaven as the backdraft tousled his grey hair and tore the thin, wool blanket off his useless legs.

'Still coming,' Reagan said.

'Kick it!' Greymarch yelled. He had to crane his head out the side window to see the street in front of them.

'What?'

'The windshield! Kick it out. I can't see for shit.'

Reagan tried to lift his legs up over the dash, but there wasn't enough room. He frantically clawed under the seat for the release. He thought he had it, but came away with an ice scraper – *who* the *fuck* keeps an ice scraper in Los Angeles?, he couldn't help but think – and tossed it out the window. He reached down again and found the handle that allowed him to push the seat back.

Greymarch swerved back and forth like a drunkard, intermittently side-swiping parked cars. Reagan hauled his legs up over the dashboard and scrunched down in the seat to get as much leverage as possible. He launched a two-footed kick at the centre of the window that extended the cracks, but didn't pry loose the sheet of glass. The impact sent spasms of pain through his injured ankle. He drew his legs back to ready another kick, when a hail of bullets exploded in through the missing rear window shattering the front windshield for him. It went flying off into the air.

'*That's* fucking service!' Greymarch shrieked and ratcheted up the speed.

Greymarch took another sudden hard left, bounced off a Federal Express truck and fishtailed before righting himself off a parked Honda. More horns blared behind them, but their pursuers found a way through and started shooting again.

'Glove compartment,' Greymarch said, taking a sharp right.

Reagan popped open the tiny door and pulled out a Browning .22. He considered turning it on his captor, but didn't see the point.

'What am I supposed to do with this?' he asked.

'How about shoot back?' Greymarch said. He glanced over at Reagan, accidently riding up the edge of a traffic island in the process.

'At what? Pigeons? This thing isn't any good beyond ten yards. And I'm . . . I was a righty.'

'What have you got to lose?'

Reagan shrugged. The Lexus was leading the chase, half a block back. No one inside was firing at them just then. Reagan turned around and knelt in the front seat, resting his left arm against the ruins of the headrest, bracing it with his right stump. He aimed low, hoping to catch the radiator or a tyre and jerked off three quick shots. Two of them went straight through the roof of the BMW.

'I take it back,' Greymarch said. More traffic loomed ahead, so he cut left, into an alley, losing the wing mirror to a brick wall in the process. They were nearly through the narrow lane when the nose of the Lexus appeared at the far end. Reagan hopelessly squeezed off three more shots, succeeding only in hitting the mirror, which was subsequently crunched beneath the Lexus's tires.

'Damn! Who are these guys?' Reagan said.

'Blood,' Greymarch replied.

Greymarch turned right again as they came out of the alley. He slammed on the brakes without warning, sending Reagan flying backward, halfway out of the car through the lost windshield. Greymarch was instantly out of the car, gun in hand. He took up the classic shooter's stance, facing the mouth of the alley. Reagan's groans were drowned out by the rising roar of the approaching pursuer. He scrambled out of the car.

Greymarch started firing as soon the front end of the Lexus nosed out of the alley. His first shot went wide right, but the next flurry were clustered in a tight circle on the tinted windshield around the driver's head. The driver had started turning right, toward the parked BMW, but Greymarch's aim was true, because the Lexus suddenly swerved wildly out into the middle of the street.

The shotgun passenger must have grabbed for the wheel, because the Lexus jerkily straightened out. He might even have brought the car under control had the garbage truck not come along at just that moment. The truck driver tried to get out of the way, but he caught the Lexus smack in the middle of the driver's side and the car went hurtling down the street, rolling on its lengthwise axis. The garbage truck, in turn, teetered onto its side, coming to a stop only after tearing through two parked cars and bursting through the plate glass window of a discount appliance store.

Reagan counted five complete rolls before the Lexus came to a stop on its crushed roof. A series of lesser crashes took place on the street behind it as drivers frantically tried to avoid the Lexus or stopped to gawk. Greymarch was quickly back in the driver's seat, putting the BMW into motion.

'Man,' Reagan said, 'I thought only Mel Gibson did stuff like that.'

'Didn't explode, though,' Greymarch said, speeding off in the opposite direction. 'They always explode in the movies.'

'Yeah,' Reagan said.

And then it came. But not from behind.

The other chase car – an old Buick LeSabre, Reagan saw – was suddenly in front of them. Automatic fire tore off their hood and set the engine ablaze. Reagan watched as a hunk of sizzling steel flew out of the flaming engine compartment, catching Greymarch in the middle of the chest. Greymarch screamed as his shirt caught fire and he let go of the wheel as he tried to bat it out.

The BMW was slowing, but it hit the Buick at a deadly thirty miles per hour.

Reagan had a micro-second to enjoy the sensation of unaided human flight as he again went out through the windshield.

He'd never remember the landing.

THIRTY-NINE

Breathing was his first mistake.

The pain was revelatory; a series of burning, raw razor slashes down his chest that exploded into agonizing life with every movement.

Not that he was going anyplace.

He guessed he had some broken ribs. A lung might have been punctured as well and though he yearned, almost to the point of panic, to draw a deep breath, he forced himself to inhale and exhale in a slow, shallow pattern.

He lay on a dank cement floor amid stacks of crushed cardboard boxes. His bad ankle had been cuffed to an immense cast iron radiator. The cold steel edge of the manacle bit into his bruised skin, adding a soupçon of further discomfort to his misery. His arms were free, but there was nothing within reach. He half-heartedly tugged at the cuffs for the hell of it, but they were solid. The dressing on his stump had come loose and the exposed sutures oozed trails of watery pus down his forearm.

The pile of boxes obstructed his view, but he was evidently in an old factory or warehouse. A conspicuously unhappy-looking black youth with an unlit cigarette dangling from his lip leaned against one of the columns of boxes and stared down at Reagan. His red bandanna marked him as Blood and he stiffly clutched a battered assault rifle in his hands. He tucked the cigarette behind his ear before sauntering off.

Reagan winced his way to a sitting position, propping himself against the radiator. An acid, chemical smell wafted through the air and he could hear activity on the other side of the boxes. It sounded like a forklift was moving back and forth across the floor. He glanced up at the exhaust pipes and lines of fluorescent tubing in the high ceiling, noting also a criss-cross pattern of narrow catwalks. He thought he spotted a couple of guards perched up on the metal mesh walks, but it was too dark to be sure.

Reagan felt a tickle in his throat and tried to ignore it, but the harder he tried not to think about it, the more the desire to cough built up. He did everything he could to suppress it, gritting his teeth and forcing himself to take tiny swallows. It finally came out as little more than a heavy wheeze, but the pain it ignited in his chest was more than enough to bring tears to his closed eyes.

When he opened them, Titus and Morgan were looking down at him. Titus flashed a broad grin, but the gang leader looked pissed. Several armed Blood shifted nervously in a half circle behind them.

'Hey!' Titus said. He grabbed his crotch. 'It's my mystery date.'

Reagan groaned.

'What you want to do?' Morgan asked.

'I want to fuck him,' Titus said. 'And then I want to fuck him up. Let's go.'

Morgan tossed a key at one of the Blood, who unlocked the cuffs and dragged Reagan to his feet. The Blood made a face when he had to touch the pus on Reagan's infected arm and he wiped his hand on the back of Reagan's shirt. Reagan screamed as the kid yanked him up off the floor.

It only made the pain in his chest that much worse.

Reagan didn't remember it, but he must have blacked out briefly, because when he opened his eyes again they were out of the cul-de-sac formed by the boxes and walking across the middle of the warehouse with Titus in the lead.

Reagan found it hard to think about anything other than the agony in his ribs, but got the sense that the warehouse served as some sort of laboratory operation. A dozen or more Blood, all armed, were clustered on mattresses and old couches haphazardly arranged on one side of the building. The other half of the warehouse was neatly partitioned, though, and the chemical smell much more distinct. Reagan caught sight of a couple of Asian men in white lab coats, who quickly darted out of sight as the procession moved past. Visions of Tunnel danced through the back of Reagan's groggy head, but wouldn't quite cohere.

Reagan stumbled over a tangle of cables taped down to the floor. The Blood who half-dragged/half-carried him jerked him painfully back to his feet, but lost his grip on Reagan's sweaty shirt. The detective tumbled sideways to the hard floor, screaming again as he made rough contact.

Titus stopped and turned around, shaking his head and placing his hands on his hips disapprovingly. The Blood soldier reached down to grab Reagan below the left armpit, but Reagan shook him off and pulled himself to his hand and knees. He paused a moment to gather his strength, determined to ignore the pain and stand up on his own. He made it to a quasi-sitting position when the body dangling above Titus's head caught his eye. He couldn't make out the face, at first, but then he recognized the remains of the figure's clothing.

Greymarch hung face down, his body roughly parallel to the ground. He'd been suspended from two metal grappling hooks attached to thick steel cables leading to a small crane in the rafters. One hook was imbedded in Greymarch's back, directly between the shoulder blades. The other had been impaled in his rectum. His legs dangled and his arms were splayed in front of him; he looked like a bargain basement superhero flying drunk.

Greymarch's thick, diseased blood oozed down his right leg, collecting in fist-sized globules at the end of his toes. Every few seconds another drop surrendered to gravity and splattered on the floor below. More blood slopped out of a gaping wound in his belly and a half-foot or more of wormy intestine poked out of the gash like the beak of a nestling emerging from its egg.

Greymarch's face looked like it had been soundly beaten with a steel mallet. A wad of flattened red putty in the centre now passed for his nose. His eyes were swollen shut, the skin purple and black, and the right ear – presumably the left, as well, but Reagan couldn't see – was missing. Greymarch's tongue lolled from his open, bloody lips and to the extent that Reagan could tell in the murky light, many of his teeth appeared to have been knocked out.

His only movement came from a gentle swaying of the lengthy cables. Reagan couldn't tell if he was alive.

He prayed Greymarch was already dead.

'And we have some lovely parting gifts for you, too,' Titus said. A few of the Blood laughed nervously, but Morgan's expression didn't change.

Reagan whimpered.

*   *   *

Titus sat on Reagan's chest, squeezing the cop's nostrils between his thumb and forefinger. Reagan's arms were pinned beneath him, trapped by the big man's muscular thighs.

'What do you think about power?' Titus asked.

Reagan tried to toss the big man off him with a buck of his hips, but Titus merely struck him again on the side of the head with his fist. Reagan saw stars.

Titus pressed his palm down over Reagan's open mouth, cutting off his air. Reagan tried again to shrug Titus off, but he couldn't budge him an inch. Pins of darkness dotted his vision. He tried to bite Titus's hand, but the grip was too tight. The blackness had just about overtaken him when Titus relaxed his grip.

Reagan gasped for air. Titus leaned back, scratched the dark stubble on his neck. For perhaps the hundredth time since his ordeal had begun, Reagan scanned the room for a weapon, a tool, *anything* he might use to fight back. There was only Titus's gun, resting on the desk across the room.

It might just as well have been a thousand miles away.

'I like it,' Titus said. He leaned forward and pressed his hand over Reagan's mouth again. The more Reagan struggled, the harder Titus squeezed. Reagan felt little electric shocks exploding in his head and racing up and down his spine and wondered if he was experiencing a series of strokes. He gave up the fight and Titus again loosened his hold.

'Power, I mean,' Titus said. 'It's totally awesome.'

Reagan sucked in air as hard as he could. The pain in his ribs was exquisite, but his mind just shouted: *breathe, breathe!*

'You must get off on it, too, or you wouldn't be a cop. Especially in this town. Most people don't really understand power, though. I find that. Do you?'

Titus reached down to deliver a not-so-playful squeeze to Reagan's testicles. Reagan squirmed again, gritting his teeth. He fastened on Titus's eyes. Titus looked at him very intently, though with no discernible emotion. Reagan shot back waves of white-hot loathing.

'I think you do,' Titus said. He broke out in a smile and stood up. Reagan shrugged his arms out from under his body. The circulation had been so effectively cut off that they felt like two floppy sacks attached to his shoulder. He tried to shake them, forcing the blood to flow with pins-and-needles fury. He reached down to massage his sore testicles with his good hand.

'What the fuck do you want from me?' Reagan spat.

Titus dropped back to his knees and snaked his arm toward Reagan's crotch, covering Reagan's hand with his own. Reagan tried to cup himself, but Titus squeezed harder, using Reagan's fingers to crush his own testicles. Reagan resisted with all he had, but it wasn't much and not nearly enough. Titus forced Reagan to slowly cram his balls up into his body. Reagan shuddered with resistance. An inchoate sound formed in his throat, growing in volume and pitch as Titus effortlessly increased the pressure.

Then he just let go.

'I want you to know what power is. I want to make you totally understand.'

'I think I get it,' Reagan squeaked.

'No,' Titus said, 'you don't. I know your type. I've seen them, listened to them, *killed* them all my life. You think power comes from a gun or a badge or . . . a vote.' Titus sniggered.

'But do you know where power really comes from? It rises from fear. And fear comes from pain. That's what I've learned. I've been there, felt it myself. I've been raised up by it, like some old time martyr. It's a spiritual thing, pain. It can be purifying. Pain and fear. They go together like love and marriage.'

Titus stood up again and walked over to the window that looked out on the warehouse floor. He casually turned his back on Reagan, but the cop could barely move, much less contemplate an assault.

'The nice thing about fear – and pain – is that there's so damn much of it. It's everywhere you look. Like oxygen or water. And if ever there's not enough, well, don't worry, we'll make more!'

'Is that what the Blood are for,' Reagan choked. 'Carthay?'

Titus shrugged. 'They're like your hand there. I squeeze them and they squeeze balls. If that hand gets to be a problem, hell, I'll just tear it off and throw it away. Turns out that's sort of fun.'

'And Bernouli?' Reagan said.

'Another hand job.'

'And all this pain. And fear. What's . . . what's the fucking point?'

'The point?'

Titus turned around. He looked genuinely surprised. Then he grinned.

'It's just for the bloody hell of it,' he said and laughed.

Titus walked back over to Reagan. The cop covered his groin, but Titus made no move toward it. Instead, he began to strip off his clothes. Reagan watched as Titus threw off his shirt and pants and stepped out of his briefs. The circle of pustules ringing his crotch were red and erect. Like his cock.

'Let's see if we can't teach you a little something about fear,' Titus said.

Reagan tried to get up and launch himself at Titus, but he moved like a fly in aspic. Titus sent him sprawling back to the floor with a single kick to the head.

'I'm gonna fuck you,' Titus said, straddling Reagan. 'Then I'm gonna suck you dry and eat you.'

FORTY

Though the prison ward was as quiet as the morgue at night, Arsenio couldn't sleep. He'd recovered sufficiently that his passive restraints had been replaced with metal cuffs. His ankle was manacled to the iron bed frame, which was itself bolted to the floor. Though the inner rim of the cuff was lined with a rubber pad, it was still annoying and uncomfortable. He normally liked to sleep on his stomach, but the way the cuff was threaded through the frame forced him to lie on his back.

They'd had him up and walking around several times during the day and he had to admit that he felt surprisingly well. His chest and arm both itched and he still had a little trouble taking deep breaths, but all things considered he couldn't complain. By afternoon, he'd even made it into the bathroom on his own – he was mortified by having to crap in the bedpan – and it was there that his spirits started to fall again. One of the other inmates – a one-eyed Crip bodybuilder called Motor Mother, big as a house and meaner than acid – taunted him about a reward that the Blood had reportedly placed on Arsenio's head. Arsenio didn't know how the Crip could have obtained the information, but he couldn't doubt the likelihood that it was true. He was afraid that Motor Mother was going to move on him then and there, but a guard came in and headed off any possible confrontation. It seemed to Arsenio that the guard also eyed him like a prime cut of meat, but at least he didn't threaten him.

Though all the prisoners were manacled for the night, Arsenio was too plain scared to go to sleep. He'd heard stories over the years, from his older brother and other gangbangers, about how easy it was to ice anyone in stir. He figured he was probably safe enough in the hospital ward, but even then he wasn't *that* sure. The guards got pretty lackadaisical at night, sometimes sneaking off for a drink or a joint or a stand-up quickie with a nurse – at least that's what they *said* when the nurses weren't around.

And he knew from what the doctors told him and given how well he felt, that he'd be moved out of the hospital and into a regular prison ward in a couple of days at most. He reckoned that represented his current life expectancy.

What he thought about most, as he lay there in the semi-dark, stewing in his fear, was Diane. Everything had gotten so crazy, so out of hand so fast, that he had almost lost sight of how he'd been drawn into this mess to begin with. His intention had been to avenge her murder – it seemed a pretty ludicrous quest given his current situation – but despite himself he got caught up in the whirlwind lifestyle of the Blood. He was loathe to admit it, but there was an excitement to it, a visceral sexiness and thrill that he'd never had a taste of before.

He'd never had any interest in the gangs, hadn't even *thought* of them in terms like 'sexy' or 'exciting', though almost everyone he knew – from his dead brother on down to his supposedly sainted but equally deceased sister – was involved with them one way or another. Because of his brother's fate, his Nana had been adamant that Arsenio avoid any hint of involvement. Her firm hand had served him well through his childhood and adolescence in South-Central. At least, up till now.

And her reward, he tortured himself, was a broken heart and soon, no doubt, another dead grandchild.

Arsenio felt tears form in his eyes as he considered what he had wrought. The sorrow turned to anger as he thought about Morgan and he refused to accept the responsibility for all that had occurred. He was, he knew, just a prop for the big boys. Like his brother had been long ago. And like Diane. Used by the Morgans of the world and his white master. And by cops like Reagan, who dealt people like Arsenio as if they were playing cards. Well, he supposed, the cop had got his. Folded his hand, as it were.

Arsenio couldn't quite remember what became of Reagan in the final mêlée at Bernouli's place. He assumed that the cop must have been killed in that massive volley of gunfire that took out the Blood. Arsenio wanted to be able to laugh about the cop, but he had grudgingly started to feel a bit of warmth toward

Reagan. It was stupid, god knows, but he couldn't deny that it was true.

The sound of a key in the locked ward door caught Arsenio's attention. The only other sounds were a few throaty snores and the odd nightmare fart. He felt something tighten in his gut when he saw the guard at the end of the ward go out, pulling a pack of cigarettes out of his breast pocket. The guard slipped outside without relocking the door behind him.

Arsenio studiously scanned the ward and held his breath, wary of signs of movement. He practically jumped at the sound of a clinking chain, exhaled sharply seeing it was only another manacled patient tossing in his sleep.

He felt a surge of relief when he heard the ward door open. The relief faded fast when he saw that it wasn't the guard coming back in. Arsenio's fear mounted as the figure strode down the aisle toward him through the ward. It was a woman in hospital greens and he relaxed again. He hadn't seen her before, but her confident, comfortable swagger and the stethoscope draped around her neck like a feather boa made her out a doctor. The residents didn't normally visit until the morning, especially with the guard away, but several new inmates had come in that afternoon and perhaps one of them required special treatment.

Arsenio half-closed his eyes to feign sleep in case the doctor looked his way. His was the next-to-last bed. As the doctor glided past the other beds, his sense of menace again started to rise. It seemed to him that the doctor was heading straight toward him, looking right at him. And he saw now that she carried a small bag in her left hand. He wanted to close his eyes and pretend to be asleep, but as she drew closer he found his eyes widening as the unease in his belly grew to full-blown terror.

The doctor – he prayed she *was* a doctor – stopped at the foot of his bed and briefly lifted the attached chart. She looked up at Arsenio and didn't seem the slightest bit surprised that he was wide awake. Despite his dread, Arsenio couldn't help but observe how pretty she was. Her eyes seemed to glisten, even in the ward's semi-darkness, and her lips looked like they tasted of honey. To Arsenio, she looked like one of those TV women JuJu and Lutece always jived about fucking, because they knew no way in the world that they ever would.

She reached into the bag as she came around the side of the bed and Arsenio got ready to scream. He knew the kind of connections that Morgan had, and had no doubt but that he could find a doctor to do his killing for him. Hell, what could be neater than a little lethal injection right there in the hospital. It wasn't like there'd be any major probe into the death of a cop-killing gangbanger.

The doctor came closer until Arsenio could read her name off a dangling County-USC ID badge: Ewing, Judy. As her hand – she had tiny fingers, Arsenio noticed – emerged from the bag, Arsenio inhaled, all set to yell bloody murder if she brought out a needle or a gun. But she pulled out a keyring. Arsenio's fear turned to puzzlement. He was about to say something when she laid a soft, tiny finger across his open lips to silence him. She then pressed it to her own lips.

Arsenio was confused as hell, but he didn't say anything as she sat on the bed and leaned over him to unlock the ankle cuff. The little metallic click as the cuffs snapped open seemed to echo like a gunshot through the ward. Arsenio scanned the rows of beds, but no one stirred.

The doctor reached back into her bag. Arsenio half-expected her to pull out a needle. Instead she tossed orderly's blues on the bed and indicated with a gesture that he should put them on. He hesitated for a moment and watched her watch him. He decided finally that, whatever the hell was going on, his best bet was to trust her.

He stood up, but had trouble removing the hospital johnny with his arm in the cast. The doctor shook her head and glanced toward the far doors before helping him to shrug it off.

Although it was fairly dark and the situation anything but romantic, Arsenio blushed slightly standing naked before this beautiful woman. His exposure didn't appear to register with her at all. In fact, she was looking toward the ward doors even as she held the loose pants out for him to step into. He managed to pull them up on his own, but needed more help getting the top on over his arm. He sat back down on the bed, feeling slightly winded, as she handed him the soft hospital slippers. He stopped to rub the raw skin around his cuffed ankle, but she silently snapped her fingers at him to hurry him along. No sooner was he on his feet she pulled him to her to escort him back across the ward.

She held him tightly as they made their way quickly toward the exit. The wound in Arsenio's chest tightened up and started to throb, but he was suitably distracted from it by his fear.

They'd made it all the way to the exit before Judy drew to a halt. She hesitated at the double doors and, to Arsenio's mixed horror and delight, pulled a fairly righteous-looking handgun out of her bag. She flicked off the safety before pressing one of the doors open a couple of inches and peering down the hall. She quickly drew the door closed again, dragging Arsenio off to one side, and held the gun up beside her cheek. Arsenio could feel her heart pounding against his arm as clacking footsteps grew louder outside the door. They simultaneously drew deep breaths as the footsteps sounded just outside the ward and passed right on.

Judy pressed her ear to the door and nodded to herself when the echo faded completely. She again inched open one of the doors and peered down the hall. Then she opened the other to glance down the corridor in the opposite direction.

As she completed her surveillance, Arsenio happened to look back to the ward. He inhaled sharply when he saw Motor Mother, in a nearby bed, glaring back at him. Motor Mother smiled; not a pretty thing. He didn't wear his eye patch at night and the scarred hole in his face gaped like a puckered, displaced asshole.

Arsenio couldn't breathe or move, even to tug a warning signal on his saviour's sleeve.

Motor Mother sat up, clinking his ankle cuff against the metal bed frame in the process. He leaned forward and ran his dark tongue over fat, coffee-coloured lips.

Arsenio thought he was going to pee in his pants.

Motor Mother flashed Arsenio a thumb's up and somehow winked with his missing eye. Then he lay back down, turning his back to Arsenio and the woman.

Judy jerked Arsenio out of the ward and rushed him down the empty hallway. They heard a metal tray clatter behind them and moved a little faster into the nearest stairwell. As they bolted down the stairs, Arsenio's chest started to hurt in earnest, but somehow it didn't really bother him.

He wondered if Motor Mother thought Arsenio was being led to his freedom or to his doom.

He wondered himself which it might be.

He wondered a lot about human nature.

FORTY-ONE

The explosion caught them both by surprise.

Staggered bursts of automatic weapons fire came from the warehouse floor. Screams and shouts in English and Spanish echoed from all corners of the building. A second explosion went off, shaking the floor of the loft and sending Titus sprawling from on top of the prone Reagan. Another explosion followed almost immediately, bathing the room in orange light. Titus sprang to his feet and ran to the window. He thrust his head out then quickly ducked back in as a spray of bullets traced him into the loft.

Reagan rolled as far from the window as he could, curling himself into a tight ball as lead chunked into the wall above him. He chanced a look up and saw Titus back at the window, gun in hand, firing up at one of the catwalks. Titus held his ground as answering fire came back toward the loft, taking a hit in the left shoulder.

It didn't faze him at all.

Titus emptied the gun at a spot on the catwalk and a body tumbled down from the metal walkway, arms windmilling in a futile attempt at flight. The soon-to-be-dead assailant went by quickly, but Reagan could see that it was a young Latino. He guessed that the Blood were under attack from another gang. Sagrados, probably, avenging the Blood attack on their meth lab.

Titus tossed the handgun aside and ran to a narrow steel cabinet. Two heavy padlocks secured a thick metal bar across the doors. Reagan saw Titus reach toward his pocket, then register that he wasn't wearing any pants. Thick blood, the colour of Mississippi mud, oozed from the gunshot wound in his shoulder. Titus grabbed the ends of the thick bar and growled. The muscles in his back tensed as he set his legs like a weight lifter and pulled on the bar. More dark blood spurted out of the wound as Titus shuddered with effort, but he was rewarded a few seconds later when the hinges holding the bar in place snapped loose and the doors flew open.

Inside were two mean looking pieces of firepower: a Calico Carbine and a Vietnam-era grenade launcher. Titus slung the grenade launcher onto his naked back and fastened an ammo belt studded with film-canister sized charges around his waist. He held the carbine in the crook of his right arm and slapped a 100-shot magazine into place. He awkwardly tucked a second magazine into the ammo belt.

Titus peered back toward the window then dashed around toward the hall that led to the stairs. He turned and pointed the barrel of the Carbine at a spot in the middle of the detective's face and Reagan knew that the end had come. He decided to face it bravely.

'Fuck you, you bloodsucking sack of shit,' he said to Titus.

He heard the shots.

Except they came through the window and tore up the floor at Titus's feet. Titus leapt back and tried to train the rifle toward the window, but the onslaught was relentless. Several bullets ricocheted around Reagan and he flattened himself and scooted under a desk for protection. The assault halted for a moment and from under the desk, Reagan saw Titus's bare feet come back toward him only to retreat again when a fresh stream of bullets poured in through the window from a slightly different direction. Two snipers sat up in the rafters; they had Titus pinned down. The other half of the loft was out of their range, so Reagan scurried out from under the desk, still hugging the floor, and headed for the far corner.

Titus was stuck at the far side of the loft. Through the doorway, the two men locked eyes. Titus tried to crawl back into the bedroom far enough to swing the carbine's barrel around at Reagan, but every time he tried he was routed by another burst from the catwalks. Reagan silently cheered the snipers and prayed that they were well-stocked with ammo. The stand-off went on for several more minutes. Shrieks and screams and machine gun fire sounded all over the warehouse and rising plumes of smoke rose up toward the roof.

Finally, with an angry yell, Titus gave up on Reagan and headed for the stairs that led to the warehouse floor. Reagan heard a spray of bullets follow him and then Titus returning the fire. A Spanish curse was yelled from the roof and another sniper went hurtling past to the floor below.

Reagan scrambled to his feet, keeping low, and assessed the situation. He was weak, hurt and unarmed and in the middle of a major gun battle. Titus would surely return at the first opportunity to tear Reagan several new assholes and then he'd probably fuck him in each and every one. There was no way he could follow Titus toward any exit downstairs. He'd be a lumbering target, subject to attack from all sides.

He looked around the loft again. The smell of burning chemicals grew thicker in the air. Several fires must have started downstairs and the temperature was rising.

Reagan felt panic begin to stir when he spotted Titus's discarded Browning on the floor. He dropped down to all fours – threes really, without his hand – and crawled over to it. As he suspected, the clip was spent, but somehow just holding the piece helped to keep panic at bay. He pressed the cool metal to his sweaty brow and listened as the battle raged below. He rolled onto his back and took another look around.

It was just sitting there. On the floor.

A full 9 mm clip.

The clip didn't fit the Browning, but the bullets sure as hell would. He quickly thumbed them out and popped them one by one into the empty Browning clip, slapping it into the pistol grip. He chambered a round into the breach.

'Fucking-A!' he said.

For the first time in a long time, Reagan felt like he had some mastery over his fate. He only had the twelve bullets, true, and if it came down to it he would have to shoot with his left hand, which was like cutting diamonds with a meat axe, but he still felt a whole lot better than he had only moments before, staring at oblivion down the barrel of Titus's carbine.

Reagan cautiously peered around the corner of the window. A fresh spray of bullets sent him diving back to the floor. The brief glimpse afforded a view of a war scene. Though the smoke grew denser, he saw half a dozen bodies sprawled on the floor below and one or two hanging from the catwalks. He thought he saw the hooks from which Greymarch had been hanging, but there was no sign of the body. He noticed something pale and fast dart across the floor toward the loading dock and guessed that it was Titus. The guess was confirmed by a grenade explosion that sent a shudder through the walls of the building.

The concussion toppled the steel cabinet where Titus had kept his heavy artillery, nearly crushing Reagan's good ankle. Another explosion from below caught Reagan's attention. It wasn't until he turned back around that he noticed the door that the cabinet had concealed.

Reagan scrambled to it on his knees, shoving the cabinet out of the way. He stood up and leaned on the door. It was deadbolted shut. He tried to slip the bolt, but it had rusted through and wouldn't budge. He looked around for something to pry at it with, found the steel bar that Titus had torn off the front of the cabinet. He tucked the Browning into his waist – remembering his own warning to Greymarch about such behaviour – and wedged the end of the bar between the bolt and the door. The action was awkward with his left hand and the bar slipped out twice before he managed to jam it in.

The noise level from below had abated, but the smoke grew thicker inside the loft. The metal walls of the warehouse glowed orange and red. Reagan feared that Titus would return at any moment. Using his left hand and the stump of his right arm he pushed down on the lever for all he was worth, grunting with effort and sweating profusely from the combined exertion and building heat.

The old bolt snapped off the frame and the door opened inward. His momentum sent him tripping over the threshold.

He tumbled to the floor of a dark and musty storeroom. He pulled the Browning out of his pants as smoothly as he could, which meant he only dropped it once. It was hot here, too, but the air wasn't near so foul as in the loft. He took a deep breath even as the first tendrils of white smoke filtered in from below.

The room was dark and he couldn't find a light switch, but the flames from the warehouse were bright enough to cast a glow even in here. Reagan forced himself to his feet, panting for breath. He hurt *everywhere*. He might have just given up and said the hell with it all, but the only thing worse than his fear of Titus was the fear of burning alive.

His first look around the room filled him with despair; it looked like nothing more than a forgotten storage area heaped with rodent-gnawed boxes and a few odd pieces of junky office furniture. He stared out into the smoke in the loft and started to contemplate the necessity of following Titus's path down the stairs and through the burning warehouse.

Then he saw the second door.

It was a large steel affair, half-hidden behind an upended desk. He didn't know where it might lead, but it had to be better than where he was. Reagan dashed over to it, pushing the desk over and out of the way. He cautiously touched a finger to the metal and breathed a sigh of relief that it felt cool. Though he could hear the crackle of fire in the loft outside and feel the intensity of the heat, it was still dark enough by the door that he had to bob and weave to get a good look at the lock.

A key-operated deadbolt was set chest-high above a horizontal release mechanism. Reagan pressed at the release, wasn't surprised when the door didn't budge. He took a step back and threw himself at the door, leading with his left shoulder.

He bounced off with nothing but a fresh ache to show for the effort.

The store room grew brighter as fire took hold of the bedroom. It was hard for Reagan to breathe even in here and he started to choke.

Part of the loft collapsed to the warehouse floor. If gunfire was still being exchanged out there, Reagan couldn't hear it above the noise of the fire.

Reagan stood, staring at the locked door. A tongue of flame licked the doorway behind him and the floor sagged slightly under his feet

He took a step to his left and levelled the Browning at the deadbolt. His hand shook, but he steadied it in the crook of his right arm. He took a deep breath and squeezed the trigger.

The bullet dented the metal half an inch to the left of the deadbolt, ricocheted off the door frame with a sound like a tin bell and whizzed past Reagan's right ear.

'Fuck!' he yelled.

He took another step to the left, aimed a little harder and squeezed off two quick shots, the first was high, but the second hit the lock dead centre, blowing it right on out the door. Through the hole where the lock sat, Reagan could see street lights.

He pressed the release lever on the door. It wobbled, but it still wouldn't open. He leaned over and eyed the lock, saw that the bolt protruded out of the door and into the jamb. He stepped back and fired twice more at the bolt. The heat from the fire now singed the hairs on the back of his neck.

Reagan smacked the lever again and, at last, the door squeaked open. He was greeted by a draught of fresh, night air that got sucked into the building, fuelling the flames behind him. He felt the heat licking at his back and dashed through the doorway onto a narrow metal balcony. The balcony had no railing and he almost tumbled over the side to the ground, thirty feet below.

With the flames crawling toward him across the storeroom, Reagan slammed the steel door shut behind him. The fire seemed to scream defiance. He leaned back against the door, but it quickly grew so hot that he had to step away.

He saw that the balcony must once have been part of a fire escape that had gone to seed. A metal ladder led down from the edge, but didn't connect to anything. Reagan saw where a second landing had once been attached to the wall down below, but all that remained of it was a few old bolts and some lines of rust on the wall.

Smoke spewed out the door through the missing lock and along the cracks. Through the tiny hole, he could see that the flames were eating up the storeroom. The metal walls of the warehouse sweated heat.

Reagan heard something crash inside, guessed it was the floor of the storeroom. He felt the balcony shiver along with the building.

He heard sirens now in the distance, saw the lights go out at a Golden Arches on Jefferson Boulevard.

He looked down at the earth below, saw what looked like some scrubby shrubs.

Reagan tucked the gun back in his waist, the metal warm against his belly. He stepped over the edge of the balcony, lowering himself down the shaky metal ladder. Even the rungs were starting to get hot. The door to the balcony he'd just quit blew open and flames exploded out through the open passage above him.

He went down step by step, till there was nowhere for him to go. He crouched on the lowest rung and grabbed onto the one above it with his left hand. He slipped his feet off the ladder and allowed himself to dangle, still a good fifteen feet off the ground.

His arm tremored with the effort of supporting his weight. He twisted in the slight breeze and felt the building shake again. The rung got *very* hot.

Reagan let go.

FORTY-TWO

'Jesus Christ!' Judy whispered.

'And I've got the stigmata to prove it,' Reagan said.

Judy grabbed his arm to help him into the Semper Fi mansion, but Reagan roughly shook her off. No more relying on anyone, he decided, no more taking orders. From here on out he did everything on his own, in his own way and to hell with the consequences. He was through being L.A.'s punching bag.

He limped in, bracing himself with a makeshift crutch fashioned from a length of rusted pole he'd salvaged from a dumpster. The Browning was still tucked in his waistband. When he turned around, Judy saw what could only be dried blood the colour of burned jelly apples smeared across the back of his shirt. A dark patch stained the seat of his torn trousers as well and his face and arms were dotted with cuts, scratches and multi-hued bruises of varying size. The wound on his stump ran with mustard-coloured pus.

Reagan made his way over to a couch in the foyer and dropped heavily onto the cushions. He tossed the crutch away and watched it clatter noisily across the floor. One of the hospice patients, a skeletal young man wearing a flowing white robe and pink bunny slippers, stuck his head out of the TV room and gasped at the sight of Reagan. He looked back and forth between Reagan and Ewing, but Judy was at a loss for words and just shook her head. The patient started to say something then noticed Reagan's Browning and quickly disappeared.

'You can't stay here,' Judy said. 'There'll be questions.'

'I ain't going no place,' Reagan replied.

'Let's just go back into the guest house. You need attention.'

Reagan stared at her for a minute before agreeing with a nod. Judy again reached out to help him, but Reagan wouldn't let her. As he slowly got to his feet, Judy retrieved the crutch and held it out to him. He took it and haltingly followed her down the hall and out the rear of the mansion.

'What happened?' she asked when they got outside. 'Where's Calvin?'

'He's dead. I think. He didn't look too good anyway. Titus hung him up by his ass from a meat hook. Sliced him up, too. I think they used to call it "drawn and quartered".'

'Christ!' Judy said. She looked more incredulous than upset. As if informed that the new Pope's name was Goldberg.

'Yeah, well, it didn't look too nice.'

'What happened?'

'Titus's crew – Blood – were waiting for us. They know about this place, in case you didn't realize.'

'Shit!' Judy said.

'Yeah. I'd say Titus is ten steps ahead of you from here to St Swithun's Day. We played demolition derby up and down Hollywood till they caught up with us.'

'It was on the news,' Judy interrupted. 'I should have known Calvin was involved. Six people were killed.'

'Things are tough all over,' Reagan sneered. 'They took us to a Tunnel lab over on the west side. Titus had already had his fun with Greymarch when I came around. Then he started in on me. Fortunately he was interrupted before . . . well, I'd rather not say any more.'

Judy unlocked the door to the guest house and ushered Reagan inside. He limped over to the bed where he'd been a captive only hours before. He happily flopped down on it. Judy retrieved some first aid supplies and set right to work on his messy stump. She knew it had to hurt like hell as she cleaned out the wound, but Reagan didn't so much as flinch. It made her shudder.

'How'd you get away?' she asked.

'The dumbest fucking luck in the world. Another gang launched a raid on the place a couple of hours ago. Sounded like Sagrados to me – payback probably – but I couldn't tell for sure. God bless 'em, whoever they are. From here on out gang wars are okay-fine by me. It was like fucking Sarajevo in there.'

'What happened to Titus?'

'Got me. Last I saw he stormed off with a grenade launcher

and an attitude. The lab went up in flames and I managed to crawl away in the confusion. Mother of a fire, too. Probably be the lead on tonight's news. Shit. I got banged up some getting out, but I managed to jack a car. And here I am.'

Judy had cleaned the wound, which was infected but not as bad as it originally looked. She started to apply a fresh dressing, then paused. 'How come?' she asked.

'Huh?'

'Why are you here, detective? Why aren't you back at your police station making a report?'

Reagan looked her in the eye, saw she was studying him. He pulled his arm back and examined the septic stump. It was a truly ugly thing and for the first time since Titus inflicted the injury, Reagan was struck by the irrevocability of what had been done to him. With all that had happened, he hadn't had time to really think about it beyond the immediate pain. He suddenly felt overwhelmed by the immensity of the loss. He was overcome with sorrow that quickly gave way to an intense and burning anger.

'Because this is personal,' he said. 'And I see now that there isn't any other way to deal with Titus.'

Judy nodded and offered a hint of a smile. 'Maybe you're not as dumb as Calvin thought.'

'Hey, I'm not the one hanging from a meat hook,' Reagan said.

Judy nodded again, but this time Reagan thought she looked a little sad. She finished applying the dressing and was about to start work on his various other injuries when she looked up with a curious little smile.

'I almost forgot,' she said.

'What?'

'A friend of yours is here.'

'I don't have any friends,' Reagan said. 'Any more.'

'Don't be so sure,' Judy said.

Reagan was so happy that, taped ribs and all, he actually swept Arsenio up in a big hug when he saw him. Arsenio wasn't quite so overcome, but he didn't complain. Reagan took a step back and looked the kid over. Though it had only been a few days since he'd first seen the boy at his grandmother's house, Reagan thought that Arsenio looked a lot older. Even wearing slippers and an oversized plaid bathrobe. The defiance in his manner when Reagan and Brolin pushed their way into his family's grief was still evident, but where before Arsenio had worn it with pride, now he seemed to carry it like a burden.

'How the hell did you get here?' Reagan asked, with a big smile. He sat back down on the edge of the bed, gestured Arsenio into a chair.

Arsenio shrugged and glanced over at Judy. 'I sprung him,' she said.

'Sprung? From where?'

'Lock-up ward at County,' Judy said.

'Say what?' Reagan looked back and forth between them.

'Piece of cake,' Judy said.

'Maybe with a file inside,' Reagan said.

'I had a little help, a little phenobarb,' Judy said. 'You'd be surprised how easy it was.'

'Probably not. But I think I'm past being surprised by anything. Why'd you spring him?'

Both Reagan and Judy stared at Arsenio and it made him nervous. He shifted back and forth from one slippered foot to the other and stared at the floor.

'I thought he might come in handy,' Judy said. 'He's seen a lot, knows a lot.'

Arsenio looked up at her with a scowl, but Reagan nodded. 'Very handy,' he agreed.

'*He* got a name you know,' Arsenio said.

'Sorry, Arsenio,' Reagan said. Arsenio seemed surprised by the apology. 'Do you understand what's going on here?'

Arsenio shrugged again, nodded at Judy. 'She told me some of it. I ain't saying I believe it all.'

'It's not easy to believe, I know. Bizarre fucking shit, ain't no doubt. And it goes way beyond Morgan and the Blood. Way beyond what happened to Diane.'

Arsenio jerked his head toward Reagan.

'I know that you're looking to get even for her. I remember everything you told me and I understand you want your revenge.' Reagan held his stump up in front of the boy's face. Arsenio's lip curled. 'I got reasons for revenge, too. That cocksucker took my hand, he took my partner and . . . he took everything from me. Except my life and I intend to use that to take him *down*. He's got plans for some serious shit that'd make the carve job on Diane look like a day at Disneyland. I know that's tough to hear, but that's how it is. Do you understand?'

'Yeah,' Arsenio said. 'Yes.'

'That's good. Because I still need your help in this. And if it all goes down right, maybe together we both get our revenge.'

'S'cool,' Arsenio nodded.

'All right. Tell me everything that's happened since you got away from Witherspoon.'

It took a while for Arsenio to get going, but once he started telling the story, he found he could remember every incident and feeling, and that it felt good to tell it all to someone else. He offered up every detail he could about Morgan and the Blood, including every shameful thing he himself had done, from the firebombing of the Sagrados' lab to his Tunnel-driven near-rape of Lanise. He broke down a couple of times and the full tale took a while to tell.

'Where would Morgan go to chill?' Reagan asked, after the story was told. 'I mean, outside his crib.'

'There's a big lab I saw once, in an old factory . . .'

'It's history,' Reagan said. 'Where else?'

Arsenio thought for a minute, shaking his head. 'I don't . . .'

'What is it?' Reagan asked.

'I never saw it myself, but once I heard JuJu talk about another place what Morgan's man – must be Titus – set up for when they had to like turn out some extra product fast. He say even Morgan had to dress like the man when he go there, else the local Five-O's pop him just for driving that side of town. JuJu say . . .'

'What?'

Arsenio peered over at Judy and blushed. 'He say it so white there, even the pussy afraid to be pink.'

Reagan bit his lip as Arsenio blushed. 'But where is it?' he asked.

Arsenio shook his head. 'That's all I know.'

'It's up in the valley,' Judy said, nodding.

'What?' Reagan said.

'Titus owns a bunch of property. He's got a place in Simi Valley. That has to be it.'

'How do you know that?'

'I told you, I have friends.'

'These the same friends who helped spring the kid from County.'

Judy nodded.

'Who are they?' Reagan asked.

'There are . . . others,' she shrugged.

'Others? You mean like you. And Greymarch.'

'Yes. Moulded by Bernouli's hand. The ones who weren't in with Titus or who he hasn't killed yet. I . . . help supply their needs – infected blood and Tunnel – and they do things for me in return. It's a mutual dependence. '

'Will they help us now?'

'I think so,' Judy said. 'Yes. Of course, they will. It's the chance we've been waiting for. Part of our survival technique has been to try to keep tabs on Titus's operations. Calvin was the main player, but others are involved as well.'

'Okay,' Reagan said.

'What are you going to do?' Judy asked.

'You know specifically where Titus's place is?'

'I'm sure I can find out.'

'I've got an idea,' Reagan said. He stared off vacantly, idly fiddling with the new dressing on his wrist. 'Simi Valley is almost *too* perfect. Titus must have a sense of humour after all. But we have to make sure we know that's where Titus and the Blood are holed up. The big lab is gone. The police already knew about his Malibu house and Morgan's crib is way too hot. If he has someplace else you don't know about, we're screwed.' He looked at Arsenio. 'But if they've already got a lab set to cook in the valley, then that's most likely where they'll run.'

'What you thinking?' Arsenio asked.

'The Sagrados gave me an idea. You a Clint Eastwood fan by any chance?'

Judy made a face, but Arsenio nodded enthusiastically. 'Man with no name,' he said.

'Exactly. You know *Fistful of Dollars*?'

'Shit, yeah!'

'What in the world are you talking about?' Judy asked.

'How about *Yojimbo*?' Reagan asked her.

'You mean the Kurosawa film?' Judy said.

'I had a feeling you were the art house type. Ever read *Red Harvest*?'

'Huh? Just what are you planning?' Judy asked.

Reagan sighed. 'I've got to make a call.'

Judy tried to send Arsenio back to the mansion to get some rest, but he refused to budge. She fetched a cordless phone from the main house, but Reagan told her it was no good. He told them he'd be right back.

He limped out to the street, stopping to pick up a heavy stone from the mansion's front garden. He walked up the block until he found a parked car with a cellular phone carelessly left on the seat. He smashed the window and grabbed the unit, dashed back to the guest house with the prize.

'Why'd you do that?' Judy asked him when he returned.

'Call tracing,' he explained. 'The number comes up on a digital display while the phone's still ringing. They'd be here before we could get out the door. But you can't use it to trace location with a cellular phone.'

Reagan punched the number on the lighted keypad and handed the phone to Judy. 'Just hand it back to me unless his wife answers,' he said.

Judy moistened her lips with her tongue. Her eyes darted around the room as she counted the rings. A sleepy, male voice answered after number three and she quickly handed the phone to Reagan who cleared his throat.

'Talk to me,' the voice on the other end demanded.

'It's Dennis, Carmine. If Loretta's up, don't say my name out loud. In either case, take the phone out to your den.'

'Jesus!' came the response, followed by a brief silence then: 'Hold on.'

Reagan heard Donatelli say something to his wife, heard the echo of the Captain's footsteps as he walked out of his bedroom, closing the door behind him.

Nice phone, Reagan thought.

'Dennis?' Donatelli said. He no longer sounded sleepy.

'Yeah, Carmine. It's me.'

'Christ on a crutch! Where are you? Are you all right? What in the goddamn hell are you doing?'

'I can't tell you where I am, Carmine. And you can toss the number 'cause I'm cellular and I'm moving.'

'Bastard.'

'I stepped deep in the apple sauce this time, Carmine. I'm up to my fucking eyeballs.'

'Dennis, you have to come in. The DA's ready to hang you with everything since the Black Dahlia. That massacre at the Bernouli house. We found your piece and your . . . your ring.'

'Was it still attached to my finger?' Reagan said.

'That's . . . what I was wondering.'

'Yeah. It's mine. Was mine.'

'What the fuck happened, Dennis? Brolin and McLeod, that

asswipe Bernouli and the Blood? God in heaven, they had to carry
McLeod out in a dozen plastic bags.'

'I know. I saw it all. And I've seen a lot since. I . . . There's
nothing I can tell you to make it clear. I can't explain it yet, except
to say that I'm trying to make things right. And I can't do that if I
come in.'

There was a silence, briefly interrupted by a whisper of voices
crossing the line like ghosts from who knows where. Reagan
heard Donatelli's heavy breathing, imagined his jowls bobbing
up and down with every laboured inhalation.

'Dennis . . . Brolin was killed with slugs matched to your piece.
With your goddamn prints all over it. Jesus, Dennis, her head
looked like a rotten pumpkin.'

It was Reagan's turn to breath hard. He closed his eyes and
saw a picture of Brolin sulking while he drove or cheering for the
Dodgers on TV.

'I didn't kill her, Carmine. Whatever else, you have got to
fucking *know* that I did not kill Jenny Brolin.'

'I don't know what I know anymore. I thought I knew
you. But . . . I don't know.' Donatelli offered a raspy half-
laugh that faded quickly. 'I sure as hell don't know what
you want.'

'I need you to do something, Carmine. Something very big and
very important.'

'You gotta be kidding me.'

'Do you hear me laughing?'

'What the fuck do you expect me to do for you, Dennis? I mean
put yourself in my position.'

Reagan didn't respond. The only sound was Donatelli's breathing. Reagan didn't want to say what he had to say. But he had
to say it.

'St Clare,' Reagan said.

Donatelli forgot to breathe and a dead silence set in between
them.

'Carmine?'

'There are markers you don't call in, Dennis.'

'I know that.'

'That's the way men live. What makes them men.'

'I understand that.'

'And?'

'I'm calling in St Clare. I wouldn't do it if there was any other
choice in the world.'

Neither man said a word for a while as Donatelli thought it over. 'What do you want?' the Captain finally asked.

Reagan told him and Donatelli said he'd think about it. 'How do I reach you?' he asked.

'Don't be an ass, Carmine. I'll call you tomorrow night, same time. Different phone, so don't waste your energy.'

'I don't know what you have and haven't done, Dennis, but I know one thing: you killed something here tonight. Something between us.'

Reagan felt a heaviness in his chest and an itch in his stump. The heartache felt worse. 'I know that Carmine. But there's no other way. I hope you'll be able to see that in the end. I . . . Carmine?'

'What?'

'Do you *remember* St Clare?'

'Do I . . . ? Do I remember my mother's goddamn name?'

'This – what's happening here, what you can help me make right — this makes St Clare look like a spinster librarian at a tea party.'

More silence. Then: 'We'll see, Dennis. We'll just have to see.'

Donatelli hung up. Reagan held the dead phone to his ear for a minute before flicking it off and tossing it aside. Both Arsenio and Judy were staring intently at him, the doctor looking sad, the boy confused.

'Who's St Clare?' Arsenio asked.

'Time to bolt,' Reagan said. 'Titus is probably still regrouping, but it won't take long before the Blood show up again.'

'But what about the hospice?' Judy said. 'I can't just leave the patients for the gang.'

'They'll be all right. Titus has your number here, but he doesn't care about them. And it's time you introduced me to these friends of yours.'

Judy pursed her lips and furrowed her brow. It made her look like a little girl. *Pretty goddamn cute*, Reagan surprised himself by thinking.

For a fucking vampire, he remembered.

'Okay,' she said. 'But let me collect a few things and at least try to get someone else on call.'

Reagan nodded his approval, then realized she probably had to go grab a fix.

'Who's St Clare?' Arsenio asked.

FORTY-THREE

'Are you all right?' Judy asked.

'I don't know,' Reagan said. 'I've got one of my hinky feelings again. Like we're not alone out here.'

'I thought that was the whole idea.'

Reagan nodded and scanned the dark street, but saw nothing out of the ordinary. He glanced over his shoulder through the rear window, saw no movement among the handful of cars parked in the lot. At least one of them looked abandoned. Reagan hoped that the Simi Valley cops didn't decide that this was the night to come collect it. Arsenio dozed in the back seat of Judy's Saab, clutching an empty McDonalds cup to his chest. The Hamburglar grinned up at Reagan.

He turned his attention back to the boarded-up store across the street and down the block. The That's My Baby furniture store. Christ, he thought, could you possibly come up with a cornier name? No wonder the place had gone out of business. The closed store served as a perfect front for Titus, though. The few other shops on the block closed early and the street terminated in a dead-end a half-block past the store, so there was no through traffic at all. The private lot in the rear had a nice little loading dock with zero visibility from the street. Daytime activity at the store might raise some eyebrows, but you could haul a big rig in at night and no one would be any the wiser.

Judy squirmed in her seat. Reagan expected her to complain about having to go and pee – he hated female partners on surveillance – but she'd been a trooper so far. He'd use one of the McDonalds cups if the need arose, but he wasn't too crazy about the idea of relieving himself with her sitting beside him.

'Is this what police work is like?' she asked, raising her sore rear out of the seat.

'Some of it. Isn't lots of doctor stuff boring?'

'Not like this,' she said. 'Think anything will happen?'

She'd already asked twice. 'Can only hope,' he told her again.

In fact, there was no guarantee that anything would go down at all. They were pretty sure that Morgan was inside – Arsenio had identified Tamara entering the store with some groceries – but there was no sign of Titus. And even if he showed, the plan depended on a whole lot more ifs:

If Donatelli came through getting word out to the Crips without setting a trap of his own.

If the word reached the right ears.

If the Crips believed the story and if they had the balls to do what Reagan hoped they would.

Reagan was counting on a lot.

'This is crazy,' Judy said. She obviously had a few of the same doubts.

'Maybe. But the gangbangers are pretty predictable. Not stupid, just predictable. They live in a narrow world with limited options. When they see a chance, they usually go for it. And a Simi Valley payback should be more than they can resist. Rodney's still King in the 'hood, you know. And they all remember the trial in Simi Valley.'

'But how can you trust this Donatelli to do what you asked? Why would he go along with it?'

'I can't be sure, but we have history,' he said. He looked at her and smiled. 'I live in a narrow world with limited options.'

Judy didn't smile back. 'So who *is* St Clare?' she asked.

Reagan's own smile faded fast. 'Was,' he said. 'Who was St Clare.'

Reagan leaned back, resting his arms in the spokes of the steering wheel. He stared straight ahead, toward the street. Only his lips moved as he told the story.

'When I got my shield – this is about ten years ago – I was partnered up with Carmine out of Pacific division. We were part of a detail working a serial rapist who'd been going wild in the South Bay. He'd been pegged to a dozen really brutal rapes between Palos Verdes and the Marina over the course of eight months. About half the victims were pre-pubescent girls and the last couple he'd killed afterward.

'Carmine was crazy obsessed with finding this motherfucker. It just ate him up. It happens like that sometimes, a perp'll just push your buttons. See, Carmine'd had a sister who was raped as a kid. We're talking years before, but this freak brought it all back for him.'

'St Clare,' Judy said.

'That was the mofo's name,' Reagan nodded. 'To make a long story short, I was young and ambitious and tripped to the guy. Actually, I got lucky. I had a junkie snitch who narked him for a pass on a PCP bust. Turned out they had the same dealer.

'Me and Carmine go after this raping bastard, only to find out he's connected. He's some real estate wheeler-dealer working for the goddamn Arabs in a Marina land grab, and he's alibied up the wazoo all the way back to the Great Train Robbery.'

'So what'd you do?'

'We hunted him,' Reagan said. 'He was careful for a while, but these freaks can never stop. Me and Carmine traded off-shifts tailing the guy, knowing that he'd slip sooner or later.'

'And did he?'

'Oh yeah. We caught up with him after he grabbed a little girl at a 31 Flavors. But we were a little too slow. When we busted in on him, he'd already killed her. He was still going at her when we nailed him. Right away the scumbag is on his hands and knees blubbering that he's a sick man and he needs help. Carmine looked over at that little girl, all purple and bloody, the bastard's cum still dripping down her chin. Carmine just pulls his piece and shoots him in the heart.'

Reagan looked up in the rear-view mirror and saw that Arsenio was awake and listening to the story.

'You've got to understand,' Reagan continued, 'Carmine's the most by-the-book son-of-a-bitch I ever knew. He wouldn't take a jelly doughnut without plopping down his four bits. I bet he hasn't so much as jay-walked since. But like I say, sometimes they punch your buttons and you run on some kind of primal instinct.'

A pair of fast-moving headlights sped around the corner, heading in their direction. The three of them slumped down in their seats as the car, a dark Porsche, zipped by. It was hard to be sure in the dark, but Reagan would have bet good cash money that it was Titus sitting behind the wheel. The Porsche turned up the driveway of That's My Baby and disappeared behind the building.

'Was that him?' Arsenio asked. There was a tremor in his voice.

'The gang's all here,' Reagan said. 'Now if the gang will just get here, we can rock and roll.'

They sat quietly for a while. Reagan spun out possibilities for the scenario he hoped would unfold. It was Arsenio who broke the silence.

'What happened with St Clare?' he asked.

Reagan wanted a cigarette very badly, but wouldn't risk lighting one up in the car. Instead he twisted nervously on a dashboard knob.

'Carmine handed me his gun and told me to place him under arrest. I stuffed it back in his holster. St Clare had a gun, too. I stuck it in the dead fucker's hand and fired a round off over Carmine's head.

'It was easy to work up a story. The hard part was getting Carmine to agree to it . If he hadn't been in shock, I think he would have told the truth. As it was, we'd nailed a baby-raper so no one asked too many questions. Who gave a fuck? We filed our reports, gave our statements. Carmine's promotion came through a few months later and I got a new partner.

'Neither of us has ever mentioned St Clare's name until I called him the other night.'

No one said a word for a long while. Reagan had to pee and decided he couldn't do it in the cup. He slid outside, crawled behind the abandoned car and peed from his knees. Judy smiled at him when he slid back behind the wheel as if she had won some sort of unspoken contest. It made him think of Brolin.

It was just after midnight when the line of dark cars, headlights off, rolled slowly down the street and pulled up in front of the furniture store.

Reagan was reaching for the assault rifle when the first sounds of gunfire exploded in the night.

'Make the call,' he yelled to Arsenio, and threw open the car door.

FORTY-FOUR

They'd agreed in advance that Arsenio would stay with the car, keep the engine running and his eyes open. Arsenio'd put up a bit of a squawk, but Reagan suspected that the kid was just as happy to keep out of any direct confrontation with Morgan and the Blood. And he didn't blame him. Reagan's cop instincts cried out to him that Judy should stay behind as well, but she was determined to see this through wherever it led and he remembered Greymarch's gleeful warning to him about her facility with a gun. Given that he had to shoot left-handed, Reagan figured she'd almost certainly be a better shot than him anyway.

And she was the only back-up he had.

Reagan led the way as they ran across the street, heading away from the Crip assault on the Blood stronghold. He cradled a Thompson 10 mm assault rifle in the crook of his damaged right arm. The weapon had been converted from semi to full automatic status and was fitted with a custom-made 50-round magazine with 180-grain plated hollow point ammo. He had a half-dozen extra clips belted around his waist, along with a .45 calibre Smith and Wesson revolver. He would never have carried that particular piece as a cop – there were already too many Dirty Harry wannabes on the LAPD – but the weapons had been procured by Judy's friends and, given his present circumstances, Reagan was more interested in raw stopping power than image. Though he'd spent the afternoon practising with both weapons, he knew his accuracy would be questionable at best. With a little trial and error he'd figured a way to hook the Thompson's front stock over his stump for balance and adjust for the recoil. Still, his ultimate success would depend on the ability to take an enemy out by hitting him once, anywhere, with a high-powered load.

Judy carried a converted Tec–9. It lacked the range and sheer killing power of the Thompson, but was lighter and far easier to handle. She had a handgun with her, as well, but Reagan knew that if it came down to relying on her .38 special, they had very big problems. Reagan suggested that she wear a vest, but she just laughed at the notion, insisting that her organelle-aided constitution would serve her far better than Kevlar could.

With just that constitution – specifically, Titus's – in mind, Judy also carried the most important weapon of all: an animal tranquillizer pistol that dangled at her waist. The trank darts were filled with a solution Judy had been working on for some time, designed to directly inhibit organelle function. Though Titus – and she – could sure enough be killed with standard weapons, it required a sustained and massive assault. The drug had been developed to speed the kill with just such an occasion as this is in mind, though of course she hadn't been able to test it. They could only hope that it would work as intended.

Reagan planned to empty a clip or two of the hollow points into Titus to be safe.

Reagan saw that the Blood were quick to answer the Crip attack. The flashing muzzles of their automatic weapons poked through gaps in the boarded-up windows of the big store. As Reagan and Judy raced around the block of shops to come up on the rear of the furniture store, they heard a whoosh followed by the reverberating WHUMP! of an explosion that shook the street like a good-sized tremblor, shattering glass and lighting up the night.

'RPG,' Reagan said with a smile. 'Rocket Propelled Grenade. They're all the rage these days with the colours. Crips hijacked a truckload last year off an Army base.'

'Think it'll bring the cops?' Judy asked.

'Not if your friends do their job.'

'They'll do it,' she said without doubt. And almost on cue, the sound of a distant explosion could be heard even above the riffs of gunfire around That's My Baby. Judy spotted a lick of flame dancing up into the sky near the centre of town and pointed it out to Reagan. He nodded and smiled.

'That should keep 'em busy for a while,' he said.

Their plan had called for Judy's associates to set off a series of controlled explosions in key spots around Simi Valley upon receiving Arsenio's call that the Crip assault was going down. The explosives were rigged in commercial areas where casualties were likely to be minimal, but property damage high. Places where police and fire attention would intently focus before responding to any calls about a problem at an abandoned furniture store. The idea was not to overplay their hand and compel the local authorities to call for outside help too quickly, but to stagger the blasts just enough to divert the locals from the main event. Reagan knew the way cops thought and how a local police chief would rather sip his own vomit than admit that he had a situation his force couldn't handle. It was precisely that kind of thinking that had made the '92 Rodney King riots the disaster that they were.

Two more explosions in quick succession greeted them as they turned down a narrow walkway that ran behind the store fronts. Though one of the explosions definitely came from Titus's lair, Reagan couldn't tell if the second was merely an echo bouncing off the hills or more handiwork of Judy's comrades. They heard the low wail of sirens in the distance, but the sound faded off in a different direction. The staccato rhythms of gunplay grew louder as the walkway opened out into the parking lot behind the furniture store.

Peering around the corner of the building, Reagan saw four black youths in baggy khakis hastily cramming crates into the back of a white van. A smiley-faced logo for Glassman's Frozen Banana-on-a-Stick was stencilled on the vehicle's side, though Reagan doubted that the crates contained much in the way of frosty treats. Three more Blood with Uzis stood guard, nervously swinging their gun barrels back and forth from the rear of the store to the driveway that led to the street. So far the Crips hadn't attempted anything beyond a frontal assault, but the Blood were ready to respond if they did.

Reagan ducked back behind the edge of the building. Judy was so close behind him that he stepped on her foot, nearly tripping himself. He fell back against the brick wall as she reached out a hand to steady him. He covered his embarrassment by inspecting the rifle, slapping the bottom of the clip.

'Blood,' he whispered. 'Seven of them in the back, at least three armed. They're loading boxes into a truck.'

'What do we do?' Judy asked.

'I'm going to take out the three with guns. They're standing together. Not too bright. You cover the others.'

'What do you mean cover?'

'Go for the legs. Spray your fire knee-high. And keep an eye on the back door. Got it?'

Judy nodded.

Reagan lowered the barrel of the Thompson and took a deep breath.

'Let's go!' he said.

Arsenio needed to pee real bad.

Twice he opened the car door to go do it and twice he shut it just as fast, worried about what would happen if Reagan and Judy should need him just as he started to whiz.

He pounded his hands on the rim of the steering wheel, his palm so slick that it slipped once and bounced off the horn pad, setting off a slight bleat. Arsenio's heart froze and he all but turned white at the sudden noise, but the short blare was lost amid the larger din of the Blood–Crip firefight.

He dropped his hands to his lap and pressed at his crotch, trying not to think about the burning in his bladder. He madly jiggled his legs up and down on the balls of his feet, painfully bouncing his thighs up into the lower crescent of the steering wheel. He let go of his crotch and started fiddling with the knobs and buttons on the dashboard, till he realized he wasn't sure how to turn on the headlights and got scared he'd flip them on by accident.

His hands went back to his crotch.

Oh man, he thought, I have *got* to go.

He opened the door again, stuck a foot out and heard a loud explosion from the furniture store. He pulled his leg back in and closed the door, reaching for the gear shift. Across the street he saw a tall Crip jump up and down in a little jig as he lowered what looked like a small bazooka from his shoulder. One whole side of the storefront went up in flame as dense smoke billowed into the night. A burning body staggered through the orange fire and out into the street before being cut down by Uzi-spray. Three seconds later a hail of bullets from inside the store caught the dancing Crip across the midsection and he collapsed to the ground like a failed soufflé.

'Shi-iii-i-it,' Arsenio cursed and started jiggling his legs again.

The battle grew more intense as a cadre of Crip gunmen formed a line and sprayed the front of the store with bullets, shredding the plywood window boards into excelsior. As the wooden barricades fell apart, Arsenio saw that a second line of corrugated steel shutters had been erected behind the plywood front, with irregularly cut gun ports and viewing slits for those inside. The Crips continued to fire at the shutters, but few of the bullets seemed to penetrate the steel. The ricochets sounded like ball-bearing popcorn in a cast iron pot.

Smoking Blood rifle muzzles protruded through the ports spitting bullets in all directions.

I can always pee in my pants, Arsenio thought, *so what? Not the end of the world. Who's gonna know in all this shit?*

A brief lull in the assault was filled by the sound of an explosion from another direction entirely. Arsenio reckoned it was someone on *his* side – whatever that meant these days. And though he had cheered the idea of Judy's friends blowing lily-white Simi Valley to pieces – he remembered Rodney, too – he found there was no immediate comfort to be taken in anything happening around him this night.

Shit, he thought, *I can not pee in my pants.*

Another explosion drew his attention back to the storefront, as one of the Crip cars went up in a mini-mushroom cloud. Shards of glass and steel flew every which way. A piece of fender neatly sliced off the arm of a Crip soldier and Arsenio watched as the arm, complete with Uzi still spitting bullets, slid across the street before disappearing down a sewer grate.

He couldn't take it any longer. The firefight was heating up again and the sound of gunfire was now coming from behind the store, too. He assumed that the doctor and cop were in the thick of it and wouldn't be needing him just then. If he was going to do it, this was the time.

Arsenio slipped the door open and crawled out of the car. He scrambled around to the back where he couldn't possibly be seen by anyone on the street. He kept his head down below the level of the car roof and unzipped his fly.

He closed his eyes and tried to ignore the bursts of automatic weapons fire. Perversely, nothing would come. Another incredible explosion shook the ground as he managed to pee. He looked up and saw a ball of flame rise up from the back of the furniture store. He shook off the last few drops and tucked himself back in his pants, feeling a residual squirt in his shorts.

His fly was half-way zipped when the cold hand grabbed him by the back of the neck.

Controlled bursts, Reagan repeated to himself, *controlled bursts.*

He emptied most of the clip with the first squeeze of the Thompson's trigger.

His aim was way off. He only hit one of the three gunmen, catching him right across the knees. But the kid reflexively threw his arms out for balance as he tumbled down, squeezing his Uzi's hair-trigger in the process. The Uzi-fire all but tore the head off of the second guard, whose grue exploded into the face of the third. The blinded Blood dropped his Uzi, spinning like a pinwheel in his desperation to scrape his buddy's brain bits out of his eyes. Reagan re-aimed and emptied the clip at the whirling target, using the hollow points to blow a soccer-ball sized hole in his chest.

Judy came out of the alley right behind Reagan, darting left as he went right. She froze for a moment, stunned by the sight of the grievous bodily harm inflicted by Reagan's ejaculating Thompson, instinctively switching into doctor mode and thinking what needed to be done. Just as quickly, she was shocked back to reality when two of the Bloods emerged from the van with Glocks in their hands. She started to yell a warning to Reagan, who was struggling to change clips with one hand, before remembering that she held a loaded machine pistol out in front of her. Without further hesitation, she squeezed the trigger, aiming, as Reagan had told her, along a knee-high line across the enemy's legs.

Both gangbangers went down clutching at the remnants of their throats. Though she was a good five yards away, Judy could hear the slushy noises of the bubbling blood as it spurted out between their splayed fingers.

The two remaining Blood must have been unarmed, because they made a bee-line toward the open door leading to the back of the store. Reagan was still fumbling with a clip as he saw them. He thrust the Thompson between his knees and reached for the .45. With astonishing smoothness, he pulled the gun out of his shoulder holster and squeezed off two quick shots. The first went wild high, but the second caught the more distant runner just as he approached the door. The bullet hit him in the right kidney, tearing a big chunk out of the kid's side. The Blood stumbled to his left, running smack into the wall and sliding to the pavement. A smear of dark red, like a sick slug's trail, marked the wall where face met brick.

The second runner was six feet behind, but didn't slow when his partner went down. Reagan took a deep breath, caught him in his sights and started to pull the trigger when he heard Judy scream, 'Get down!'

Reagan dropped without hesitation. He heard the tut-tut-tut of an Uzi and felt the bullets sear the air an inch above his scalp. He rolled across the tarmac parking lot, turning his .45 in the direction of the gunfire. The first guard, whose knees he'd taken out, had gotten it together and dragged himself over to his Uzi. The kid was lowering his sights toward Reagan when a new burst from Judy's Tec–9 tore the gun right out of his hands. The Uzi bounced up into the kid's chin, snapping his head back before clattering across the lot. In the instant the kid's soft neck was exposed, Judy cut it open with the remainder of her clip.

Reagan acknowledged her with a wave of his gun then tucked the .45 back into its holster. Still on the ground, using his knees to brace the Thompson, he slapped a fresh magazine into the rifle and scrambled to his feet. Judy had already popped a new clip into her piece and darted toward the back door, gripping the machine pistol tightly against her belly. The other Blood had disappeared inside, so Reagan knew that there might be a welcoming party waiting for them. He hoped that with the Crip offensive still going strong – and from the sound of machine gun fire, it was – Titus and Morgan weren't sufficiently fortified here to pitch a battle on two fronts.

Reagan resecured the stock of the rifle over his stump and edged toward the entrance to the furniture store when Titus appeared in the doorway.

His jet black shirt was torn in several places and blotched with wet stains. The dark circle of a bullet-hole, oozing gunge, gaped like a weepy third eye in the hollow of his left cheek. Reagan couldn't imagine how such an entrance wound wouldn't be fatal until he saw the matching hole in the other cheek. The two dark circles marked his face like perverse clown make-up framing a horrible rictus of a smile. Several of Titus's teeth had been shattered and a piece of his lower lip flapped loosely against his chin.

Titus held the grenade launcher in his hands. It was pointed directly at Reagan's feet.

I'm dead, Reagan thought, but made the effort to lift his rifle anyway. Titus's warped smile grew wider, then drooped as he looked down at a dart that seemed to have sprouted from his right arm.

Judy stood off to the side, the tranquillizer gun in her hands.

Titus let loose an inchoate yell and started to swing his weapon around in her direction when Reagan caught a movement out of the corner of his eye. Titus saw it too and jerked the barrel of the launcher thirty degrees back the other way. Reagan followed the weapon's arc and saw a Crip standing at the end of the driveway, balancing an RPG on his shoulder. Quicker than a heartbeat he heard the low-pitched cough of Titus's grenade launcher followed immediately by the susurrant hiss of the RPG. Faster than he could think, Reagan threw himself to the ground and rolled. He prayed that Judy was smart enough to do the same.

The explosion was massive.

The shock-wave lifted Reagan a foot off the ground, the heat searing his exposed flesh. He landed hard on his damaged right arm sending hot needles of pain through his body. Thick smoke swirled around the parking lot and for ten seconds it was impossible to catch a breath. Reagan felt around for the Thompson, but couldn't find it. He pulled the .45 out of his holster and tried to peer through the murk for Titus.

The upper floor of the furniture store was on fire. Flames danced out of a hole in the wall torn by the RPG. Reagan pointed the barrel of the revolver toward the doorway below, but the entrance had collapsed under the debris.

There was no sign of Titus in the rubble.

A bus-sized crater smouldered back where the Crip had been standing. Some of the asphalt was on fire, but there no trace of the gangbanger. Reagan figured that the Crip must have been carrying spare grenades on him. There was no other way to account for the sheer intensity of the blast. And if so, there wouldn't be enough of the kid left to bury in a pill box.

Some of the smoke drifted away, but more poured out of the side of the store. Reagan scrambled to his feet, noting movement beside the rubble where the door had been. He saw the Thompson lying on the ground and grabbed it, but found he couldn't bear the pain of balancing the rifle on his injured arm. Reluctantly, he tossed it aside in favour of the revolver.

Reagan stumbled toward the rear of the store, the .45 held stiffly in front of him. As he drew close enough to make things out through the murk, he saw that Judy was trying to climb out of a big metal Dumpster. She staggered around inside it, but couldn't drag herself over the lip. Reagan ran over to help, peering over his shoulder for any sign of Titus, Blood or Crips.

Reagan holstered the gun and reached in toward Judy. Her face and upper torso were a mass of cuts and abrasions, but none of them looked too bad. She seemed to have trouble getting her balance and he had to grab her from behind to pull her out of the trash bin. Her machine pistol lay under some rubbish and he grabbed it as well. There was no sign of the trank gun.

As Judy wobbled around holding her head, Reagan watched for activity from inside the store. He could still hear scattered machine-gun fire coming from the front, but there was no sign of Titus. Judy came up behind him and rested her head on his shoulder.

'Are you okay?' he said.

She didn't answer.

He turned around and raised her chin. She had trouble focusing. She looked like a dazed cartoon character, lacking only little birds and stars circling her head.

'Are you okay?' he repeated to her face.

Judy frowned. She cupped her hands over her ears and shook her head, losing her balance again in the process. Reagan steadied her.

'What?' he said. 'What is it?'

She pointed at her ears.

'I'm deaf,' she said. 'Bloody hell.'

Reagan wanted to cry. He expected the authorities to show up any time now. Even with the mayhem Judy's friends were wreaking around town, there was no way that last blast wasn't going to attract attention. He had to hope the locals were spread thin enough that he'd have time to go in after Titus and finish the job.

The sound of machine-gun fire from out front seemed to have slackened. It wouldn't be a surprise if the blast had sent the Crips into retreat as well. There was no way to know how many Blood were left inside, but if he was going to make a move it was now or never.

Judy was still wobbly. She had to lean against the edge of the Dumpster to stay on her feet. Reagan didn't like the idea of leaving her out here, but she didn't appear to be up to walking much less backing him up in an assault. Besides, she'd already nailed Titus with one of her magic trank darts. With any luck, that would do the job.

Reagan checked the clip in the Tec–9 and grabbed two more off Judy. He retrieved the Thompson and handed it to her, gesturing for her to hold the fort where she was. She tried to protest and follow him, but after stumbling to her knees with her second step, accepted that she wasn't going any place. She hunkered down away from the heat of the burning furniture store.

Reagan peered up at the flames that consumed the upper half of the store. The wood crackled like crushed peanut shells and embers swirled around the parking lot, rising like demons in the updrafts. The RPG had thoroughly demolished the rear entrance, but several new gaps had been breached in the store's back wall. Visible heat emanated from the burning building.

Reagan took a deep breath and found that the air parched his throat.

He tightened his grip on the Tec–9, checked for falling debris and offering a brief and silent prayer, ran into the building.

FORTY-FIVE

Reagan walked right into a dead black girl sprawled in an easy chair. A thick, yellow substance dripped out of her open mouth and her neck was twisted at an awful angle. At first, Reagan thought it was cum, but when he saw the singed Entenmann's cake box clutched in the girl's burned fingers, he realized it was just banana cream filling. Reagan heard a creak, looked up and jumped out of the way as a hunk of smoking wood crashed down from above. He could see straight up to the flames through a large hole in the ceiling and realized the girl had been sitting in the room above and had fallen – chair, cake and all – through the hole in the floor when the RPG hit.

What the hell was she doing eating cake in the middle of all this? he wondered.

He didn't muse on it overlong. With the muzzle of the machine pistol leading him like a divining rod, Reagan crept through the maze of boxes and old furniture that littered the back room. The fire hadn't spread down to the ground floor yet, but it was getting hard to catch a decent breath in the acrid, swirling smoke. The gunfire from outside had abated and the roar of the fire was the omnipresent sound.

The only illumination was provided by the flames above and Reagan had a hard time finding his way around the back room. Several times he tripped over odds and ends strewn across the floor: rotten bits of furniture, spent hypos and, he saw as he poked through some of the boxes, enough 9 mm ammo to arm a battalion.

Or at least a street gang. Reagan exhaled sharply. The place was going to go up like Dresden once the fire worked its way down here.

He moved a little faster.

The sound of gunshots – handgun, small calibre – led him to the main part of the store. He had to climb over another bank of cardboard boxes to get over to the door. His foot went through the top of one box sending him sprawling. He managed not to yell out, but knocked over a whole row of cartons in the process. He trained the gun at the door, expecting Titus or one of the Blood to come rushing in, but they either didn't hear him or were too busy to pay any mind.

As Reagan got to his feet, he peered into the crushed box. It was half-filled with small, brown bottles labelled with the name of a chemical he couldn't pronounce and had never heard of. With one eye still on the door, he unscrewed the top and gingerly sniffed at the liquid. The stuff smelled like acetone and it burned his nose hairs. It had to be an ingredient in the Tunnel manufacturing process. Which meant that there were probably other chemicals around as well. He replaced the bottle and glanced back toward the flames.

Forget Dresden, he thought, *this place'll go up like Hiroshima.*

Two more shots from the front of the store caught his attention. As he worked his way around toward a doorway he heard another pair of shots. A bullet-ridden oak door that opened out into the main part of the store stood slightly ajar, swaying on its creaky hinges. A hot draught blew across the threshold. Several of the rounds had penetrated right through the thick wood, affording Reagan an irregular line of peep-holes onto the action up front. He had to duck his head back and forth from hole to hole to get a decent view of the scene.

What he saw was a slaughterhouse.

He couldn't discern the entire length of the former showroom area, but he counted eight bodies lying on the floor by the fortified front windows. They were all Blood foot soldiers and a few squirmed in pools of their own blood. Since no one was shooting into the store from the street, Reagan assumed that the surviving Crips had lit out for home. He didn't have a clear view out to the front, but saw a flickering glow through the impressive Blood fortifications.

Titus was the only figure on two feet. He went from one prone figure to another, kicking each sharply in the balls. If the body moved, he put two bullets into the back of its head. Reagan noted that Titus held the gun in his left hand. His right arm, which had taken the hit from Judy's trank dart, dangled limply at his side. The sleeve was torn away and the forearm had swelled hideously to several times its normal size, like Popeye on a spinach OD. Titus had taken several other bullet hits as well and though wet patches of dark blood dappled his clothes, the injuries seemed to slow him down not at all.

Another piece of the ceiling collapsed somewhere behind Reagan and flames began to creep down the walls of the back room. Reagan readied himself to charge through the door, gun blazing, before the fire reached the ammo and chemicals. Titus had his back turned to the door and Reagan prepared to make his move when Titus turned around. Reagan froze, but saw that Titus wasn't actually looking his way. Instead, he smiled and blew a kiss at someone out of Reagan's view. Titus took a few steps toward whoever it was, half-facing Reagan's position, killing any chance for Reagan to take him by surprise.

Reagan pressed his cheek against the jamb to peer through the crack between door and frame. He saw that Titus was talking to Morgan. The gang lord also lay on the floor, leaning against an overturned crib. Morgan had taken several bullets and gasped for breath through his open mouth. Saliva and blood drooled down his chin as he looked up at Titus in disbelief. It was difficult to hear above the crackle of the fire, but it was clear that Morgan was pleading for his life. The clincher was the sadistic smile on Titus's face.

'. . . can't,' Reagan heard the gang leader say. He missed the rest of it except for something about 'homies' and 'your boy, your boy.'

Titus laughed – hysterically, Reagan thought – in response. So hard that he had to lower the gun. Reagan saw a gleam of hope rise in Morgan's eyes as the muzzle drooped, but it faded fast as Titus leaned over and pressed the barrel of the gun against Morgan's temple.

Titus squeezed the trigger three times.

Morgan only jerked once.

Titus lowered his mouth to the wound in Morgan's head and briefly sucked at the blood that pumped out of the dead body. He licked his lips and walked away from Morgan's corpse without a second glance. He had again turned his back to the door and Reagan knew that this was it. He secured his grip on the stock of the machine pistol and pressed his finger against the warm curve of the trigger. He wedged his stump into the gap between door and jamb and took a deep breath.

He flung the door open, swung the barrel of the gun toward Titus and squeezed the trigger.

The first spray of bullets caught Titus across the small of the back. The force flung him forward and out of further harm's way as Reagan emptied the clip in panic. Titus screamed as he hit the ground and the pistol flew from his hand. Reagan quickly ejected the spent magazine. He pressed the weapon to his chest with his right arm and grabbed for another clip with his good hand. He smoothly slapped it into place even as Titus started to roll across the floor toward one of the bodies. An Uzi was wedged under a Blood corpse.

For all his injuries, Titus was inhumanly fast. He had the Uzi in hand and pointed at Reagan as quickly as Reagan was able to swing the muzzle of the Tec–9 back at Titus.

Reagan squeezed the trigger.

He felt the vibrations in his bones.

He saw the Uzi jerk in Titus's hand as dark blood geysered in the air.

He heard the cacophonic, polyrhythmic jam of the two sputtering weapons.

He smelled his own precious blood as searing lead tore holes in his soft flesh.

The impact of the bullets propelled Reagan backward through the open door. As he stumbled across the threshold, he heard an explosion behind him as flames met ammo and he was suddenly moving forward again, though his feet didn't touch the ground. He flew, as in a dream, all the way across the room, his flight aborted by contact with the steel shutter that spanned the front window of the store.

Reagan barely held onto consciousness as he landed in a pile on the floor. He smelled burning and felt an intense heat. A few seconds later it hit home that his clothes were on fire. He rolled onto his back to snuff the flames. He continued to roll until he simply couldn't move any more and came to a stop on his back.

He had no idea where the gun went. He decided it didn't matter when he found that he couldn't move his left arm. He glanced down at himself and saw that the front of his shirt was sopped with blood. He was able to breath and decided that at least his lungs hadn't taken a direct hit. His heart seemed to be beating, which he decided was quite a good sign. He'd been gut shot, though.

He turned his head to the left to glance at the store behind him. He heard bullets popping in the back room as the flames ate up more of the boxes of ammo. Fire arced across the entire rear of the showroom. Bright orange licks crawled up Morgan's corpse and rapidly consumed the body. The smell of burnt flesh was thick as a swarm of flies.

Reagan heard something slosh across the floor. He mustered the energy to turn his head to the right, succeeding on the third try. He was too tired, too plain worn out to be crestfallen by what he saw.

Titus dragged himself across the showroom toward Reagan with one arm. The top half of his body was a mass of shredded flesh and black-red liquid. His chest pumped fluids and was smeared from right to left with a broad brushstroke of blood. He had a butterfly blade gripped between his teeth, the knife edge turned inward, cutting into his snarled lips. His eyes were black specks of death.

Man, Reagan thought, *does he ever looked pissed.*

Reagan looked around for a gun, saw that the nearest piece was five yards away. He tried to move toward it and had to laugh at the idea. Expending what little energy he had left, he managed to swivel himself around so that Titus was approaching his feet. He could lift his head just enough to stare Titus in the eye. The contact seemed only to spur the son-of-a-bitch on.

Several more explosions rocked the rear of the store as Titus continued his slow crawl across the showroom. For the first time, Reagan felt the pain in his gut and considered that there'd be worse to come. Taking in the look on Titus's face, thinking about McLeod, Reagan wondered where Titus would start to slice.

Titus grabbed onto Reagan's ankle as soon as he was within reach. He dug his fingers into the flesh and pulled himself up until he could perch atop Reagan's legs. He removed the knife from his mouth, licking the blood off his lips before spitting it in Reagan's face. His aim was pretty good considering he had gaping holes in both cheeks. Reagan could see his tongue through the rent flesh.

'Fwmmm fwanna fwoo oo fo ffad,' Titus breathed through his ruined mouth. 'Ooor fwannna feat oor ffffuffin' ffallff.'

Titus raised the knife up in his fist, the point of the blade unmistakably aimed at Reagan's crotch. Reagan tried to lift his arm to ward off the blow, but could only manage to flail his stump a few inches off the ground.

Titus smiled broadly as the arc of the knife headed down. Reagan was fascinated at how he could see his own pale features reflected in the silver of the blade. He thought he looked remarkably at peace.

The first bullets blew the knife out of Titus's hand, taking three fingers with it.

The second burst sent him flying off Reagan and spinning across the floor.

Greymarch stood in the middle of the showroom, a smoking AK–47 in his scarred hands. He wore a peculiar assortment of ill-fitting clothes and looked more dead than alive. Plugs of singed hair sprouted like weeds from the burned patches that covered his skull. The fire's livid red was reflected in his bone-white skin and glassy eyes.

He looked, to Reagan, like an avenging angel.

Titus again started to drag himself across the floor, but Greymarch cut him off with a new burst of bullets. Titus rolled onto his side, bleeding from a score of wounds and glared daggers at Greymarch. He tried to say something, but only coughed up bile-coloured ichor. It spilled out from the holes in his cheeks as well as his lips.

Greymarch silently limped over toward his prone enemy till he stood directly above him. Titus balanced himself on his left arm, weaving back and forth. He managed to tilt his head back and glare up at Greymarch.

'Ffufff ooo,' he stammered. More dark liquid percolated out of his cheeks.

'Uh-uh,' Greymarch rasped. 'Fuck *you*. To death and ever after.'

Greymarch stepped back and pointed the barrel of the gun at a spot in the middle of Titus's forehead.

He squeezed the trigger, emptying the clip.

He reloaded and did it again.

The third time, Titus lacked any head as such to aim at, so Greymarch emptied the gun into the remains of his torso.

He walked away without so much as another glance at the body. Greymarch popped another clip into the gun as he approached Reagan. The cop looked up at him with a broad smile.

'Man, oh, man,' he wheezed. 'Did you ever make my Christmas list.'

Greymarch didn't smile. 'You left me behind, scumbag,' he croaked.

'Huh?' Reagan said, his joy starting to fade. 'What do you mean?'

'You left me hanging there. You left me in the shit.'

Reagan tried to read Greymarch's expression and saw nothing human there. Nothing left at all.

'I thought you were dead,' he said. He knew it was a waste of time.

'You left me,' Greymarch said again. He hefted the gun, pointing it at Reagan.

'Fuck,' Reagan said.

The dart caught Greymarch in the right eye before he could pull the trigger. The bullets cut a furrow in the floor beside Reagan's head as tiny shards of linoleum ricocheted into his neck.

Greymarch dropped the gun and clawed at his face, screaming at the top of his lungs. The trank dart had plunged right through the soft tissue of the eye. Only the tail-end of the four-inch dart poked out of the socket.

Judy staggered in through a breach in the front of the store, the trank gun held stiffly in front of her in both hands. She'd clearly forgotten that the gun only shot one dart at a time.

'Oh, baby,' Reagan cried. 'Come to Santa.'

Greymarch collapsed to the floor. His back was arched and his hands continued to tear at his eye as his whole body convulsed. It appeared to Reagan that the flesh around the wounded eye swelled and contracted. Greymarch screeched in hoarse agony as he flopped around on the ground.

Judy still looked a little unsteady as she made for one of the tossed Uzis. She checked the clip and walked slowly over to Greymarch. The convulsions had abated, but he continued to emit nail-on-chalkboard screeches. Judy straddled his body and stuck the barrel of the gun in his open mouth.

'Forgive me,' she said, 'I know what I do.'

She didn't flinch as she pulled the trigger. It seemed to Reagan that Greymarch didn't stop convulsing until the entire clip had been spent, but he couldn't tell and didn't really want to know. Judy tossed the gun away. She stared down at the corpse for a long minute and Reagan was sure he heard her sob once before she got up off the body.

The fire was within a dozen feet of them when Judy came over to examine Reagan. He tried to smile at her, but found that the muscles wouldn't respond. She tore his shirt off and looked down at the damage done to his belly. He tried to read her expression and couldn't. She had already shifted into doctor mode.

He felt very cold and turned his face toward the roar of the flames. He didn't know if he succeeded or not, just that he suddenly felt better.

He heard a sound that might have been sirens.

Or perhaps heavenly music.

FORTY-SIX

Reagan stepped out onto the deck to light a cigarette. A light drizzle fell, but the breeze was warm and he could even see a few breaks in the clouds drifting in from over the ocean. He glanced down the muddy slope to Pacific Coast Highway, saw a blood-red Jag facing the wrong way in the southbound lanes near Gladstone's. Traffic crawled in both directions, the pathetic L.A. drivers panicking as usual in the wet weather.

Reagan looked across the expanse of the canyon, to the gutted shell of Titus's mansion. It had burned down sometime in the last two or three days. Titus had likely torched it before retreating to Simi Valley. Or one of his cronies did it afterwards. Judy reckoned that there were still a few of them left. With Titus gone, she didn't see them as a big problem. Reagan wasn't sure he agreed, but didn't care to argue about it.

The house they were crashing in had been obtained because it afforded the view of Titus's former digs. It belonged to a member of Judy's 'secret circle', though Reagan had yet to meet the man and Judy was none too forthcoming about his identity. Reagan shrugged to himself as he thought about it and took another drag.

The cigarette tasted like shit.

He smoked it anyway.

His stomach itched like crazy. He was determined not to scratch, since it only made things worse. He compromised by rubbing at the sore spots with the stump of his wrist. It didn't actually relieve the itching, but it made him feel a little better. Like the cigarette.

Judy had already warned him that there'd be changes and that they were unpredictable.

'Caramel popcorn,' she'd replied when he told her about the cigarettes.

'Huh?' he said.

'It was my favourite treat in the whole world. I'd get a big old tub of the stuff with the sugar-coated peanuts and rent a weepy movie. Man alive, I'd be in hog heaven for two hours. Now I think it tastes like bleached cardboard.'

'It *always* tasted like bleached cardboard,' Reagan told her. 'You just had the veil lifted from your eyes. And how can any reasonable person compare caramel corn with nicotine?'

But he reckoned she was right. *Unpredictable*, he thought again. Well, that pretty well summed everything up.

The glass door slid open behind him and Arsenio strolled out onto the deck. He peered up at the rain and frowned, crossing his arms over his chest. The boy was even thinner than when Reagan had first met him. Haggard looking. Reagan's eye was drawn again to the large lump on Arsenio's scalp where Greymarch had pistol-whipped him after finding him in the car on the night of the final assault. Arsenio was lucky that Greymarch hadn't killed him outright, given his state of mind. Or lack thereof. Still, Reagan thought, Arsenio didn't look much like a boy anymore. Yet another thing that had been taken from him.

'Got a nail?' Arsenio asked.

'You're too young to smoke,' Reagan said.

'Not any more,' Arsenio replied, echoing Reagan's thoughts. Reagan tossed him the pack. Arsenio lit up off the smouldering butt. He coughed a little as he dragged and smiled, trying to hide it.

Reagan watched the boy, waiting for him to say something more. Arsenio pretended to stare out over the ocean, but his eyes kept flicking back to Reagan. He took a final, weak puff on the half-smoked Marlboro, coughed again, and tossed the butt off the balcony.

'What?' he asked.

'That's my question,' Reagan said.

'Nothing.'

'Tell me.'

'What you think?'

'I don't,' Reagan said, 'so I'm asking.'

'She wouldn't talk to me,' Arsenio sighed.

'Not at all?'

Arsenio shook his head. 'She just stared at me for a minute then went back inside the house. She picked up the phone and called the police. You believe that? My own Nana narking me out.'

Reagan summoned a mental image of the stern, precise old woman. He had no trouble believing it at all.

'I'm sorry,' Reagan said.

Arsenio nodded.

'About everything, Arsenio . . . about everything.'

Arsenio looked up at the cop. He could have laughed at the uncomfortable expression of apology that didn't quite work on Reagan's face.

He just didn't feel like laughing.

'Least Morgan's dead,' Arsenio said. 'Least there's that.'

Reagan wanted to say more, but didn't know what. He started to try when he felt the spasm rip through his guts. He swayed on his feet and had to reach out for the rail to stop himself from falling. Arsenio ran over to support him and helped Reagan into a wet deckchair.

Another spasm doubled Reagan over. He coughed up some greenish-grey bile and spat it onto the deck. Arsenio curled his lip at the sight – and the smell – but kept a hand on Reagan's shoulder.

The spasm passed and Reagan was able to sit up again. The colour had blanched from his face and he was racked by a case of the chills.

'You okay?' Arsenio asked. He was glancing back through the glass doors, looking for Judy.

'M'all right,' Reagan said. The chills passed as quickly as they came. He patted Arsenio's hand on his shoulder in thanks. Reagan's hand felt like a block of ice.

'Everybody pay a price,' Arsenio said.

Reagan nodded.

Reagan was still breathing hard, but the rain had dwindled to a fine mist. The sun was even peeking out over the beach now, though the traffic was still backed up on the highway below.

'You call what's her name? Your aunt in Chicago?' Reagan asked.

'She ain't really my aunt.'

'You said.'

'Yeah. She say I could stay with them. I told her I had some trouble, but she don't ask no questions.'

'You want to do it?'

'I got a choice?'

Reagan shook his head. 'Not that I can see. You've got a stack of warrants here.'

'I can't never shake them, can I?'

'No,' Reagan said. 'Not unless I can get back in.'

'That gonna happen?'

'I don't know,' Reagan said. 'I just plain don't know.'

Reagan had finally spoken with Donatelli, but didn't resolve anything. He couldn't answer all the captain's questions and he still wasn't ready to come in. Donatelli told him that a warrant had been issued for him, but Reagan didn't mention that to Arsenio. Reagan himself didn't know what he was going to do.

There were other things to settle first. Things he would have to get used to.

As if on cue, another spasm rocked Reagan's insides. He puked up a cup's worth of bile this time and groaned loudly as the shivers tore through his system. Arsenio tried rubbing his back, but Reagan pushed him away. It was two or three minutes before Reagan could straighten up in his chair. The sun had vanished and the rain picked up again.

'I'd better go inside,' Reagan rasped.

Arsenio helped him to his feet and opened the sliding doors for Reagan, who baby-stepped his way across the carpeted living room.

'You need some help?' Arsenio asked.

Reagan waved him off, shaking his head. 'We'll talk more later,' he said.

'Later,' Arsenio sighed. He followed Reagan's slow progress toward the kitchen and suppressed a shudder. He headed downstairs for the big screen TV in the den. Arsenio didn't like to be too near when they ate.

Judy was waiting for Reagan in the kitchen. It wasn't the proper kitchen, but a utility room that had been converted into a makeshift lab, with a refrigerator along one wall and some medical gear in the corner. Judy had treated Reagan's injuries there after the firefight.

Judy put on her doctor face and managed not to grimace when she saw how Reagan looked. She wanted to go over and help him across the room, but knew he preferred to do it himself. He was a stubborn S.O.B.

'It's past time,' she said as he hauled himself onto the gurney.

'I know,' was his response.

'It's not going to help if you fight it. It's not going to make things any better or any easier.'

He looked up at her with haggard eyes. 'I can't do it any other way.'

Judy started to argue, then thought better of it. *In time*, she thought.

She went to the fridge and pulled two vials of blood out of a rack in the door. She snapped one vial into her hypo and the other into Reagan's. The golden vials of Tunnel were already in place.

Another sharp spasm elicited a moan from Reagan, but it quickly passed. She held out the hypo, but he didn't take it and wouldn't meet her gaze. He unbuttoned his shirt and touched the budding tumours sprouting in a ridge below his navel, on top of the pinkish bullet wounds.

'If there had been any other way,' she said.

He nodded.

'The damage was too severe. Without the treatment you would have died.'

'I know,' he whispered.

Is that what you would have preferred?' she asked.

Reagan didn't say a word. He held his hand out for the hypo and she gave it to him. He stared at the colours.

'Blood and piss,' he said.

'How's that?'

'My school colours. Red and gold. Blood and piss.'

'Must be a good omen,' Judy said.

Reagan snorted. 'Must be,' he smiled.

They fed.

OTHER BOOKS AVAILABLE FROM ROBINSON PUBLISHING

Celestial Dogs   *Jay Russell*

A missing girl, a dead client and a string of savage murders lead
Marty Burns, a low-rent Private Eye, to demonic killers.
   'The ultimate Raymond Chandler with attitude read . . . sharp,
dark and savagely readable.' Peter James

Cybersex   *Ed. Richard Glyn Jones*

A collection of scary and erotic stories about everything from sex
on the Internet to cyborgasms, from Martin Amis, Jeff Noon,
Will Self, Kurt Vonnegut and many others.

The Best New Horror   *Ed. Stephen Jones*

Volume seven of the essential annual collection of the best horror
fiction. More than twenty terrifying tales of supernatural fear.

The Mammoth Book of Pulp Fiction   *Ed. Maxim Jakubowski*

A massive collection of seven decades of pure, unadulterated pulp
fiction in the company of such superlative writers as Dashiell
Hammett, Mickey Spillane and Ross MacDonald.

The Mammoth Book of Erotica   *Ed. Maxim Jakubowski*

Hugely successful collection of daring and erotic writing from
the best modern authors.

The Mammoth Book of International Erotica   *Ed. Maxim Jakubowski*

Top authors from around the world contribute to this new
collection of erotic fiction.

Robinson books are available from all good bookshops or can
be ordered direct from the Publisher. Just tick the title you want
and fill in the form overleaf.

Robinson Publishing, PO Box 11, Falmouth,
Cornwall TR10 9EN
Tel: +44(0) 1326 317200 Fax: +44(0) 1326 317444
Email: books@Barni.avel.co.uk

UK/B.F.P.O customers please allow £1.00 for p&p for the first
book, plus 50p for the second, plus 30p for each additional book
up to a maximum charge of £3.

Overseas customers (inc Ireland), please allow £2.00 for the
first book plus £1.00 for the second, plus 50p for each
additional book.

Please send me:

_____ The Best New Horror £6.99

_____ Cybersex £6.99

_____ The Mammoth Book of Pulp Fiction £6.99

_____ Celestial Dogs £5.99

_____ The Mammoth Book of Erotica £6.99

_____ The Mammoth Book of International Erotica £6.99

NAME (Block Letters) ....

ADDRESS ....

....POSTCODE ....

I enclose a cheque/PO (payable to Robinson Publishing Ltd)
for _____

I wish to pay by Switch / Credit card

Number _____Card Expiry Date_____